Merry Christmas

CW00549016

Dead Birds Don't Sing

Niall Illingworth

Grosvenor House
Publishing Limited

All rights reserved
Copyright © Niall Illingworth, 2020

The right of Niall Illingworth to be identified as the author of this
work has been asserted in accordance with Section 78
of the Copyright, Designs and Patents Act 1988

The book cover is copyright to Niall Illingworth

This book is published by
Grosvenor House Publishing Ltd
Link House
140 The Broadway, Tolworth, Surrey, KT6 7HT.
www.grosvenorhousepublishing.co.uk

This book is sold subject to the conditions that it shall not, by way of
trade or otherwise, be lent, resold, hired out or otherwise circulated
without the author's or publisher's prior consent in any form of binding or
cover other than that in which it is published and
without a similar condition including this condition being imposed
on the subsequent purchaser.

This book is a work of fiction. Any resemblance to
people or events, past or present, is purely coincidental.

A CIP record for this book
is available from the British Library

ISBN 978-1-83975-273-5

Dedication

For Helen, the love of my life.

Also by the Same Author

Where the Larkspur Grow
A Parcel of Rogues.

Acknowledgements

April 2020, lockdown. Ten years from now we will look back and remember what we did during that strange and frightening time. Cut off and isolated from our families and friends during the coronavirus pandemic, we reverted to long walks, box sets and jigsaws as our normal social conventions were turned upside down. In truth there wasn't much we could be positive about. But for those of us fortunate enough not to be involved in any frontline response to the crisis it did give us the gift of time. Even as a retiree, lockdown provided me with more spare time than I'd ever been used to. I decided to maximise that opportunity, and as a consequence I was able to write the majority of this book. You, the reader, will be able to say if that was time well spent.

This book is the third and last in what has turned out to be an unexpected series. It was never my intention when I wrote the first book to still be writing about Fairlea and Greenbrier County some 310,000 words later. It's been a lot of fun and I hope you enjoy this latest story but it's now time to say goodbye to West Virginia and seek other projects.

My grateful thanks goes to Debs who, as she has done for all three books, ploughed her way through the early draft and provided feedback. She must be a glutton for punishment. Thanks also go to Eunice, who once again took on the daunting challenge of proofreading the text.

Prologue

2nd May 1953. Spruce Knob Mine, Greenbrier County, WV.

'I can't remember a spring like this. Certainly not one as hot and dry this early in May. I thought it was going to be the perfect day for the Derby when I got up this morning, but it's just kept getting hotter. It's got to be 90 degrees now and we're up in the mountains, it'll be like a furnace in Kentucky and the ground will be rock hard, I don't think they've had any rain in a month. What have you got your money on? You always like a bet on the big one.'

Tom Hicks shook his head.

'Not got a bet on this time. I thought about it, but in the end, I decided not to bother. Anyway, I reckon it's a done deal. Native Dancer will win easy, especially with the ground as firm as it is. There's no value in backing the favourite, the odds are way too short. As for the others, they're just racing for second. I think I'll save my money for another day. What about you, have you got a few dollars on anything?'

'Nope,' said Joe Jarret wiping the sweat from his brow. 'I haven't had a bet in over a year, I can't afford it right now. Not after the second one came along. Money's tight, so frittering it away with a punt on the horses doesn't seem like the smartest thing to do.'

'No, you're dead right.' said Tom opening the door of the mine office. 'I've not given it up completely, but other than the Derby and the Belmont, I hardly bother with it now. Much like yourself, I can't afford it anymore. Not with the five of us.'

'Yeah, how's that working out? That woman of yours sure has a big heart, fostering like that when you've already got two of your own, can't be easy.'

Tom smiled and gave a resigned sigh.

'Let's just say there have been a few teething troubles along the way but it's nothing we can't cope with. The boy's circumstances were dire, if we hadn't agreed to take him, he would have gone to the orphanage and there was no way Carole was going to let that happen. But hey it's all good, the boy just needs some time and love invested into his life. And just in case you were wondering, it's also the reason why I never make Bursley's on a Friday anymore. I'm taking him to karate classes then, you should see him Joe, strong as an ox he is, and he's still only twelve. They've got him fighting boys two years older than he is because he's broken all the ones his own age. My younger boy worships him, and I know that's not a bad thing, but it's proving tricky.'

'Oh, why's that then?'

'It's his temper. He's only eight but I've never seen a child with such a volatile temper. He really is wild. Flies off the handle at the slightest thing. Carole struggles to control him and I'm not much better being honest. There is no way I could take him to karate. Of course, he wants to go and be like his foster brother, but I couldn't trust him with the other kids. We have a massive tantrum every Friday, as I said it's tricky.'

Joe raised his eyebrows.

'Sounds like you've got your hands full right enough. You'll need to tell me where those karate classes are, and I'll make a point of keeping well away. I'm not the biggest of guys, that boy of yours would make mincemeat of me! And as for your eight your old, I don't think I'm brave enough to meet him.' said Joe trying to lighten the mood.

'Well, it doesn't look like Dan's about.' said Tom scanning the small wood panelled office. He pushed the bathroom door open with his foot.

'He's not in the John either.'

'Well he damn well should be here. There are still men working in 'C' pit, what if something happened and the alarm was sounded? No darn use if nobody's here to respond. As the union rep I've got a responsibility for those men, I'll have a word, he can't leave this office unmanned, not while men are still working.' said Joe angrily.

Tom gave a rueful nod but didn't reply.

Joe picked up a copy of the racing news that was lying open on the desk and scoffed loudly.

'I bet he's over at the canteen watching the race. And look at this, he's got Dark Star circled at 25/1. It's a dead cert that he's over there watching it. He'll have a hefty punt on it too, you can be sure of that.'

Tom started to laugh.

'Knowing Dan, it's likely to be half his wages. He just can't help himself. He'd bet on two flies walking up a wall if you gave him the chance. Well I can tell you one thing: he's backing a loser this time. Native Dancer's unbeaten in eleven and it ain't going to get beat by some 25/1 shot.'

'God damn it,' said Joe pulling the handle of a small wooden door at the rear of the office. 'The aviary's locked, and so is the lamp cupboard. I bet he's taken the damned keys with him.'

'Looks that way,' said Tom rummaging through the desk. 'They're not hanging on the board and I can't see them in any of the drawers.'

'Well we're just going to have to go without the canary. And don't worry about the lamps, its well enough lit down there. Anyway, it won't be a problem, we're only going to be ten minutes. I just want to measure the width of the seam.' said Joe.

Both men put on their hard hats and wandered over to the lift at the end of the corridor that would take them down to the entrance of 'D' shaft, the fourth, but as yet, unmined seam of the Spruce Knob complex.

'Funny isn't it, but I feel kind of naked.' said Tom with a grin. 'I mean, I don't think I've ever come down this lift without the bird. It just feels a bit strange. What about you?'

Joe started to chuckle.

'Yeah, I know what you mean. Things like that seem a bit weird when they're so much part of your routine.'

'Exactly that.' replied Tom. 'Listen, changing the subject. Didn't you tell me that the mine inspectors were in last month and have already certified that the new seam is fit to be excavated?' Tom closed the lift's metal security gate and pressed the button to go down. 'And that's got to be good news, right?'

Joe nodded.

'Yep, that's what Mr Lawrence told me, but I just want to check. And I also want to know how much coal is down there. I was speaking to Walter Massie recently. He was part of the team that did the initial excavation last year, he told me there was potentially more than twice as much coal as any of our other seams. If that turns out to be true, then I've a few questions I'd like Lawrence to answer.'

Tom raised his eyebrows and gave his friend a knowing look.

'I've known you a long time Joe. More than thirty years if you include our schooldays and I know when somethings bothering you. So, what's up?'

Joe slowly shook his head.

'I'm not quite sure, I can't quite put my finger on it, but it's fishier than an otter's pocket. I know something doesn't add up. At the last meeting I was at, the boss said that the purchase of the Trepanner cutting machine was being put on hold indefinitely. He said the viability report they'd commissioned didn't justify the expense. That just seems bizarre, especially if what Walter said turns out to be true. We'd need two machines to mine that much coal, and anyway, the things been on order for months. Cancelling it now makes no sense. And you know the rumours as well as me, all that talk of laying men off. As the union rep I've got responsibilities, so having told you all that, you'll understand why I want to see the coal seam with my own eyes. I need to be sure of my facts before I challenge him about it. The man's as slippery as an eel. I wouldn't trust him as far as I could throw him.'

'There's definitely something unsettling about him right enough, I've always thought he was a strange character. Funny looking for a start. Six foot something, big nose and that chin of his could pick onions out a jar.

And don't get me started on that stupid tooth. Who on God's earth would want a gold front tooth? The man gives me the creeps.' said Tom with a shudder.

Joe started to laugh.

'And to top it all he's got a fucking stupid name. Who in their right mind calls their kid, Eldridge Gaylord Lawrence the third?'

'Of course, he's named after his father and grandfather.' added Tom. 'I never knew his dad, but according to Dan he was just the same. A right pain in the ass. The only one of them I can stomach is David, the youngest one,' said Joe. 'That middle brother Mitchell ain't right either, thinks he's God's gift to women and the thing is they can't stand him. I know Wilma and the other girls in the canteen put a shot of bromide in his coffee. I'm not joshing you. They reckon it helps keep a lid on his rampant libido! I'd give him a boot in the cojones if he ever tried it on with Carole.'

'No offence my friend, but that would be worth seeing.' laughed Joe. 'And while you're at it, could you give Eldridge's boy a swift boot in the stones too, he's one smarmy son of a bitch. Company lawyer! Don't make me laugh. What is he, twenty-three! The ink on his law degree is still wet! When you think they forced old Foggerty out so they could give him the job, it's a disgrace. He's another one I wouldn't trust, he's well worth the watching.'

'They do, of course, all talk highly of you,' chortled Tom.

'Bunch of shysters the lot of them.' mumbled Joe. 'Anyway, as I was about to say, I don't think any of them could come close to old Eldridge Gaylord the first. Not in the badass stakes anyway. Shot and killed

Chief Makatai so he could throw the Shawnee off their land and open this mine. He was one ruthless son of a bitch.'

'Now my friend, that's a little unfair. If I remember my history there were no witnesses and he was never convicted of anything.' added Tom sarcastically.

'True enough,' sighed Joe, 'but that's only because he and his henchmen shot all the witnesses. If memory serves, twenty-nine men, women and children were slaughtered on this mountain all because he wanted his hands on this coal. That's always bothered me. I know working here provides for my family, but I hate to think I'm helping line the pockets of the Lawrence family, not after what they did to them Indians.'

'Long time ago now my friend.' said Tom sliding the metal lift gate open.

'Aargh......fuck, ah fuck you son of a bitch. How did I manage to do that? Yelped Tom clutching the fingers of his right hand. 'God that hurts like hell!'

'Shit man let me see. Can you move your fingers?' asked Joe peering at Tom's crushed hand.

'Ah, that was fucking stupid but it's my own fault.' replied Tom trying to straighten his fingers.

'It's easy done if you're not watching what you're doing. I've caught my hand in that door before. Can you move them? If you can move them even a bit, then that's a good sign. Means they might not be broken. But look, this can wait. We'll head back up and get that hand seen to.'

Tom shook his head.

'No, it's okay, we're here now, if we're only going to be ten minutes then it can wait. Look I can move them a bit more now, I just feel a little sick, but it'll pass.'

'Okay, but only if you're sure.'

'I'm sure,' said Tom putting his good hand on Joe's back and steering him towards the entrance of the seam. They had only been walking for a couple of minutes when Tom stopped abruptly.

'I might just sit here and wait for you,' said Tom eyeing up a pile of wooden posts that were stacked against the mine wall.

'I'm starting to feel a bit dizzy and lightheaded. The air's vile too, it's not making me feel any better.'

'Not a problem, just you wait here, I'll be as quick as I can. Like I said, it won't take me five minutes to get to the coal face and measure the seam.'

Tom sat down and looked around him. There were tools and cables lying all over the floor, it was a right old mess.

'You would have thought it would be tidy if it had just been inspected. I thought mine inspectors were shit-hot on that type of thing. Trip hazards left lying about used to be an instant fail. My boy's room is tidier than this and that's saying something.' said Tom trying to raise a smile.

'Yep, it's a disgrace and damned dangerous. I'll get Dan to dig out the journal when we go back up. It'll tell us when the inspection took place. Someone must have been down here after that. There's no way it would have passed looking like this.'

Joe left Tom sitting on the posts and disappeared down a gentle slope following a line of lights into the distant gloom.

Jeezo, Tom wasn't wrong, thought Joe. The air wasn't great back there but it's rancid down here, smells like rotten eggs. This can't be right. If the air's this bad the ventilator can't be working properly and at least a third of the light bulbs look to be out. This is a health and safety nightmare.

A few hundred yards further on Joe found himself standing in front of a large set of metal gates that were secured by two padlocks and chains. Those gates don't look like the ones we have at the other seams, they look like they've just been fitted, thought Joe. Why don't I know about them, what the hell is going on?

Chapter 1

September 1993

Two hundred and sixty miles north of Greenbrier County, in the library of Moundsville High Security Prison, Lilian Taylor was beginning to feel agitated.

It was twenty-five past two and the parole board hearing was scheduled for three. When she'd returned from her lunch just before two, he had been cataloguing magazines by the photocopier. He seemed calm and prepared.

Keeping up the pretence that it was just another day, Lilian had delivered three books to the Deputy Governor. On her way back she'd stopped briefly to chat with the Prison Chaplain. She couldn't have been away for more than twenty minutes but now, he was nowhere to be seen.

A feeling of panic swept over her as she checked the bathroom and store cupboards. It appeared that history might be about to repeat itself. Lilian felt sick in the pit of her stomach. Surely, he wasn't going to blow it again.

He had already served forty-one years of a life sentence, handed down for the murder of his foster father just after his seventeenth birthday. A capricious southern judge and a solidly white jury had negated any chance of a not guilty verdict. But in a strange twist of fate, he had avoided the death penalty. Since the age of thirteen he had lived in De Witt, Arkansas with his new foster family. On the day of the murder the family had travelled east to spend thanksgiving with an elderly aunt in their former home of Alderson, Greenbrier County.

Back then, excursions away from Arkansas were rare, but if he'd killed his foster father in his home state and not in West Virginia, which had abolished the death penalty in the mid-sixties, it was likely he would have ended up strapped to a gurney having a cocktail of lethal drugs injected into his arm. In truth that may have been a preferable option, forty-one years in Moundsville had mostly been a living hell for the state's longest serving prisoner.

Since his incarceration he had already failed the parole board twice. The first time was a surprise to no one. It was standard practice to fail your first board. The second time though was both regrettable and unfortunate.

One of the board members, a sanctimonious, holier than thou woman in her sixties, had arrived with a lifetime of prejudices and her mind already made up. Things did not get off to a good start when she insisted on calling him Charles, the name given to him by his Arkansas foster family. He hated the name and since his imprisonment he'd refused to acknowledge it. Growing up as a child in Greenbrier County, he'd always gone by the name of Chas. But for the last few years, he had asked to be called Chaska. With Lilian's help, he had started to research his ancestry and discovered what he believed was his given name. His proper name was Chaska, an Indian name often given to the first-born son.

Although he had been too young to remember his birth parents, Carole Hicks, his foster mum in Greenbrier

County, had told him that he had been given the name Chas by his real parents. His own research however, had convinced him that somewhere along the line his name had simply got mixed up. That wasn't too difficult to believe as he had lived with several foster families since he was first taken into care aged four. Chas was not an Indian name, but Chaska was, and it meant the first-born son. To his mind he had never been Charles and now he refused to answer to it. The mere mention of it raised his hackles and put him on the defensive.

After she'd called him Charles the first time, he'd politely asked that the panel call him Chaska as he didn't recognise the name Charles. Then, when she did it for a second time, he was almost incandescent with rage. He finally snapped when she referred to his fore-bears as wagon burners. That was the final straw; he could take no more.

Disrespected and abused, he reacted furiously and returned her insult with several of his own. As a matter of principle, he had refused their offer to apologise. In a final act of defiance, he smashed a glass water jug against a wall and kicked over a table before he was felled by a hail of baton strikes and forcibly removed from the room. That sealed the deal. His parole was refused and after a fortnight in solitary confinement he was returned to his cell to complete his sentence.

That had been nearly five years ago and since that unfortunate incident, the world had moved on. George Bush had succeeded Reagan as President and Operation Desert Storm confirmed that when America flexed its military muscle, the rest of the world looked on and held its breath. Events in the State Penitentiary might not have gathered pace at quite the same rate, but even in prison things move on and time proves to be a great healer.

After a few months cooling off, Lilian persuaded Chaska to attend weekly anger management classes. She wanted to support him, so she'd attended the first few meetings with him. They seemed to be working and there were discernible signs that things were improving. His temper and unpredictable outbursts receded noticeably in the year following the parole board debacle and a more measured calmness now prevailed. With the stimulation of a new job in the library his life was able to return to what passed for normal in prison.

Over the last three years, he had never so much as raised his voice to Lilian, and they had formed a strong bond. She had invested a great deal of time and energy working with him and advocating his case. She understood that he'd suffered terribly and believed that his crime, heinous though it was, was committed after intolerable provocation. He had been punished enough and deserved another chance. The governor though, did not see it in quite those terms, and from the onset it was obvious that he would not be easily persuaded. He was concerned for Lilian's safety, and sceptical, despite Lilian's repeated assurances, that Chaska didn't pose a threat, well certainly not to her. Unfortunately, the beating he'd meted out to a fellow inmate nearly four years ago, remained a stain on his character and lived long in the governor's memory.

The circumstances of that incident had been most unfortunate. Finding herself alone one afternoon in the library, Lilian had been sexually assaulted by a white supremacist remand prisoner, who had secreted himself in a store cupboard after the other prisoners had left to

4

return to their cells. Attacked from behind and with a gag forced into her mouth, she had been defenceless as he straddled her and started to abuse her. Pinned against her desk, she bucked and squirmed while his evil hands ripped at her blouse and roamed all over her. Her bird like frame defenceless against his brawn.

By a stroke of good fortune, Chaska had called at the library to return a book. God knows what might have happened if he hadn't been passing. With her blouse torn open, he'd caught the assailant unbuttoning his trousers. The beating he handed out hospitalised the con for weeks and left him requiring surgery for a broken jaw and badly smashed eye socket. Many looked upon it as summary justice and no more than the con had deserved. However, Chaska's actions that day did nothing to enhance his chances of release. The governor was not alone in thinking that his violent temper had not been rehabilitated.

To Lilian the injustice was glaring. She had been signed off work for a month following the attack, but on her return, she vowed to fight for justice, and like a dog with a bone, she refused to let it go. Not for the first time, Chaska had been grievously wronged, and that sense of injustice burned deep. This needed to be put right. Eventually, fully 15 months after she had first pleaded his case, her persistence was rewarded, and the governor relented and agreed he could work as her assistant. But it was strictly on the understanding that it would be on a trial basis, and it would be closely monitored. One slip, the merest indiscretion and there would be no second chances.

Things had been a bit strained to begin with. Not much was said during those first few weeks. He was shy and uncommunicative. After nearly forty years of incarceration he trusted no one and everything Lilian did or suggested was treated with a healthy dose of suspicion.

As the months passed, she slowly began to gain his trust and it soon became apparent that Chaska was both intelligent and hardworking. He had a natural aptitude for the indexing and record keeping that were the bread and butter of library work. It was, however, through his interest in research that his academic ability really began to shine.

He had still been in high school when he was sentenced for his crime and Lilian was adamant, that if the circumstances had been different, he could have gone to college and achieved academic success. He had a fine brain. Encouraged by Lilian, he began to read which was something he had never done before. He started slowly, a book every other week, but soon he was devouring two or three books in a week. And it wasn't just any old book. He was making up for lost time and following a reading list, prepared by Lilian, that steered him through many of the great works of English literature. From Dickens to Tolstoy he read them all. The solitude to read in peace was one of the few things guaranteed in prison.

His favourite book, to which he often returned was Steinbeck's 'The Grapes of Wrath'. Although he never really said, Lilian wondered if he identified with the central character, Tom Load, who is paroled from prison at the start of the story, having been convicted of murder. Whether it was that or not, the fact remained that he must have read the story half a dozen times.

His new-found ability at research had allowed him to develop his burgeoning interest in his ancestry. Once again encouraged by Lilian, he spent endless hours ploughing through history books, academic journals and newspaper articles to gain an understanding of who he really was. His systematic research proved fruitful, he had folders full of articles and photographs, all meticulously indexed and referenced, just as you might expect from someone acquainted with library processes and with an attention to detail.

It was, however, through a chance encounter one summer's evening that things moved quickly onto a different level. At a friend's barbeque, Lilian had been introduced to a university professor who went by the name of Alan Foulis. Professor Foulis just happened to work at the Carnegie Mellon University in Pittsburgh where he was head of American cultural studies and an expert in First Nation tribes. Lilian had got talking to him about her work at the prison library and he was intrigued to hear about her new library assistant and the circumstances that had led to his imprisonment. Professor Foulis readily agreed to drive the fifty miles from his home in New Cumberland to meet Lilian and her protégé at Moundsville. That first conversation had been six months ago, but since then, Professor Foulis had visited the prison on a further two occasions and was now taking a keen interest in helping Chaska trace his ancestry.

*

Lilian's chest felt tight and her heart was starting to race. She glanced up at the clock, it was nearly half past two. With every passing minute her feelings of anxiety increased. She closed her eyes and prayed. On the rare occasions she made it to church, she always prayed for Chaska during the prayers of intercession and asked that he might be given another chance. Now it seemed that his prospect of being released might be disappearing for ever. If he wasn't sitting in that room before the board convened at three, he would probably never be freed. The thought that he'd have to spend the rest of his days in prison filled her with despair.

Sitting down at her desk Lilian picked up the phone to call 'B' block. It was a long shot, but it was just possible he might have returned to his cell to collect something prior to the hearing. As she waited for the phone to be answered she thought she could hear coughing. There it was again, a deep hacking cough. It seemed to be coming from the far corner of the office by the photocopier. Lilian stood up and went to investigate.

Two feet clad in white canvas sneakers were poking out from behind the photocopier. There he was, lying wedged between the wall and the copier with his headphones on. He looked up and smiled, a great beaming smile that made his pearly white teeth shine like gemstones. Sitting up he took off his headphones.

'I think I've properly done it this time. It's well and truly jammed and I ain't a clue where it is. I've had every damned drawer and cover out, but I can't see where it's stuck.'

Lilian let out a sigh of relief and shook her head.

'Look, never mind about that. Do you know what time it is? You've got half an hour to get yourself together and get over to the governor's corridor. The hearing will start at three sharp. Today's going to be your big day. Remember what we discussed. We've gone over the process dozens of times. You just need to stay calm, stay in control and focus. Just answer their questions, there's nothing they can ask you that you won't be able to answer. You're going to do just fine.'

The sides of his mouth creased as he smiled again.

'I feel good, well, apart from the damned cough.'

He coughed again, hacking several times into the tissue that covered his mouth.

Lilian glanced down at the trash can that was filled with blood speckled tissues.

'You're going to have to get that seen to, you've been coughing like that for weeks.'

'I know, it comes and goes a bit but it's proving diffi-cult to shift. And all the cigarettes I've smoked in this place over forty years ain't helping it, I know that. Thought I'd say that to save you the trouble of mention-ing it.'

Lilian smiled and nodded.

'Anyway, apart from the cough I feel okay, chilled even and what will be will be Lilian. Look, can you give me a minute? I just want to finish listening to this song. You were right about the music, it's certainly helped, I feel calm and ready.'

'Glad to hear that. What've you been listening to?'

'A bit of Springsteen but mostly Dylan. This is one you gave me, Planet Waves. The whole album's cool, but this song, Forever Young, is just brilliant. It's his lyrics, they're like poetry, the man's a genius.'

Lilian laughed and shook her head.

'I've got a convert. I thought you'd like Dylan. But we can talk about that later. Look, your hands are covered in printer ink. Get yourself in the restroom and get yourself cleaned up. Then I'm going to escort you to the governor's corridor, just to make damned sure you get to that hearing on time. I'm not letting you out of my sight till you're in that room, you hear me?'

Chaska laughed.

'Loud and clear, but less of the fussing, you're not my mother!'

He got to his feet and headed into the restroom.

The irony of that remark was not lost on Lilian. He may not yet know who his real mother was, but thanks to Professor Foulis he was close to finding out. The professor was analysing the photographs he'd taken of the tattoo on Chaska's neck. At their last meeting, when she was walking the professor back to his car, he told her that he was almost sure that the three arrow tips signified that Chaska was the son of an Indian chief. His name suggested that too, but there was at least some dubiety about how he'd come by the name. The tattoo on the other hand was far more compelling proof.

Although most of the tattoo had been destroyed by the scarring, just enough of the arrow tip design remained to make it identifiable. That was all Professor Foulis needed to confirm that the tattoo was important. He would need to check his reference books, but he was almost certain that the three arrows signified that Chaska was the eldest son of a chief from either the Lakota or Shawnee tribes. Lilian had been desperate to tell her friend, but he had been let down too many times before, she didn't want another false dawn, she needed to wait for the professor's confirmation.

During their last meeting, when the three of them had sat in Lilian's office drinking coffee, Professor Foulis had been repulsed as Chaska described how he'd come by the scar on his neck. He explained in lurid detail how his then foster father, a man who went by the

10

name of Earl Walker, had forced him into the kitchen, bound him to a chair and covered his mouth with gaffer tape. Unable to move, Chaska watched in horror as Walker put on an oven glove and removed a red-hot metal soup ladle which had been left baking in the Aga. Like a farmer branding a steer, Walker grabbed Chaska's hair and pulled his head to one side while searing his neck with the back of the molten ladle. Chaska had been 13 years old.

That barbaric act had been carried out with the sole intention of erasing any trace of Chaska's Indian heritage. He remembered the excruciating pain that had caused him to faint. Then being violently sick when he regained consciousness and smelt the nauseating sweetness of his burning flesh.

The scar from the third-degree burn was a constant reminder of that appalling episode. Fatefully, it did not prove to be an isolated incident. It was just the first of many acts of cruelty he would endure at the hands of his guardian and so-called protector.

It was perhaps inevitable that their abusive relationship would end in further violence. One evening in Alderson, in the aftermath of a family thanksgiving party, Chaska took his revenge. It wasn't the first time he'd witnessed the horror of Walker beating his wife to a pulp in a drunken rage. That piece of shit, the so-called family man and elder of the church, that pillar of the community and wannabe town councillor was an evil monster. His cowardly violence exclusively reserved for his traumatised wife and fostered son and administered privately, always privately, far away from prying eyes.

That night Chaska could stand no more. Picking up a baseball bat he bludgeoned the monster to death in an orgy of blood and retribution. His only regret being he hadn't done it sooner.

*

After their last meeting, Professor Foulis had indicated that he would want to consult colleagues, to verify his findings. That would take a little time, but he hoped to be back in touch by the beginning of the month. That could be any day now. The thought of knowing the truth made Lilian tingle with anticipation. But they could wait for the confirmation. Chaska had been in prison for forty-one years, another day or so wasn't going to matter, he would find out soon enough.

For now, their focus had to be on the parole hearing. If that went well, by next week he could be a free man, and perhaps they could save Professor Foulis a trip. She hadn't been to Pittsburgh in a while and she was sure that Chaska never had. The thought of a day trip together made her feel warm inside.

Lilian Taylor looked younger than her 35 years. She was petite in all senses of the word. Barely five feet tall with short dark hair which she wore in an immaculate French bob, she was delicate and small boned. She had the build of a small bird. Her most striking feature was her piercing blue eyes which contrasted strikingly against her pale milky skin. As ever, she was dressed conservatively. Black pencil skirt worn with a white blouse and navy cardigan. The plain leather soled shoes she wore clicked every time she moved on the hard-tiled floor. Her movements were busy and efficient as she flitted from one task to another. Lilian was well suited to her role as prison librarian.

It was not though, the easiest of jobs. It was a hard sell trying to get prisoners to read. They had other priorities. But just occasionally, like now with Chaska, she could pierce their resistance, and open their minds to a world of knowledge and possibilities.

The restroom door opened, and Chaska emerged looking clean and sleek. He had brushed his mane of grey flecked black hair back from his face and tied it neatly in a ponytail. Though he was now in his late fifties, he maintained the physique of a much younger man. The dividend of his daily visit to the prison's gymnasium was apparent to Lilian's admiring eye. Lean and muscular in a way that swimmers often are, he was broad chested and narrow waisted. She thought he looked magnificent.

'You're looking good,' said Lilian eyeing him up and down. 'But if you're ready, I think we should head over. Better to be a bit early. I can stay with you till it's time to go in if you'd like.'

Chaska smiled and nodded but didn't reply. Lilian locked the library door and the two friends headed outside to cross the yard to 'A' block where the governor's and administrative offices were situated. The early September air was hot and breathless. Chaska stopped momentarily and stared up at the cloudless blue sky. He took several slow and very deliberate breaths, as if he was topping up his energy with the rays from the sun.

Away to his left, in the shadow of the prison wall, his attention was caught by a solitary pigeon that was flapping helplessly against the base of the wall. The bird was covered in blood and nursing a damaged wing. Chaska knew what had happened. He glanced up to the roof of a stone outbuilding where a large ginger tom was hissing and staring down at the stricken bird.

Chaska frantically waved his arms and sprinted across the yard towards the crouching feline, its back end now swaying rhythmically, a sure sign it was about to pounce. Recognising its nemesis, the cat scrambled up the wall to the overhang of the kitchen roof and disappeared out of sight. Very slowly Chaska approached the terrified bird. Bending down he gently picked it up, cradling it between his massive hands.

'I hate that cat. I don't hate many critters, but I hate that cat. And it's always on that roof. I can see it from my cell, it's killed at least three birds this week and that's just the ones I know about. It's a killing machine. I'm gonna mention it to the Governor, I'm pretty sure it was his wife who brought it here, found it as a stray and brought it here. Well it can fuck right off, there will be no birds left if it keeps killing them. I'm going to speak to the Governor.'

Lilian grimaced and looked despairingly up at the sky. Not now, dear God, not now. Lilian knew that Chaska meant what he said. He was stubborn and not easily dissuaded. She needed to act quickly or all the hard work they had done would be for nothing. It didn't matter if he had a parole board to attend, if the bird wasn't seen to, he would be going nowhere.

Chapter 2

'Serves you right nigger! You're fucking lucky I don't whip that black ass of yours, this is a white town, you wait your turn. You don't get to fucking eat before we do. You hear that nigger?'

Ella looked straight at the boy. Like a laser pin-pointing its target, her stare punched through him to the horizon beyond. She would not be cowed. Not now, not never. She had been abused countless times before, but no buck toothed racist with his razor cut hair was going to bully her. She picked up the jar and stood motionless and mute by her car. She was petrified, but she wasn't going to run. Her grandfather had taught her not to fight back, but that same wise man also taught her why she shouldn't run. Be brave and stand tall, she could almost hear him whispering in her ear. They hate it when you don't run. They may verbally and physically abuse you, but if you don't run, they don't get to touch your dignity. And dignity is a very precious thing. Don't run and you get to keep it. You win and they lose. The haters detest that.

She desperately didn't want to cry, but at that moment it was all too much. Tears trickled down her cheeks as she watched the youths, like feeding locusts, gather up the notes and coins that had spilled from her jar. Her right arm ached from the kick that dislodged the jar from her grasp. A year of scrimping and saving was now scattered across the car lot. Money that was supposed to buy her sister's wedding present. She had only stopped off to pick up a burger for lunch on her way to the store. She'd left the Macy's catalogue, carefully marked on the front seat of her car. She knew she'd saved enough to buy the bed linen. A double quilt, various sheets, and pillowcases, all pretty in a floral pattern of pink and white roses, her sister's favourite flowers. Billie would understand, of course she would, but it was heartbreaking and just so unfair.

If it hadn't been for the recovery truck that had just pulled off the highway, she would have lost even more of her money. But the sight of the driver getting out of his truck seemed to spook the youths. She watched as they scrambled aboard a pick-up festooned in the flag of the confederacy and disappeared out the lot in a frenzy of screeching wheels.

Ella looked forlornly at the jar. There was still some notes and coins in the bottom, and they hadn't got all the money that had spilled out either. The midday sun was glinting off the coins that lay strewn across the tarmac and she could see some dollar bills that had found their way underneath parked vehicles. All was not yet lost.

Ella had just started to gather up the remaining money when she heard a voice from behind her. It was Detective Sam Coutts. He had been returning to Lewisburg Police Office from White Sulphur Springs where he'd been taking witness statements. He'd seen the group of youths surrounding Ella. His police instincts told him immediately that something wasn't right. Passing the entrance to the lot he'd glanced to his right in time to see the youth kick the jar from Ella's hands.

'I'm sorry I couldn't have got to you quicker. I saw what happened. I was passing in the car and saw the guy kicking out at you. But I couldn't stop or get turned because the highway was so busy. I'm sorry about that. Are you okay, you're not hurt, are you?'

Ella smiled weakly and shook her head.

'My arm aches a bit but it's not serious. And as for the racist abuse, that's water off a duck's back, I've been called a nigger and worse a hundred times before. Although, they don't usually assault me at the same time. So, today's been a bit different.'

'That sucks. I'm real sorry to hear that, but I'm glad you're not hurt, well not physically hurt, that's the main thing. Listen, did you happen to get a look at the vehicle they left in. I take it they did leave in a car?'

Ella nodded again as she dabbed her eyes with a tissue.

'And how many of them where in it?'

'Four guys. All white and aged I'd say between 20 and 25. They left in an orange pick-up. I think it might have been a Ford and it had a West Virginian plate. It was definitely orange, and it had a large Dixie flag on the hood.'

'Excellent,' said Sam taking out his radio from his jacket pocket. 'That's something to go on. Oh, I should explain, I'm a police officer. I'm going to broadcast a lookout for the vehicle. Which way did it go when it left here?'

Ella pointed to her left.

Sam put his thumb up as he started to speak on the radio.

'Lookout requested for an orange pick-up, WV plate, possibly a Ford, four up and with a sticker of a

17

confederacy flag on the hood. Vehicle involved in an assault in the parking lot of Denny's on the Lewisburg road. Vehicle last seen five minutes ago heading east towards Fairlea.'

As Sam put his radio away and took out his notebook, Ella was on her knees trying to recover a five-dollar bill that was tantalisingly out of reach underneath a parked van.

'Can I give you a hand there?' asked Sam taking off his suit jacket.

'Sure,' said Ella standing back up. 'I'm grateful to you for stopping by to help.'

'Just doing my job. Although I hope I would have stopped anyway, even if I hadn't been on duty. People like those guys are absolute scum. I can't understand what gets into their heads.'

'Nothing in their heads, that's partly the problem.' said Ella sitting down on a low wall. 'But it's not just a lack of education, it's about many things, but ignorance is perhaps the single biggest factor.'

'Go on I'm listening; sounds like you know what you're talking about.' replied Sam as he scrambled between parked cars picking up the money.

'Well, if you study the causes of discrimination, and that's any type of discrimination, not just racism, you'll find that much of it comes down to ignorance and a fear of things they don't understand. That's often because they've never been exposed to it before.'

'Hmm,' said Sam scratching his head. 'Plenty of people I know don't have much of an education and they might be a bit ignorant, but I'm pretty sure they're not racist.'

'Yeah, of course. I didn't say they were all racist. And anyway, there's more to it than that.'

'What do you mean by that?'

'I mean there are other factors, not just the lack of education.'

'Like what?'

'Well, based on what I've studied, and it's backed up by my own experience, I think people who have travelled a bit, visited other countries and mixed with other cultures, are much more tolerant and understanding. They don't rush to judge someone just because they don't look or speak like themselves and they aren't fazed if someone has a different religion. I'd bet you the rest of the money in this jar that none of those guys have been outside the country. In fact, I wouldn't be surprised if they hadn't been out of West Virginia. The world they inhabit is small. That doesn't excuse their behaviour, but it does start to help explain it I think.'

'Interesting, I'd never thought about it like that before. But what you say makes a lot of sense. Now I'm a bit worried about myself. I've never been abroad. In fact, thinking about it, apart from a school trip to Disney in Florida and a trip to Washington and New York with my folks, I haven't travelled much. I don't think I've been west of Oklahoma!'

'I'm sure you've nothing to worry about, but you might just be the exception that proves the rule.'

'Let's hope so,' said Sam standing up clutching a five-dollar bill. 'One more to put back in your jar. Apologies, but I don't think I introduced myself properly. I'm Detective Coutts, but please call me Sam.'

'I'm pleased to make your acquaintance Sam, I'm Ella. Ella Fitzgerald Massie, to give you my Sunday name.'

Sam looked bemused.

'Ella Fitzgerald, I've heard that name before. Isn't she some famous actress? I've definitely heard of her.'

Ella started to giggle.

'You don't know much about black female jazz singers then?'

Sam puffed out his cheeks.

'Not a thing as you've clearly worked out. I take it she's a singer then and not an actress.'

'One of the greatest. She's an old lady now, but in her prime, in the 50's and 60's, she was the queen of jazz and the blues. My mother named me after her. And my sister's called Billie Holiday Massie. You can see my mother's a massive music fan. I've got some Ella Fitzgerald CD's in the car; I could lend you one if you were interested.'

'I might just take you up on that. But before we do that let's make sure we've picked up the rest of your money. The coins won't be a problem, but this breeze will blow the notes away if we're not careful, so we better get a hurry on.'

Five minutes later they had gathered up all the money they could see and now they were sitting in Sam's car.

'You don't happen to know how much money was in the jar, do you?

Ella smiled and nodded.

'170 dollars exactly. It's money I'd saved to buy my sister a wedding present. She's getting married in a couple of months. I was going to buy her some fancy bed linen from Macy's and I'd priced it at $170. I stopped saving a couple of weeks ago when I had reached that target.'

Sam emptied the jar and started to count the money.

'There still looks like there's quite a bit here, but I'm afraid we might struggle to get all the money back that's been stolen. There's a good chance we'll be able to trace the pick-up and charge them with the assault, but I'm just being truthful when I say it's going to be more difficult getting the money back.'

Ella shrugged her shoulders and gave a rueful nod.

'There's $95.75 still here which means you're missing $74.25.'

Ella tilted her head and stared at Sam incredulously. The second he finished counting the money he had announced how much was missing.'

'Man, you're pretty swift with those numbers.'

Sam started to laugh.

'It's about my only skill. Anything to do with numbers and statistics, I like all that kind of stuff and can work most things out in my head. Words and writing on the other hand, well they're not my strongest suit. Just ask my boss at work. Drives him to distraction. He says my police reports are like a dog's dinner! And that's a pity, 'cause there's much more call for writing in the police than crunching numbers, so it's a constant battle. I was diagnosed with dyslexia at school, so writing has always been a bit of a struggle, but I get there. It just takes me longer than most to write the damned report. But hey, we can't all be like Mark Twain. Not that I've read his books you understand, but I loved Huckleberry Finn when I saw it at the movies.'

Ella put her hand to her mouth to stop herself laughing. Her knight in shining armour had a self-deprecating sense of humour and she kind of liked that. Sam didn't seem to be like any of the other guys she knew. He was white for a start. She had hung out with a few white guys, more so at college than at high school, she'd even dated one for a while. But none of them were as polite and respectful as Sam appeared to be.

'Well then, it looks like I'm the complete opposite of you. It would have taken me ages to do that subtraction. I'm pretty good with words but I'm hopeless with numbers. I was diagnosed with mild dyscalculia at school.'

Ella scoffed then continued.

'It just seemed to go in one ear and out the other. I had no capacity to retain it. I would just about be able to do my homework for that day, but by the time I was next in class I'd forgotten it again. Fractions and long division, it was like a foreign language. It nearly stopped me getting into college. Somehow, I scraped a pass, but now I do my best to avoid doing any type of calculation, it really is that bad.'

'Perhaps I should do your maths and you could write my police reports. Sounds like that might be the perfect solution.' laughed Sam. 'If you don't mind can I ask what it is you do? I'm going to need to know for my report.'

'I'm still a student,' replied Ella. 'I finished my history degree last summer and now I'm doing a Masters, at the College of West Virginia in Beckley.'

'A Masters eh! You must be a smart cookie right enough. What's your subject going to be?'

'It's going to be on the history of coal mining in Greenbrier County. I've got a bit of a vested interest you see. My grandfather, Walter Massie, was one of the first black miners in Greenbrier County, so I'd thought it would be pretty cool to do my Masters on that. I've always been interested in industrial history, and with my grandfather's connection, it just seemed like the perfect fit.'

'That sounds great. How far into it are you?'

'Not started yet. It's a two-year course but I don't officially start till next month. I'm just trying to organise where I'm going to stay. I've got the offer of a room in Fairlea which I think I might take. It's cheap and belongs to a friend of my mum's cousin. I need to be near Middleton and Spruce Knob; those were the two mines my grandfather worked at.'

'What's the address in Fairlea? I've stayed there all my days. Still live in the town with my parents but I've been saving for a deposit on a flat. Hope to have my own place sometime this year. I might have to move out of Fairlea though, not many flats there. Well not ones I can afford.'

'The house is on Seneca Trail, number 62.'

'That's the main road through the town. We're at the other end in Cedar Knoll Park. But it's a small town. You won't be more than a ten-minute walk away if you take that room.'

'Cool. I didn't think the first person I would meet in Fairlea was going to be a police officer, but there you go, might not have been my first choice, but I suppose it might have its plus sides.'

Sam wasn't sure what to make of that remark and looked at Ella quizzically.

'What's wrong with police officers? Have you ever met any before?'

Ella gave a resigned sigh. Sam seemed like a genuinely nice guy, but she sensed he might be just a little naïve.

'I've met plenty of police officers Sam. Never socially. Just when they've been on duty. I must have been stopped a dozen times by your colleagues. When they stop me, I usually end up spread-eagled against my car while they search me and my friends. They always say they are looking for drugs. Drugs or a weapon. I don't do either, but that doesn't seem to matter, they just stop me anyway. You should speak to my brother, he's been stopped more than fifty times, never been charged, but of course he looks like a drug dealer!'

'What does a drug dealer look like?' blurted out Sam without further thought.

Ella didn't answer. She just stood silently staring at Sam. He felt foolish and uncomfortable. Was she being facetious? He wasn't entirely sure as her dead pan expression was giving nothing away. He'd taken it that she'd meant that police officers abused their powers, or to put it more bluntly, discriminated against blacks. He felt aggrieved. Here he was just trying to help, to do what was right, and now he and his fellow officers, were being tarred with the same brush, and he didn't much care for the implication.

He was going to say nothing and just move the conversation on. But somehow, he felt compelled to speak. He was proud of what he did. His father had done his thirty years and Sam had followed him into the force and now he was a newly appointed detective. Not even into his third year of service he was the youngest and most junior member of the department. Sam was proud, mighty proud of that fact and the thought that he might be being stereotyped as just another officer who liked to persecute black people made him bristle. He was always scrupulously fair, he needed Ella to understand that.

Ella could see the hurt in Sam's eyes.

'Look, I can see I've touched a nerve. I'm sorry, I wasn't meaning to have a go at you. As I said, I'm grateful for your help. But it's complicated. Excuse the poor pun but it's not a black and white issue. There's plenty of shades of grey. It's just in my experience not many can see the grey. People just make assumptions.'

Sam pursed his lips.

'Part of a police officer's job is to make assumptions. We have to make sense of things we see and act quickly. We don't have time to mess about, we've got to make a decision.'

'Don't have a problem with that as long as everyone gets treated the same. But that's where it starts to go wrong. The police use lazy stereotypes. Like most drug dealers are black! That's why my brother's been stopped and searched over fifty times. It's not because he's a drugs dealer, it's because he's black and drives a fancy car.'

'Perhaps.' replied Sam quietly.

'No perhaps, Sam. I'm afraid it's the truth. My whole life people have judged me. Not for what I do or say. Not for my talent or brains, they judge me because of the colour of my skin. Black lives matter Sam, or they should do. All we're asking is to be treated equally. The same as you get treated! When was the last time you were verbally abused for being white?

Sam shook his head but didn't say anything.

'Mostly their words are like paper darts. They can be brushed off and ignored, but it gets to be like a dripping tap, it never seems to stop. Eventually they will get you. A ton of paper darts will crush you just the same as a ton of bricks will. That's the reality of having a black skin. The darts keep coming, they wear you down.'

Crikey thought Sam. This was all starting to get a bit heavy. He was so far out of his comfort zone he didn't know how to respond. None of what Ella had said had been his experience, but what did he know, he was a white boy from a predominantly white town. He'd dealt with numerous black people in his three years with the force. Now he found himself questioning whether he'd treated them fairly. If you'd asked him that question ten minutes ago, he would have said that he had. Now, after hearing what Ella had had to say, he wasn't quite so certain. It was a strange feeling. As a police officer you are used to being in charge. You're on the front foot and you get to call the shots. He didn't feel like that now. But in some strange sense he felt a connection with Ella, in a way that he didn't when he was with other girls he knew.

Ella was clearly smart and self-assured, maybe even a little sassy. She also happened to be rather attractive. Sam didn't want to stare, but as he looked at her toned arms and powerful legs he couldn't help wondering if she was an athlete, she certainly looked like one. She was wearing white sneakers, black leggings and a yellow cap sleeve T-shirt that contrasted strikingly with her dark, chocolatey skin. She was maybe only an inch shorter than him, and her sleek black hair was neatly cut around her jawline.

Sam checked his watch. It was now after one and he had someone coming into see him at the police office at two. He still had to get details to allow him to file a crime report and he would need to check Denny's for any CCTV footage and get a proper statement from Ella. Sam sensed an opportunity.

'I'm a bit pushed for time as I've an appointment to get back for. If I can get some brief details from you now, I'll raise a crime report when I get back to the office. I'm also going to need to check Denny's before I leave to see if the assault or the vehicle was captured on their CCTV. I won't have time to get a full statement from you just now, but I'm going to need that for the enquiry. Would you be able, perhaps sometime tomorrow, to meet me and I could take a proper statement from you? It doesn't have to be at the police office, perhaps I could meet you somewhere and we could grab a coffee at the same time?'

Ella smiled and nodded.

'That would be fine, I'm free all of tomorrow. You know this area, so you just tell me where and when.'

Sam had to stop himself from breaking into a beaming smile. This was police business, so he had to remain professional. Anyway, Ella had only agreed to meet so he could take her statement. It wasn't a date. She'll probably tell me all about some great guy she's been dating since high school. She's probably got plans to get married. But on the other hand, perhaps she hasn't. That was the thought he would hang onto. Either way, Sam would get his statement and anything else that came of it, well that would just be a bonus.

'How about ten thirty at Sue's diner. It's on the Maxwelton Road. It's about a ten-minute drive from here. Turn right as if you were heading for Lewisburg and take the turn off for Maxwelton. It's the second or third junction from here.'

'Fine. Sue's diner it is then. I'll see you tomorrow at ten thirty.'

Chapter 3

'Okay, let's get one thing straight. If we're going to check in at the bird sanctuary, then you're going to take some damned linctus for that cough as it doesn't seem to be getting any better. There's a Walgreen in the shopping mall a mile or so up this road. We'll get you the cough mixture and then we'll head to the sanctuary. That's non-negotiable you hear me. If you don't take something for that cough, we ain't stopping to check on that pigeon. Deal?'

Chaska nodded but remained expressionless.

'Good, I'm glad we've got that clarified. Anyway, we're going to have plenty time. Professor Foulis isn't expecting us till two and it's not yet eleven. I thought we'd pick up a sandwich and stop off at Wellsburg. There's a lovely picnic area by the edge of a forest just off the highway and you can walk up to the Shawnee falls. It's supposed to be very picturesque, I thought you might like to go, given that there's a good chance that you're a member of that tribe.'

Chaska's gave the merest of nods but remained stony faced.

'Oh, for God's sake cheer up will you. You could be back in that cell staring at those walls. You're a free man. I thought you'd be happy.'

Chaska had hardly said a word all morning. They had left the prison just after nine and swung by Lilian's house to pick him up a rucksack. The case he'd been given by the prison authorities to put his meagre belongings in was ancient and the stitching on one of the corners looked like it would give out at any time. While they were at the house Lilian had introduced Chaska to Marion, her long-time partner. He hadn't been disrespectful; in fact, they'd shaken hands and said hello before the three of them sat down and had coffee together. But there had been no conversation from Chaska. Now nearly two hours later he'd been lucky if he'd said a dozen words.

'I'm not trying to be rude, but there's just so much to take in. Perhaps a bit too much.'

For the umpteenth time that morning, Chaska coughed and spluttered into the handkerchief he was holding. Wiping his mouth, he continued.

'Where did all these Japanese cars come from? I've not seen a single Cadillac or Lincoln saloon since we've been on this highway! If it's not Japanese, it's a 4x4 with enormous wheels. That or a truck, we must have passed hundreds of them, and each one seems bigger than the last. And what's with all the food joints? They're everywhere you look. Burgers, Pizza, doughnut, and pancake places. There must be dozens of them.'

Suddenly it dawned on Lilian. No wonder he was being quiet. The world he knew forty-one years ago no longer existed. This version was bigger, faster, and brasher than the one he had known as a teenage boy. He was gobsmacked and bewildered, it was in danger of suffocating him.

Unusually for someone who had spent so long in prison, Chaska wasn't ignorant of current affairs. He'd consciously tried to keep abreast of what was going on in the world. During his long years in prison he'd read extensively and made a point each day of trying to see or hear the news. He knew about the assassinations of JFK and Martin Luther King and he understood that Castro was a friend of Russia. In '69, he'd watched transfixed as the Apollo mission landed Armstrong on the moon and he'd despaired watching the body bags being repatriated during the intractable tragedy of the Vietnam war. More recently, he'd got angry watching reports of his kinsmen being forced off their land in Oklahoma to make way for the oil pipelines that were quite literally fuelling the explosion of activity that was now all around him.

But watching the television news hadn't prepared him for the world he could now see through the car window. The billboards, neon signs and traffic, all flying by in a fury of colour, diesel fumes and advertising logos. Vehicles of all shapes and sizes thundered past, overtaking and undertaking in a seemingly desperate race to reach their destination. It was frenetic and overwhelming. Chaska felt unprepared for the land of the free.

This, then, was his new reality. This was the world he was expected to inhabit, to find work in and make his peace with. The thought of what lay ahead sent shudders up his spine. There had been no induction to prepare him for life on the outside, but his first few hours of freedom showed him there was no escaping it. He was surrounded and engulfed and it was already choking him. When he opened the door, he would step right into it and at that precise moment he couldn't feel more ill prepared. He didn't even know how to buy a stamp. It was just a little terrifying.

'This is where the Walgreen store is.' announced Lilian pulling off the road and parking next to a trolley park in the sprawling car lot.

'Are you coming in?' asked Lilian quietly.

'Sure.' replied Chaska nervously getting out of the vehicle and scanning the numerous stores that formed the front of the vast shopping mall. Right now, Lilian was his shield, his security blanket and his buffer between the world he was leaving and this new reality. For now, he wanted to keep her close.

Ten minutes later the friends emerged from the store with two bottles of cough syrup and a can of cola that, according to Lilian, would be needed to wash away the taste of the medicine.

'There should be enough in those bottles to last you a week or more. If it doesn't shift the cough it should make you feel a bit better. But that stuff's loaded with paracetamol and caffeine, so don't go drinking beer or any alcohol with it, you hear me, that could get you in a whole heap of trouble.'

Chaska listened politely. Lilian might be his security blanket and he appreciated she was just trying to look out for him, but if he was going to make it on his own, he needed to wise up and start making decisions for himself. It would just take time to get used to his new way of life. For the first time in more than forty years he was free from the constraints of prison life. He could take a shower and eat when he wanted. Hell, if he wanted to go for a walk in the middle of the night he could. He didn't need anyone's permission. There was no locked door to prevent him. He was a citizen of the world again. Free to make mistakes but also to experience life's joys. It might be a daunting prospect, but he could see the upside. This was a whole lot better than being banged up in a cell. He was going to give it his best shot.

'Right, time to get going again. The bird sanctuary is another half hour up the road. Do you fancy listening to some music?'

'Sure, why not.'

Lilian switched on the CD and started to giggle.

'More Dylan I'm afraid. I could put something else on if you want.'

Chaska smiled and shook his head.

'No Dylan's cool. And this is one of his best.' he said starting to sing along to the music.

You used to laugh about everybody that was hangin' out

Now you don't talk so loud now you don't seem so proud

About having to be scrounging your next meal

How does it feel, how does it feel?

To be without a home

Like a complete unknown

Like a rolling stone.

Chaska started to laugh.

'That pretty much sums up me right now, don't you think?'

Lilian smiled.

'Well not quite. You hopefully won't have to be scrounging your next meal. It's on me, so what do you fancy? As you said yourself there's plenty to choose from.'

Chaska leant back putting his hands behind his head and thought for a moment.

'You know what I'd like?'

'Nope.' replied Lilian. 'That was kinda the point of my question.'

Chaska grinned and chuckled.

'A McDonald's. I've never had a McDonald's. Seen that big yellow sign plenty of times in movies, but I've never had one. Don't think McDonald's were around when I got locked up. But don't ask me to go in and get it, I don't have a clue what to ask for.'

Woah, that is just weird thought Lilian. 58 years of age and he hasn't had a McDonald's. Wasn't that just the perfect metaphor to highlight a lifetime wasted in prison. Who hadn't been to McDonald's?

Her mind drifted back to the many conversations she'd had with friends, most of whom liked to argue, that life in prison was too easy. Every discussion ended the same way. It wasn't a holiday camp they were there to be punished. It didn't seem to matter what Lilian said. Her friends didn't understand, or rather they didn't want to understand, what the reality of prison was really like. But this was the perfect illustration. It was being deprived of simple pleasures, like not being able to go for a McDonalds, or take the dog for a walk or the kids to the park, that was the reality of being incarcerated. Forget having access to a T.V or being able to work out at the gym, it was not being able to do the things that most folk took for granted that made prison such a dehumanising and punishing experience. Right now, she wished her friends could witness this.

Here was a man finding joy at the thought of his first Big Mac Meal. It was a sobering moment. Listening to Chaska she was also beginning to understand why so many ex-prisoners didn't make it on the outside. Prison was like a revolving door. Out one minute back the next. She had met those prisoners countless times before and dismissed them too readily as merely repeat offenders, career criminals, who were somehow hardwired to commit crime. The reality was slowly dawning on her, most simply couldn't cope.

The one thing you didn't have to worry about in prison was making decisions. Most of them were made for you. The contrast with life on the outside couldn't be more stark. The transition was going to be hard, especially for someone like Chaska, who'd been locked up for half a lifetime. How was he going to cope? Temporary accommodation had been arranged in Wheeling by the Prison Welfare Officer, but that was only going to be for a month. After that he would be on his own. She wanted to help but she didn't know what more she could do. Perhaps she would go to church this Sunday, say a quiet prayer to the man upstairs. It couldn't do any harm.

*

'Well the good news is it looks like the pigeon is going to be okay, the bad news though, is how did I let you convince me to make a monthly donation to help run this place. I can see that hanging out with you is going to cost me a fortune.'

Chaska smiled and patted Lilian on the back as they walked back to the car.

'I'd do it myself, and will when I get myself organised and get some regular money coming in. But it's for a good cause, you heard what the lady said, they can't run the place without the support of people like you. And hey, look on the bright side, she's going to send their monthly newsletter, keep you up to date with how

Mr Pigeon and all his other friends are getting on. So that will be something to look forward to.'

Lilian scoffed and shook her head. That twenty-minute visit was an example of why she was so fond of Chaska. Sure, he had a violent past. He had inflicted a sickening level of violence when he'd sought revenge on his foster father and she wasn't forgetting that he had brutally assaulted her attacker, but that was now well in the past. Here was a passionate and caring man. Single-minded too, as the episode with the pigeon proved. If he cared about something, he would commit to it 100%. There were never any half measures with Chaska, it was all or nothing.

Surprisingly for a Friday the picnic area wasn't busy. Lilian found them a table that was shaded from the hot sun and unpacked the brown carrier bag.

'One Big Mac Meal, large fries and a coke for you and a cheeseburger, small fries and orange juice for me. Do you want ketchup or mayonnaise with your burger?'

Chaska didn't reply. He had zoned out and was studiously reading a letter that had arrived at the prison just as they were leaving this morning.

'Ketchup or Mayo?'

Lilian waved the sachets in front of his face.

'Err, Ketchup, thanks.'

'Is your letter from Carole?'

Chaska nodded but didn't look up.

'I thought I recognised the writing. She must be very fond of you. I'm sure she must have written to you every month for as long as I've worked at Moundsville, and that's more than ten years now. Weird though, how she never visited.'

Chaska finished reading and put down the letter.

35

'It's more than 250 miles away, she doesn't drive and anyway, she'll have her reasons. I'm not going to blame her for that.'

'No, of course, I didn't mean to sound critical.'

'No, I know you didn't.' replied Chaska with a shrug of his shoulders.

'But I can tell you she's been writing to me for a lot longer than ten years. I think she first wrote when I'd been in prison for a couple of years. Since then, she's written nearly every month. Occasionally I might get two letters in a month if she's got something special to tell me.'

'Twelve letters a year for forty years, that's.'

Lilian screwed up her face as she tried to do the arithmetic.'

'480.'said Chaska.

'Wow. That's a helluva lot of letters.'

Chaska stared into the distance. He had hardly touched his burger, he seemed distracted. Something was clearly bothering him.

'Is everything all right?'

Chaska bit his bottom lip.

'Not really sure. She's telling me that she's to go into hospital for some tests, but she says it's just routine and nothing to worry about. But I think I'd like to contact her, to speak to her personally, it would be great to hear her voice again.'

'Of course, you must telephone her. I've got a phone card you can use. I take it you've already written to tell her you were getting released?'

Chaska looked sheepishly at his feet.

'She doesn't know about the parole board. I didn't want to raise her hopes. And everything has happened so quickly since then, somehow, I didn't get around to it. Anyway, she's got a lot on her plate. I feel badly about that now, especially as she has to go into hospital.'

'Well, never mind. This will be the very news to cheer her up and take her mind off things. If you ask me, the timing couldn't be better.'

'Appreciate you saying that. But there's more to it than just the hospital appointment. She's been writing about it for months now.'

'Writing about what.' said Lilian wiping mayonnaise from the side of her mouth.

'The court case that's been brought against the Greenbrier Asbestos Company has just started this week. I know she's been worrying about it as she's due to give evidence for the prosecution. She worked for the company for a few years after her husband died. But that must be over thirty years ago now. The Lawrence family opened the company not long after they sold off the Spruce Knob mine. A lot of the folk who worked in the asbestos factory were women, like Carole. It was a big employer in the area for twenty years or more. And a godsend for many families whose men folk had lost their jobs in the mine.'

'How did they end up losing their jobs? I thought you said they sold the mine.'

'They did, to the West Virginian Mining company. But they were modernising big style. Bringing in new fancy cutting machines and a conveyor belt for getting the coal out of the mine. With the new technology they didn't need as many men, so lots of them lost their jobs.'

'Ah, gotcha. But why is it such a difficult time for Carole?'

'This latest case is opening old wounds. Many years ago, Carole had been part of a group that tried to sue the Lawrence family after her husband and his friend, Joe Jarret, were killed in a mining accident. That was a terrible time for her. She had been struggling with mental health issues for several years. Her illness was the reason I was fostered with another family. With a husband and two kids of her own to look after it had all become too much. She couldn't cope and social services persuaded her that I would be better off if I went and lived with another family. I know that she bitterly regretted that decision, she told me often enough in her letters. Then, when Tom died a few years later, it all came to a head. With the case lost and no compensation from the mine she struggled to put food on the table. The stress of it all brought on a full-blown nervous breakdown. It was years before she fully recovered and got properly back on her feet. And, of course, it meant she had to leave her job in the asbestos factory. It was impossible for her to stay on after she'd been part of the group that had tried to sue the Lawrences.'

'Goodness, that is really sad. I didn't know any of that. Why didn't you tell me any of this before?'

'There was nothing you could do about it, so I didn't want to burden you with it. Anyway, it looks like lightening may be about to strike twice.'

'What do you mean by that?'

'The current court case, the one that's being brought against the asbestos company, is trying to get compensation for gross negligence. The workers were handling raw asbestos and exposed to its dust and fibres for years. They didn't even give them face masks to wear! A few years after the factory closed former employees started dying of respiratory illnesses, asbestosis mainly, lots of people died and now hardly anyone's left to fight the claim. The families have been trying to get the company into court for years. Carole is one of the few former employees still alive and she reckons that's only because she moved off the factory floor into an office job after a few months. She wasn't exposed to the asbestos to the same extent as the others.'

'That is shocking. You hear about the dangers of asbestos on the news, but I never even knew that they manufactured it in West Virginia.'

'The factory has been closed for more than ten years now. The family shut it down when the first employees were starting to fall ill. They took their money and got out. There's another irony to all of this. The three Lawrence brothers, who ran the mine and then the asbestos company are still alive. Old men now, but wealthy old men, enjoying the trappings of two businesses that ruthlessly exploited their workers and gave them nothing by way of compensation.'

Lilian slowly shook her head.

'That just ain't right. Doing that to honest folk who were just trying to earn a living.'

'Just another example of the rich exploiting the ordinary worker. Happens the world over from what I've read.'

'I don't care that they're old men, I hope they are having to give evidence and justify what they've done.'

Chaska sighed and shook his head.

'Apparently not. According to what Carole's told me, the case is being defended by Aiden Lawrence. Well not him personally, but lawyers he's instructed who are acting on behalf of the family. Aiden's the son of Eldridge Lawrence, the oldest of the brothers. He's a lawyer himself and was heavily involved in the running of the mine and the asbestos company. He made it a limited company shortly before it was wound down, and because of legal stuff I don't understand, that has somehow protected the family from personal liability. It's more complicated than that, but it looks like none of the brothers will be forced to take the stand.'

'Shit, no wonder she's angry. I'd be furious if I were in her shoes. Some folk just seem to get a raw deal in life, you being a case in point. And by the sounds of it, Carole Hicks has been equally unfortunate.'

Chaska smiled weakly.

'The Hicks were a great couple. I loved my time with them. It's where I got to love birds. Tom used to breed the canaries they used in the mine. He had an aviary in his backyard, and I used to help him feed and look after the birds. The mine paid him a bit extra for doing it, but it was always a labour of love. He just adored those birds. And after he died, Carole kept the birds on. She's still got some. I don't think she has as many as Tom used to have, but I know from what she tells me in her letters, that it somehow keeps her connected to him, and I kinda get that. Reckon I would have done the same if it had been me. I would love you to meet Carole, she was just the kindest person and had the biggest heart. She's just like you.'

Lilian blushed, she didn't know what to say.

'Apart from the Hicks, you're the only person who's every taken an interest in me. Respected, spoken up and looked out for me. I want you to know how much I appreciate what you've done for me. You see Lilian, the thing is, I don't know how I can ever repay you for that kindness.'

Chaska's voice tailed off. What he'd said was heartfelt but now his voice sounded brittle. He was starting to get emotional.

'Please stop.' said Lilian putting her hand to her mouth to stop herself crying. 'You don't need to thank me for anything. You've given me more than I've ever given you. But please stop, you're going to make me cry, and I don't want to cry. Not right now.'

'Jeez, I'm sorry, I didn't mean to upset you.'

'It's fine. Honestly it is, but can we change the subject? You were about to explain about the court case and why Carole is so upset. Tell me about that?

Chaska clasped his hands together and leant forward on the table.

'I know she's been agonising about the case for months. She's a key witness and a lot is resting on her testimony. The result of the case might depend on it. She desperately wants to see justice done. Not just for all her co-workers who have died, but also for her husband. She's convinced that the Lawrences covered up his death. They made out that it was his own negligence that led to him being killed. Carole hasn't had a dime from them, and if she can't give her evidence, it's possible that the family might get off with it again.'

Lilian blew out her cheeks and shook her head. Reaching down she picked up her handbag and started to rummage through it.

'Here, this is what I was looking for.' she said holding up a small card. 'It's a $5 phonecard. Don't know how much is left on it, but there will be enough for you to call Carole.'

Lilian turned and pointed to a phone booth that was attached to the side of the toilet block.

41

'Think I'm going to have to get you to dial for me, don't have a clue how to use that card.'

'Sure.' said Lilian getting up from the table. 'I take it you've got her number.'

Chaska nodded producing a diary from his jacket pocket.'

'Got it right here.'

Ten minutes later Chaska returned to the picnic table and sat down. He looked pensive.

'Is everything alright?'

'Think so. She got all emotional when she realised it was me.'

'I'm not surprised. She hasn't spoken to you in over forty years, and as you never wrote to tell her you were being released, she must have got a right shock when she heard your voice.'

'Yeah, I suppose. Maybe I didn't think that through properly, I shouldn't have surprised her like that.'

'No harm done I'm sure, and I bet she was thrilled to hear from you.'

'I couldn't get a word in for several minutes. She kept telling me how.......But never mind all that now. I'll tell you about it in the car later. Anyway, I'm glad I phoned when I did. She's going in for her tests tomorrow. Her attorney has told her that he expects her evidence to be heard on Wednesday or Thursday next week. So, all going well, she should be out the hospital and home in plenty of time.'

'Well that will be a weight off her mind,' said Lilian gathering up the empty burger boxes and depositing them in a trash can. 'She'll still get to give her evidence. The Lawrence family might get what they deserve yet!'

'I hope so, but don't hold your breath, the justice system doesn't always work that way.'

Lilian gave Chaska a knowing look.

'Right then, what about a walk up to see the waterfall? It's only five minutes up this path. We're still in good time for Professor Foulis, despite the detour to visit that blessed bird sanctuary.'

Chaska smiled and started to follow Lilian up the path.

'Quick question. Do you know how I could get myself to Fairlea? I'd like to go and see Carole. My accommodation in Wheeling is booked for a month. I'll not be away long, just a few days, but I feel I should go, I won't feel right if I don't go.'

'From what you've told me I can understand that. You should go. It's important to you, and Carole will be made up to see you. But you're going to have to remind me, where's Fairlea?'

'It's at the other end of the state, in Greenbrier County.'

'Greenbrier County. Is it near Lewisburg? I think that's the only place I've been to down that way.'

'Yep. It's only a few miles from Lewisburg.'

'Well in that case, you could get a bus from Pittsburgh to Charleston and then a connecting bus to Lewisburg. After that you're on your own but I expect there will be a bus from Lewisburg to Fairlea. Failing that you could get a taxi.'

'Sounds like a plan.' said Chaska high fiving Lilian.

'Great. I'll be able to drop you at the bus station after we've finished with Professor Foulis.'

Chapter 4

In the conference room of Lewisburg Police Office, Lieutenant Charlie Finch, Sam Coutts and numerous other detectives were seated together on the far side of the room underneath an enormous framed map that depicted the Greenbrier Police jurisdiction. They were waiting for the Chief to arrive. This was not going to be any old meeting. Unlike his predecessor, the new Chief of Police, John Bowater, rarely did public appearances and he was not given to hyperbole. He was an intrinsically shy and serious man, speaking in public, perhaps surprisingly for someone of such high office, was just not his thing. He disliked it so much that he never chaired the regular morning meetings, preferring to delegate that responsibility to his deputy.

Bowater was a fully signed up stats and procedures man. Statistical reports and policy documents were his natural territory. He studied everything in minute detail, from the number of fixed penalty tickets his officers issued to how many toilet rolls the office got through each month.

John Bowater was what was referred to in the Force as a headquarters man. He had been brought in by the Police Authority after the suicide of Chief Wilder. A wise head, much needed, they said, to steady the ship after such a traumatic incident. Well if invisibility was a requirement for stability, then John Bowater was your man.

So today was a rare occasion, a collector's item even. It was the first time that the new Chief had deemed it necessary to address all his detectives together.

His appointment five months ago had been very low key. There were many working in the Lewisburg office who still hadn't met him. Even more damning, they probably wouldn't recognise him, even if you'd shown them a photograph. He was anonymous and carried all the charisma of a pot plant. Watching paint dry was more exciting than Chief Bowater.

It had come to Charlie's attention that the Chief had never been a detective, and his discomfort when he was around them was palpable. That was certainly one reason why Charlie had seen so little of him. Like many senior officers, Bowater had spent most of his service pushing paper through various roles and ranks in police headquarters. It was a long time since he'd had to face an angry man. Clever? Most certainly, but a leader? Someone the troops could relate to and would run through a brick wall for, probably not.

From Charlie's perspective his anonymity had its advantages. Up till now he hadn't interfered or micro-managed the way Wilder used to. Charlie had a free hand to run the department the way he wanted. Set his own agenda and prioritise as he saw fit. But there were disadvantages too. It was difficult getting the Chief to make a decision. Even for seemingly straightforward issues. That was because decisions can be dangerous things. They make you accountable, responsible, subject to scrutiny in a way that can be uncomfortable and challenging. Bowater was the classic fence sitter, a procrastinator and hedger of bets. The sooner he could get a problem off his desk the better, it was then someone else's responsibility.

But that thought process exposed a serious level of naivety. Bowater couldn't just delegate or magic things away. The previous chief had too many faults to mention them all, but shirking responsibility certainly wasn't one of them. Ewart Wilder had always been up for the challenge. So, no matter what Bowater thought or how hard he tried, he couldn't shake off the fact that he had vicarious responsibility for all his officers and civilian staff. It was that thought that kept him awake at night and a bundle of nerves for the rest of the time.

Learn how to manage your manager, had been a favourite saying of Mike Rawlingson, Charlie's former boss and close friend. Chance would be a fine thing thought Charlie, as he watched Bowater nervously shuffling his notes at the lectern next to the screen. How do you manage the invisible man! Up till now everything had been fine. For several months nothing had crossed Charlie's desk that he couldn't deal with. It was routine, mundane even and though he didn't like to admit it, occasionally boring.

Charlie knew the warning signals all too well. When things were this quiet you can drop your guard and become complacent. He remembered what Mike had told him. When it's quiet, when apparently nothing's happening, that's when you should be at your most alert. Have your antennae up because the others won't. And remember, things can change in an instant. Crime will still be happening, it's just that at that moment, you won't know anything about it.

Charlie chuckled to himself. As usual Mike had been right. As a young detective learning his trade, he had found it irritating just how often Mike had been right, but that irritation had long since passed. Charlie missed the wise counsel of his friend, but it had been the many lessons that he'd learned from his mentor, often during the most innocuous of enquiries, that now allowed him to lead his team with confidence and a level of professional expertise that was the envy of many.

Charlie glanced across to the Chief who was carefully reading through his papers while making occasional notes with a black Montblanc fountain pen which he clutched tightly between his talon-like fingers. Bespectacled, with an unusually large nose and prominent Adam's apple, his neck was long and scrawny. His shirt collar looked at least a couple of sizes too big, and like a puppet head on a stick, it gave the strange illusion that while his collar and tie remained static, his head was rotating. Charlie tried not to laugh, but for some strange reason, he couldn't get the image of an agitated ostrich, spinning its head round in all directions, as it tried to ward off the next threat of danger, out of his head.

Charlie hadn't given it much thought before, probably because he had spent so little time in the Chief's company, but studying him now, he decided that his boss was a very strange looking man. The Chief looked older than his fifty-two years. He had thick shiny grey hair swept back from his face and held stiff with lashings of Brylcreem. Around six-foot tall, he appeared taller because he was so bony and angular, the opposite of most officers his age, who carried the evidence of years of fast food and fast living around their waists. The Chief could never be described as a physical specimen. Puny would be unkind but it was nevertheless accurate. Not that any of that should matter. But as Charlie stared at his leader, somehow it did.

Charlie shook himself and tried to concentrate. He had drifted off, daydreaming about demented ostriches, and had managed to miss the Chief's opening remarks, not the best example to set his junior officers. But what the hell was he on about? The Chief nodded and Sergeant Joice, who was operating the laptop brought up the next slide.

<u>West Virginian Police Authority</u>
New Code of Conduct for Officers
Complaints against officers made by members
of the public

For fuck's sake, thought Charlie, is this for real? The first occasion the Chief speaks to the troops and he's lecturing us about professional standards and how the public can make a complaint against us. Way to go boss! That will get them on your side. Charlie couldn't believe what he was looking at.

The presentation lasted nearly forty minutes. It had been received in stony silence. Other than Charlie's obligatory words of thanks at the end of the presentation there had been no questions. Sergeant Joice looked embarrassed as he handed out copies of the slides and explanatory notes. The detectives sat expressionless staring at the Chief. For several moments nobody moved or said anything. The Chief blinked first. Standing up he straightened his tie making sure his gaze didn't meet those of his subordinates. Picking up his briefcase he ghosted out of the room and headed for the sanctuary of the third floor.

'What the hell was all that about?' asked Angela turning around to look at Charlie as the conference door clicked shut.

'We're not discussing it here.' replied Charlie tersely, 'I want you, and the other supervisors in my office in five and we'll discuss it there. I'll speak to the rest of you later, you'll get your chance to have your say, but let's get back to work, there are crimes to solve, so let's get at it.'

There were mumbles and shakes of the head as officers picked up their papers and left the room, but not much was said as they disappeared along the corridor. They were still shell-shocked at what they'd just heard.

'Steve, do you want to join us? Looks like you could do with a coffee?'

Sergeant Joice gave a resigned sigh.

'Would rather have a stiff whisky being honest, but sure, a coffee would be good. I'll give you a bit of background about all of this. Don't want you detectives thinking I've been brown nosing the Chief. You see he cornered me the other day when I was on the top floor and asked if I knew anything about PowerPoint. Stupidly, I said a little, but that was before I had time to think. The next thing I know I'm the Chief's bagman for these damned presentations. You're the third one he's done, still five more to do. I'm like a pariah now, no one wants to sit with me in the canteen. Why the hell are Professional Standards, from Headquarters, not doing these inputs? This is doing my head in I can tell you. The worst of it is, I've still got my day job in Roads Policing to do, you should see the hours I'm putting in just now doing two jobs. The Mrs is going nuts.'

'The things some people will do to get that next promotion.' laughed Angela putting on the kettle.

'Fat chance of that.' scoffed Steve slumping down in a chair. 'But it's a lesson learned. I'll be keeping a low profile from now on. And just so you know, when I found out you were this morning's audience, I did come and try and warn you, but neither Angela, nor you were in your office. I didn't think I should tell Sam or any of the others without you knowing, so that's why you went in blind, sorry about that.'

'Nothing to apologise for, we've all been there. And anyway, I don't want you thinking that any of my detectives don't think it's an important subject. I'm all about fairness and treating people right. It's just the timing of it. He's hardly said a word to any of us, let alone discuss crime or the work we do. Then he rocks up out the blue and gives a lecture about our conduct. It just leaves a bad taste and does nothing for anyone's motivation. But nobody's blaming you.'

'Good to know,' said Steve stirring his coffee.

'Look,' said Angela waving her notes in the air. 'It's got the Chief's name at the bottom of these and it's dated October '92.'

Steve looked up.

'He wrote them and devised the input when he worked in HQ. It's his baby. It's why he's so precious about it.'

'Explains a lot.' said Charlie. Before he could continue there was a knock at the door.

'Come in.' shouted Charlie.

The door opened and standing there with a smile as wide as the Greenbrier river was Sam Coutts.

'What are you looking so pleased about?' asked Angela beckoning him to come in and sit down.

'I'm looking for the Pontiac car keys. Someone said you had them Sergeant. I've got a detection pending, and get this, when I charge them, our detection rate for the year will hit 70%. That will be the highest it's been for 3 years.'

'You really are a geek,' chuckled Angela as she searched her jacket pocket for the car keys. 'The Chief is going to love you, he's nearly as big a stats man as you. You better watch yourself, Sergeant Joice was just saying he could do with someone else being the boss's bagman.'

Sam's smile withered instantly.

'Sergeant Brown's just joshing you, but seriously, if the detection rate has hit 70% then that is great news. Hey, if you're lucky I might buy you a beer in Bursley's.'

'Been a while,' said Angela cheekily. 'Anyway, what's your detection for, is it that assault and racial incident you came across last week?'

'That's the one. I've managed to get three of the four identified from the CCTV tape I got from Denny's. It's the Sill brothers and Linton Webb. I can't make out the fourth guy in the truck, but maybe one of them will spill the beans. It would be good to get all four charged.'

'Play one off against the other when you bring them in for interview. That's how we usually get them to burst ,' said Angela with a smirk.

'Not going to work this time. I've just been down seeing Sergeant Lang in the custody suite. He says it will have to be a caution and charge. Apparently too long has elapsed since the crime was committed, so we're struggling for a power of arrest.'

'Since when?' said Angela indignantly.

'Since the Chief gave Sergeant Lang and the other custody officers new procedures regarding powers of arrest and detention. And because all three of them are well known and on file we don't need to arrest them for fingerprints. So, as I said, I've to charge them, but I've not to bring them in.'

Charlie narrowed his eyes and shook his head. He turned and stared at Sergeant Joice.

'Don't look at me boss, I'm just his PowerPoint man. I know diddly squat about new custody arrangements.'

'I've had next to nothing to do with the man for six months, now in the space of an hour he's got me really pissed off. This ain't going to help us to our job one bit. Wilder was a dick, but he would never have sanctioned this piece of crap.'

'Right that's enough Angela. I'll keep my counsel till I know all the facts, but till I do, we'll play it by the book. Gordon Lang's a good guy, we ain't going to get him or anyone else in bother by asking them to do something against procedure. So, suck it up just now and I'll look into it.'

'Fine.' said Angela realising that she was in danger of overstepping the mark.

Angela Brown was a hardworking and tenacious detective, but she was new to her role as a Sergeant. Leadership, and all that it involved, was not a skill that was coming easily. She had become used to looking out for herself, and at times she had sailed close to the wind, but now as a supervisor, she had responsibility for the actions of others. Leading by example was all very well but charging headlong at problems was not always the solution as Angela had occasionally found out to her cost. There was more than one way to skin a cat. She just needed to be a little less headstrong and find other, more subtle, approaches to resolving problems.

Angela looked at Sam.

'Have you got a neighbour organised to go with you? You should take Ryan, it will be good experience for him.'

Sam shook his head.

'Well that had been my plan, he seemed right up for it, then when I explained the case and where we were going, he suddenly remembered that he'd arranged for someone to come into the office to see him. Something about an outstanding enquiry he had from when he was still in uniform. I've had a look in the office, but everyone else seems to have disappeared, so I'm a bit stuck to be honest.'

'Where's your enquiry?' asked Steve rinsing out his mug. 'If it's anywhere near White Sulphur Springs then I might be able to help. I'm meeting a Roads Engineer, on the mountain road after lunch, regarding the fatal last week when the old boy careered off the road at the bluff bend. But that's not till two. So, I've got a couple of hours if that's any use. We could do your enquiry and then if you didn't mind hanging on for me, we could kill two birds with one stone.'

'Perfect, that works for me.' said Sam putting his thumb up. 'My enquiry is over at Addison, so not that far away. I don't want to drag you away if you've other things to do Sergeant, but it sure would be a help.'

'Not a problem. Must be fifteen years past since I was an acting detective, but it'll be just like old times. I'll have to go in uniform though, we don't all get to cut about in fancy suits.'

Angela stroked her chin as she looked Sam up and down suspiciously. Something was different about him. He was wearing a very smart three-piece grey suit and a pair of highly polished black brogues. His hair looked different too. Short and neat, it looked like it had been recently cut.

'Is that a new suit?'

Sam nodded sheepishly but didn't reply.

'And you've had your hair cut, and those look like new shoes. You brush up well. Is there something you want to tell me?'

Sam's cheeks burned crimson; he didn't know where to look.

'I knew it.' said Angela slapping her thigh. 'It's female intuition you see. You've met a girl, and I'm going to guess that she's helped you pick out that suit and suggested you should get your haircut. Am I right Detective Coutts?'

'Pretty much,' replied Sam quietly.

Angela started to laugh.

'A detective's training isn't just good for solving crime. I'd noticed a few days ago that you were looking smarter. That suit fits properly for a start, but I didn't say anything. But good for you Sam. Having an interest away from work is important. You spend way too many hours in this place. You'll need to let us meet her, bring her to Bursley's, Lieutenant Finch was just saying it was time he bought you a beer.'

Sam stared down at his feet. So far, he'd only been out with Ella a couple of times. He wasn't counting the coffee they'd had when he was taking her statement. But after plucking up the courage to ask her out, they had been out for some food and been to a drive-in movie. It was early days, but they were getting on great and just Like Angela had said, Ella had picked out his suit and suggested he buy the brogues to go with it.'

Charlie had been sitting at his desk watching his newest member of the department squirm with embarrassment at Angela's interrogation. It was time to end his discomfort.

'Okay, if we can get this conversation back on track it sounds like we've got the perfect solution. We're obliged to you for your assistance Steve. Always good to have both sides of the organisation working collaboratively. Good for team cohesion. Crikey, perhaps I should run up and tell the Chief, might even bring a smile to his face.'

*

Half an hour later Sam and Steve were approaching bluff bend on the mountain road.

'There's a lay-by another couple of hundred yards on your right. You can park there.'

Sam parked up and the two officers walked down a sharp incline to where some yellow police tape was strung between a gap in the metal barrier.

'Just morbid curiosity on my part you understand, but I wanted to see it for myself. Hope that doesn't sound creepy,' said Sam staring over the abyss. 75 feet below a small red hatch back lay pulverised having smashed hood first into a massive boulder.

'Don't worry about it. You're no different from anybody else, it's part of the human condition. We need to know, to see things for ourselves. It helps us to understand.'

'That, or we're just a bunch of nosey dudes, who can't help ourselves. A bit like those rubberneckers you see at the scene of road accidents.' added Sam.

'Yeah, I suppose.' said Steve who was now sitting on the twisted barrier.

Sam bent down to examine a set of skid marks that were burnt on the road.

'Jeezo, I take it these were made by that car. '

'Afraid so. Must have realised that he was going too fast and braked hard, but it was far too late. He's been unable to take the bend and has gone straight through the barrier and smashed headfirst into that boulder.'

Sam winced at the thought.

'The barrier looks kinda flimsy, no way it could stop a vehicle if it was travelling at any speed.'

'That's why I'm meeting the Roads Engineer. We're going to have to put a much bigger and stronger barrier on this bend, or it will happen again, and then the brown stuff really will hit the fan!'

'The way the tracks disappear over the edge like that, reminds me of a ski jumper launching themselves off one of those giant ski jumps.'

'Yeah, I know what you mean. I hadn't thought about it like that before, but I can see where you're coming from. You won't be surprised to hear that the old boy was killed instantly. And get this, when the troops got here, his CD player was still playing.'

Steve started to laugh.

'What's so funny?'

'I suppose it's not funny, but it tickled me. It was an ACDC CD that was playing. I like to think the old guy went out to 'Highway to Hell' playing at full volume. That would be the perfect way for an aging rocker to go!'

'It must have been like that final scene in Thelma and Louise when they career off the edge of the cliff. I know it's wrong, but now I can't get that image out of my head.'

'Don't worry yourself about it. That's just police gallows humour speaking. We all do it. It's a type of coping mechanism, and by God you need one doing a job like this.'

Sam scratched his head.

'Yeah you're right. I've not been in the job long, but I can recognise it in myself. It's like a protective shell that you build around yourself, it lets you keep things at arm's length, where it can't hurt you.'

'Yep, I think you've summed it up pretty well,' said Steve patting Sam on the back. 'Now time to get a shift on. What was the address in Addison we're looking for?'

Twenty minutes later Sam pulled up outside a dilapidated wooden bungalow on the edge of Addison. The front and roof of the building were covered in grey wooden shingles. To the side of the house stood several large pine trees. Their fallen needles formed an inch-thick apricot coloured blanket that covered two thirds of the roof. Several of the shingles on the front of the house were missing and others appeared split or badly warped, twisted by years of exposure to the rain and hot sun. In front of the rickety garage stood an orange Ford F-Series truck with the flag of the confederacy emblazoned on its hood.

The front yard resembled a junkyard. Rusting old scaffolding poles and assorted pieces of scrap metal littered the parched lawn. In a narrow border in front of the house, a row of wilting chrysanthemum plants, desperately in need of some water, struggled to lift their heads from the compacted soil. Their presence, the only evidence that someone was trying to make the place look homely.

'Well it ain't no des res that's for sure,' said Steve getting out the vehicle. 'Looks like a scrap metal yard.'

'According to their intelligence file, they do a bit of wheeling and dealing. Expect a lot of this stuff is stolen. They've got several convictions for theft but proving old metal like this is stolen is a nightmare. It's rarely stamped and most of it never gets reported.'

Steve nodded in agreement.

'A lot of it comes from old yards and railway sidings. And those old beer kegs over there,' said Steve pointing to the side of the garage, 'they look like they might be aluminium. They're worth a fair bit when melted down. And you can bet your bottom dollar that they will have had any markings that could distinguish them removed.'

'Correct.' said Sam walking over and examining the kegs. 'I'll put an intelligence log in when we get back to the office. But that will be for another day. I need to sort this enquiry first.'

'Do you want me to cover the back? Wouldn't be the first time that the Sill brothers have tried to do a runner from the police.'

'Good thought,' said Sam taking his police radio out of his pocket. 'I'll give you a shout if they answer the door.'

'And I'll do the same.' said Steve waving his radio in the air. 'It's a long time since I've had this much excitement, I should get out and about more, this is what we all joined the job for.'

Sam waited for a minute to give Steve enough time to get round to the back door. Glancing to his right he noticed that one of the front rooms had its curtains drawn. Perhaps they aren't up yet. Neither brother has a regular job, and it's only midday, so early yet by their standards!

In the short time he'd been in the job, Sam had noted that people like the Sill brothers often kept unusual hours. They didn't conform to normal social conventions. They preferred to do their work at night, under the cover of darkness and away from prying eyes.

Sam knocked on the door with the end of his radio. There was no reply. He waited a few seconds then knocked again harder. He stood back from the door and looked to his right. The twitch of the bedroom curtain gave the game away. Someone was in.

Sam was about to rattle the door for a third time when the door opened.

'Come in Detective Coutts,' said Steve with a beaming smile. 'Darren here was just going out the back when he met me. I explained that we're looking to have a word with him and his brother. He's kindly agreed to delay his trip to the store to speak to us. Isn't that right Darren?'

Darren made a strange grunting noise and looked down at his feet. He was tall and skinny, and his milky white skin was unblemished apart from a large brown mole on his left hip that poked out above the waistband of his shorts. Like his older brother, his reddish blond hair was cut to the wood, giving him a strange almost skeletal like appearance. He was naked apart from a pair of grey fleecy shorts.

'He was in that much of a hurry to go and get his shopping that he forgot to put on some shoes! Isn't that right Darren?'

Darren nodded but didn't look up.

'I see.' said Sam pushing the bedroom door open with his foot and peering into the room. There was no sign of Sean.

'And where might your brother be?' asked Sam who was now examining a long white cotton robe that was hanging on the back of the door.'

'In case you're wondering that robe belongs to our mom,' said a surly voice from the other end of the hall. 'She's in a drama group, it's a costume for one of their plays, not that it's any of your business.'

Sam put down the robe and turned around to speak to Sean who had emerged from the bathroom.

'Didn't think it was your style somehow.' said Sam sarcastically.

'What is it you want?' asked Sean doing up the belt on his jeans.

'Can we take a seat and I'll explain why we're here.' said Sam.

'No, you can tell us what you want and then leave. We've got stuff that needs doing.'

'Yeah, we can see that you're busy people.' quipped Steve who was leaning against the kitchen door.

'Fine then.' said Sam opening his folder, 'I want you both to listen very carefully to what I'm about to say.'

Chapter 5

'Come in, come in.' said Professor Foulis ushering Lilian and Chaska into his spacious office overlooking the university's quadrangle. 'Perfect timing, I was just about to make a cafetiere of coffee, and I've bought a red velvet cake to help us celebrate your freedom Chaska. Please, give me your jackets and have a seat.'

Professor Foulis took their jackets and Chaska's fedora and hung them up. He embraced Lilian, kissing her warmly on both cheeks. The vigorous handshake he greeted Chaska with, a clear indication that he was delighted to see him.

With the welcomes over, Lilian and Chaska sat down on an ancient leather settee by the window that was surrounded by piles of books and academic papers.

'And may I say, many congratulations Chaska. I couldn't have been happier when Lilian telephoned to tell me the news. Please, make yourselves comfortable, I've got lots to tell you.'

For the next ten minutes the three friends sat drinking coffee and catching up on each other's news.

'Would you rather have a cookie?' asked the professor noticing that Chaska had hardly touched his cake.

'No thanks, I'm fine really,' said Chaska before another bout of coughing brought his explanation to a halt. He took out his handkerchief from his shirt pocket and covered his mouth.

'Apologies, I don't mean to be rude, but I'm just not that appetized right now.'

'It's that blessed cough,' explained Lilian. 'He only ate half his burger at lunchtime. Maybe time you took some more linctus. It must be nearly four hours since you had the last lot.'

Chaska retrieved the bottle from his jacket and took two spoonfuls which he washed down with a mouthful of coffee.

Professor Foulis peered over the rim of his glasses and smiled warmly. He opened his briefcase and removed two sets of photocopied notes. He handed one of the sets to Chaska.

'Okay, we could small talk all day, but I think it's time we got down to business.'

Chaska nodded and started to read the report.

'Page one is just some introductory words, but if you'd like to turn to pages two, three and four I think you'll find what you're interested in.'

Chaska tuned over the page and continued reading. For the next few minutes, he sat expressionless as he read through the report. Eventually he put down the notes. A small but discernible smile creased his lips.

'How certain can you be that this is accurate?' asked Chaska.

'About as certain as I can be without there being a DNA test. The three-arrow tattoo is most definitely Shawnee. There is no doubt about that. And we also know that they only ever used it to denote the firstborn son of the chief. So, that being the case, I'm 99% sure that you are a direct descendent of Chief Makatai. He was the leader of the Shawnee people when he was killed at the massacre of Spruce Knob in 1869. By my reckoning Chief Makatai would have been your great grandfather.'

Chaska pondered for a moment.

'That makes sense,' he said putting down the report. 'I thought I must be a member of a tribe local to that part of West Virginia. After I was taken into care I was placed with local families, so from my research I reckoned I must be either Shawnee or Lakota. They both lived in the area. I've read a bit about both tribes and I know about the massacre, and about Eldridge Lawrence who was supposed to have shot the Chief. He wanted the land so he could get his hands on the coal reserves.'

Professor Foulis clasped his hands and blew out his cheeks.

'That was about the strength of it. There was big money in that coal. To a great many people's surprise, Lawrence was charged with murder and there was a trial, but I'm afraid it was no more than a show trial. It was never going to go anywhere. He was a well-respected local businessman. There was no way any jury back then was going to convict him of the murder of some Indians. I don't want that to sound callous, but it's the truth I'm afraid. I've included an appendix that covers the incident at Spruce Knob.'

Chaska raised his eyebrows and nodded gently.

'I know about thirty of the tribe were murdered that day. And that included many women and children. It doesn't get much of a mention in the history books. Thirty dead Indians was neither here nor there in the greater scheme of things. Not when you compare it to the likes of the Tonkawa or Oak Run massacres when hundreds were killed.'

Professor Foulis nodded sympathetically.

'They were bleak times alright.'

'That's an understatement. But there's something else that I want you to know. It's not just the massacre that connects me to that mountain and Eldridge Lawrence.'

Professor Foulis looked puzzled.

'How so?' asked Professor Foulis wiping some cream away from the side of his mouth.

Chaska put down his cup.

'It was a long time ago, but when I was 12, I lived with a family called Hicks in Greenbrier County. They were, without question, the nicest family I was ever fostered with. Tom Hicks, my foster father, used to work on the mountain at the Spruce Knob mine. He and a colleague were killed in an accident in May of 1953. That was another tragedy I can tell you.'

'My goodness, I'm sorry to hear that. And what a strange coincidence. I mean losing two people in such unfortunate circumstances.'

Lilian looked at Professor Foulis and frowned.

'It was a sight more than two. I thought you said 30 Shawnee lost their lives at the massacre. If Chaska was related to Chief Makatai, then presumably he must be related to others who died that day.'

'Absolutely.' acknowledged Professor Foulis. 'That's a fair point. I hadn't really thought about it in that way.'

Lilian continued.

'I already knew about the death of his foster father, Chaska told me about that. But I hadn't appreciated that so many people had lost their lives in the massacre. That really is shocking.'

Professor Foulis nodded in agreement.

'And I'll tell you another thing.' added Lilian. 'What happened on that mountain and at the trial was blatant racism. No other term for it. I don't care that it was more than a hundred years ago. That shouldn't change anything. They would have convicted the Shawnee quick enough if things had been the other way around. It's disgusting.'

Professor Foulis sighed.

'I won't give you an argument about that Lilian.'

Chaska made a face and stood up.

'Can we go back a bit. I'm now confused. I think I'm right in saying the Lawrence family started mining the land eighteen months after the massacre.'

'That's correct . We've got all the documentation regarding that.' replied Professor Foulis.

'Yes, yes I understand that. But what happened to the rest of them? I mean the rest of the tribe. There must have been more than thirty of them, they didn't all die in the massacre.'

'No. You're right again. From what I've been able to establish, it appears that most of the tribe who weren't killed made their way west to Wyandotte in Oklahoma. That's where the Shawnee were originally from. We can't be sure how many of them made that journey, but we do know that the Spruce Knob Shawnee were not a big tribe, so the numbers probably weren't huge.'

'Okay, I follow that. But what I'm really interested in then, is what happened to my immediate family? You say in the report that there is no record of my family being in Wyandotte.'

'I'm afraid this is where it starts to get a bit tricky. We've no way of knowing for certain, but my best guess is that for some unknown reason, your immediate family decided to stay behind in West Virginia.'

Chaska looked sceptical.

'But why would they do that? Surely, it would have been better to stick together and go with the others to Oklahoma.'

'I don't think we'll ever know the real reason why they didn't go. But I suspect, as the direct descendants of Chief Makatai, your family were reluctant to give up what had been your home for generations. But I can tell you something, with the rest of the tribe gone, life would have been very difficult. I could almost guarantee that they would have faced terrible discrimination and it would have been a very isolated existence.'

Chaska shook his head in quiet resignation.

'And what about my grandfather and father. Is there anything you can you tell me about them? They would have been the next two Chiefs.'

'I'm sorry, but I can't find any information about either of them. The story just seems to go cold for more than fifty years. I haven't been able to establish what happened to your grandfather or your parents for that matter. The only thing I can tell you is your parents were called Chaska and Wahpea Quatah. That much was recorded on your adoption papers.'

Chaska put his head in his hands and sighed.

'For some reason you were taken into care when you were four. That was in September 1938.'

'Do we know why he went into care, did his parents die?' asked Lilian.

'We just don't know. At that time, it wasn't un-common for the authorities to remove Indian children from their parents and take them into care. There was a mistaken belief that it was somehow better for the child. Seems crazy now, but there you have it.'

Professor Foulis tapped the paper with his finger.

'Most of what we've been discussing is included in the report. There's a lot to take in, so I appreciate you'll have to read it a few times.'

'Just one more thing for now Professor. It's being annoying me since I started to research the massacre. How come they were able to get away with killing all those women and children. The newspaper articles that I read in the library reported that many of those killed, including the Chief, had been shot in the back. Surely that suggests that they were trying to run away. Women and children wouldn't have had guns or weapons.'

Professor Foulis shook his head despondently.

'I know, and it leaves a very bad taste doesn't it. But I'm sorry Chaska, those were different times. If I'm being completely candid, I think it was a miracle that there was any trial. There wasn't any appetite for justice back then. Well not for indigenous people. For years, your ancestors were considered savages by people like, well, white people, like Lilian and me. And look how we treated the Negro in this country. I'm ashamed to say that the history of white America is very sullied when it comes to how we've treated minority groups. Of course, that doesn't make what happened right, but it does help to start to explain things; I think. As ever, the context is important.'

Lilian looked unconvinced.

'Well, I for one think it's a disgrace. And I'll tell you something else. I don't think things have moved on that much in recent times. Racism and discrimination against First Nation people, is still just as bad. Look at Chaska's case as an example. I don't believe the state would have kept a white boy in custody for more than forty years. Not for a killing someone when he was seventeen and after severe provocation.'

'You may well be right.' said Professor Foulis topping up the coffee cups. 'I suppose if you're a privileged white male like me, then it's difficult to fully understand the impact of such prejudice, especially if it doesn't directly affect you. But I hear what you say. The discrimination is undoubtedly still there, it just manifests itself in more subtle ways now. I hope I'm wrong, but I suspect you will experience your fair share of that Chaska, now that you're a free man.'

Lilian got up and looked out the window.

'I've been worrying about that, ever since the news that you were being released came through. Promise me you'll try and turn the other cheek. I couldn't bear the thought of you being back in prison. The authorities won't need a second invitation to lock you up again if something happens out there.'

Chaska smiled at Lilian; he was touched by her concern.

'I'm going to do my best to not get involved. I've wasted enough of my life in a prison cell, I don't intend to go back inside.'

Professor Foulis stood up and took off his glasses.

'I'm not sure what use an aging academic like me can be, but if you ever need anything, anything at all, please don't hesitate to get in touch. If I can help you in any way, I'll be pleased to do so.'

'And you know that that goes for me too.' said Lilian sitting back down and squeezing Chaska by the hand.

'You're both very kind and I appreciate your concern. I want you both to know that. But I'm under no illusions as to how tough it's going to be.'

Chaska thought for a moment and then scoffed.

'Our journey here this morning proved that. It was almost overwhelming, I couldn't believe the noise and the amount of traffic on the roads, it was a different world to the one I'd left. And after we leave here, I'll be on my own. I know the transition is going to be difficult. But I also know, if I'm going to make a go of it, then I'll need to stand on my own two feet. And that's what I intend to do. I'm the great-grandson of a Shawnee Chief. My people have lived through adversity, their spirits will stand with me, I have nothing to fear.'

'Absolutely. And good for you Chaska.' said Professor Foulis who was now hastily rummaging through various papers that littered the top of his desk.

'You just reminded me. I've got a paper here somewhere that I want you to have. It's not quite finished, but it's just final proofing that still needs to be done. It's an article I've written for an academic journal, it's about the history of the Ghost Dance. Do you remember we were talking about it at the prison when I was last there?'

Chaska nodded.

'Well I thought it might be of interest to you. And what you just said, about the spirits of your ancestors standing with you, jogged my memory. Ah, here it is.' said Professor Foulis holding up the paper.

'It's quite a long article I'm afraid, academics can be a bit long winded, we like the detail you see. But you can read it at your leisure. I think you'll find it interesting because the Shawnee adopted the Ghost Dance.

It originated in Nevada in 1889 with the Paiute tribe, but it spread like wildfire and we have hard evidence that it was used by the Shawnee and many other tribes.'

'What's the Ghost Dance when it's at home?' asked Lilian who hadn't a clue what Professor Foulis was talking about.

'Well, I suppose the best way to describe it would be to say it was like a religion. It was certainly widely adopted in much the same way as religions often are. In essence it was a ritual circle dance, performed to reunite the living with the spirits of the dead. Your people believed that through the dance the spirits of their ancestors would be stirred, and they would then return and fight on their behalf. This in turn would make the white colonists leave their land. And when that happened, peace and prosperity could return to their people. There is a lot more to it than that, but that's a brief overview of what it was about.'

'I'll look forward to reading it.' said Chaska taking the report from the professor. 'I had seen it mentioned a couple of times during my research without really knowing what it was about. It sounds fascinating. One thing's for sure, I'm going to have plenty time to read it.'

'Excellent.' replied Professor Foulis.

'This isn't your only copy, is it?

'Don't you worry about that; I can print another one off the computer. It only takes seconds. I can't tell you what a difference these new computers are making to my life. And it's not just teachers like me saying that, ask any of the students. They love them, it's making everyone's life that little bit easier. When you think how we did it for years. I don't know how we ever found the time.'

'Just one more thing to get my head round when I'm out there.' chuckled Chaska. 'Lilian had a computer at the library, but I could only do very basic stuff on it. I'll need to learn more about them.'

'You and me both.' said Lilian.

'You should definitely do that. That would be a great use of your time. It's the way forward. Ten years from now every college, workplace and home will be using them. Enrol on a college course and learn how to use one properly. It's amazing what they can do. You'll never be without a job if you can master a computer, mark my words.'

'I'll bear that in mind.' said Chaska handing Lilian her jacket and putting on his own.

'Oh, one last thing before you go.'

Professor Foulis reached into his jacket pocket and pulled out an envelope.

'It's just a few dollars, enough to buy you a couple of decent meals, to help you get started. Please take it, I'll not take no for an answer.'

Chaska accepted the gift with the grace with which it had been given and hugged Professor Foulis warmly.

'It's a token, that will tide you over for a couple of days, nothing more. You'll find out soon enough that life is expensive, everything needs to be paid for. On that point, have you given any thought how you might provide for yourself in the future?'

'I'm going to find work. I know that won't be easy for an ex prisoner, but I'm prepared to do anything. I'm not afraid of hard work and intend to pay my way.'

Lilian glanced at her watch.

'But that won't be for a few days yet. Chaska is going to Greenbrier County to visit an old friend who's in hospital. I'm dropping him off at the bus station. There's a bus to Charleston at four and its nearly half three now so we'd better get a move on.'

'She was my foster mother a long time ago. Tom, her husband was the man I told you about who died in the mining accident. The Hicks were great foster parents to me, so I want to go and see her. It's been a long time.'

Professor Foulis smiled and nodded.

'You've got a good heart Chaska. Your ancestors would be proud to know that their Chief is a good man. Safe journey and make sure you keep in touch. We'll speak again soon, I'm sure of it.'

*

'Thanks again for your help Steve.' said Sam as the two officers parked their car and walked across the yard to the rear door of Lewisburg Police Office. 'Not a perfect result, but three out of four ain't bad I suppose.'

'I wasn't surprised that the Sill brothers didn't burst. I've never known them to co-operate with the police about anything. Linton Webb on the other hand, now he must have found himself a backbone. I've had numerous dealings with him over the years, thinks he's a boy racer in that old Camaro of his. But he usually folds like a pack of cards when you interview him. But not this time. I expect the Sills have a hex on him. He'll be scared shit-less of them.'

Sam punched in the security code and opened the door.

'It would have been good to trace the fourth guy. I might still get him, I've my suspicions as to who it might be.'

'Still, something positive to tell Ella. Did you say it was tonight you were seeing her?'

'Yep, meeting her after work for a bite to eat. Oh, and I'll send you a copy of the report when it's done. You might find yourself cited to corroborate the caution and charge.'

'No problem. It will be just like any other day in Roads Policing. I never seem to be away from the court. Don't have to give evidence too often though. Most plead guilty on the day, it lets them hold onto their licence for as long as possible you see. They can keep driving till the last minute. Complete waste of my, and my officers' time. But that's the justice system for you. It was never designed to benefit cops.'

'Think this one will go to trial unfortunately, don't see the Sills pleading, do you?'

'Unlikely, but we can live in hope. And don't go writing some longwinded Hans Christian Andersen fairy tale. Stick to the facts and keep it brief. That's my mantra with police reports.'

Sam started to laugh.

'What's so funny about that?' asked Steve.

'You've clearly not heard about my legendary report writing skills.' chortled Sam. 'Not one of my strengths I'm afraid. It will be short and to the point, you can be sure of that.'

'Just like it should be.' replied Steve. 'And you can't be that bad, you'd never have made detective if it were that bad.'

With that Steve bounded up the stairs to his office while Sam headed to the uniform bar where Sergeant Lang was unpacking a large box full of stationery on his desk.

'How did you get on with your enquiry, did you manage to trace them all?' asked Sergeant Lang noticing Sam.

'Yeah, fine thanks. I've charged three of the four. Still don't know who the fourth guy is but I'm going to trawl through all the intel logs for the Sill brothers. Check who they've been associating with. I might get him that way.'

'Good shout.' said Sergeant Lang putting the box on the floor. 'And sorry about this morning; if I could have accepted the arrest I would have. Jeez, I can just imagine what your old man would have said if he were still the Custody Sergeant.'

'Well perhaps it's just as well he's retired.' said Sam trying to be diplomatic. 'And look, no worries, it's not your fault. Charlie says he's going to have a word with you and then he was going to take it up with the Chief.'

'He's already been on the phone. Charlie that is, not the Chief. I can't believe the Chief never copied him into the memo. How could anyone, let alone a Chief of Police, think it unnecessary to let your senior detective know about new custody arrangements. That's just bizarre.'

'Totally.' said Sam pouring himself a drink from the water cooler. 'Expect it won't be the last surprise this Chief has in store.'

Sam walked across to the window that looked onto the rear yard. Leaning against the car wash talking to a young female officer was Acting Detective Ryan Mulroy.

Although Mulroy was only a couple of years older than Sam, he had considerably more police service. He had been applying to be a detective for years, and he had made no secret of the fact that he resented Sam's recent appointment. By right he felt that that position should have been his, fortunately those making the decision saw things differently. He wasn't even interviewed for the job. Now he had to make do with an acting position, a six-month attachment to prove he had the necessary qualities to be a detective. If his first few days in the job were anything to go by the signs weren't promising. He was lazy and had a real smack for himself. His arrogant attitude was partly on account of having an uncle who was an Assistant Commissioner in Charleston. Mulroy thought he was untouchable. His failure to get an interview for the vacant detective's post should have been a wake-up call, but Mulroy wasn't the sharpest tool in the box. He was blissfully unaware of what Lieutenant Finch and Angela thought of him, and now he was ploughing on as he normally did, putting all his energies into flirting with the attractive new recruit, who might just be naïve enough to be impressed with his sharp suit and smart talk.

Sergeant Lang joined Sam at the window.

'He's never away from that poor girl. He's like a fly round horse shit. Expect she's gonna need to learn the hard way, there's no point either of us telling her he's a complete dofus.'

'Tell me this Sarge, did anyone appear at the office this morning looking for Ryan?'

'Not that I'm aware of. What time are you talking about?'

'Last couple of hours. He was supposed to meet a witness as part of an enquiry he has.'

Sergeant Lang shook his head.

'Nobody's come in asking for him, and I've been in since seven. Is it important?'

'Probably not. I just wondered that's all. It was something he said to me this morning. But it'll keep, I'll deal with it later.'

'Look, while you're here, what are the plans for Charlie's 40th I take it you're arranging a night out for him.'

Sam nodded.

'Sergeant Brown has it in hand. Bursley's after work for some beers. I know it's going to be a Friday, the 17th springs to mind. I think his birthday might be the 27th, so it will be around then.'

'Fine. Count me in. Are we chipping in for a gift? Happy to be included if we are.'

'Yep, that's the plan, I'll let Sergeant Brown know, she's collecting the money. I think she said we're going to get him new running gear as he's been going on about needing to get fit again.'

'Do you think your old man will be going? It would be good to see him again. How long is that he's been away now?'

'It's coming up for a year. It doesn't seem that long does it? I'm not sure if he'll make Bursley's, he's always fishing on Fridays nowadays. but I know he and my mom are going to the official party at the community centre at the end of the month. They got their invitation the other day. I think it's the day before his actual birthday. Captain Rawlingson and his wife have been invited to that, I know that much. It would be great to see our old boss again and hear how he's getting on in Chicago, but I'm not sure I'll get to see him, Chris and I have volunteered to cover the late turn that Saturday, it'll let others who have known Charlie longer get to the party.'

'That's very decent of you Sam, in hindsight perhaps you should have told Mr Mulroy that he has to work, it looks like he could do with a kick up the backside.'

'Now why didn't I think of that.' said Sam laughing. 'But there might be time yet, nothing's set in stone.'

Chapter 6

Twenty minutes into his journey and Chaska was beginning to regret sitting so far back on the bus. His initial intention was to have taken the back seat, but having said a prolonged goodbye to a tearful Lilian, that seat was already occupied by a Latino looking woman and her two small children who were now sprawled across the bench seat sharing an enormous bag of potato chips. He had been surprised at just how busy the bus was, so having got on, he headed straight to the second last row on the driver's side, as it was one of the few double seats that was still unoccupied.

He had wanted to sit near the back as he needed to keep the other passengers in front of him. It was an old habit he had developed in prison. Whether he was in the canteen or in the library, he always tried to sit with his back to a wall and with his foe in front of him. That way you could negate the chances of being attacked from behind, a not uncommon occurrence in a prison.

The problem with the seat he had chosen was that he was sitting directly above the rear wheels, so every time the bus went over a bump or hit a pothole, the shock transferred through the thin fabric seat and up his spine to his teeth, which rattled together unpleasantly. His feeling of discomfort was compounded by the smell of diesel fumes that caught the breeze and drifted in the open window every time the bus stopped at a junction. They hadn't yet left the Pittsburgh city limits and it was already starting to give him a headache. He was in a quandary. Should he close the window or leave it open? The bus was stiflingly hot, and to make things worse the air conditioning didn't appear to be working. He pondered his options for a moment before deciding that suffering the occasional whiff of exhaust fumes was preferable to the furnace that the bus was in danger of becoming.

Either way, it didn't seem to be affecting his fellow passengers on the rear seat, as they were now tucking into tortilla wraps and bottles of Mountain Dew.

Another ten minutes passed, and the urban sprawl of the city gave way to the peaceful tranquillity of the country. This was rich farming land. Chaska stared out the window transfixed. Mile after mile of fields, full of ripening corn and soya beans were interspersed with fields of livestock. Cattle and hogs mainly, but occasionally some leggy sheep, their thickening fleeces a strange shade of terracotta fashioned from the loamy red soil of the fields that were dust bowl dry.

As the bus meandered its way south into Braxton County, the fields of livestock gave way to apple orchards, immaculately ordered, and neatly pruned, each tree branch groaning under the weight of ripening fruit. There were also peach trees laden with tangerine coloured orbs, just asking to be picked. Nature's bounty was everywhere you looked.

What few people Chaska had seen since the bus left the city, were mainly farm labourers breaking their backs filling boxes of late summer vegetables. Every couple of miles, either at the side of a farm road or in a layby, was a vender sitting patiently under a makeshift awning, hoping that a passer-by might stop and part with a few dollars. Business was slow as they tried to offload the last of the tomatoes and courgettes. The real money spinners, the corn and apples wouldn't be ready for another week or two. But their time would come, and then the farmers would start to see some return for their labour.

There must be easier ways to make a living mused Chaska as the bus streamed past. He could see it was honest toil but sweating all day under the hot sun didn't hold much appeal. He would investigate other means by which he could earn his living.

By the time the bus had reached Sutton, Chaska was almost asleep. He had been up early, and it had already been a long and emotional day. Also, the road they were currently on had recently been re-laid which made for a much smoother and quieter journey. The rhythmic rocking of the warm bus as it rolled along was relaxing and sleep inducing. Chaska pulled his hat over his eyes and settled back in his seat. There was still more than three hours to go till he was due to arrive in Charleston, more than enough time to catch up on some sleep.

He hadn't been asleep very long when he awoke with a start as the bus came to an abrupt halt. The air doors swung open and a young black girl, aged about seventeen, got on. She was weighed down with two large sports bags which she wore over each shoulder. She was carrying several folders and a purple coloured water bottle. As she struggled to find her ticket, the bottle slipped from her grasp and rolled up the central passageway. She made a valiant attempt to retrieve it, squeezing herself past an entanglement of feet and small children. Chaska watched as the water bottle evaded her grasp and rolled further up the aisle. It was halfway to the back of the bus when suddenly it slewed to the left and then stopped.

An ashen faced white youth had trapped it underneath his caterpillar boot. Aged about twenty, the youth was wearing a white t-shirt and bleached blue jeans. The look was topped off by a grey baseball cap that bore the number 311 on the front. Another youth of a similar age sat in the window seat. He was bareheaded and was sporting a couple of days growth. His red t-shirt had the slogan, 14 Words, emblazoned in white letters across the front. Seemingly oblivious to what was happening, the youth in the window seat sat engrossed in a magazine.

''Excuse me sir,' said the young woman politely. 'Can I have my water bottle back please?'

The youth in the cap sat motionless staring straight ahead. There was not a flicker of acknowledgement.

The young woman repeated her request, but again she was blanked as the youth stubbornly ignored her. Chaska watched as the girl bent down to pick up the bottle that was now firmly wedged under the youth's foot.

'Don't you fucking touch me nigger, you hear me.' hissed the youth venomously. 'You sit that pretty black ass of yours down right now. But don't you fucking touch me.'

The young woman recoiled in shock and stepped back. His barbs of hate dripped easily from his rancid tongue. You could have heard a pin drop. Only the very youngest stared. The other passengers, both men and women, looked straight ahead. This wasn't their fight. They didn't want involved. This was between him and her.

'You're standing on my water bottle, please give it back to me.' said the young woman bravely.

For a third time the youth ignored her request.

Chaska had seen enough. He slid from his seat and approached the smirking youth.

'This young lady would like her water bottle back. She's asked you politely three times. So, stop being a dick and give the lady back her bottle, 'cause I ain't going to ask you a second time.'

The youth sneered at Chaska, then turned to his friend who had stopped reading and was now paying attention.

'Hey Carter, looky here, this prairie nigger wants me to give this negress her bottle back. What do you think? Do we take instructions from an Indian?'

Before the other youth could respond Chaska leant forward and grabbed the youth by the throat ramming him back against his seat. Squeezing his neck, he whispered menacingly in his ear.

'I ain't here to play your silly games boy. Now give the lady back her bottle or I'll smash your fucking teeth down your scrawny neck. Is that clear?'

The youth, squirmed in his seat, gasping for breath as Chaska tightened his grip. He was turning the colour of a ripe tomato. He made the merest of nods and then lifted his foot. The girl moved quickly and retrieved her bottle. She smiled at Chaska, mouthing thanks, before sitting down towards the front of the bus.

'Okay, good.' said Chaska letting go of the youth's throat. 'Glad we now seem to understand each other.'

The youth didn't reply. He was rubbing his neck and studiously trying to avoid making eye contact.

'Now, there's just one more thing I need you and your friend to do for me. I don't know where you are heading, but no matter, you're both getting off at the next stop, 'cause if you don't, you and I are going to pick up from where we were a moment ago. Clear?'

There was a moment's hesitation before the youth muttered a barely audible,

'Clear.'

Five minutes later the bus came to stop by some labourers' cottages in the middle of nowhere. The youths got off without a backwards glance. Their middle finger salutes as the bus pulled away their pathetic final act of defiance.

The remainder of the journey passed uneventfully. As chance would have it, the bus was continuing onto Lewisburg after a twenty-minute break in Charleston. By the time the bus pulled into Lewisburg bus station it was less than half full. The girl with the water bottle had got off at the stop before shouting thanks and giving Chaska a grateful wave.

Chaska picked up his rucksack as the other passengers filed off the bus. He was the last to leave as he'd let an old lady and her aged spaniel go before him. Just as he was about to step off, the bus driver spoke to him.

'You did a good thing there my friend, I hadn't realised what was going on, but the girl told me before she got off the bus. She was mighty grateful to you.' said the driver as he squeezed himself out of his cab and walked round the front of the bus to the side door.

The driver was black and aged about 30. He was of average height and carried the evidence of his appetite around his middle. He was several stones overweight and walked with a pronounced limp.

'I couldn't stand by and watch that. Couple of bully boys that's all they were. Picking on a young woman like that.'

'They weren't just any bully boys; those rednecks were Klan.'

Chaska wasn't sure what the driver was talking about.

'The guy with 311 on his cap, and the dude with the slogan on his t-shirt. They are Klan.'

'What, Ku Klux Klan?'

The driver started to laugh.

'Where you been bro, what other Klan would it be?'

Chaska shrugged his shoulders.

'I didn't know the Klan was still on the go, I thought it'd died out years ago.'

'Still active round these parts I can assure you of that. And they're becoming more brazen all the time. They don't seem to care no more who knows about it. Got so bad us brothers gotta watch ourselves, parts of this county ain't safe no more.'

'Huh. Just shows you eh. I had no idea.'

'The 311 on the dudes cap is a Klan symbol.' explained Leroy. 'K is the eleventh letter of the alphabet. 3 times 11 equals KKK. And the guy with 14 words on his shirt. That's another Klan slogan. It's to do with securing the future for white children. Honestly, I'm not joshing you bro, if they weren't Klan, they were definitely white supremacists. Pure scum. As I said, you did right by that girl.'

Chaska was gobsmacked. None of that had registered with him. Of course, he knew about the KKK, but he wasn't aware what the symbols stood for. But somehow this was now making sense. He cast his mind back to the time in the prison library when he'd interrupted the attack on Lilian. The prisoner who'd attacked her had 311 tattooed on his knuckles.

'Well, white supremacists or not, I ain't standing by watching a lady being abused like that.'

The driver smiled and thrust out his hand.

'I'm Leroy by the way where you headed for?'

'Chaska. My name's Chaska.' he said shaking Leroy by the hand. 'I'm just visiting. I'm here to see a friend who's in Fairlea County Hospital.'

'Looks like you're here to stay a while.' said Leroy eyeing Chaska's large rucksack up and down.

'Well not really. It's a bit of a long story. But I'm only here for a day or two. Can I get a bus from here to the hospital?'

Leroy nodded.

'There's one on the hour, leaves from bay 12, takes you right to the door. But you've just missed one. It's five past eight now. Anyway, you will have missed visiting, I'm sure that finishes at seven thirty. You'll not be able to go till tomorrow. Where are you staying while you're here?'

Chaska sighed wearily.

'Not sure being honest. Somewhere cheap. Is there anywhere you'd recommend?'

'Well the YMCA is cheap, but I wouldn't recommend it. A few weird characters hang out there if you know what I mean.'

'I think I get your drift.' said Chaska despondently.

'Look, I'm about to clock off and I stay about ten minutes from here. It's just a studio apartment, but you're welcome to crash on the couch, if you'd like. Won't cost a bean, and I feel I owe you for helping one of my sisters like that.'

'That's mighty kind of you, but I don't want to impose on you. The YMCA can't be that bad.'

'Believe me it is. Look, it's no trouble, really it isn't. And anyway, I could do with the company. I'm fed up staring at my own four walls.'

Chaska smiled.

'Fine, but only if you let me pick up some food for us.'

'Nope.' replied Leroy. 'I made an enormous bowl of mac and cheese yesterday and there's still loads left. It needs eaten, so if you're okay with mac and cheese we'll have that. You can pick up a six pack if you'd like, could do with a beer, it's been a long day.'

'Deal. You lead the way to the liquor store.'

*

The third-floor apartment on the corner of West Randolph Street was small and compact. But it had a homely feel, it was bright and airy and freshly decorated. Compared to the 6'x 8' prison cell Chaska had spent the last forty years in it seemed positively palatial.

Leroy removed a steaming bowl of mac and cheese from the microwave while Chaska searched a drawer for a bottle opener. Having located it he flipped the beer lids and placed two bottles of Budweiser on the kitchen table.

'Now be real careful with this, there's chorizo in it. It will be burning hot, and so will the melted cheese, so don't say I didn't warn you.'

'Just a small portion for me thanks. It smells great, but I'm not that hungry, I had a big lunch.'

'Well I'm starving, must be six hours since I ate anything. I mean ate any proper food. I'm not counting the bag of pretzels, that was just a snack. Well cheers then Chaska.' said Leroy lifting his beer.

Chaska clinked his bottle against Leroy's.

'Yeah, cheers. And thanks again for your hospitality, it's much appreciated.'

'Not a problem my friend. Now, you were telling me you were a scaffolder in New York. Sounds like an interesting job, you must have seen a few things working on them skyscrapers for nearly thirty-years.'

Chaska gritted his teeth. He was already regretting having said that to Leroy as they'd walked back to the flat. He hadn't wanted to lie, but Leroy had been curious. Not unnaturally, he had wanted to know about Chaska's past, what he did, where he lived. It had caught Chaska unawares; he wasn't prepared for it and now he was caught telling a circle of lies.

With hindsight it would have been better to have told the truth. As Mark Twain famously said, 'If you tell the truth you don't have to remember anything.' Of course, Leroy was just being polite, making small talk, but he wasn't sure how his new friend would react to hearing that his house guest had done forty-one years in prison for murder. That could kill any friendship stone dead. Chaska was beginning to despair. He couldn't remember exactly what he'd said half an hour ago. His lies were in danger of unravelling. If he said anymore, he would likely contradict himself. That's the trouble with lying, the story just keeps changing, it's nearly impossible to keep track of what you've said. He shuddered at the thought that this might be his new reality. Would every day be one big lie? He had a guilty secret. A secret that every man jack would want to know.

At that precise moment, he needed to change the subject and get Leroy talking about himself. He needed a hook, something that would distract Leroy. As fortune would have it, the photograph that was hanging on the wall opposite looked like it might provide the very thing.

'Is that you in the photograph?' asked Chaska pointing at the picture.

The photograph was of a young man dressed in a red football shirt and black leggings. Lean and muscular, he was kneeling on one leg holding a helmet. On the ground next to him was a large gold coloured trophy.

'Yep, sure is. Running back for the Georgia Bulldogs, that was taken in my sophomore year. I had just been voted the player of the season and was starting to make a name for myself in college football. Then in an exhibition game at the end of the season I tore ligaments in my knee. It ended my football career and the knee's never been right since.'

Chaska blew out his cheeks and shook his head.

'That's a real shame, I'm sorry to hear that.'

'I'm over it now. That was eleven years and five stones ago. Can't keep the weight down since I did my knee. Eat too much, can't run, it's a vicious circle.'

'So, how did you end up driving a bus and living in Lewisburg?'

'I dated a girl in college who came from here. We moved up when she graduated. I dropped out of college. I wasn't academic, and with the football scholarship gone, I decided to cut my losses and move up here with her.'

'Are you still seeing her?'

Leroy laughed and shook his head.

'Lasted less than a year after we moved here. I started on the buses just to earn some money. Turns out she didn't much fancy a fat bus driver, wasn't quite as sexy as the college football star with ambitions to be a pro. So, she dumped me.'

'Man, that's tough.'

Leroy snorted and put his head in his hands.

'Sure is, bet you're glad you're not me. Funny how your life doesn't turn out how you intended it to.'

'I know what you mean.' said Chaska quietly taking a sip of his beer.

'And the ironic thing is, she met some rich boy and moved to Richmond, while I'm stuck here in this tiny apartment and driving a God damn bus.'

'Does sound like you got a raw deal my friend. Here, have another Bud, it'll help dull the pain.'

Chapter 7

The heat of late summer lingered in the smell of freshly mown grass as the temperature nudged north of 80. A refreshing westerly, strong enough to bow the branch ends of shady maples brought welcome respite from the baking sun. Ella sipped her lemonade and looked at her watch. It was after seven, Sam was late.

On the fence near to the picnic table was a small black backed bird with a peach coloured flank and a white breast. Ella had recognised its distinctive sharp metallic song instantly. There was no mistaking it. It was an eastern towhee.

As a small child, she had been taught to identify bird songs by her grandfather, Walter Massie. The towhee's song was one of the first she learned as the attractive small bird was a frequent visitor to her grandparents' garden in South Carolina. Ella leant across the picnic table and crumpled up the remains of a half-eaten cookie that was still in its wrapper. She threw the crumbs to the side of the table and watched as her fearless friend flew down from the fence and hoovered up the tasty morsels. The towhee sang a song of thanks and flew back to its perch.

'Is that a canary I can hear singing?' asked Sam who had just appeared from the car lot.

Ella looked at Sam scornfully.

'No. It's an eastern towhee. Sounds nothing like a canary.'

Sam shrugged his shoulders.

'Sorry. I should just keep my mouth shut. I only said a canary because I know they sing. But every time we're out I seem to say something that confirms my ignorance. How do you know about all this sort of stuff? Seriously, I'm starting to feel kinda stupid.'

Ella laughed.

'I only know about bird songs because my grand-father taught me. And I'm an expert on canaries because he used to have one in his front room. And as for their song, once you've heard it, you'll never forget it. It's melodious and soft, like the sound of water rolling over rocks. Then there's a series of deeper clicks that sound like water dripping into a bucket.'

'Who knew.' replied Sam with a surprised look on his face.

'Do you remember I told you that my grandfather had been a miner?'

Sam nodded.

'Well, it wasn't uncommon for miners, often after they had retired, to keep a canary as a pet. Kept them in touch, I suppose, with their former life.'

Sam's eyes lit up.

'And the mines kept canaries because that was the bird the miners took down the shaft with them to detect if there was any carbon monoxide. The colourless and odourless killer. I remember that much from school.'

'Exactly.' exclaimed Ella. 'See you're not as stupid as you think you are. Anyway, enough of all that. Are we eating? I'm starving.'

'Sure,' replied Sam leaning in and kissing Ella on the cheek. 'Sorry, I'm a bit late. I was dictating the police report for your case, I've got some good news about that.'

'Excellent. You're going to tell me that you've got the rest of my money back.'

Sam grimaced and bit his lip.

'Eh, no, sorry that's not …'

'Don't look so alarmed, I'm kidding you. I wasn't really expecting to get it back.'

'No. Well. Anyway, I've now charged three guys with assault and racial abuse. I'm pretty confident we'll get a conviction for the assault. Not sure how the racial abuse charge will play out. That's going to be your word against theirs.'

'I'll take my chances; I'm looking forward to having my day in court.'

'Don't get your hopes up, it might not get that far. Expect their attorney might try for some sort of plea bargain.'

'No way. Those dirty lowlifes aren't going to walk away from this one.' bristled Ella.

'Okay, let's just wait and see, shall we? There isn't anything we can do about it right now.'

They went into the restaurant and sat in a booth next to the window. The waitress at the counter gave them a cursory nod. Sam passed Ella a menu.

'And how was your day, what have you been up to?'

'Called in at the university this morning and picked up my timetable. First lecture is a week tomorrow. I also got some info on the orienteering club. I enjoyed that when I was at university so, I thought I would give that a go while I'm at Beckley. It's a great way of staying in shape.'

'Orienteering eh. I've never tried it. Is that why you gave up your athletics?'

'Partly. I just got a bit bored with the track. Being honest, I realised that I wasn't going to win anything as a 400 metre runner. I was good but just not that good. A friend on my course suggested that we should try orienteering. I had done a bit of map reading in the scouts and enjoyed that, so combining it with the running seemed like a perfect solution. Plus, you get the bonus of being out in the wilderness, amazing what you see when you're out in the forest. We could give it a try if you'd like.'

Sam smiled. He hadn't done any fitness work for a while. He was fully committed to his job and was now working long hours, which came with the territory when you became a detective. He had let his fitness slip and for the first time in his life, he'd put on a little weight. This might be the perfect opportunity to do something with Ella and lose a few pounds at the same time.

'Sounds great. I'd be up for that.'

Sam looked around trying to catch the waitress's eye. The restaurant wasn't particularly busy, but they'd now been sitting for the best part of five minutes, and no one had come to take their order which was strange. Usually when Sam ate here, he was in and out in no time.

'Service is slow tonight!'

Ella raised her eyebrows and gave Sam a knowing look.

'What? I've only known you a couple of weeks, but I know that look. What are you thinking now?'

'It's slow because you're sitting with me.'

Sam frowned and shook his head.

'I'm telling you it is.'

Ella pointed towards a booth at the other end of the restaurant.

'That couple over there. They came in after us and they've already got a drink and ordered their food.'

Ella tilted her head towards a man who was sitting alone over to their left.

'Likewise, he's already eating, and he arrived after us. You've never been in here with a black person before.'

'Na,' said Sam screwing up his nose. 'You're overthinking this, she's just forgotten we're here. I'll give her a shout.'

Ella smiled and sat back in her seat.

'You've got a lot to learn Sam Coutts. But you better get used to this if you're going to go out with me. This sort of thing happens all the time. You don't notice it because its subtle. It's never in your face, but this is classic, I can't tell you how many times this has happened to me.'

Ella had just finished speaking when the waitress appeared.

'Sorry about your wait, what can I get you?'

Sam didn't say anything until the waitress disappeared with their order. Ella knew exactly what was coming next.

'See. She was tied up doing other things and then apologised for our wait. You shouldn't be so quick to judge.'

Ella started to laugh.

'You still don't get it do you? As I said before it's subtle. But when you start to see it, you can't not see it. It's part of a power game. Designed to keep people like me in our place.'

'I'm sorry Ella, but I don't see it like that at all. What power? She's a waitress!'

'Okay.' said Ella opening her bag and taking out a notebook. 'Bear with me on this one, I want you to do an exercise with me.'

Sam shrugged his shoulders.

'Sure, whatever you want.'

Ella tore two pages from her notebook and handed one of them to Sam.

'Have you got a pen?'

Sam nodded and took out a pen from his jacket pocket.

'Good. Then I went you to write the heading, White Heterosexual Male, at the top of your page.'

Sam looked bemused but did as he was told. Ella then divided her page into two columns. At the top of the first column she wrote, Black People. On the other column she wrote, Women.

'Okay, I think we're good to go. Now, I'm going to give us, say, five minutes to complete this exercise. What I want you to do is write down a list of derogatory terms that describe White Heterosexual Men. As many as you can think of. We're both going to end up with some not very nice words as I'm going to the same for my two categories, which is appropriate, since I'm both black and a woman. Right, have you got all that?'

'Not sure.' said Sam screwing up his nose again. 'So, I've only to write down terms about White Heterosexual Men, is that right?'

'That's it. And remember it must be a derogatory term and it must be one that only describes that particular group. So, don't write down fat or stupid, that could apply to any of the groups. Okay, clear? Are you ready to begin?'

'I think so.' said Sam apprehensively. He still hadn't the first idea where Ella was going with this.

'Great. Three, two, one, begin.'

Sam watched nervously as Ella began to write.

Nigger, coon, porch monkey, sambo, wog, jigaboo, her list seemed to go on and on. And that was just her first column, she hadn't even started the second one yet. Sam looked down at his blank page and chewed the end of his pen. Come on, come on, how difficult can this be? Eventually, after what must have been a good couple of minutes, he wrote, redneck underneath his heading. By the time another two minutes passed he was squirming in his seat. He was beginning to realise where Ella was going with this.

He hadn't managed to think of a second term and now he was doubting whether even redneck would make the qualifying criteria. His page, naked apart from his one feeble attempt, stared back at him pitifully. He glanced across at Ella, who was now sitting with her arms folded. Both her columns were full. Bitch, whore, slut, he didn't need to read anymore. He felt like a complete dick. He was starting to get this. Sam wasn't stupid. He'd had a college education, but he'd never been confronted with anything like this before. The scales were starting to fall from his eyes. He looked across to Ella and gave a rueful nod.

'White Heterosexual Men are the power brokers aren't they, they are the dominant group.'

'I'm impressed.' replied Ella.

'That's what's this is about isn't it? It's about groups of powerful people, and how they use that power to define and control other minority groups. So, people like me, the police, the president and politicians, judges and lawyers, the common denominator is that they are almost always white.'

'Now I'm very impressed. You've pretty much nailed it. The power group is invariably the majority group. There are exceptions to that rule like apartheid South Africa, where the blacks were the majority group but didn't hold the power, but as a rule of thumb it holds pretty true. Interesting isn't it, how difficult it is to find derogatory terms to define the majority group. You see, as a group, they actively suppress that kind of thing. Why? Well, because they can. As you said yourself, they hold the power.'

Ella looked at Sam's sheet.

'I see you could only come up with one example.'

'I'm not even sure that it counts to be honest. It could cross over into another group. Could you have a gay redneck?'

Ella smiled. 'Unlikely I'd say, but I suppose not impossible, but I'll give you that one.'

'But how does it work for the waitress then? She's a woman, and they are often a minority group, they certainly are in the police.'

'Ah, but she's also white. And in this instance, it's the fact that she's white and I'm black that makes her powerful. It trumps the fact that she's also a woman. But it is all about the context. But usually you'll find, it's the white group that holds sway. They call the shots. And if the group happens to be white, male, and heterosexual then you've got testosterone overload. You won't find a more powerful group than them, well I can't think of one.'

Sam blew out his cheeks and sat back in his chair.

'Wow, here was I thinking I was heading out for a burger after a busy day. This stuff is starting to make me feel very insecure. Since I met you, it's like I'm looking at the world through a different lens. And that's all happened in a fortnight.'

'And you say that as if it's a bad thing. I know it's challenging, but it's hugely interesting don't you think. Knowing stuff like this will make you a more rounded person. It will let you understand the world we live in better, that was a big part of it for me. The more we know and understand, the less likely we are to discriminate. That's why it's so important that we teach people these things. I think we should teach it in every school. The country would be a much better place if we did.'

Sam looked at Ella and smiled. She was a beautiful girl. Smart and with a caring heart. He felt a warm glow inside. This was only their fourth date. But it felt like he was now in a relationship. A proper relationship, one where he could call Ella his girlfriend. It was stimulating and exciting and he was mighty glad that he'd been fortunate enough to meet her.

Chapter 8

The view from Carole Hicks room on the second floor
of the county hospital was spectacular. Standing by the
window you could see the treelined ridge of the
Allegheny Mountains in the far distance, running like a
spine up the eastern border of the state. The rounded
peaks of Spruce Knob and Thorny Flat, crystal clear
against the cobalt blue sky, rose up from the ridge like
the humps of a Bactrian camel.

It was now early September and the first colours of
fall were starting to appear on the white ash trees that
lined the entrance to the hospital. The intense heat of
the summer was on the wane and the air, particularly in
the early morning, now had that invigorating freshness
that had not been felt since spring.

Chaska stared out the window, captivated by the
beauty of the mountains. Carole had pointed out Spruce
Knob, easy to identify as the highest peak in the range.
Chaska felt drawn to it, compelled to visit and re-engage
with his spiritual home. But that would have to wait.
He was here to see Carole. Support her at this difficult
time. But right now, he was giving her some space.

Not much had been said since he arrived nearly
twenty minutes ago. Carole had been simply overcome
with emotion. Forty years of guilt and torment had
come spilling out and now every time she looked at

Chaska she burst into tears. It was all too much. When Chaska had enquired where Carole's room was, the nurse at the desk had been at pains to explain that she wasn't to get too excited as she was due to have an exploratory operation that afternoon, as the consultant suspected she might have an obstruction in her bowel. But since she arrived yesterday, her blood pressure had been up and down and if they didn't get it under control, the operation would have to be postponed for another day. They had also detected an irregular heartbeat, which was just compounding the problem.

Chaska knew that his presence wasn't helping. If she wasn't crying, she was wanting to hold him and hug him and tell him how sorry she was for letting them take him into care. At times she was beside herself with grief.

The alarm on her monitor had already gone off once as her heart raced and spiked into the red zone. The nurse who responded told them if it happened again, she would have to ask Chaska to leave. They needed Mrs Hicks to remain calm. So, for the last few minutes, he had been standing quietly by the window as she regained her composure.

'Oh my, look at me. I'm so sorry about this,' said Carole drying her eyes with a tissue. 'It's just that I can't begin to tell you what it means to see you, to talk to you and be able to hug you. But I'm not going to cry again. I want to hear about you and your plans. I can't begin to imagine what you must have been through. It breaks my heart just thinking about it.'

Chaska came across and sat down in the chair at the side of the bed.

'You don't have to worry about any of that now. There's plenty time for that. I'm going to stay a couple of days so there will be ample time to catch up on all that stuff. For now, you have to concentrate on getting your operation and then getting well, so you'll be able to go home.'

Carole smiled and looked at Chaska.

'I just feel so vexed. Life can be so unfair. Look what happened to you. And, of course, losing Tom in the accident. It was almost unbearable. It was forty years ago but I remember it as if it were yesterday. The pain has never really gone away. And then, when I think what happened to Eric, well it's been a rough ride.'

'Yeah, I know it's been tough. But tell me about Eric. I was thinking about him earlier, has he been in touch? I mean does he know that you're in hospital, or that the court case has started?'

Carole shook her head.

'No, he doesn't know. I did get a birthday card in May, but I haven't heard from him since. But that isn't unusual. Julie is trying to get hold of him for me, I spoke to her yesterday. She was going to contact the hospital in Savannah. As far as I'm aware, he's not been in the hospital for a while, but we know he keeps in touch with them, helps him keep on an even keel. They're very good with him. We're hoping they might have an address.'

Chaska leant forward and took hold of Carole's hand.

'Let's hope so. It would be good for both of you to see each other again.'

'He's not a bad boy. But after his father died, he did go off the rails. His mental health was never that great, but by the time he reached twenty, he had developed full blown schizophrenia. He must have been in and out of that hospital a dozen times over the next twenty years. Things did get better for a while. The treatment seemed to work, but every so often, something would happen to trigger his illness and he'd find himself back in the hospital.'

'Was he ever able to work and hold down a job?'

'He was always working when he wasn't in the hospital, fruit picking mainly. He used to travel up and down the east coast. He loved the sunshine, so he spent a lot of time in Florida picking oranges and peaches. But he would go as far north as Pennsylvania. He never had his own place. He lived in caravans on the farms mostly. But the lifestyle suited him. He was never the most sociable boy, so he was happy enough in his own company.'

'And what about Julie? I'm sure the last time you wrote to me she was living in Tennessee.'

'Yep, she's still there. Working in an elementary school in Clinton. She never remarried after the divorce. But both her girls are married now. No great grandchildren yet, but I live in hope. When I spoke to her last night, she said she's going to come up for the weekend. You'll get to meet her if you're still around.'

'That would be nice. It was so long ago the only thing I can remember, other than she was two years younger than me, was that she had beautiful long auburn hair.'

Carole smiled again.

She's still got it, but she wears it a lot shorter now. She's still as pretty as a picture, well I think she is, but I'm her mom so I'm biased.'

Chaska laughed.

'And quite right too, moms are supposed to be biased.'

Chaska looked at his watch. It was just leaving twenty-five to two. There was still more than twenty minutes of visiting time left, but he didn't want to overstay his welcome, or for that matter, make Carole overly tired. He stood up and was about to suggest that he should leave when Carole reached across and grabbed him by the wrist.

'I know you'll have to go in a minute, but before you do there's something I must tell you.'

'Sure.' said Chaska sitting back down. 'What's on your mind?'

'I've not been able to get it out of my head for days now. But with the court case about to start I didn't know what to do. I understand that it doesn't directly affect the case against the asbestos company, but it's definitely connected. Those Lawrence brothers have behaved despicably. They've schemed and covered things up right from the moment Tom and Joe Jarret were killed. And I know for a fact that the truth never came out about their deaths.

Carole eyes welled up again and tears started to run down her face.

'I'm not sure I'm following you. What is it that's happened and how is it connected to Tom's death?'

Carole wiped her eyes with another tissue.

'It was sometime last week. Wednesday, I think. I had an unexpected visit from Rosemary Latimer. Her husband, Clifford, worked with Tom at the Spruce Knob mine. He was the company secretary back then. I wasn't aware, but she told me he had died a few weeks ago.'

'Okay, I'm with you so far.'

'I hadn't spoken to Rosemary in nearly thirty years. But when she called at the house, I knew straight away

103

who she was. I used to occasionally see her in the town. Dressed to the nines in her fancy clothes. The Latimers moved to a big house at Lake Tuckahoe, shortly after the mine was sold. I don't know what Clifford did for work after he left the mine, but they weren't short of money. They were forever going away on Caribbean cruises.'

Chaska scratched his head.

'Sure, but what of it. Why is that important?'

'She arrived at the house carrying a box. A large cardboard boxed stuffed full of folders and documents. She told me it was the Spruce Knob Mine archive. Her husband had kept it in their attic for all these years and now she wanted me to have it. She said it contained all the minutes and important papers from the time the Lawrence family first opened the mine.'

'Ah, I see. I take it the box is in the house and you want me to get it. Is that it?'

'Well, no, that isn't it. I think the box is now in Lewisburg library. Being honest, I was a bit confused and didn't know what to do with it, so I suggested she give it to the library. I think they keep stuff like that, especially if it's local and got some historical interest.'

'Definitely. I expect they'd be happy to have it. But why was she trying to give it to you?'

Carole shook her head.

'Apparently before he died, Clifford wanted people to know the truth. Rosemary told me he was ashamed of what he'd done. She said a couple of days before he died, he was very agitated and wanted to get something off his chest. He didn't want to go to his grave with a guilty conscience. The way she described it sounded like a death bed confession.'

'A confession about what?'

'About what happened at the time of Tom's death. You see they lied about that, covered up what really happened. The Lawrence brothers made sure the truth never came out. They didn't want to jeopardise the sale of the mine, so they paid them off. Gave Clifford Latimer and others, thousands of dollars to keep quiet. According to Rosemary some of the other men were threatened with violence. They said they would get their wives and kids if they spoke up. That frightened them, so the truth never came out.'

'And did she tell you that the truth about what really happened is in the archive?'

Carole nodded.

'Clifford Latimer was told to destroy all the records. As the company secretary he was responsible for minuting board meetings and knew everything that was going on. She told me the Lawrences got him to falsify documents about mine inspections and the purchase of new equipment. As I said, they were desperate to sell the mine and would do anything to make sure that happened. '

'Did she show you any of those documents? I mean the ones that had been changed.'

Carole shook her head.

'The documents didn't appear to be in any order, I only looked at them for a few minutes, but I couldn't make head nor tail of them.'

Chaska leant back in his chair and looked at the ceiling.

'Hmm. So, all you've got right now is her word, you haven't seen any physical evidence?'

'No, not yet. But the worse bit was that she told me that when the police were called in to investigate Tom's accident, the Lawrences got Clifford and others to testify that Tom and Joe had been found dead in part of the mine where they weren't authorised to be in. And they said they'd ignored safety instructions and had gone down the shaft without a canary. And get this, they said when they were found they weren't wearing hard hats and didn't have lamps with them. That's when I knew they were lying. Joe Jarret was the union rep and a stickler for health and safety. He wouldn't have done anything that put himself or Tom's safety at risk.'

Chaska tapped his chin and thought for a moment.

'Okay, that all makes sense. But this is what I don't get. Why, if Latimer had been bought off like you said, did he not just destroy the documents. That would seem like the obvious thing to do. It would have got rid of a lot of incriminating evidence.'

'I know. I thought that as well. I asked Rosemary why he'd kept the documents. She said she thought it was some sort of insurance policy. To make sure he still had something on the brothers if he ever needed it. So, in the future, if anything did come to light, he could use the archive as evidence against them.'

'I see. And as he knew he was dying, he wanted to be reassured that someone else knew about the archive. He could then die with a clear conscience, knowing that at the very end he'd tried to do the right thing.'

'Yeah, something like that.' said Carole with a weak smile. 'And I thought as you've had experience working in a library, you might be the very person to look into it for me. I don't know when they're going to let me out of here, and to be honest, I don't think I've got the energy for it anymore, not at my age.'

Chaska stroked Carole's hand.

'I'd be happy to do that for you. I'm not sure what we do then, but I could call in at the library tomorrow and see if I can get a look at the documents.'

'You're a good man Chaska, I'll sleep better now that I've told you, I needed someone else to know about this.'

Before Chaska had a chance to reply, he had another coughing fit. This time his hacking cough sounded loose and wet. He excused himself as he searched his pocket for a tissue.'

'Here, please take one of mine.'

Carole passed Chaska the box of tissues from the table next to her bed.

'That cough sounds dreadful, that's the third time you've coughed since you've been here. Are you taking anything for it?'

Chaska nodded and showed Carole the bottle of linctus which he'd produced from his pocket. He turned his head away and spat the lumpy mucus into the tissue which he wrapped and deposited into a trash can.

'Well make sure you keep taking it, sounds like that coughs got a way to go yet.'

'Don't worry about that. I've only been taking the mixture for a couple of days, it ain't had a chance to sort me out yet, but I'm sure it will.' said Chaska reassuringly.

'Look, is there anything else I can do for you before I go? Do you need anything else brought in?'

Carole pondered for a moment.

'I don't think so. I've got all the night clothes and toiletries I need.'

Then a thought came into her head.

'But now that you ask, there is one more thing if you don't mind. Could you call at the house and check on the canaries? I remember how you liked to help Tom look after them. There are only five left now, and they will be the last ones. I'm just getting too old to look after them. They live in a small aviary in the back yard. The gate won't be locked, and the food is in a wooden box next to their cage. If you could fill the feeders and refresh their water, I'd appreciate it.'

Chaska smiled.

'Not a problem, it'll be just like old times. I'll call in when I leave here.'

Carole looked concerned.

'But you'll not know where the house is?'

'I've got the address and a good tongue in my head, I'll find it, you don't have to worry about that. Now you get some rest and hopefully when I see you tomorrow, you'll have had your operation. I'll come in the evening and give you an update about the archive.'

'I'll look forward to that.' said Carole lying back and closing her eyes. 'And with a bit of luck you'll get to meet Julie, she should be here by then.'

The nurse came into the room just as Chaska was leaving. As she was checking the bedside monitor, she noticed a bloodstained tissue in the trash can.

'Is that your tissue in the trash Mrs Hicks? Have you cut yourself?'

Carole shook her head.

'No, no, I haven't. Is something wrong?'

'No, nothing's wrong, everything's fine.' replied the nurse as she watched Chaska disappear down the corridor.

'And good news, your blood pressure and heart rate are pretty stable, you might get that operation yet.'

Chapter 9

The following morning, Chaska was making scrambled eggs in the kitchen of Leroy's apartment.

'Do you want one or two pieces of toast with your eggs?'

'Stupid question. You don't get to be the size of me eating one slice of toast. I'm going all in, give me two of them bad boys!' laughed Leroy. 'I'm gonna need my energy, I'm back on the Pittsburgh run today.'

'Fine, then two it is.' said Chaska searching the cupboard for some plates.

Leroy pulled out a chair and sat down at the table.

'And as I said to you last night, you can stay here as long as you like. It's really not a problem bro. Being honest I'm enjoying the company and if you can stand sleeping on the couch, then it's all good.'

'Appreciate that. It won't be for more than two or three days, but it's a big help and I owe you my friend, it's real hospitable of you.'

Picking up a ladle, Chaska spooned the creamy eggs onto the toast and presented them to his host who immediately smothered them in tabasco sauce. Although he didn't say as much, Chaska was mighty pleased with his efforts. Cooking, even making something as simple as scrambled eggs, was not something you ever got to do in prison. Other than a slightly burnt pan, there was nothing much wrong with his first attempt. Still flushed with the success of his culinary efforts, he poured two large mugs of coffee and sat down at the table.

'Bit of a strange question, but do you have any idea when the library opens?'

Leroy thought for a moment.

'Nine I would have thought. Won't be earlier than that but it could be later, why do you ask?'

'I've an enquiry to do on behalf of my friend in the hospital, so I thought I'd head over this morning.'

'Fine. I'll walk you along if you like. It's quite near the bus station and I've to be there for about nine. My bus leaves at half past.'

It was just approaching five to nine when Chaska reached the library. The plain and rather mundane rectangular shaped building was made of red brick. It was typical of public buildings built in the sixties that can be found in small towns across America. The architect of the Lewisburg Public Library was not going to win any awards for its design.

Finding that the front doors were locked, he sat on the wall outside and waited. Bang on the hour the bolts slid open and a smiley lady in her late forties opened the doors.

'That's a healthy sign,' she said cheerily, 'it's not often we have someone waiting for us to open up, but I like that, the early bird catches the worm as the saying goes.'

Chaska tipped his hat and followed the lady to the reception desk where she sat down. The name on her desk said Mary Winters, Assistant Librarian. The uniform rows of neatly ordered bookshelves, and wooden trolleys stacked full of returned books, were just like those he had worked with in Moundsville. The place even smelt the same.

'My name's Mary and I'm one of the library assistants. What is it I can help you with today?'

Chaska removed his hat and smiled politely without giving his name.

'I'm here on an enquiry for a friend who's currently in hospital. I'm trying to track down a box of documents that I believe may have been given to the library recently. It's the archive of the Spruce Knob coal mine.'

Mary's face lit up.

'I know exactly the box you're referring to. It came in sometime last week. I'm afraid we haven't had a chance to go through anything yet as we've been a bit busy, so none of it has been catalogued or referenced. As you'll see there is rather a lot of it. But you're welcome to have a look at it if you'd like.'

'That would be great if it's not too much trouble.'

'Just give me a minute and I'll get it, it's somewhere in the back store.'

A couple of minutes later Mary returned carrying a large cardboard box.

'Hope you're not in a hurry, there must be hundreds of documents in here.'

Chaska smiled and shook his head.

'No ma'am, I'm in no hurry, the one thing I've plenty of is time. Please, can I take the box from you, it looks kinda heavy.'

'Yep, you most certainly can,' said Mary handing over the box. 'There's a private reading room just over there. It might be the best place for you. It's got a large table which might make things a bit easier. It'll let you spread out all these folders and documents.'

'That sounds ideal thanks.'

'Right, good. Follow me then. I'll get the door for you. Is there anything else you need?'

'I've got a pen, but I've stupidly forgotten my notebook, if you could give me some paper that would be good.'

'No problem, you can have one of my notepads, I've got plenty. They're about the only freebies we get working in a library. I'll go and get you one.'

By the time she returned with the pad, Chaska had started to unpack the contents of the box. Folders were stacked to one side, minutes of meetings and other miscellaneous documents piled neatly on the other. This was all so familiar. His methodical nature would have meant he would have done it anyway, but Lilian and been at pains to explain the benefits of an organised approach when he began working in the prison library, and for the next two hours Chaska set about the task of sorting the piles of paper.

By eleven o'clock he was done. Every piece of paper had been sifted and now he was surrounded by various documents all neatly stacked in chronological order. He had made a decent start.

There had been a moments excitement earlier in the morning when Mary had rushed into the reading room to remind Chaska that no drink or comestibles could be consumed on the premises. She felt slightly foolish when she discovered that it was cough mixture he was taking. To make amends, she fetched him a spoon and some napkins should he need to take anymore. She also provided him with an array of coloured post-it notes as it was clear that her handsome visitor had begun cataloguing the various documents. She had a vested interest in assisting him, it would save her having to do it later. Ploughing through a mountain of archive material was not a job Mary was relishing.

As the clock ticked towards six, Mary started to tidy her desk and shut down the computer as she prepared to lock up and go home. The good-looking man with the mane of grey flecked dark hair and broad shoulders had been hunched over the table hard at work for nearly nine hours. He hadn't even stopped for a lunch break. Come to think of it, Mary wasn't sure if he'd even left the room to visit the restroom. Whatever it was he was doing; he seemed totally immersed in it.

Mary stuck her head around the reading room door.

'Sorry to interrupt, but I'm afraid I'm going to have to ask you to finish up. We close in ten minutes.'

It was then that she saw it. The swish of his hair momentarily revealing his past as he spun round to face her. She caught her breath to suppress a gasp. It looked angry and sore. The skin around the cicatrix was pitted and raised. It was the colour of weak coffee. A lattice work of skin where the flesh had melted then set. It disappeared from her gaze as his hair fell back.

Chaska looked at his watch. He hadn't noticed her stare.

'Just about done. I'm just going to finish this document then I'll be with you. Won't be more than five minutes.'

He had started his research by reading through the minutes of the monthly company board meetings. Each set wasn't particularly long but there were hundreds of them to check. He could see that this was going to be a lengthy task. He'd already written several pages of notes, just based on what he'd read so far. Looking at the piles of paper on the table he reckoned it would take him at least a week to get through all the documents. And that would be just a skim through, it would take forever to read and digest every word. He needed to come up with a better plan.

Then, quite suddenly it came to him. He tapped his forehead with his fists in frustration. He felt foolish for not thinking of it earlier. He didn't need to waste time reading every document. Some history geek would no doubt do that one day, but right now he didn't need to. He had to focus on what Carole had told him last night. He did the arithmetic in his head. He had gone to prison when he was 17. That was 1952. Tom Hicks was killed in the accident a year later and according to Carole, the mine had been sold not long after that. Those were the salient dates. If the Lawrence brothers had documents doctored and coerced people into lying, it would be around that time. He would come back tomorrow and concentrate his efforts on that period. He felt refreshed and invigorated, now he was getting somewhere. What had seemed like an almost impossible task just a few minutes ago was now suddenly manageable. As he carefully put the documents back in the box, he felt uplifted. Tomorrow promised to be an important day.

'We're open till 8pm on a Thursday, if that's any help.' said Mary closing the door behind Chaska. 'And we'll be open again at nine tomorrow. I take it you're going to need to come back?'

'That's a given. You weren't joking, there's a mountain of the stuff to go through. I'll be in first thing tomorrow; I'm only just getting started.'

Mary watched him go from the window. There was something about the man with the scar on his neck that was beguiling. She had wanted to talk for longer, to find out who he was and why he was there. It was mysterious and intriguing, exciting even. Mary couldn't wait till tomorrow.

*

Leroy was grilling hamburgers when Chaska walked into the kitchen.

'Good timing bro, I'm not long in myself. Fancy a couple of burgers for your dinner?'

Chaska glanced at the table. A bowl of sliced tomatoes, cucumber and some tired looking lettuce sat in a bowl on the table. The wilting wet leaves of the aging lettuce clung forlornly to the sides of the glass bowl. It did not look particularly inviting.

'I'll just have a little of this salad if that's alright. I had a big lunch and I don't think I could manage the burger.'

'Suit yourself. But I ain't wasting these burgers. Just means I'm going to eat all four myself, but that won't be a problem, I'm as hungry as a horse, as my grandpa used to say! And help yourself to dressing, there's some ranch in the fridge. And the kettles just boiled, so I'll have a coffee if you're making some.'

Chaska poured two mugs of coffee, then took a fork and side plate and helped himself to a portion of the lifeless salad which he picked at unenthusiastically while Leroy spread mayo on the buns.

'You going to the hospital tonight?'

Chaska nodded.

'I thought I would. Carole should have had her operation yesterday, and I said to her that I'd visit tonight. I'm just going to finish this and go if you don't mind. You said the bus left on the hour?'

115

Leroy put his thumb up. He couldn't speak as he had taken an enormous bite of his burger.

'Before I go. Do you happen to have a sharp knife or a bradawl I could borrow? I need to put another notch in my belt. I'm struggling to keep my jeans up. It would save me buying another belt if I can put another couple of holes into this one.'

Leroy started to laugh as he wiped his fingers with a napkin.

'Not a problem I've ever had my friend.' he said patting his ample stomach. 'But sure, I've got a knife you could use. Never heard of that other thing you said, so I'm pretty sure I ain't got one of them. But there's a swiss army knife in the top drawer by the sink. Help yourself.'

*

That's more like it thought Chaska as he walked up the drive to the entrance of the hospital. For the first time in days he hadn't needed to keep pulling up his jeans. He'd added two holes to his belt and now it felt as though his jeans might actually stay up. It was clear that he'd lost some weight. That wasn't a surprise as he hadn't been eating normally. He just didn't feel appetized. He put it down to the damned cough that still showed no sign of going away. But at least he wasn't smoking. Amazingly, he hadn't particularly missed the cigarettes. He'd stopped when his cough had got bad, but he wasn't suffering from any withdrawal symptoms, which surprised him, as he'd smoked heavily from the day he'd arrived in prison. That, at least, was something. The nagging cough was bad enough without going 'Cold Turkey' because he couldn't have a cigarette.

Nobody was at the nursing station when he arrived at the ward, but as he knew where Carole's room was, he cleaned his hands with the sanitiser, then joined the steady trickle of visitors processing along the corridor, eager to see their loved ones. He stopped abruptly as he arrived at the room and checked the nameplate on the door. He was sure this was the right room, but there was no name on the door. The bed was empty but had been freshly made. Perhaps she had been moved to another ward after her operation. There was someone in the room though. Sitting in a chair staring out the window was a casually dressed woman in her mid-fifties with striking auburn hair. It was Carole's daughter, Julie.

Chaska stood at the door for a few seconds trying to make sense of what was going on. Julie hadn't noticed him and appeared caught up in her own thoughts as she peered out into space. After a few moments Chaska broke the silence by gently knocking on the door.

Julie slowly turned around to face him. Her reddened eyes gave the game away, she had been crying. Something dreadful had happened.

'You must be Chaska.' said Julie quietly. 'I was waiting until you arrived. When I spoke to her on the phone, Mom said you had visited and would be coming in tonight. I'm sorry to have to tell you this, but she didn't make it through the operation. Her heart just gave out and she never regained consciousness. I didn't even get a chance to say goodbye.'

Julie's voice was brittle and raw. She dabbed her eyes with her handkerchief, breathing deeply as she fought to keep her composure.

Chaska didn't know what to say. He was stunned. Carole had seemed fine when he'd left her yesterday.

117

Okay, she was in hospital, but she'd told him it was a minor operation and there was nothing to worry about. She'd said she'd expected to be home in a couple of days and was determined to give her evidence in the case against the asbestos company. Less than 24 hours since he'd seen her, he was being told she was dead. This was just awful.

Chaska couldn't remember the last time he had cried. He steadfastly refused to cry when he was in prison. He remained resolute and unbowed. Crying would somehow show he was weak, vulnerable even. He wanted none of that. He was a proud man who had fallen victim to a judicial system that was never concerned with defending the rights of people like him. But now, standing in a hospital room, watching a bereaved daughter mourn her mother, he felt an overwhelming sense of sadness. Other than Lilian, Carole Hicks was the only woman who had ever shown him any love and affection. His heart ached and watery tears filled his eyes.

Unable to find the words he wanted to say, he walked across to Julie and hugged her. He held her tight for several moments as she sobbed into his shoulder.

'I don't know what to say but I'm just so sorry.' Chaska's voice was cracking with emotion. He let go of Julie and looked into her eyes.

'Your mom was just a beautiful person with the kindest heart.' his voice tailed off. It was all he could do to stop himself from breaking down.

Julie smiled and passed him a tissue. He wiped his eyes and sat down and for the next twenty minutes the childhood friends talked about Carole, and Julie's father Tom, and brother Eric and their childhood memories of the eighteen months they had spent as a family. The happiest time of Chaska's life.

'I'm just so glad that I've been able to track Eric down. It would have been dreadful if I hadn't been able to get hold of him.'

Chaska nodded.

'I take it the hospital had his address?'

'Yes, fortunately. He'd been in to see them recently and told them where he was staying. He's been picking tobacco on a farm in South Carolina and I've now got the address. The local police are going to contact him. I've asked that they let him know that mum has died, that way I'll know that he'll get in contact with me. He can phone me at the house. I'm going to stay there for a few days till I get things sorted.'

'That's good that you know where he is. Look, if there's anything I can help you with, please just ask. I've been staying in Lewisburg but I'm going to the mountains in a day or so. I've got some business at the library to attend to first, then I'm heading for Spruce Knob for a few days. But just say if I can assist with anything. I'd be happy to help.'

'That's real kind of you. I know about the archive and the library. Mom was thrilled that you were going to look into it. And as for everything else, I've already contacted funeral directors, they will start to make arrangements when the hospital issues the death certificate. And I thought I'd go and see the minister tomorrow. Mum was still attending the Baptist church. She didn't go every week, but I know she tried to get along at least once a month. I'm hoping the funeral can be there.'

'What about the court case, would you like me to contact her attorney?'

Julie shook her head.

'No need thanks. I've already spoken to them. I was going through mum's stuff and found their number in her diary, so I called them there and then and explained what had happened. They were very nice on the phone, but I asked them about the case. I wanted to know if mum not being able to give her evidence would affect it.'

'And what did they say?'

'Of course, they couldn't be certain, but they said it would make things more difficult. I think much of their case was going to be built around mum's testimony. But that's not important right now. Nothing's going to bring her back.'

Julie shook her head and blew her nose. She was desperately trying not to start crying again.

'You've done so well on such a difficult day. If you're absolutely sure there's nothing I can do for you, can you give me your telephone number, so I'll be able to contact you. I would like to stay for the funeral if that's alright.'

'Yes, you must. Mum would want you to be there. And Eric will want to see you so you must stay. He used to think the world of you. It was a big blow to him when you left us.'

'And I'll be happy to see him. It's been a long time. Just as long as he doesn't want to fight with me.'

Chaska started to chuckle.

'Do you remember how he always wanted to wrestle with me and your dad? He wasn't the biggest, but he was strong and when he lost his temper, he was like a whirlwind, I've still got a scar on my forehead from when he threw that glass ashtray at me.'

Julie smiled and nodded.

'Yep, I remember that day. I was a little scared of him when he lost his temper. I'm sure it was all part of his illness. He was never violent to anyone that I was aware of. That's not why he was sectioned. He just got so frustrated with himself and later on, he started to self-harm. It all got too much after dad died. But he's much older now and better able to cope. Well I hope he is.'

Chaska got up and put on his jacket. He put the telephone number that Julie had written down in his pocket and was about to leave when Julie suddenly remembered something.

'If you really don't mind, there is something you might be able to help me with.'

'Shoot.' said Chaska putting on his hat.

'The canaries. I'm going to need someone to take the birds. I'm allergic to them. I come out in a nasty rash if I go anywhere near them.'

'Yeah, I remember you being allergic to them. Probably the reason I ended up helping your dad with them. But sure. I'll get something organised don't you worry about that. And I'll call you in a couple of days, hopefully Eric will have been in touch by then and you'll have more information about the funeral arrangements. You look after yourself, and as I said, I'll be in touch.'

Chapter 10

Ella had parked in a clearing at the end of the forest track. It was another beautiful September afternoon and all around, seasoned maple and birch leaves danced and whispered in the light breeze, their red and orange hues, a tantalising foretaste of the main event that was still some weeks away.

She had decided to come a bit earlier than she'd originally intended as Sam had telephoned to say there was no chance of him finishing work sharp. He had too much to do. She'd told him where she was going if that changed for any reason, and they'd arranged to meet later for a bite to eat. He'd wanted to come, but if she'd waited until he finished work, they wouldn't have been able to complete the route before it got dark. Anyway, she had agreed to do a run with him at the weekend, so this afternoon was now just some extra training as far as she was concerned.

Ella opened the tailgate and took out her sports bag. The college had provided her with a map and today's run was going to be a gentle four miles following forest tracks over mainly flat ground. She unfolded the map and studied the trail where eleven orienteering stations had been numbered and marked with red flags. It didn't look overly complicated and the club secretary had assured her that it was an ideal route for a first training run. She was confident that she would be able to manage the run, it was the map reading she was more concerned with. She hadn't done any orienteering in her last year of her degree as she had been concentrating on her studies, so it was more than eighteen months since she'd last had to navigate using a map. She was searching the bottom of her bag looking for her compass when the blast from a shotgun ripped across the treetops sending roosting pigeons in all directions.

Someone must be out hunting she thought as she zipped up her bag. But as it didn't sound particularly close, she didn't give it much attention. And in any case, the route to the first station was going to take her in the opposite direction.

She was tying her shoelaces when the second blast came. This time it sounded closer. Nervously, she looked around, but she couldn't see anybody. She was about to put her bag away when she noticed two youths emerging from the trees a hundred yards to her left. The youth wearing the grey baseball cap was carrying a shotgun broken over his forearm. The other youth appeared to be holding a squirrel by its tail. The wretched creature twitched and curled, it was clearly not dead.

Ella watched as the two youths walked slowly towards her. They stopped about twenty yards away, they stared at her but didn't speak.

'Are you going to be eating that squirrel?' asked Ella in a voice designed to show that she wasn't intimidated by them.

'I don't know what the fuck it's got to do with you, but this here is vermin.' snarled the youth carrying the shotgun. 'We don't eat vermin, expect you do though. Do you want it?'

The other youth held the miserable creature aloft.

'You could have at least put the poor thing out of its misery.' said Ella defiantly.

'Good point missy.' replied the youth carrying the squirrel.

Ella watched horrified as the youth put the squirrel on the ground and crushed its head with the heel of his boot.

'Hope that satisfies you missy. You still want it for your supper?'

Ella stood rock still staring at the youths. She felt sick in the pit of her stomach. She needed to get away before the situation escalated. She was about to turn and get into her car when she sensed someone behind her. In an instant she had been grabbed and thrown face down on the ground. Rough calloused hands grabbed her wrists and forced her arms behind her back. A plastic cable tie pulled tight secured her hands. Someone pushed her face into the grass. Frantically she kicked out as she gasped for air. Darkness enveloped her as a foul-smelling sack was forced over her head. A single defiant scream, all she could muster before a gag was forced into her mouth and tied around the sack. Ella knew she was in serious trouble.

She heard the grumble of a diesel engine nearby. The hessian sack offered no protection and the smell of diesel fumes made her want to vomit. Not a word was spoken but the threat of menace was everywhere. She felt the dead weight of a second person lying across her legs. Petrified and helpless, her ankles slammed together with the pull of a plastic tie.

Face down and immobilised, Ella was struggling to breathe. Fear gripped her like a vice, paralyzing and overwhelming, the only sound her throbbing pulse pin sharp in her ears.

Unable to fight back her survival instincts kicked in, she needed to think clearly if she was going to stay alive. Desperate to stay calm, she took repeated shallow sniffs as she fought to control her breathing. Rancid fetid oxygen bled into her lungs, it was toxic and evil, but it would keep her alive, her senses hadn't been dulled, she was still thinking clearly.

Unceremoniously, she was grabbed under her armpit and spun over onto her back. She felt the rope bite into her ankles as it pulled tight around her feet. The engine revved and car doors slammed. The rope tightened and she shot forward. She was now being dragged through the forest by her feet.

Instinctively she raised her shoulders to protect her head from hitting the hard ground. Although years of gruelling gym sessions had strengthened her core, Ella didn't know how long she would be able to keep her head from striking the ground. It must only have been a few seconds, but her neck and shoulder muscles were already starting to ache. Stones and pinecones ripped the skin from her back and legs. Searing, fiery bursts of pain pulsated through her body as she bumped and scraped across the forest floor. With eyes tight shut and gritted teeth she willed it to be over.

Ella had no idea how far she had been dragged, or for how long. She could no longer hear the engine, so in the silence she lay perfectly still resting her head on the ground. Her whole body hurt. A hot, numbing, stinging pain, like when salt hits broken skin. Her pain receptors were fully functioning. She hurt so badly she convinced herself that she must have broken something. Everything hurt, every damn thing. Tentatively she moved each limb in turn. Miraculously, nothing appeared to be broken.

The sound of a stick breaking underfoot told her she was not alone. Her aching body tensed once more in preparation for another assault. The smell of stale body odour leached under her head sack. Now she could hear the rasping sound of heavy breathing, someone was close by. Ella could hardly dare to breathe.

She felt the rope being untied and removed from her feet first. Then coarse hands grabbed her fingers holding them tight while her hands were cut free. She heard the briefest sound of heavy boots crunching on parched ground before the silence returned.

Fully five minutes must have passed before she dared to move. Slowly, she sat herself up and untied the gag and the string of the sack. She pulled it off and gasped for air, like a diver returning to the surface, she filled her lungs with the fresh forest air. Turning through 360 degrees she scanned the trees looking for her assailants. There was no sign of anyone. She was sitting on a patch of soft grass within a circular shaped hollow that was surrounded by tall trees. It looked like she was sitting in a Roman amphitheatre. On either side of her were vehicle tracks which ran in a straight line for as far as the eye could see.

Ella looked at her wrists. They were raw and bleeding from where the plastic tie had cut deep into her flesh. Tentatively she reached under her T-shirt and touched her back. Gritty and wet, she winced at the stinging pain. She removed her blood covered hand and wiped it on the grass. The cuts and grazes that covered her arms and legs told a similar story.

She examined the plastic tie that still bound her ankles together. With nothing to cut it with she tried snapping it with her hands which she instantly regretted. It was locked fast and her efforts caused her nerve ends to jangle spitefully.

Ella knew that she needed to get medical attention. Her head throbbed, and she was now feeling sick. The remains of her lunch came up in rhythmic waves. She spat out the sour tasting bile and wiped her mouth with a clump of soft grass. It was a small blessing but having vomited she started to feel a little better. She decided to try and stand and see if she could move. She needed to get back to her car.

Hauling herself to her feet she tried to shuffle forwards. With her ankles bound so tightly it was almost impossible. It was all she could do just to stand up. In ten minutes, she was lucky if she'd managed a hundred yards. It was exhausting and she still couldn't see the end of the tree line. She looked at her watch, it was approaching six, there was still more than two hours till it was dark. She decided to stay where she was and conserve energy. At least it wasn't cold. She lay down in a shaft of sunlight that burned through a break in the trees. Warm and comforting it soothed her aching body.

Ella had told Sam where she was going so when she didn't turn up at the diner, he would come looking for her. He would find her car and then he would find her. It was just a matter of time. She closed her eyes to wait.

Ella woke with a start. A large slavery dog was licking her face and nudging her with its enormous paws. She hadn't been aware that she'd dozed off, but through hazy eyes she looked up to see a middle-aged woman carrying a dog lead striding towards her. She was only a hundred yards or so away. Dog-breath, thought Ella, had never smelt so good.

'Willow, Willow, what's that you've found?'

The golden retriever sniffed and licked her discovery as if it was some tasty treat.

'Willow, Willow leave her be, come here. Oh my God what's happened to you, are you okay?'

Ella sat up and patted her rescuer. She looked at the woman standing in front of her and tried to speak. No words came, just a cascade of tears and desolate sobbing. Ella was shaking uncontrollably; she was an emotional wreck.

Chapter 11

The following morning, Angela was reading the overnight crime report in Charlie's office when she saw Sam's car drive into the rear yard.

'That looks like him now boss.' called Angela from the window. 'I'll go down and get him and bring him up.'

'I'd appreciate that. And bring him straight up would you. He'll be stressed enough without everyone asking how his girlfriend is.'

A few minutes later Angela walked in with Sam at her side. Charlie gave a welcoming smile and asked them to have a seat.

'Coffee's made and help yourself to a doughnut. Sergeant Brown is looking after us this morning.'

Charlie passed Sam a mug of coffee and sat down.

'First up, how's Ella doing. Are they going to be keeping her in?

Sam sipped his coffee and took a bite of his doughnut.

'She's doing remarkably well thanks. Doctors wanted to check her overnight but she's pretty sure they're going to let her out this afternoon. She knows she's been lucky. Superficial cuts and bruises, but nothing more serious than that.'

'That's good to hear. That was a helluva ordeal she's been through. Look if you need to get back to the hospital it's not a problem. Sergeant Brown's got things covered at this end. In fact, we were just waiting to get an update from you before we head down to the locus. Steve Joice has got a couple of uniforms sealing off the area and scenes of crime are already down there.'

Sam put down his mug.

'Ella's mom is on her way up. She's coming up on the bus from Charlotte and should be at the hospital by lunchtime. I'll go over after lunch and run them to her digs if that's alright. Her mom's going to stay with her for a few days.'

Angela smiled.

'That will cheer her up, nothing against you Sam but there's nobody quite like your mom when you're not feeling well or something traumatic like this has happened. She'll make sure Ella gets lots of TLC and that's what she needs right now.'

Sam nodded.

'Yep, you're right. But she's going to be okay. She was talking of taking me orienteering at the weekend. We won't be doing that of course, but it does show you how resilient she is. This won't keep her down. And anyway, I'm going to make sure we get the scumbags who did this.'

Charlie put down his mug and looked at Sam.

'I've not known you that long, but you're cut from the same cloth as your father, and I mean that in a good way. I know you want to be involved and can sense that you're itching to come to the crime scene with us.'

Sam smiled again. He was desperate to be part of the investigation. Ella had been the victim of two horrible racist attacks in the space of a fortnight, wild horses wouldn't stop him from getting involved.

'But there's just one thing you need to understand. Sergeant Brown will be leading this enquiry. You've got too much personal interest to be directly involved. We can't let emotion get in the way of the investigation. Sergeant Brown will be dealing with it, and I've asked her to bring Ryan along. It will be good experience for him. He's at court this morning but Sergeant Brown will brief him later.'

'That's fine, sir, I understand that. But I would like to go down to the locus if that's okay. Hope to hell we can get some forensics! This has got to be a racially motivated crime, just like the other one was. And there's every chance the Sill brothers and their cohorts will be responsible for this one as well!'

Angela picked up a pen and the incident report and sat down next to Sam. Talking of forensics, you'll know that we've seized her clothing for examination. I haven't had a chance to look myself, but I'm told there might be some fibres on her socks. Brown fibres, perhaps they came from the rope they used to tie Ella's legs. Anyway, we'll see, but we'll get it checked out. And on that point, remember to take a set of fresh clothes for her when you go to the hospital.'

'Yep, I will do, I was remembering.'

'Okay good. Look, it says on the incident that Ella saw two guys with a shotgun coming out of the woods. You've spoken to her; did she have anything to say about that?'

'Well she can say for sure that neither of them was the youths who assaulted her at Denny's the other week. The guys she saw yesterday were white and about the same age, but neither of them was the Sills. But she also told me she was attacked from behind and that she was

131

grabbed and tied up by at least two other people, there may well have been more. She never got a look at them, but they could easily have been the Sill brothers.'

Before Angela and Sam could continue their conversation, Charlie intervened.

'Okay let's just take a time out shall we. You see this is the problem when you're too closely involved with an enquiry. Objectivity can go out the window. Now I'm not saying the Sills aren't involved, but at this moment we just don't know. And speculating like that isn't helping. Sergeant Brown will investigate all lines of enquiry, you can be sure of that. And while it sounds like it might be a racially motivated crime, we can't be certain of that either. So, I don't want to hear any more accusations. let's do what we were trained to do and keep an open mind.'

Sam bit his lip to stop himself from blurting out. His frustration was in danger of getting the better of him. There was no doubt in his mind that the crime was racially motivated. Ella had been set upon and badly assaulted by a bunch of racist thugs. They could easily have killed her. As far as Sam was concerned there wasn't any other explanation. He was hurting, and he wanted to argue the point and stand up for his girlfriend, but he was experienced enough to know there is a time and a place to disagree with your boss, and right now, this wasn't it.

*

Forty minutes later Angela parked up the Pontiac at the end of the track near to where some yellow barrier tape was loosely tied between two large trees. Just beyond the tape was Ella's blue Toyota, still standing where she'd left it yesterday afternoon. As the three detectives approached, Dave Richardson and Zoe were finishing dusting the tailgate for fingerprints.

'Any joy?' asked Angela as the officers approached the vehicle.

Dave looked up with his familiar deadpan expression. After nearly twenty years as a scenes of crime officer, his face was almost impossible to read. Dave Richardson would have made a fine poker player. He didn't like to speculate; hard evidence was his game and he was too long in the tooth to be drawn into second guessing what may or may not have happened. He would leave that to the detectives, that was their job.

'Well I'm getting lots of lifts from the car, especially around the tailgate. But as usual we'll need elimination prints from the car owner before we can say anything about the prints.'

'Fine,' said Charlie bending down to look at Ella's sports bag that was sitting a couple of feet from the car.

'Was the car locked?'

'Nope.' replied Dave removing his protective gloves. 'So, we've taken prints from inside the vehicle as well.'

Charlie nodded and peered in the rear window.

'Good. And it looks as if nothings been touched. There's a jacket and a handbag still lying on the back seat, and the bag over there looks intact as well, so theft probably wasn't a motive. What about blood, vehicle tracks or anything else for that matter?'

'Not picking up any tyre marks. No surprise really the ground is rock hard. But we may have some blood on a pinecone halfway down the track. Looks like there are some fibres attached to it as well. I'll show you where we found it on our way down. I take it you want to have a look at the clearing where the girl says she was dragged to.'

'Sure, you lead the way, we don't want to walk across any potential evidence.'

'Don't think you'll have to worry about that this time, we're really struggling to get any forensics if I'm honest.'

Ten minutes later Dave and the three detectives arrived in the clearing where Ella's ordeal had ended. Steve Joice was sitting on a fallen tree talking to one of the uniformed officers who was protecting the scene.

Steve got up and walked across to meet Charlie and the others.

'Really sorry to hear about what happened to Ella, Sam.' said Steve putting his arm on Sam's shoulder.

'She won't think much of Greenbrier County, or some of the folk who live round here. She's had a tough time of it. Can you pass on my best wishes when you see her? I'd like her to know we're not all like those assholes.'

Sam managed a weak smile.

'I'll do that, and I appreciate your concern.'

Dave turned to speak to Charlie.

'From what we know, this is where they untied the rope and cut her hands free. We were hoping we might find the plastic cable tie, but we've gone over this area with a fine-tooth comb and found nothing. The only thing we came across was some burnt wood fragments in the centre of the clearing, but I don't think they're connected in any way. Probably left there after somebody made a campfire.'

Steve shook his head and wandered back to the fallen tree. He looked perplexed.

Sensing something was bothering him, Angela went across to have a word.

'What's up? I can tell by the look on your face that somethings annoyed you.'

Steve pursed his lips and nodded.

'I don't think Dave's right about this one. I mean about the campfire. I don't think there's been a campfire here.'

'You don't. What makes you say that?'

'Come over here and I'll show you.' said Steve walking to the centre of the clearing.

As Charlie was still talking to Dave, Sam wandered across to join Angela and Steve.

'As I said, I think Dave's got this one wrong. His theory about the campfire doesn't stack up. Look, these are the burnt pieces of wood he was talking about.'

Steve pointed at several small pieces of charred wood that were lying close together in the grass.

'If this had been a campfire you would expect to see some scorched earth, or at least find some burnt grass. But as you can see, there isn't any.'

Angela stared down at the fragments of wood on the ground.

'Hmm, yeah you're right, other than the wood, there's no sign of burning at all.'

'And two more things. Look at the grass just in front of the trees over there.'

Steve pointed to the edge of the clearing about 30 feet from where they were standing.

'I know we're standing in a bit of a dip, but follow the edge of the grass right around, it almost forms a complete circle. And if you look closely the grass at the edge is much flatter than the grass here in the middle. It looks to me like it has been trodden down, and quite recently too.'

Angela and Sam looked at each other and nodded.

'Okay, I wouldn't argue with that. But what's the other thing? You said there were two things.'

'Take a look at that large white oak over there, this I think, may be the clincher.'

Steve nodded towards a majestic old oak tree that towered above the others on the far side of the clearing.

'Do you notice anything about that tree?'

Angela and Sam stared at the tree. Angela looked bemused and shook her head.

'Not sure I'm getting anything. Just looks like a gnarly old tree to me.'

Suddenly, Sam's eyes widened, he had noticed something.

'I think I can see what you're on about. The trunk of the tree is burnt. There's a ten-foot scorch mark up the bark.'

'You've got it.' said Steve.

'I'm still not getting it. Where am I supposed to be looking?'

'Look at the trunk about six feet up from the ground.' replied Steve pointing at the tree. 'Then go up another ten feet and look along that thick branch on the left. Can you see? It's all charred as well. I'd say something shaped like a cross has been placed against that tree.'

'Okay, yes, I can see it now, but it doesn't look like a cross to me. Looks more like an upside down 'L' shape.'

'You would see it as a cross if there was burning on the other side. But there's not a branch on the right-hand side that low. That's why it looks like an upside down 'L'.

'Yep, I'm with you Steve.' replied Sam. 'It looks to me like someone has put a burning cross against that tree.'

'But even if you're right, why would anyone do that? And what's it got to do with the attack on Ella?'

'It might not be connected at all. But it looks to me like this has been used as a meeting place.'

'A meeting place for what?'

'The Klan that's what.'

'Woah,' said Angela shaking her head. 'You mean the Ku Klux Klan, that Klan?'

'Yep, the very one. I'm no expert, but I know they hold clandestine meetings in secluded places and stand in a circle around a fiery cross. I don't know what the hell else they do, but it looks to me like this might be a place where they hold their secret meetings.'

'I didn't know that the Klan was still a thing, I thought it died out years ago.' said Angela.

'I thought that too, until I read an article about it recently. It talked about the fourth incarnation of the Klan and how it was making a comeback in states right across the country. I suppose you just don't expect to find it on your doorstep.'

'And if what we've found here is related to the KKK, then it's hardly a stretch to connect it to what happened to Ella yesterday.'

'Yep, that's exactly what I was thinking.' replied Steve.

'Guys, over here, come and have a look at this.' shouted an excited Sam who had made his way to the base of the oak tree. 'There's several small bits of burnt wood here that look just like those other ones.'

Angela and Steve walked over to Sam.

'I think you may well be right.' said Angela bending down to get a closer look.

'We'll get SOCO to photograph the wood fragments and the scorch marks. And with any luck, when they get the wood back to the lab, they should be able to confirm that it's come from the same source. Top work Steve, there a detective's job for you any time you want it.'

Steve laughed.

'It's funny but this has put me in mind of old Trevor Wilks, do you remember him? Carnaptious old bugger, been retired years now. I only ever got to work with him occasionally, but I learned more from working with him than just about anyone else in the job. He always used to say get your head up and look around. He said most cops never did. Too busy looking at the ground he said, so they missed things. I've never forgotten it. So, I always scan a crime scene, top to bottom. That's why I noticed the scorching on the tree.'

Sam nodded.

'He's got a point. Don't think anyone's ever pointed that out to me before. I'll remember that, it's good advice.'

'If he's the guy I'm thinking of, he retired when I had a couple of years' service. He was a uniformed cop, wasn't he? I don't remember him being a detective.' said Angela.

'Uniform all his days. Too much of a maverick to be a detective. The bosses hated him, they thought he was a disrupting influence. But he was just different. Smart too. That's often why the top brass don't like someone. They hate it when they know a mere cop is smarter than them. Trevor was one of those. But I liked him, and as I said, learned loads about how to be a good cop from him.'

'Sam do us a favour and go and ask Charlie if he can come over. Looks like Dave is on his way back to his car, so give Zoe a shout on the radio and get her to meet

138

us here with a camera and her box of tricks. Charlie can give Dave the heads up later and tell him what Steve here has found. It means we don't have to embarrass Dave. It's not like him to miss something like this, but we're all human, even SOCO miss things occasionally.'

Steve smiled to himself. That was smart thinking on Angela's part. No need to point out Dave's oversight in front of the Lieutenant and the others present. That could be dealt with back at the office later. She's learning, thought Steve, she's going to make a cracking Sergeant.

Chapter 12

Mary had noticed that the reading room light was on when she was hanging up her jacket. The long-haired stranger with the fedora hat hadn't been in at all yesterday, but here he was today, head down and pouring over a pile of paper that was neatly stacked in front of him.

Today was Thursday and Mary was due to start work at eleven and work through till the library closed at eight. She had twenty minutes until the start of her shift, so she went into the office and put the kettle on. She was intrigued by her mysterious visitor whose name she still didn't know. She couldn't help wondering what he was up to. By the time she came out of the office her curiosity had got the better of her. She tapped politely on the glass window of the reading room door.

Chaska looked up and smiled. Mary smiled back and opened the door.

'I'm sorry to disturb you but I was wondering if you needed anything. I was expecting to see you yesterday and had looked out the box, but you didn't appear. I hope everything's okay?'

'Everything's fine thank you, but something came up yesterday and I couldn't come in. Sorry if I put you to any trouble looking out the box.'

Chaska was polite but non-committal. He was reserved by nature and had a healthy suspicion of anyone trying to pierce his privacy. A loose tongue in jail could cost you dear and he had learned to keep his cards close to his chest.

'Oh, no it was no problem. I didn't mean it like that.'

Mary's face flushed crimson. The last thing she wanted was to give the impression that he had put her to any trouble.

'Anyway, I wanted to tell you how impressed I was with how much you'd managed to sort in just one day. You've saved us hours of work, you certainly seem to know what you are doing, have you experience of archiving?'

'A little. But that was a lifetime ago. But a bit of organisation does makes things easier. It's helped me to get on with things this morning. I've now located all the documents I'm interested in, which is just a fraction of what's in that box. With any luck I should finish what I require to do today. You did tell me you were open till eight tonight, didn't you?'

'Yep, Thursdays are always our late-night opening.'

'That's good. I'm going to try and have everything done by then. But as you mentioned it, there might be something you could help me with, do you happen to have a photocopier I could use?'

Mary smiled and nodded.

'Sure. There's one on the other side of the reception desk, but it's ten cents a copy to use that. Look, I'm about to make myself a coffee, there's a copier in the office you could use for nothing, and I could make you a coffee if you like, expect you could do with one. But you'll need to have it in there, remember the rules, no food or drink in the library.'

'Sounds like you've got yourself a deal.' said Chaska getting up from his chair and stretching. 'All this sitting is giving me a sore back. And I don't think I introduced myself Mary, I'm Chaska, pleased to make your acquaintance.'

'How do you know my name? I'm not wearing a name badge.'

'No, but I can read. Your name's on the reception desk.'

'Hmm. Yes of course it is. You aren't a police officer by any chance, are you?'

Chaska chuckled.

'Afraid not. Never been one of them and somehow I don't think they'll have me now.'

Mary didn't know what that was supposed to mean but it didn't matter. She had broken the ice and now she knew her handsome visitors name.

Chaska picked up his notepad and a pile of papers and was about to follow Mary into her office when he started to cough and splutter. He pulled out his handkerchief to cover his mouth as the hacking continued.'

'Apologies,' he said wiping his mouth. 'It's this damned cough, just can't seem to shift it.'

Mary smiled politely and held the door open.

'You better take some more of that cough mixture if you've got it with you.'

'Won't be without it just now.' replied Chaska patting his pocket.

'You should take some with your coffee. I'll get you a spoon. Now, how many copies do you need?'

'Just one of each thanks. Your copier looks a bit more complicated than the one I'm used to. I think you're going to have to show me how it works?

'Sure, but it's really quite straightforward. Give me your first document and I'll show you.'

Chaska handed Mary a set of minutes which she tapped on top of the copier to make sure all the pages were straight. They were minutes from a board meeting dated February 1953. Mary couldn't help but notice the names of the attendees listed in the first paragraph of the front page. Eldridge, Mitchell and David Lawrence were the first three names mentioned.

Mary scoffed and made a face.

'Sorry, I don't want to pry, but I couldn't help noticing the names of the Lawrence brothers on your report. Are they part of your investigations?'

Chaska could tell by the sarcastic tone of Mary's voice that she was less than impressed.

'Yeah, they are, together with a few other things. I take it then that you know of them?'

Mary gave Chaska a withering look.

'Everyone in this town knows of the Lawrence brothers. Bunch of rogues. My father worked at the Spruce Knob mine for a short while, but he never had any time for the Lawrences. They made themselves rich on the back of their workers and then right out the blue they sold the mine. Many men lost their jobs. My father wanted out anyway, so he left and became an Insurance Clerk. I'm really glad he did, or he might have gone to work in the asbestos factory. Did you know they opened that after they sold the mine? Talk about out of the frying pan and into the fire.'

'Yes, I was aware they had been involved in that. In fact, isn't there a court case ongoing. I thought some former employees and their families were trying to sue

143

the company for compensation. Somebody told me that many of their former employees had died of asbestosis.'

'That's correct, the court case started last week. But I'll not hold my breath. Aiden Lawrence, that's Eldridge, the oldest brother's son, is one slippery customer, he's contesting the case. He's a lawyer himself, worked at both the mine and the asbestos company. He'll have made sure that his father and uncles are kept at arms-length. It will end up the same way as the case against the mine did. They'll walk away scot free, mark my words, the families won't get a dime.'

'If you're typical of the rest of the townsfolk, it doesn't sound like there's much love lost between you and the Lawrence family.'

'That's an understatement. When you have time, you should take a walk round the graveyards in Lewisburg and Fairlea, they're full of victims who died from respiratory illnesses picked up from working in the mine or the asbestos factory. My family were lucky, we are one of the few who didn't lose anyone. So, you're right, I think it would be fair to say that the Lawrence brothers aren't top of everyone's Christmas card list!'

Chaska heaved a sigh and shook his head.

'I wouldn't give up hope just yet. If they've managed to get the company into court, there must be a chance that they'll be found guilty.'

Mary shook her head.

'I very much doubt it. It's been all over the local news this week. And just last night they were reporting from the steps of the court when who should appear out of the building but Aiden Lawrence and his defence team. All smiles and clapping each other on the back. And I think I know why they appeared so happy.'

'Go on, I'm listening.'

'Now I didn't know the lady myself, but I heard yesterday that one of the key witnesses for the prosecution had died suddenly, and now there's speculation that the trial might fold. Whether that's true or not I don't know, but I think it helps explain why Aiden Lawrence was looking so pleased with himself.'

Chaska opened his notepad and started to write. He didn't disclose that he knew the lady Mary was referring to. Instead he sensed an opportunity to fill in some gaps in his knowledge.

He already knew, even after just a cursory read through of the documents, that he could prove that important pieces of information had been doctored. He had uncovered two sets of board meeting minutes that had been completely re-written. Both the original minute and the re-written version were in the box. He would need to go over them in fine detail, but on first reading it appeared that the mine inspection scheduled for April 1953, was completely spurious. In fact, from what he had read, no inspection had ever been arranged.

In other altered minutes it stated that the purchase of new cutting equipment had merely been delayed, when the truth, as disclosed in the original document, was that no new equipment was to be purchased ahead of the sale of the mine. The doctored minute also erased any mention that the mine was to be sold.

It was still early days, he'd only been at it since nine this morning, but his notepad was already filling up. It was abundantly clear from the discrepancies he had already discovered that the scale of the cover up was considerable. Now what he really needed, was more information about the three brothers. Information that was unlikely to be found in the archive.

He already knew that the brothers were still alive. Likewise, Eldridge's son, Aiden. He was also aware that the company secretary, Clifford Latimer, had recently passed away. And of course, he knew all about the deaths of his former foster father, Tom Hicks and former union rep, Joe Jarret. It was the other names he knew nothing about. Who was Dan Tomkins or Walter Massie? Their names frequently appeared in documents. Could either of them be still alive? They would be old men now, but it was possible. If they were alive, they might hold the key as to what really happened more than forty years ago.

From what Mary had already said it was clear that she knew a bit about the Lawrence family and their companies. Perhaps she might also know who Tomkins and Massie were. No time like the present, thought Chaska. It was time to pick Mary's brains.

'Can I ask if the names Dan Tompkins or Walter Massie mean anything to you?

Mary raised an eyebrow and sipped her coffee.

'I know about Dan Tompkins alright. I used to sing in the same choir as his wife. The other name doesn't ring any bells though. Massie did you say, Walter Massie?'

Chaska nodded.

'Nope. Can't say I've ever heard that name.'

'That's not a problem, but what can you tell me about Dan Tompkins?'

'I can tell you that he's a real pain in the ass. Must be in his early eighties now. It's a miracle that he's still alive. He's got a chronic drink problem. It used to be gambling but somehow, he managed to kick that. Just when his poor wife thought their lives might return to normal, he went and discovered drink. He must have an addictive personality. It finally did for their marriage and she moved away. I haven't seen her in years. But you'll find him most nights in Ruby's bar on South Street. I often see him going in when I'm on my way home from here.'

Chaska scribbled that information into his notepad.

'Do you happen to know what he did in the mine?'

'Well he wasn't at the coal face. I know he didn't go underground. I seem to remember he worked in the office. Not sure how I know that but perhaps, Val, his wife, told me. Either that or dad might have mentioned it. If you go to Ruby's after you're finished here you could ask him yourself, as I said, I'm sure he's in there most nights.'

Chaska nodded.

'I'll do that, thanks. I'll try and get a word with him tonight. Look Mary, while you're here, is there anything you can tell me about the brothers? Do you know if they still live around here?'

'Mitchell, the middle brother still does. He has a big house that looks onto the eighteenth fairway of the Greenbrier Country Club. He's never off the golf course apparently, even at his age. My neighbour regularly plays nine holes with him, and his wife uses the spa. Aiden, Eldridge's son lives locally too. Somewhere up in the mountains. He skis and cycles. You'll see him dressed head to toe in lycra out on his bike, he's a fitness fanatic.'

'And what about Eldridge and David, the youngest brother?'

'Eldridge moved to Chicago when the asbestos factory closed. He lives on an estate in some gated community outside the city. Our local newspaper did a feature on him a few years ago. That's why I know where he lives. Not sure about the youngest one. I did hear that he'd found religion and was living in a commune near Huntersville, but that could just be gossip. I do know there was a falling out, and he never had anything to do with the asbestos company. I'm sure he left the mine around the same time my father did. I'm sorry I can't confirm that for you, but my father died five years ago.'

'Oh, I'm sorry to hear that. Please accept my condolences. But that has been most helpful, you've filled in a few blanks for me. You won't find any of that information in the archive.'

Mary smiled and looked up at the clock.

'Just glad to be of help. But look, it's nearly eleven, I'll have to get going. You carry on with your photocopying and just close the door when you're finished. I'll let Jane, my colleague, know you're in here. Is there anything else you need before I go?'

'Just one more thing if you don't mind. I'm looking to get my hands on a book. It's called, 'Massacre at Spruce Knob.' I looked it up on your computer and it said you had a copy and it wasn't out on loan. But it wasn't on the shelf where it said it would be. Do you have any idea where it might be?'

'Hmm. I'll go check for you. If it's not marked out on loan, then we should have it. Most likely it's been returned but hasn't been put back on the shelf yet. There's a whole pile of returned books waiting to be gone through. I'll make that my first job this morning.'

A little while later Chaska was sorting through his photocopies when Mary came into the office holding a book.

'Good news. Just as I suspected, it was in the pile of returned books. Do you need it just for reference today?'

Chaska shook his head.

'Don't think I'll be able to get to it today; I've still got too much of the archive to plough through. I was hoping I might be able to borrow it for a few days, only thing is, I'm not a member of the library.'

'Well, we can easily fix that, you could join. I'll sign you up now if you like. All I need is your name and an address and we're good to go.'

'Yeah, I know the process but there's just one problem. I don't have a permanent address. I'm only in Lewisburg staying with a friend for a few days. So, I don't think that is going to work.'

Mary pondered for a moment.

'Okay fine. How about this for a solution. I'll take the book out using one of my cards. You can have the book for as long as you need it, then just give it back to me. I'm bending the rules a little, but no one's going to know other than you or me. What do you think?'

'I think that will work just fine. And I'm grateful to you, you've been most obliging. And thanks for the coffee and letting me use your copier, it's been a big help.'

Mary's heart fluttered. She was smitten by the handsome man with the long hair and the terracotta coloured skin. He wasn't like the other customers she was used to dealing with, the worst of whom treated her like an unskilled receptionist. Chaska was mannerly and polite, she wanted to know more about him. If it wasn't so obvious, she would have turned up at Ruby's after work just so she could see him again. But that would be crass, he had important business to attend to. Anyway, she was mannerly too, she would bide her time, and see if another opportunity might present itself.

For the next eight hours Chaska never left the reading room. Whatever it was he was doing he appeared totally engrossed in it. It was just approaching seven thirty when she saw him putting on his jacket and hat and getting ready to leave.

Chaska smiled and placed the box of papers on the reception desk.

'There still a bit more to do, indexing for example. But at least it's all now in chronological order. I've also separated and ordered the minutes and other documents, so navigating through it is quite straightforward. I've maybe saved whoever asks for it next some head scratching, I hope so anyway. But I've got all that I need now.'

'It certainly looks like you've done a good job.' said Mary sifting through the box. 'Archiving isn't really my thing, so I wasn't looking forward to having to tackle it. But It looks like it's almost done, even I should be able to finish it off.'

'And I'll tell you another thing.' said Chaska putting his photocopies into a folder. 'You weren't wrong about those brothers; they've been ruthless and have a lot to answer for. If anyone had known back then what I now know then they would have ended up in prison. Well, two of them would. I'm not sure that David, the youngest one was involved to anything like the same extent. There's evidence that he tried to stop what the other two were up to. That part's not particularly clear, but I know for certain that the other two were a pair of shysters. I wouldn't trust either of them. Same goes for Eldridge's son. For someone who was only in his early twenties, he had a lot of influence. From what I can gather, he had his fingers in most of the pies and, as the company lawyer, knew exactly what was going on'!

'I think you've got them to a tee. That's always how my father described them. He had no time for the Lawrence family.'

Chaska buttoned up his jacket and picked up his folder.

'Anyway, enough of all that. I don't want to keep you from what you've got to do. But I'd like to thank you again for all your help and it was real nice meeting you.'

Then with a smile and a tip of his hat, he was gone. Mary watched out the window as he crossed the road and disappeared into the night. She felt sad that he had gone. Meeting Chaska had been the highlight of her week. There was still half an hour till closing, the last thirty minutes of the late Thursday shift always seemed to drag. She was hungry and a little weary, right now she wanted to be home with her feet up. That or in Ruby's bar having a drink with her mysterious friend. She glanced up at the clock. There was still twenty-eight minutes to go, this was as slow as a wet weekend and clock watching wasn't helping.

By quarter to eight the library was empty. Mrs Deans, an eccentric old spinster in her late seventies and a Thursday night regular was, as usual, the last to leave. She had finally decided to borrow 'The Pelican Brief', but only after Mary assured her that it had nothing to do with underwear and wasn't too racy. Mary was busy shutting down the computer and switching off the photocopier when the door opened and a man eating a slice of pizza from an open box walked in.

'I'm afraid you can't come in with that.' said Mary fixing the man with a stern stare. 'No food of any kind is allowed in the library, and anyway, I'm just about to lock up, the library closes at eight.'

The man looked at his watch and shrugged his shoulders.

'I'm not wanting any books or anything, I'm looking for the guy with the long hair and fedora hat. I was told he might be here.'

Mary wasn't sure how to respond. What did this strange looking guy want with Chaska?

The man was aged around fifty and stick thin. He skin was the colour of mahogany and he had heavy tan lines visible underneath the edge of his short-sleeved shirt. His jeans looked badly in need of a wash. There was something about him that made Mary feel uneasy.

'Not sure who you're talking about.' replied Mary with a dead pan expression. 'Can't say I remember seeing anyone fitting that description and I've been here since eleven. So sorry, I can't help you, but as I said, you'll need to leave, you can't come in here eating pizza.'

The man stood motionless not saying anything. Then, quite theatrically, he took another bite from the slice before returning it to the box and slowly closing the lid. Without another word, he turned around and walked out of the building.

Mary sighed in relief and slumped into her chair. The stranger hadn't been abusive, nor had he threatened her, but she still couldn't help feeling unnerved. Who the hell was he? And what did he want with Chaska? She wondered if she had done the right thing by not saying where he was. He might be completely genuine. He could be a friend, family even. But then again, he could be anybody. She decided she would mention it when Chaska next came in. The only trouble with that was she didn't know when that might be. He hadn't actually said. But he would need to come back sometime, if only to return the book he had borrowed.

*

The barman in Ruby's was drying glasses when Chaska walked in. The bar wasn't particularly busy, at a rough count there were less than ten customers in the place. Chaska scanned the room looking for his target. As everyone else looked under forty it had to be the old fellow sitting gazing into space nursing a beer at the end of the bar. He seemed oblivious to Chaska's presence. The old man's bulbous nose and florid complexion told the story of his struggles with the bottle. He did not look a well man.

'What can I get you?' asked the barman putting down his dish cloth.

'I'll have a glass of whatever he's drinking' replied Chaska gesturing towards the old man. 'And pour one for him too would you.'

The barman frowned and leant forward on the bar.

'Not sure that's such a wise move my friend. Buy him a drink and you'll never get rid of him. And he's on his last warning, if I catch him pestering my customers for drink then he's out. He really will be in trouble then, this is the only bar in the town he can still drink in, he's already been barred from all the others.'

A thin smile creased Chaska's mouth.

'So, he's drinking in the last chance saloon then?'

The barman's frown broke into a smile.

'Yep, quite literally he is. So, don't say I didn't warn you.'

Chaska picked up the two beers and pulled out a stool at the end of the bar.

'I'm guessing you must be Dan Tompkins.' said Chaska holding out a beer.

The old man took the beer and looked Chaska up and down suspiciously.

'And what if I am, who's asking?'

Chaska held out his hand.

'My name's Chaska, I'm a friend of the Hicks family. I was hoping you could help me. Someone told me you used to work at the Spruce Knob mine, and might have known my foster father, Tom.'

The old man narrowed his eyes and tentatively reached out to shake Chaska's hand.

'Sure, I knew Tom Hicks. He might have even called me his friend once. But that was a long time ago. He's been dead over forty years and look at me, I'm still here. Seems like the good Lord has forgotten about me!' said the old man lifting his eyes to the ceiling and taking a slug of his beer.

'If there were any justice in this world, he would have taken me a long time ago. But I reckon this is kinda my punishment. Keeping me here, so each day I wake up and the nightmare continues. One day, I reckon quite soon, he'll call me up and I'll face my judgement. Reckon Tom and Joe will be there too, so they'll get their say. They'll get their chance to get even.'

Chaska had no idea what Tompkins was on about. But he could tell his mind was troubled.

'Get even about what my friend?'

154

The old man drained his glass and shook his head.

'I sold them out. Same as what Judas did to the good Lord, I sold them out. I did it for more than thirty pieces of silver mind, $2,000 was my price. I might have got more, Cliff Latimer got more, but $2,000 was my price for selling out my friends. It's cost me a wife, family, everything I ever had. God damn it, at least Judas had the courage to kill himself. I don't even have that. So here I am, a pathetic alcoholic, just waiting. Waiting for that fateful day when he'll call me up to judge me.'

Chaska raised the empty glass in the direction of the barman who poured another beer.

'Dan, I can see how hard this is for you, but I need you to tell me what happened. I know you didn't kill those men. They died of carbon monoxide poisoning. You weren't responsible for that.'

Dan took another drink of his beer and looked Chaska in the eye.

'I am to blame. It wasn't just my fault, but I'm still to blame. I've never told anyone this before, and I don't really know why I'm telling you.'

Dan put his head in his hands.

'I wasn't there. I should have been in the office to give them the bird and the lamps, but I was over in the canteen watching the race. It was the 1953 Kentucky Derby. Dark Star beat the odds-on favourite. It came in at 25/1. I won a fortune. But I should have been sacked for leaving the office unattended. No one was there when the alarm was sounded. Them poor boys died because of me and then I sold them out. Took $2,000 to say they were in an unauthorised part of the mine without the bird or lamps. They even made us testify that they weren't wearing hard hats when we found them. Latimer and Walter Massie were with me, and I swear to God we found them with their hats on.'

Chaska pursed his lips and nodded.

'Even if all that was the case, the real blame still lies with the Lawrence brothers. They were the ones who deliberately ran down the mine so they could maximise their profit when they sold it. They were the ones who didn't place the order for the new machinery and cancelled the mine inspection because they didn't want to spend any money ahead of the sale. If the inspection had gone ahead, they would have discovered the carbon monoxide in that seam and those men wouldn't have died. Look Dan, I've seen the papers, the actual minutes of the board meetings. It was their actions that created a dangerous mine that killed Tom Hicks and Joe Jarret.'

Dan looked incredulous.

'But they said the mine wasn't viable, they were on the brink of going bust. That's why they sold it. They got me and the others to tell lies so that the sale still went through, ain't that the truth?'

Chaska shook his head.

'That's only partly true. You see they never released the report about the fourth seam. If I remember right, I think it was 'D' seam. It had up to three times as much coal as the other three seams. The coal was deeper down and more difficult to get at, but it would have kept the mine going for years.'

Dan laughed ironically.

'And God damn it,' continued Chaska, 'that's what happened. The West Virginian Mining company brought in new machinery and mined that seam for years after. But those coal reserves were the only real asset the Lawrences had when they wanted to sell. So, as I said, they deliberately ran the mine down and laid men off. It was all so they could maximise their profits. I reckon they bought you and the others off because they didn't want anything to come out that might jeopardise the sale. You see, if the management had been shown to have been negligent, then any deal to sell the mine would probably have fallen through.'

Dan drained his beer and put down his glass.

'Woah, this is the first time I've heard any of that. So how do you know all this?'

'As I told you, I've seen the documents. All the board meeting minutes, and papers about the proposed sale. They are all in an archive that Clifford Latimer kept. He'd been given instructions to destroy everything by the Lawrences, but for some reason he didn't, and now I've seen the documents I know the truth. Those brothers are the real guilty party here. You're just a pawn in their game, they exploited you for their own ends.'

Dan looked up at the television at the other end of the bar and ruefully shook his head.

'And look they're still at it.'

Dan nodded towards the screen where a news reporter was standing on the steps outside a court building.

'That's the local news reporting from the court a couple of blocks down the street. There's a case ongoing between the Lawrence family and their asbestos company. They shafted those workers the same as they did with the miners. And from what I'm hearing they'll likely get away with this one too. I heard that Mrs Hicks had passed away real sudden. She was the prosecution's best chance of getting a conviction. With her gone, I reckon the games up. Old Eldridge's son,

Aiden is as slippery as an eel. Smart though, he'll have made sure that the family are protected. You mark my words. They won't find the Lawrences guilty.'

'Expect you might be right about that. I got to see Carole the day before she died. As you said it was very sudden. Really sad too, she was a great lady, much like her husband was. I don't know anything about the case against the asbestos company, but if they did something similar to what they did to those miners, then they are as guilty as hell.' said Chaska sliding another beer towards Dan.

Dan sucked the froth off the top of the glass.

'They'll get their comeuppance one day the same way I will. They'll need to stand in front of the good Lord and justify what they did, they'll be no hiding place then. They'll get what's coming to them.'

'Well, perhaps we won't have to wait too long. I hear they're very old men now.'

'The three brothers are. But it might be a while before Aiden meets his maker. He's only in his mid-sixties. He could be around for years yet.'

'Oh, you never know, I'm a great believer in fate and nobody knows what might be around the corner! What goes around comes around as they say. We're just going to have to wait and see. Look, while I'm here, there's one last thing I'd like your help with. Can you tell me anything about Walter Massie? I've drawn a blank as far as he is concerned. Do you know if he's still alive?'

'Can't tell you that I'm afraid. I lost touch with him immediately after Tom and Joe died. He left Spruce Knob to go and work at the Middleton mine. I take it you know he was a Negro?'

Chaska shook his head.

'First black miner to work at Spruce Knob. One of the first in West Virginia if my memory serves. I didn't know him that well. He was friendly with Joe Jarret, if I recall. He knew Tom as well, but Joe was his big pal.'

'And do you know if the Lawrences bought him off, like they did with you and Latimer?'

Dan grimaced and bit his lip.

'Not sure about that. I've thought about it often enough. But the rumour at the time was he and his family had been threatened. I mean properly threatened with violence. Some even said that the Klan were involved. I believe he gave his testimony to save his family. He moved out to White Sulphur Springs when he went to work at Middleton. Don't know what happened to him after that. But the fact he went straight to another job suggested to me that he hadn't taken money. I reckon they put the frighteners on him, and he feared for the safety of his family. He's not guilty to the same extent as me and Latimer are. I would have done the same if I'd been in his shoes. This is a white town you see, and it was worse back then. Not easy being a black man in a white town. And that's before the Lawrence's henchmen come after you.'

Chaska took out his notepad and scribbled down some notes. He nodded to the barman who poured another beer.

'Listen, I'm grateful to you.' said Chaska passing Dan the beer. 'You've filled in a lot of gaps and what you've told me makes sense. But remember what I said to you. The real guilty parties are the Lawrence family. You didn't kill those men. Those brothers did that. You might want to mention that when you see the good Lord. And from what I hear he's a good guy, so he'll see

159

you alright, I'm sure of it. But anyway, let's hope that won't be for some time yet.'

Chaska smiled and tipped his hat.

'Good speaking to you.' replied Dan lifting his glass. 'And thanks for the beers, been a long time since anybody bought me a beer.'

Chapter 13

Early the following morning, Detective Sergeant Angela Brown, Sam Coutts and Scenes of Crime Officer, Zoe Marchbanks were deep in conversation outside Sam's parents' house in a quiet side Street in Fairlea.

The white door of the garage that adjoined the chalet style property had been freshly daubed in shiny blue paint. 'NIGGER LOVER,' was written across the door in three-foot high capital letters. Sam had discovered the graffiti when he was leaving to go to the police office that morning.

'Are you nearly done?' asked Angela.

Zoe put down her camera and nodded.

'I've got all the photographs I'll need. I'm just going to get a scraping of the paint and then I'm done. I'll be with you in a couple of minutes if I can find where I've put the damn phial.'

'That's fine take your time. We don't want to miss anything, but it'll be good to get back and give Charlie a briefing before the morning meeting starts. He'll want a full update ahead of that. And just checking Sam, you said you got in at roughly 2215 last night and discovered it at 0620 this morning. So, we can assume it's happened sometime between then?'

'Yep, that's right. I'm certain it wasn't there when I got back from Ella's last night. Look, I take it I can try and get it cleaned off when you're finished? I want to try and get it off before my folks get back. Good job they've been away for a few days. It'll just upset mom if she sees it and my dad will have a fit, you know what he's like. Never had the longest fuse when he was in the job and I can assure you it ain't got any better since he retired.'

'You take your time, we'll see you when we see you, so there's no hurry. I'm not sure what you'll need to get that off. Any ideas Zoe?'

'I should think white spirit should do it, but you might be better with a branded paint remover. That's metallic paint and it's been done with a spray can, I can tell you that much.'

'How do you know they've used a can?' asked Sam.

'Because there aren't any drips. If they'd painted it on with a brush, you'd expect to see drips where it's run, but as there aren't any, I'm almost certain its been sprayed on.'

'Good to know.' said Angela taking a note of it in her pocketbook. 'It looks to me like the type of paint they spray cars with. It's got little bits of gold fleck through it that makes it sparkle.'

'Yep, I would agree. I'll know for certain when we test it. And it's a very unusual shade of blue. Almost aquamarine, you don't see many cars driving around that colour. I'll make some enquiries and see if I can get an exact colour match and brand for you.'

'That would be useful. If we know the colour and type of paint, we might be able to trace where it come from. Can't imagine too many stores round these parts sell that type of paint.' remarked Angela.

Sam looked sceptical.

'Who's to say it was even purchased from round here. It could have been brought in from anywhere.'

'That's true. But I reckon whoever did this is local. Probably the same individuals who assaulted Ella the other day, they've probably seen you and Ella out together. Too much of a coincidence for it not to be. And if that proves to be the case, then you can bet your bottom dollar that the spray can has come from a store round here.'

'Better not let Charlie hear you say that.' said Sam sarcastically. 'He bit my head off when I suggested that the incident at Denny's a couple of weeks ago was related to the assault on Ella.'

'Hey steady on, that's a bit of an overreaction. He was just trying to be objective.' replied Angela. 'You've got to remember that it's the Lieutenant's job to keep an open mind. Ours too. But he can't get ahead of himself, he has to be sure of the facts. I'll make sure that I give him a thorough briefing about what's happened here, you can be sure of that. And as I'm also leading the enquiry into who assaulted Ella, I'm not going to miss any opportunity to link the two incidents.'

'Good to hear.' said Sam who was now rummaging through a box of old rags looking for a cleaning cloth.

'I'd just like to say how sorry I am that you've had to put up with this shit, especially after what happened to Ella. And apologies I didn't ask. How's she doing? I heard she got out of hospital.' said Zoe.

'Doing well all things considered thanks. Her mom's come up and is staying for a few days which has been a big help.'

'Will you tell Ella about what's happened this morning?' asked Zoe innocently.

Sam nodded.

'She'll want to know. It will take more than a few racists to put Ella off, or me for that matter. She's an unbelievably strong woman. But I'll tell you one thing, going out with Ella has opened my eyes. She told me right from the off that it would happen, but stupidly I didn't believe her. I believe her now alright. Black people do get treated differently, almost every day they're subject to some form of discrimination. You see it in bars and restaurants and how folk look and speak to them in stores. That's the low-level stuff. Then, you get more serious incidents like this. I mean blatant, in your face racist incidents, committed by people who don't have half the brains or decency of Ella. They're weak and ignorant fuckers, and I despise them.'

'Gosh, that really sucks Sam. I'm sorry to hear that. I can't begin to imagine what gets into some folk, they're just horrible individuals and as you say, pig ignorant with it.'

*

In his office at Lewisburg Police Office, Lieutenant Finch was checking overtime returns and chatting to Dave Richardson. Charlie looked at his watch.

'If you're pushed for time I could come back, I know who've got the morning meeting to prepare for.'

Charlie shook his head and closed the file.

'No, you're fine. I've asked the deputy if he can put the meeting back half an hour. Angela's on her way back and I want to speak to her ahead of the meeting. I take it you heard what happened to Sam's garage this morning?'

'Yeah. Came in this morning to find a note from Zoe. She's at the house with Angela doing the scenes of crime. Starting to look like we're dealing with some serious racists. It's been a while since we had to deal with anything like this.'

'Yep, it looks kinda like it. I've got a meeting with the Chief later this morning, I need him to understand what we're dealing with here. You should have seen the hassle I had with his secretary just to get to see him. She says I can have ten minutes. Must be a busy man, but I'm none the wiser what he does all day. None of it seems to involve the detective division. But joking aside, he needs to appreciate how serious this is becoming. And as one of his own officers is now involved, I want to know that I've got his full support. This is going to need some dedicated resources if we're going to crack it.'

Dave puffed out his cheeks and sighed.

'Good luck with your meeting. He's a strange one right enough. I've not had many dealings with him, but he seems so insecure every time I speak to him. You don't expect your Chief to be a bag of nerves. If Wilder had still been around, he would have eaten him for breakfast. Can't decide which of the two I'd prefer. At least with Wilder you knew where you stood.'

'I know exactly what you mean.'

'Look Charlie, while it's just the two of us, I wanted to apologise for the other day. Steve Joice was right. Those bits of wood we discovered under the tree, are the same wood that was in the centre of the clearing. It was never a campfire. I don't know what I was thinking of. Just twenty minutes earlier I had been telling you that I didn't want to be drawn into making predictions. And there I was doing just that. It was a schoolboy error and I feel kinda foolish being honest. It's the type of thing I'm always telling my team to avoid.'

'It's not an issue Dave. Show me the man who never made a mistake and I'll show you a liar! We all do it, but I'll say one thing, you make fewer mistakes than most of us, and that certainly includes me. I should write a book on the ones I've made. It would be a long read.'

Dave smiled as he handed Charlie a typed report.

'Appreciate that. But it's been a good wake up call. Anyway, this is just a short report on the wood and the other SOC we did at the locus. It's short because there's not much to tell.'

Charlie quickly perused the three-page report.

'It says here that the wood fragments were from a white oak tree. Is that significant?'

'Yes and no.' replied Dave. 'I don't think it will be of any use evidentially. But it might give you a bit more understanding about how the minds of these suprema-cists work. You see the white oak is an indigenous tree to North America. And in that sense, they view it as being pure, they wouldn't use a tree that wasn't native. It also helps, of course, that it's called a white oak. They like that. Also, you'll see from the photo on the second page that the scorch marks that we found on the trunk of the tree, were almost certainly made by a burning cross. The outline shape is pretty clear if you look closely.'

Charlie nodded.

'Hmm, so just to confirm, you're telling me that the choice of wood is important. I mean they didn't choose it by accident.'

'Oh, it was no accident. From the research I've done I think they deliberately chose to make the cross out of white oak. And it was also a white oak tree they placed the burning cross against. That wasn't done by chance. Seems it's all part of their rituals.'

Before he could elaborate further there was a knock on the door and an out of breath Angela stumbled into the office. She was bent over trying to catch her breath.

'Sorry, boss, can you give me a minute.' Angela took several deep breaths.

'I sprinted up those stairs to catch you before the meeting starts, but all it's done is prove how out of condition I am.'

'Take your time, the meetings been put back so no hurry, it's all good.'

While Angela was regaining her composure, Dave got up to leave.

'Oh, I forgot to say, thanks for the invitation. Arrived in the post yesterday. Rachel and I will be delighted to attend. Forty eh, creeps up on you unexpectedly doesn't it?'

'That's great, glad you can both make it. And as for being forty, I can't quite believe it. I'll have twenty years service at the end of the year as well, not sure where the time goes.'

Dave scoffed.

'You'll still just a boy to me. I remember when you started. You've not changed that much. A couple of pounds heavier perhaps but aren't we all. Gordon Lang was telling me earlier that Mike was coming down for your party. It'll be nice to see him again. Good cop Mike, always liked him.'

'One of the best. Without doubt the most able detective I've worked with. I learned most of what I know from him. Wouldn't be sitting here now if it wasn't for Mike. He and Susan are coming down for the weekend and staying with us, so you'll get plenty chance to have a catch up.'

'Looking forward to it.' said Dave as he headed out the door.

'Right Sergeant, after you've given me the heads up as to what's happened at Sam's place, you and I are going to make a point of getting to the gym. Looks like we both need too. A healthy body leads to a healthy mind and all that. Think we might need both, if the last couple of weeks are anything to go by. Now what can you tell me about Sam's garage?'

*

In the kitchenette of Leroy's apartment, Chaska was stacking boxes of burgers into the bottom tray of the freezer. He placed a box of beer on the kitchen table and sat down. Tearing a sheet of paper from his notebook, he took out his pen and started to write.

'To Leroy,
You'll find a few boxes of burgers in your freezer which I hope you'll wash down with some of these beers. It's just a small token of my gratitude for the hospitality you have shown me. It was much appreciated, and of course, way better than the YMCA would have been. You were right about that. I'm just sorry I couldn't have given you more.

I've decided to head to the mountains for a while. I've got some unfinished business that needs taking care of. After that, who knows. I might just jump a bus and see where it takes me. Life is short and death is long, so it's time to start living.

Yours in friendship,
Chaska.

Chaska folded the note and put it on top of the box. He closed the front door behind him and headed into town. It was a sunny September morning and he was on his way to see Julie. Hopefully, she would have news about her mom's funeral arrangements. He fully intended to return to town for that. But before he called on Julie, he had somewhere else to go.

Returning to Leroy's apartment last night, he had passed an old house that was undergoing major renovations. In the driveway he'd noticed a large skip, stuffed full of broken up pieces of furniture and other household items. In one corner, wedged under a pile of old floorboards, Chaska had spied a rusty old birdcage. It had been difficult to get a proper look last night as it had been getting dark, but now, gazing at it in the daylight, it looked like it might be just what he needed.

He approached the front door and rang the bell. The door was opened by a middle-aged lady wearing blue overalls and a face mask. She removed the mask and smiled.

'Can I help you?' she asked politely.

'Sorry to bother you ma'am I can see you're busy, but I was wondering if I could take the birdcage that's in your skip. I mean if you're throwing it out would be alright if I took it away.'

'You do know it's broken.' said the lady coming down her front steps. 'The lock on the door is missing, and its very rusty. It belonged to my father. He used to have an African Grey parrot but that was years ago. I'd forgotten I had the cage. It was when I was clearing out the attic that I came across it. The parrot died not long after my father passed away, and that was more than ten years ago now.'

Chaska removed his hat.

'I'm sorry to hear that.' he said solemnly. 'I mean about your father, not the parrot. Well, I suppose I'm sorry ...'

The lady interjected before he could explain any further.

'I think I know what you're trying to say and that's kind of you. But as I said, that was a long time ago. So sure, you help yourself if you think it would be of any use. One less thing for us to throw away. Are you getting a parrot, is that why you need it?'

Chaska smiled and shook his head.

'It's not for a parrot, I've a few Canaries that I need to move out of an aviary, so it would come in handy to do that.'

The lady started to laugh.

'They'd better be very fat canaries. The gaps are way too big; they would just fly away.'

Chaska chuckled.

'I appreciate that. I'll need to modify it with some mesh or you're right, they won't be in there very long.'

'Look, there's rolls of chicken wire round by the shed. It's all different sizes if I remember. Some of the smaller stuff might do. You're welcome to help yourself to it.'

'That sounds like it might be just the job. Is it okay if I go and take a look?'

'Not a problem, follow me, I'll show you where it is.'

An hour later Chaska was standing in the aviary attempting to coax the last of the canaries into his makeshift cage. The chicken wire he'd fitted to the inside of the cage was the perfect size. The canaries weren't small enough to get through it. He'd fixed the door with a heavier piece of wire and knocked off all the loose rust. It might not have been the most attractive birdcage in the world, but the canaries didn't seem to care. Judging by the noise they were making they were as happy as a clam. They were singing their little hearts out as he filled the food trays with fresh seed and water.

The kitchen door opened, and Julie appeared carrying a tray of cookies and iced tea.

'I'll say something Chaska, you're certainly resourceful. They look right at home in that parrot cage. Have you got a new home for them to go to?'

'I'm working on that.' replied Chaska stuffing the box of bird seed into the side pocket of his rucksack. 'But till then, they'll stay with me. Anyway, it's going to be one less thing for you to worry about.'

Julie sat down on the kitchen steps and passed Chaska a glass of the iced tea.

'I'm pleased you're going to be able to make the service. Mom was always very fond of you. I could come and pick you up if you like. If you give me the address where you're staying, I'd be happy to do that.'

Chaska drained his glass and wiped his mouth.

'That's real kind of you, but you'll have other things to do on Monday. I'll make my own arrangements; it won't be a problem. I'll see you at the church for two.'

'Well, if you're sure, that will be fine. It's the Baptist Church on Cedar Street. There's not much parking at the church, so most folk park at the cemetery and walk through the lane. Its less than five minutes away. It's a small white panelled building, you can't miss it.'

'Gotcha.' said Chaska putting on his rucksack and picking up the birdcage. 'I know where the cemetery is, I'll find it no problem.'

'And you must come back to the house afterwards. I'd love you to meet my daughters, and Eric of course, and one or two close friends will be there. It'll just be some sandwiches and coffee, but it'll be a good chance for a catch up and to talk about mom. She would have enjoyed that. She always liked the gossip.'

Chaska smiled but didn't reply. As he closed the gate behind him, he smiled again and tipped his hat.

'Here, hang on a second. Please take these cookies, you didn't take one with your tea, but I want you to have them. I'll only eat them all if you don't take them, and I could do without that, believe me.'

'Sure.' said Chaska accepting the cookies which Julie had carefully wrapped in kitchen roll. 'I'll have them with my supper later.'

It was only a ten-minute walk from Carole's house to the bus depot. But in that time, he must have been asked at least three times where he was going with a parrot cage full of canaries. At the depot, Chaska looked up at the information board trying to work out which bus he needed to get.

'Can I help?' asked a small middle-aged man who was walking past wearing a driver's uniform.

'Hope so.' replied Chaska scratching his head. 'I'm trying to get to Spruce Knob. I think I need to get the bus to White Sulphur Springs.'

The bus driver grinned.

'You're in luck that's my bus it's Number six, leaves in five minutes from bay six. You're not by any chance Leroy's friend, are you? You sure as hell look like the guy he was describing to me. Don't take this the wrong way, but there aren't many folks cutting about Lewisburg with long hair and a fedora hat.'

'Yep, I'm that man. Now you've got me worried, what's he been saying about me?'

The bus driver started to laugh.

'Don't worry about that. It was all good. I think you made quite an impression. I don't think he'd met anyone like you before. Hey, is that birdcage with you?' asked the driver who had only just noticed the cage full of canaries.'

Chaska nodded.

'Where the hell are you going with them. You do realise Spruce Knob's a mountain, don't you? It's not a town. There's just a few farms scattered in the foothills, but nobody really lives there, it's in the middle of nowhere.'

Chaska nodded again.

'Yeah, the birds are with me and I know Spruce Knob's a mountain. I'm just visiting it, so, for now, the canaries are staying with me.'

The bus driver laughed again.

'Well good luck with that. It's a three mile walk in from the road end. That's as close as I can get you. Then after that you've still to get up the mountain. At least there's a decent path but it's nearly 5,000 feet to the summit. It's the highest peak in West Virginia. And I'll guarantee you one more thing.'

'What, you're gonna tell me it's got spectacular views?'

'No, that's a given. I was gonna say you'll be the first idiot to have climbed it carrying a birdcage full of damned canaries.'

Chaska smiled then started to laugh. Even he could see the funny side of it. He picked up the cage and followed the driver onto the bus.

'How much to where I'm going?' asked Chaska rummaging in his pocket for some change.

'Don't worry about that, this one's a freebie.' replied the driver with a wink. 'Leroy's done me a couple of short notice shift changes recently, so I owe him. And as you're a friend of his, you can have this one on me. And I'll give you a shout when it's time to get off, 'cause as I said, it's in the middle of nowhere.'

*

'Has anyone seen Ryan?' asked Angela sticking her head round the detectives' office. 'He's supposed to be meeting me here. We've got interviews to do in Addison and we should have left ten minutes ago.'

Blank faces looked up and shrugged their shoulders. Nobody seemed to know where he was. Muttering her frustration, she headed down the stairs to see if he was in the canteen. On her way she bumped into Sergeant Lang who was heading up to see Charlie.

'Ah, the very person, glad I bumped into you.' said Gordon rummaging in his pocket.

'Someone told me that you're collecting money for Charlie's 40th.'

Angela nodded.

'Excellent. In that case can you stick $20 on the sheet from me.' said Sergeant Lang waving a $20 bill at Angela.

'Yeah, sure, I will, thanks.'

'What's up with you? You've got a face like thunder?

Angela frowned and screwed up her nose.

'Is it just me, or are all new starts complete dicks? Ryan Mulroy was supposed to meet me in my office ten minutes ago and now he's gone AWOL. He's only just started in the department. He's supposed to be keen. Impress the boss and all that. Well he ain't impressing me. His attitude is all wrong.'

'Yeah, I think Mr Mulroy would piss me off as well. Although I don't think you can say they're all like that, but I know what you mean. It's just a job now isn't it. They like the money, just not the hours or the graft. Well most of them. There are exceptions of course. Young Sam for one.'

'Yep, you're right. I shouldn't tar them all with the same brush. But it's just so different from when you and I joined. I would never have dared to be late, not with some of the bosses I had.'

'Anyway, in answer to your question, I can tell you he's in the back yard, sniffing about that young blonde new start. See in future when you can't find him, track her down and he won't be far away.'

'Good to know I'll bear that in mind. The solution to this might be to have a word with the newbie. Warn her about the perils of dating a colleague, it rarely seems to work out, and never has in my case. Keep your work and your love life separate, that's what I say.'

Gordon chuckled.

'Sound advice; don't think I ever went out with anyone in the job. The current Mrs Lang was a lab technician. She smelt of formaldehyde occasionally, but I'll not hold that against her, there are worse things she could have smelled of!'

Angela grimaced. At that moment she couldn't think of any examples, but that was just typical of Gordon's dry sense of humour. She had half a mind to forget Ryan and ask Gordon to neighbour her. He was a cops' cop. Although he was now getting on in service and could be a bit set in his ways, he was solid and reliable and 100% loyal. He had all the qualities that appeared to be lacking in the wannabe detective who couldn't walk past a pretty girl.

Angela opened the back door and yelled across the yard.

'Ryan, step away from that officer and get your ass over here now. You're late and we've got police work to do. And here, you drive.' she shouted throwing Ryan a set of keys. Her startled colleague spun round and caught the keys just as they smashed into his chest.

'Now get in the car and pin your ears back and listen to me. Because if you don't, your tenure in this department will be short, I can promise you that.'

Chapter 14

It was approaching midday by the time the bus pulled into a layby at the side of the road. The temperature was climbing into the eighties and the cloudless bluebird sky was still and calm. There wasn't a hint of breeze, it looked set to be another scorcher.

In the far distance the twin peaks of Spruce Knob and Thorny Flat shimmered seductively in the hot sun. Their western slopes sparkling like crystal as the sunlight glinted off outcrops of ancient quartzite.

A wooden signpost bleached blond by the elements pointed the way, its faded lettering affirming what the driver had said. Three miles to the foothill of the mountain. Next to the signpost, at the mouth of the path, sat a rusty metal bench and an empty trash can. The only evidence that people visited this remote outpost.

The bus driver took off his cap and wiped the top of his head with a handkerchief. He was as bald as a coot and his head glistened with sweat. He picked up his water bottle and took a large swig.

'Better keep your hat on my friend, it's going to get mighty hot. Won't be surprised if it hits 90 this afternoon. They say this is the start of an Indian Summer. Hope you've got some water with you? cause' you're gonna need it!'

Chaska picked up his birdcage and rucksack and stepped off the bus.

'Packed a couple of bottles. It won't be cold, but it'll keep me going. Anyway, I won't run out, I can top the bottles up from one of the creeks that run down to the Greenbrier river. My map shows at least three, so I should be fine for water.'

'If you say so.'

The driver poured some water from his bottle onto a handkerchief and dabbed it on his face.

'Look, before you go, what time does the bus pass here on its way back to Lewisburg? I need to be back in town for 1330 at the latest on Monday.'

The driver looked at his timetable.

'If it's a Monday, you'll need to get the 11 o'clock. It'll pass here about 1125 hrs. Don't miss it. There won't be another one till 1325 and that'll not get you there in time.'

'I'll not miss it; don't you worry about that. And I'm grateful to you, thanks for all your help.'

The Driver shook his head and smiled.

'Not a problem my friend, but I still can't believe you're going up that mountain with them birds. I've seen a lot of weird things driving this bus over the years, but a guy climbing a mountain with a cage full of canaries is right up there. I'll need to tell the boys in Ruby's that one, that'll give them a laugh.'

Then with a toot of the horn the bus was gone. Chaska watched it disappear over the hill. Sitting down on the bench, he took out his library book from the front pocket of his rucksack. On the inside cover was a detailed map of Spruce Knob. The map showed the river and creeks, and the Spruce forest that dominated the lower slopes. The path he was to follow was delineated by a dotted line. About two thirds up the mountain, the ground appeared to plateau and open out into an area of relatively flat land. On his map it was called Yellow Rocks, named after the enormous outcrop of limestone, that formed huge slabs of granular yellowish rock. That was where he was heading for. Ever since Professor Foulis had confirmed his bloodline he had felt drawn to the mountain. With each passing day the desire had grown stronger, it was like searching for a drink in a desert. But today he would quench that thirst, today he would reach his nirvana, Yellow Rocks, the place where Eldridge Lawrence murdered Chief Makatai.

He looked at his watch. It was nearly ten past twelve. He reckoned it would take him the best part of an hour to cover the first three miles. That would take him to the base of Spruce Knob and the start of the steep climb up the southern ridge towards the summit. Yellow Rocks was at roughly 3,700 feet. Factoring in the cage and rucksack he had to carry, regular water stops, and the mushrooms he was intending to gather, he decided it would take him the best part of four hours to reach his destination. If all went to plan, he would be there by four o'clock.

He had only been walking for twenty minutes when he spied what he was looking for growing in a damp mossy knoll underneath the cover of some mountain ash trees. They were psilocybe azurescens, the most potent of the hallucinogenic mushrooms that proliferated throughout West Virginia. Perfect, thought Chaska, bending down to take a closer look. He sat down on a rock and took out his notebook unfolding a sheet of paper that contained coloured pictures of various types of fungi. He was no expert, so he needed to be certain. But from what he could tell from the picture, these looked like the real deal, these were magic mushrooms and more to the point, there were dozens of them. Professor Foulis's paper on the 'Ghost Dance' had referred to the fungi and how they were often used to induce a trance-like euphoria when his ancestors performed their ancient rituals. If he was to reach out and connect to the spirits of his forefathers, he needed to be sure that he had picked the right mushrooms.

Chaska had never used any type of hallucinogenic drug before. The opportunity had never presented itself. He'd been incarcerated since the age of seventeen, so the only drugs he had tried before he went to prison had been tobacco and alcohol and even that had only been the odd beer. This, therefore, was unfamiliar territory. But it would be a means to an end and with the full moon due tomorrow night, the plan that he had been developing since his last meeting with Professor Foulis, looked like it would now come to fruition.

The innocuous looking fungi stood about five inches tall, their slender grey stems supporting a large convex cap. Chestnut in colour, it was similar in shape to the hats often worn by farm labourers in the paddy fields of Asia. Within a few minutes, he had filled a paper bag with about 30 of the largest specimens. They had a mild, slightly farinaceous smell that belied their powerful reputation. The full potency of the mushrooms would only be revealed when they were chopped up and boiled to make an intoxicating broth.

Up till now the canaries had been strangely quiet. Now, quite suddenly, all five birds started to sing. Trilling and chirping quite frenetically, their chorus starting a chain reaction from other passerines perched high up in the surrounding trees. Melodic and manic at the same time, like an orchestra warming up before a performance, the twittering of birdsong filled the air. Chaska had never heard anything quite like it. Was it some kind of warning signal? If canaries could detect carbon monoxide down a mine, then perhaps they were picking up something sinister from the bag of freshly picked mushrooms. Whatever had prompted them to start singing, it showed no signs of abating. For the next few minutes, he lay back in the warm grass as the forest choir performed their repertoire.

In a frenzy of escaping wings, it suddenly went quiet. Completely silent. Chaska looked at the cage. The five songbirds were mute and huddled together on a single perch near the bottom of the cage. He scanned around him; it didn't take long to find the reason for their silence. The choir had been muted by the arrival of a red-tailed hawk who was now nonchalantly preening its wing feathers high up in a balsam fir tree. The choir knew from experience that the hawk wouldn't tolerate their concert, if they were to sing another day, then today's practice was at an end.

*

The do not disturb light had been on outside Lieutenant Finch's office for the last fifteen minutes. He felt stressed. He loosened his tie and leant back in his chair with his eyes shut trying to relax. It took a lot to get Charlie Finch riled. His calmness in stressful situations set him apart from most other detectives and was a primary reason why Mike Rawlingson had recommended him for the Lieutenant's job. But today his patience had been stretched to its limits by a Chief of Police who was self-evidently way out of his depth.

The meeting he had scheduled for that afternoon had lasted less than ten minutes. Charlie had quickly realised that he and the Chief were on a completely different page. It was incredibly frustrating and dispiriting, so he'd excused himself and left. If he'd stayed any longer, he would have said something he would have later regretted. All that would achieve would be to make his job of overseeing the investigation and managing the department even more difficult than it already was.

It was clear from the start that the Chief had read Charlie's briefing note. Annotations and underscores, in spidery turquoise ink, were all over the paper. And from his first response it was also clear that he didn't agree with Charlie's view that the incidents involving Ella and Detective Coutts were racially motivated and almost certainly connected.

Charlie had encountered such intransigence before, he had seen it many times in junior officers who despite their training, struggled to leave their personal prejudices at home or see the other point of view. The shocking thing about today's encounter was that it was Greenbrier County's most senior officer who was in denial and refusing to accept that his jurisdiction was in the grip of violent racists.

That was worrying enough. But what really shocked Charlie was the Chief's suggestion as to how the problem should be resolved. In his view it was simple. The matter would go away if his detective officer ended his relationship with his black girlfriend. He even suggested that as the officer's line manager, it was Charlie's responsibility to tell Sam that he should end his relationship immediately. The relationship, the Chief

182

had mused, was the causal factor of these problems. End that and the problem goes away.

Charlie was stunned. He was so taken aback that it took him a moment to digest the idiocy of his boss's remarks. Gathering his thoughts Charlie had tried to reason with the Chief, but it was apparent from his dismissive reaction that the issue was not up for debate. Charlie was simply staggered. How could a Chief of Police hold, and more to the point articulate, such racist views? This was a classic case of victim blaming.

From the first time he met the Chief, Charlie had suspected he was weak. None of his subsequent encounters, few and brief as they were, had made him change that initial assessment. He had gone to today's meeting expecting the Chief to try and seek the path of least resistance and keep the enquiry at arms-length by letting Charlie and his team get on with it. Just keep him apprised of developments. That's what they usually said when they wanted to distance themselves and didn't want hands-on involvement. This though was different. It was abundantly clear that the Chief didn't want to hear about these incidents again. He had suggested a solution and now it was down to Charlie to magic it away. The man was hopeless. He lacked any form of moral compass and had been promoted way beyond his level of competency. In the face of such stubborn resistance, Charlie had picked up his folder, excused himself and left the room.

In the detective's general office, Sam was checking witness statements when Angela and Ryan walked in the door.

'Does anyone know if Charlie's got someone in with him? I could do with a word, but I see he's got the do not disturb sign on.'

Sam looked up and shook his head.

'I'm pretty sure he's not with anyone. Stuck his head round the door looking for you on his way back from his meeting with the Chief. He didn't say much, but I've seen him look in better moods if you get my drift.'

Angela sighed and blew out her cheeks.

'That sounds like it didn't go well. Okay then, no time like the present.' said Angela lifting the phone. 'We might as well get all the bad news over at one time.'

Sam didn't like the sound of that. Sergeant Brown and Ryan had just got back from interviewing potential suspects in Ella's abduction and assault case. If he was reading the mood music right, it didn't appear that things had gone to plan.

'Hi boss, it's Angela, sorry to disturb you but I thought you'd want an update regarding our enquiries this morning.'

'Yep, sure. Hope your day as been more fruitful than mine. Come through and I'll stick the kettle on, although it's a stiff bourbon I'm needing. Don't think the coffee's going to cut it after the meeting I've just had.'

Sounds like his day might be even worse than ours thought Angela putting down the phone. She turned to Ryan who was unwrapping a sandwich at his desk.

'Working lunch for you.' said Angela in a serious voice. 'I need you to update the case file and then I want intelligence logs put on for all five of those jokers, they might think they're being smart, but I know a lying toad when I see one. They'll get what's coming to them, I'll make sure of that.'

Ryan looked less than impressed but didn't say anything. He put down his sandwich and went and retrieved the case file that was lying on Angela's desk.

'And I'll see you when I'm finished with the Lieutenant.' said Angela nodding towards Sam. 'And don't look so concerned, I'll make sure that you're fully up to date with what's gone on.'

Sam's heart sank. He didn't have to wait for Angela's update, he was long enough in the tooth to know that the interviews had gone badly. He was desperate to be able to give Ella some good news for a change. But it appeared that for now, that would have to wait.

The door was open by the time Angela reached Charlie's office. She walked in and sat down in front of his desk.

'I've brought cookies, in the absence of any bourbon it's the best I can do I'm afraid.'

'Appreciate the sentiment.' said Charlie getting up to make the coffee. 'Now before I tell you my tale of woe, how did you get on? Are we any closer to being able to charge anyone with the assault?'

Angela shook her head.

'Nope.' said Angela despondently. 'It was really weird. All four of them claimed to have an alibi. They all said they were at the bowling alley that afternoon. We spoke to the Sill brothers first, that Sean one is a right cocky pain in the ass, he told us that Riley Muntz, he's guy who manages the alley, would confirm that they were all bowling that afternoon.'

'And did Muntz confirm that? I take it you checked.'

'Oh, he confirmed it alright. He also volunteered that his CCTV had been broken so we'd have to take his word for it. It was all just a little contrived. I hadn't even asked about his cameras and there he was telling me they weren't working. Of course, it's working now

I checked, he said he managed to fix it himself a couple of days ago.'

'Did you ask to see the tapes?'

'Yep. And there weren't any for the day of the assault or the following day. He could have just removed them ahead of us coming of course. Judging by the smirks on the Sills faces I suspect that they had all discussed this beforehand. I'm going to make some enquiries to try and establish a link between Muntz and the others. I mean a link other than them knowing him from the bowling alley.'

Charlie handed Angela her coffee and sat down.

'And the other two you spoke to, remind me of their names?'

'Linton Webb and Perry Blackley.'

'Yep them. I take it the response was much the same.

'Exactly. The conversations were almost identical. Which was a surprise because Webb is usually as nervous as a kitten when we speak to him. But not this time. I'm telling you the four of them, well five, if you include Muntz had got together and discussed what they should say when the cops came calling. It was as if someone had tipped them off. I'm telling you boss; they weren't surprised to see us.'

Charlie leant back and put his hands behind his head.

'Well that could be lifting the lid on a whole new can of worms. But from what you've said that would make sense. Especially if they were as well rehearsed as you say they were. I take it Ella hasn't been able to help. I presume you've shown her photographs.'

Angela raised her eyebrows and stared at Charlie.

'Ahem. Yes, I've shown Ella photographs and she hasn't picked any of them out.'

Charlie could tell he had hit a nerve.

'Just checking that's all. It wouldn't be the first time a simple thing like that has been overlooked. It wasn't meant as a dig at you.'

'Apologies, I know it wasn't. It's just my frustration showing through, that's all. Anyway, enough about my day. Yours sounds like it might be even worse. Do you want to talk about it?'

Chapter 15

Ella waved and blew a kiss as the bus pulled out of the depot onto the main road. Her shoulders sank and she let out a weary sigh as she watched her mother frantically waving back and blowing endless kisses from the back of the bus.

'Are you okay?' asked Sam putting his arm around her shoulders. Ella smiled and snuggled into his embrace.

'I'm fine. Honestly, I'm just fine. But there's only so much love you can put up with. I know she meant well, but four days was long enough. I was starting to drown in all those hugs and kisses. It was just a bit full on. I'm not used to that level of affection anymore. It was a bit suffocating.'

Sam wasn't sure how he should respond. Was he being too tactile? The last thing he wanted to do was annoy Ella, so he released his arm and stood awkwardly at her side not saying anything.

'You can put your arm back where it was, thank you very much. That wasn't a subliminal message, but after four days of mom's TLC I just need a bit of a break. That's all I meant.'

Sam replaced his arm.

'She's a great lady. Quite full on but she's got boundless energy and she's a lot of fun. But I can't wait to meet your dad. I know you said he was the quiet one, no wonder, he'd have to be, living with your mum. He wouldn't get a word in edgeways.'

Ella started to laugh.

'And you'll know what I mean about the house being clean. If she wasn't talking, she was spraying disinfectant on some working surface and cleaning. Sometimes she was doing both. Then when she did shut up, on went the music. You must know every Ella Fitzgerald and Billie Holliday CD by heart now. It was starting to do my head in. I'd forgotten just how obsessed she was with the pair of them.'

Sam smiled and hugged Ella. She must be feeling better, she's back to her opinionated old self. Ella was more like her mother than she would care to admit.

'Right, what would you like to do now? We've got Max in the car and we don't need to be anywhere for the rest of the day, so it's up to you. Where do you fancy going?'

'I thought we might head out to the country and walk up Spruce Knob and try and find the old mine. It'll be great exercise for Max, and I'd like to see where Grandpa Massie worked. He was quite famous, I think I told you, he was the first black miner to work at Spruce Knob. I'm starting to research it for my dissertation, so it would be good to see where it all actually happened.'

Back at the car Sam filled Max's water dish.

'Sounds good, I'm up for that. You know I've lived here all my life and I've never climbed Spruce Knob. Closest I got was a school trip when I was about 10. They took us to study the wild-flowers and look for newts. But that was in the woods at the bottom of the mountain, I've never been up it so just as I well I've got boots in the car.'

'Shall we pick up a sandwich to take with us. We could stop by Annie Mack's, it's on the way?'

Sam shook his head.

'I've got water and some snacks in my rucksack, but I thought we could stop at Ming's on the way home and have the early bird special. It's a buffet, you can eat as much as you like.'

'Okay fine, that suits me. I've heard people at the college talk about Ming's, they say it's really good, but it'll be a first for me, it'll give me a chance to see what all the fuss is about.'

'Great. I don't think you'll be disappointed. If you like Chinese, you'll love Ming's. And there's nothing like a decent walk to work up an appetite. Right Max, up, that's it boy, in you get. Good boy.'

Half an hour later Sam parked up in the small visitor car lot on the east side of the mountain. There were maybe only half a dozen other cars there, which were surprisingly few considering it was a Saturday. Sam got out and walked across to the pay machine to get a ticket while Ella put on Max's long lead and stuffed some poo bags and doggy treats into Sam's rucksack.

Sam walked back to the car looking pleased with himself.

'Result.' he exclaimed. 'There's a notice on the machine saying it's out of order so the parking is free.'

Ella shook her head and laughed.

'Whoo-hoo, you've saved yourself a dollar, good for you.'

'Every little helps.' said Sam patting his pocket. 'Now, which way are we heading?'

Ella opened out her map.

'It looks like we have two choices. We could take the old mine road. I don't think it's been used since the mine closed, but it's certainly still marked on the map. Alternatively, we could take this path here.'

Ella pointed to a dotted line that meandered its way up the eastern ridge.

'It looks a bit longer, but I reckon it will be a more interesting walk. Better chance of seeing some wildlife. How will Max be with that? He won't chase after a deer if we see one, will he?'

Sam laughed.

'No danger of that. Max is better trained than I am. He's really my dad's dog. We got him when he was 15 weeks old and dad spent months training him. He was supposed to be a police dog, but German Shepherds are prone to problems with their hips. There's nothing really wrong with him, but he failed the initial assessment, so he's been the family pet since then. But he's an excellent dog, biddable and well trained. He'll not chase a deer, squirrel or anything else for that matter. Well, not unless I tell him too.'

'Well in that case, we'll take the path. And I think we can safely take this off.' said Ella removing Max's lead.

By two in the afternoon the sun was high overhead and stiflingly hot. In the absence of any breeze, the air was alive to the sound of stridulating crickets and various bugs and beetles who seemed to have set up home in the huckleberry bushes that lined the mountain path. A few yards in front of them a black capped chickadee energetically flitted from shrub to shrub feasting on the insects disturbed by the crunch of a boot on the hard-baked path. To the rear trailed Max, falling further behind as he stopped to sniff and decipher the scent of previous travellers.

'Clever things birds.' remarked Ella as she watched their feathered friend devour yet another juicy bug. 'He'll stay with us till he's had his fill and then he'll fly off and find a shady spot to rest up while he digests his lunch.'

Sam chuckled.

'I'll tell you something, he might not be very big, but he sure can pack those crickets away. That's at least ten he's had.'

'Feast or famine you see. Most animals and birds will take the opportunity of an easy meal when it presents itself. There're not like us, they can't be sure where their next meal will come from.'

Sam stopped and scoffed loudly.

'Well then they're exactly like me. Wait till you see me attack the buffet in Ming's. I'll be going at it like there's no tomorrow, just like Mr Chickadee over there.'

'Well if that's the case, then it will just be an example of gluttony, something you'll share with a great many of our species unfortunately. And for what's it's worth, greed is never a good look.'

Sam felt immediately deflated. He was just trying to be funny. But not for the first time, his attempt at humour hadn't come over quite as he'd intended. He wasn't sure if Ella was aware that he was just joking. Now he felt a little foolish.

Ella sensed his unease.

'Look, I'm just joshing with you. I know you're not a glutton, look at the size of you for a start, there's hardly a pick on you. It's me that should be worried. Now that I'm not doing my athletics the weight will slip back on if I'm not careful.'

'Oh, I don't think you've got anything to worry about on that score, you look in pretty good shape to me.'

Ella smiled and planted a kiss on Sam's cheek.

'Kind of you to say so. I think that's why I like you, you're such a gentleman.'

Sam sat down on a rock and opened his rucksack. He passed Ella an apple and a bottle of water.

'Well thank you sir, you're just proving my point.'

Sam grinned and took out the map.

'How much further do you reckon it is to the mine?'

Ella glanced over Sam's shoulder.

'Do you see that area marked Yellow Rocks. I think that must be those rocks we can see in the distance.'

Ella pointed up to a series of rocky outcrops that dominated an open area of ground over to their left. I'm almost certain that must by Yellow Rocks. The mine is further round to the right and not quite as high up. If you look here the path forks just above those trees. If we take the right fork, I think it should take us right there. I don't think it can more than 15 minutes or so from here.'

'Well that's good news. I'm starting to feel kinda hot. I should have brought a better hat. This baseball cap isn't protecting my neck and I don't have any sun cream.'

Ella grinned and removed Sam's cap. She turned it round and put it back on his head, so the peak was protecting his neck.'

'Simples. Just a shame not everything in life can be so easily fixed.'

Ella picked up the rucksack and put it on her back.

'I'll take a turn. I can't go on about equal opportunities if I don't practice what I preach. So, let's be having you. It can't be too much further.'

Another half a mile up the path they came across a large wooden sign. Painted on the sign in red capital letters were the words, 'OLD MINE WORKS, DANGER KEEP OUT.' A couple of hundred yards beyond the sign they could see a large metal gate that was locked by means of three enormous chains and padlocks. Coils of razor-sharp barbed wire sat on top of an eight-foot palisade fence that ran along either side of the gate. Fifty yards beyond the gate was the entrance to the mine itself. Sealed and fortified by a solid metal door. The sign above the entrance read, 'DANGER of DEATH, KEEP OUT.'

Sam started to laugh

'That sign above the door is just there in case you were in any doubt that you shouldn't be here. I bet you it would be easier getting into Fort Knox than it would be trying to get past this level of security.'

Ella shrugged her shoulders.

'I don't really know what I was expecting, I didn't think we'd be able to get in, but someone is sending a serious message aren't they? They don't want you coming any further, so this is as close as we'll get.'

Ella took off the rucksack and sat down on a post by the palisade fence. She was about to pass Sam her water bottle when she noticed a cardboard box lying on the ground immediately in front of the metal gate. Ella went over and picked up the cream coloured box that was about the size of a shoe box. There was no lid on the box but lying at the bottom was what appeared to be three dolls. Identical in size and colour, the 9-inch dolls had been roughly fashioned from old corn husks. They were lying face down and each doll had a large masonry nail driven into its back.

Ella picked up a doll and turned it over. The corn husks had been crudely stitched together with what looked like twine and its featureless face and body made it impossible to tell what gender it was supposed to be. Apart from the nail, the only other thing of note was its hands which had been painted bright red.

Ella turned over the other two dolls. They were identical to the one she was holding. This was just weird. Why would anyone leave three corn dolls outside the entrance to the Spruce Knob mine? And more to the point, why were their hands painted red and why did they all have nails sticking out of their backs?

Sam scratched his head as he stared at the box.

'What do you make of this then?' asked Ella passing Sam the box. 'You're the detective. Any idea why three corn dolls with nails in their backs would be left in a box by the mine.'

'Haven't a clue.' replied Sam examining the box. 'But they've not been left by accident. Someone's gone to a lot of trouble making them and then bringing them all the way up here. It's got to mean something. No idea what, but the nails in their backs suggest something sinister don't you think? Somebody's not happy with something, that's my take on it.'

'What should we do. Shall we just leave them here?'

'Nope.' replied Sam taking a plastic bag out of his rucksack. 'I'll take them into the office to show Angela and Lieutenant Finch. If they're not important then we can throw them away, but if they are, well we've done the right thing and kept them. I'll tell you something, I don't think they've been here long. I know it hasn't rained for days but there's no water marks on the cardboard and the red paint hasn't run. Also, the box

195

looks remarkably clean, the dolls aren't even covered in dust. It's a strange one though. By leaving them here, someone is trying to make a statement or send a message. The question is, what are they trying to say?'

*

On the other side of the mountain Chaska was busy making his final preparations. Tonight, he would honour his ancestors. Tonight, he would perform his ghost dance.

Using a penknife, he had spent the last hour carving the words 'Malakai, Chief of the Shawnee People,' into the soft bark of a red cedar tree growing just below the rocks. Underneath, he had carved 28th May 1869, the date of the Spruce Knob massacre. Now, away to his right, the glowing orb of a burning September sun was fast disappearing over the western ridge of the Allegheny Mountains, he felt a strange sense of excitement and anticipation. In another two hours everything would be ready.

He had previously read that it would be several hours before the effects of the magic broth would fully kick in. More than an hour had passed since he'd boiled up the mushrooms and drank a mug of the bitter tasting liquid. But within the last few minutes, he was starting to feel the first physical effects of the brew. He felt light-headed and a little unsteady on his feet, this feeling, would apparently pass, and then feelings of euphoria and ecstasy would gradually start to take effect. He leant back against a slab of rock to steady himself. The rock, hot from the sun's rays was soothing and comforting. He felt its power being absorbed into his body, through his skin and bones, like a battery on charge, he could feel his energy levels starting to climb.

He had spent most of the morning gathering feathers and wildflowers which he had meticulously attached to a leather thong which now hung loosely round his neck. Using the charcoal from a burnt stick, he had adorned his face and arms with the tribal marks of his forbears. Professor Foulis's paper had detailed illustrations of the markings which his unskilled hand had tried to faithfully replicate. He had done all he could to prepare. Now all he could do was wait, for the sun to set and the full moon to appear.

As he lay against the rock, he felt his chest tightening. His breathing was becoming more rapid and shallow. Negative thoughts attacked him from all directions worming their way into the dark recesses of his mind. Could he really be a member of the Shawnee tribe? Was he the great grandson of Chief Makatai? Could he prove that he carried his DNA? Even if he did, what did he know? He knew nothing about those people, or their language or culture. He was a fraud, an ex con, not fit to call himself one of them. He shut his eyes. Bright rainbow coloured lights flashed in the darkness and his skin felt hot and tingly. Beads of perspiration appeared on his forehead, then on his naked torso and arms. Was it just the symptoms of the broth, or was it his feelings of inadequacy? He couldn't tell, but either way he felt transfixed and unable to move from the rock, it felt like he was being held in some form of suspended animation, he was seized by feelings of anxiety and fear.

Twenty minutes of torment passed, but with it came a reassuring calmness. His breathing regulated and slowed to its normal pace and he was no longer sweating. Like a sugar rush, he felt suddenly energised, joyous and connected to this special place. He fingered the scarring on the side of his neck. He didn't know his people, or their ways or language, but he could connect to them through this place. These were the rocks they had rested on. This earth was the ground they trod. It was here that they bled and died. The red cedars, towering and ancient were his witnesses. They had lived through it. The slaughter of the innocents. Chaska gazed all around. This place is what connected him to the spirits of his ancestors. This was their land. Yellow Rocks, the home of the Shawnee, the home of his people. He felt euphoric, this was his moment.

Chapter 16

A line of mourners stood respectfully waiting to shake hands and pass on their condolences. It had been a lovely service and Julie was pleased at how many friends and former colleagues had packed into the small church. As her mother's death had been so unexpected, no instructions had been left about what type of service her mom would have wanted. So along with her brother Eric, and with guidance from Mr Collins the Minister, Julie had chosen the hymns and readings for the funeral. At Eric's request, the organist played 'The Ballad of Davy Crockett,' as his mom's coffin was brought into the church. It was a moment of humour and the congregation smiled warmly, but it had been a family favourite and one Eric remembered singing with his mom when they made pancakes together when he was a small child.

All that had been fine, beautiful even. It was the next part that Julie wasn't looking forward to. She took out her handkerchief and wiped a tear from her eye. She was still emotional from the minister's lovely tribute and thoughtful prayers. But this was her duty. She wanted to make her mom proud, so she stood with her younger brother, determined to thank everyone who had been kind enough to attend.

It had helped that Mr Collins had known Carole personally. He had been her preacher for more than fifteen years and his eulogy was gracious and heartfelt. For those listening from the pews he had captured the essence of a kind and compassionate lady, who despite living for forty years as a widow, had remained strong and resolute. Carole Hicks had faced many challenges in her life, but she had been supported through these difficult times by her children and her many friends. Hers had been a life well lived.

As the line of mourners thinned to the last few, Julie looked around anxiously in case she had missed him. The one person she had expected to see but who wasn't there was Chaska. He had been adamant that he was going to attend, he had said so quite clearly when she last spoke to him. But he was nowhere to be seen. Her brother would be devastated. He desperately wanted to see the man he had admired and looked up to all those years ago. Julie was worried that something must have happened. Chaska wouldn't just not turn up, he was a man of his word, and he'd said he would be there.

Julie smiled warmly when she saw the last two mourners in the queue. It was Mrs Jarret and her son Henry.

'Lovely to see you Mrs Jarret. Thank you so much for coming. You more than anyone know what my mom went through. You lived that too. But she's at rest now, no more worries. I hope she's with my dad.' said Julie looking up to the heavens. 'It wouldn't surprise me if Joe is with them. Your husband and my dad were great buddies according to mom.'

Mrs Jarret smiled and kissed Julie on the cheek.

'That they were. It's incredible to think we lost them more than forty years ago. It's a long time to be a widow. But enough of that. Let's remember your mom for the great lady she was.'

Mrs Jarret turned to her son.

'Do you remember Henry? I think the pair of you were in the same year at school.'

'Yes, of course I remember Henry, but I think you were in the year above me.' replied Julie holding out her hand.

Henry shook hands with Julie then scribbled quickly on the chalk board he was carrying.

'So sorry for your loss. It's nice to see you again. It's been a while.'

'That's kind of you Henry. I do hope you and your mom can come back to the house. It'll just be family and a few friends over coffee and some sandwiches. But it'll give us a chance to catch up properly and talk about mom.'

Henry smiled and put his thumb up. It was now almost a year since he had lost his power of speech, the result of being smashed in the side of his head by a rifle butt. Ralph Portman, the man convicted of the assault, had been sentenced to eleven years in the state penitentiary. There was no question about it, Henry had been through a traumatic twelve months. The worst part was his lifelong friend, Eustace Brownlie, had died in tragic circumstances at the Deans estate, the same night he had been assaulted.

In the last year, Henry had undergone two operations to repair the damage to his cheek and temporal plates. Remarkably, his brain was still functioning normally, it was only his speech that hadn't recovered. That wasn't for the want of trying. He had undergone hours of intensive therapy, but it had been to no avail. He could make sounds and sometimes say the odd word, but for reasons that were baffling his doctors, he couldn't but sentences together.

By way of compensation, he had become a dab hand with his chalk board. He was never without it. Whether it was in a store or having a drink with friends, Henry, known universally in the town as Screech, had absolutely no difficulty keeping up with conversations. He was quite literally, the fastest draw in Greenbrier County.

Eric had been waiting patiently while his sister talked to Mrs Jarret. But now he could wait no longer. He was three years younger than Screech, but growing up, he'd been part of a group of boys that had hung out together and played softball in the park. In summer they'd camped in the mountains, built rafts and swam in the Greenbrier river. Chaska had been part of that group, Eustace Brownlie too. It may have been more than forty years ago, but seeing Screech standing there brought back a flood of happy memories. Eric put out his arms and embraced his friend with an enormous bear hug.

'Good to see you Screech. Mom told me what happened to you. Helluva thing. Devastated when I heard 'bout Eustace. Them Portmans were real bad asses. Wilder too. How that son of a bitch made Police Chief I'll never know. I mind the beatings he handed out to you and Eustace. I had a few beers the night I heard he'd shot himself. Good riddance I say.'

Eric's voice grew ever louder as a steady flow of expletives filled the air.

Out the corner of his good eye, Screech caught sight of Julie. He could tell from her expression that she was feeling anxious. Her brother had always been a volatile character, now was not the time to get him angry or excited, not at his mother's funeral. Screech reached for his board.

'*Greetings bro. We'll talk more at the house. Did I hear that Chas was released from prison?*'

Eric nodded and a great beaming smile engulfed his face. In the blink of an eye, Screech had skilfully changed the subject and calmed Eric down. Screech was sharp and wily. He had the instincts of a fox. In his own way, much like Carole Hicks and his mother, he'd not had it easy. His father had died when he was five and he'd lost the sight in one eye when he was eight. Life had been tough for Screech Jarret. But despite these challenges, he'd proved himself to have a good heart, and he made a point of looking out for those who were in need or vulnerable. He was no angel, he'd been in jail plenty of times, but he never stole from the poor or took advantage of the needy. He was a con with a conscious.

'Do you need a lift back to the house. My daughter brought her car and there's space in mine too.' asked Julie trying to keep the conversation on track.

'We're okay thanks, Henry brought his truck.'

Eric turned to his Mrs Jarret.

'Why don't you go with Julie, Mrs Jarret. I could catch a ride back with Screech. We haven't hung out since we were kids, I'd like that, be like old times.'

Screech smiled and high fived Eric.

'Great. That's sorted then.' said Julie. 'We'll see you back at the house. And if you're there first Eric, stick the kettle on and put the pigs in blankets in the oven.'

The journey back to the house took less than ten minutes. Julie was helping Mrs Jarret up the front steps when Screech and Eric pulled up outside the house. The slam of the passenger door suggested all was not well.

'Did you have the fucking radio on, did you catch the local news?' shouted Eric who was waving his arms about manically.

Julie turned around and shook her head.

'No, we were chatting, we didn't have the radio on. Why what's happened?'

'Radio Greenbrier are reporting that the trial has folded, some fucking judge has said there is insufficient evidence to proceed. They were broadcasting live outside the court. Them brothers have done it again, they've walked away scot free. I hate them Lawrences, I fucking hate them.'

Eric stormed passed his sister as she opened the front door nearly knocking Mrs Jarret over in his haste to get into the house.

'Oh, that is terrible and today of all days. Why did it have to be today?' said Julie.

'At least Carole was spared the misery of having to hear that. That's twice I've been kicked in the guts by that family.' said Mrs Jarret clearly shocked by the news.'

'My goodness, I'm so sorry. That was insensitive of me. You've suffered the pain every bit as much as we have. It's just appalling but if I'm honest I'm not surprised. I didn't want to tell mom, but I had a feeling this would happen. It just shows you doesn't it, there's one law for the rich, and another one for the rest of us.'

Screech scribbled on his board and lifted it up for Julie to read.

'That is really shit. And talking of shit, I hope the Judge's next one's a porcupine!'

Julie put her hands to her mouth to stop herself laughing.

'Too true Henry, I couldn't have put it better myself.'

*

Over at Lewisburg Police station, Charlie Finch was photocopying statements in the general office. As usual, Sam was head down and hard at work at his desk. It was quarter to six and Charlie had it on good authority from Liz, the cleaner, that Sam had been in before her that morning. And as she started at 0545hrs, it meant he was now into his thirteenth hour at work.

'Time you weren't here, Sam. Whatever it is you're doing it can wait. So, get your jacket on and get out of here. And that's an order. And remember what I said to you earlier, if we get a chance to sit down with Angela tomorrow, we'll discuss that box of dolls you brought in. Typical of you to come across something weird like that. You've not been with us long, but I've come to expect the unexpected when you're around.' said Charlie with a laugh.

'Two minutes boss and I'll be finished. Just doing you a briefing note about those dolls. I'm on the last paragraph so just about done. Anyway, I've to pick up Ella from the library and it closes at six, so I'd better not be late. I promised I'd take her for coffee and cake, so I'll need to get a shift on. Ella doesn't do late, she's always on time. What about you, are you heading home?'

Charlie made a strange grunting sound and shook his head.

'If only. I'll be here for at least another couple of hours. The Chief wants his senior management team to meet the new head of the police authority for a 'get to know you session' in his office. Starts at seven.'

205

'Hope he's feeding you? Long time to wait to get your dinner if he's not.'

'It's a finger buffet apparently. Well that's according to Sergeant Lang who met Steve Joice in the yard. Steve was apoplectic apparently. Seemingly the Chief told him to go to Annie Mack's and pick up the buffet, and get this, after that he's to stay on so he can serve the coffee and soft drinks.'

Sam burst out laughing as he put on his jacket.

'I shouldn't laugh but poor Steve. He will be hating that. It was bad enough when he had to work the PowerPoint for those presentations, but this will piss him right off.'

'Lesson in there for you, detective. Don't let a new Chief learn your name too quickly or you'll end up like Steve and become his bag man for god knows what. I've seen it happen before. Better just keep your head down till the new boss finds his feet. That way you'll be left alone and won't end up getting a using like old Steve. I don't think he's going to be able to live it down.'

'Good advice, sir, I'll bear that in mind. By the way, my dad was just saying last night how much he's looking forward to your party. But you'd better keep your wits about you. You know what he's like. I expect he'll have something up his sleeve, he always enjoyed a practical joke.'

Charlie Laughed.

'You don't have to remind me. I remember the time he emptied the contents of the paper punch into the vents in Mike's car. It was like a blizzard when he switched his engine on. So, I'll be keeping a close eye on your old man.'

'Glad to hear it. How are things going, have you much to do before Saturday?'

'Not really thank God. My good lady is taking care of most things like the catering and decorations. I've been told I've just to turn up. And while we're talking about the party, it was good of you and Chris to cover the late shift. I know Angela and the others are grateful to you.'

'Not a problem, just happy to help.' said Sam taking his car keys out of his pocket. 'And I'll see you tomorrow, I hope your meeting isn't too deadly, and pass on my regards to Sergeant Joice. I can't wait to see him. He's going to get ribbed about this one for weeks.'

*

Over at Lewisburg library, Ella was chatting to Mary Winters at the reception desk. She had spent the afternoon looking through the Spruce Knob archive. She'd gone to the library more in hope than expectation. She had thought there was a reasonable chance that with Spruce Knob being a local mine, the library would have some information about it, but when Mary told her that they'd recently acquired the archive, well, Ella thought that Christmas had come early. The documents would be a great help as she started work on her dissertation, and just to cap things off, the first set of minutes she had picked up included the name of her grandfather as being present at the meeting. That had made her day.

'Thank you so much for your help.' said Ella handing Mary the box of documents. 'This is going to be really useful. I can see myself spending a lot of time in here. And the archive is so well ordered, everything's in chronological order, it's quite straightforward to follow.'

Mary gave a wistful sigh.

'Well it had nothing to do with me or anyone that works here. A man came in last week asking about the archive. We'd only had it a few days and nobody had got around to cataloguing it. He spent endless hours sorting through it and then indexing and referencing it. He's the one you should thank. He did all the hard work.'

'Well he's done a terrific job, he clearly knew what he was doing.'

'I'm sorry we don't have anything on the Middleton mine. But you might want to try the library in White Sulphur Springs. It's more local, they may well have information about it.'

'I'll do that.' said Ella looking at the clock. 'Now I'd better go, I'm keeping you back and I know you close at six. And anyway, with any luck someone will be waiting outside for me and they promised to take me for coffee and cake, so I don't want to be late for that.'

Mary smiled and sighed again. She wished a certain someone with long dark hair and a fedora hat was waiting outside for her. It had been four days since she'd lent Chaska the book, and she hadn't seen hide nor hair of him since.

Sam was just pulling into the library parking lot when Ella came out the front door.

'Good timing.' said Sam leaning across and opening the door for Ella. Ella got in and hugged Sam.

'How did you get on. Did they have any info about the mine?'

'Yep, loads.' said Ella with a beaming smile. 'Couldn't believe my luck, they had the complete archive from the mine. Someone handed it in a couple of weeks ago.

Documents explaining how the mine came to be opened, procurement invoices, there were even copies of all the company board minutes. The first one I looked at even had my grandfather's name on it. So, yeah, I've had a great day. What about you?'

'All fine thanks. Not as exciting as yours by the sounds of things, just mundane stuff I had to catch up on, but it's all good. Now where do you want to go for coffee?'

'Anywhere's good. So long as they've got cake. I've had a craving for something sweet all day.'

Twenty minutes later the waitress in Benny's diner appeared carrying a tray of coffee and sweet treats.

'Here come the calories.' announced Sam licking his lips. 'Yikes, Ella, look at the size of that meringue. You won't know whether to eat it or climb it. It's enormous.'

'Who's having the blueberry cheesecake?' asked the waitress putting down the tray.

'That'll be me.' replied Sam putting his napkin on his lap. 'looks like I've made a decent choice, not quite as big as your meringue, but close enough. Right, get stuck in and enjoy. You deserve something nice after the last couple of weeks you've had.'

Ella didn't reply. She was too busy demolishing the creamy delight that covered her plate. Five minutes later she was done. She pushed her plate to the side and sipped her coffee as Sam continued his struggle with the cheesecake. He was stuffed, but he'd paid good money for the cakes, so he wasn't going down without a fight.

Ella looked out of the window. Something had caught her attention. At the far side of the parking lot was a youth wearing a grey baseball cap. He was standing talking to guy in a smart suit who appeared to be with a younger girl who was standing a few feet away. She was wearing a denim jacket over what appeared to be some type of uniform. Her dark blue pleated trousers looked incongruous with her jacket. Ella stared at the youth with the cap. There was something familiar about him.

Before she had a chance to speak, Sam pointed out the window and blurted out.

'I work with that guy, that's Ryan Mulroy. He's just started working with us, he's the new trainee detective.'

Ella looked confused.

'Who is, the guy in the cap?'

'No. the guy in the snazzy suit. And the girl who's with him is also a cop. I should have known; she must be dating him. Well more fool her, he's got some reputation. He thinks he's God's gift to women.'

'Never mind about them, see the guy in the baseball cap? I'm sure it's him.'

'Sure it's who?'

'The guy with the shotgun. Remember I told you I'd seen two guys who'd been squirrel hunting, just before I was grabbed and had that sack put over my head. Well, I reckon that guy in the cap was the one with the gun.'

Before Ella could say anything else, Sam grabbed his jacket and headed out the diner. He'd better be quick, as the girl and the guy in the suit were now walking towards a car parked on the far side of the lot. There was no sign of the guy in the baseball cap.

Ella watched as Sam sprinted across the lot. He got to the car just as it started to reverse out of its parking space. After the briefest of conversations Sam smacked the roof of the car and ran across to the other side of the lot. Ella lost sight of him as he disappeared round the end of the diner.

A few minutes later Sam returned and approached the vehicle which was still parked in its space. There was still no sign of the guy in the baseball cap. The driver got out and started talking to Sam. Ella hadn't a clue what was going on but judging by the pointing and waving of arms she could tell Sam was frustrated. Five minutes later he returned to the diner and sat back down.

'You didn't find the guy in the cap then?'

'Nope.' said Sam despondently. 'Don't know where the hell he went, he just seemed to disappear into thin air. By the time I got round to the other side of the building there was no sign of him.'

'That's not your fault, that's just unfortunate. What did your colleague have to say about it, I take it he must know the guy if he was speaking to him?'

'You might have thought, eh!' scoffed Sam, 'but apparently not. Ryan says he's seen him around, says he thinks he lives local, somewhere in the Lewisburg area, but he only knows him to nod to. Says he doesn't know his name.'

Ella made a face.

'So, what were they talking about? Seemed to be chatting for quite some time for a couple of guys who don't know each other.'

'I know. Ryan said the guy was asking where he got his suit. Said he had a wedding to go to and needed to get a suit and wanted to know where he'd got his from.'

'Huh. He didn't look like the type of guy who would ever wear a suit to me. But there you go. What about the girl, what's she saying about it?'

'She isn't saying anything. Hardly said two words. But she doesn't know who he is. It looks like we've hit the crossbar with this one. But if the guy is local, he'll come again. That's what we always say in the office. It's only a matter of time, Ella. But we'll get him, and the others, I'll promise you that.'

Chapter 17

Thursday, September 23rd

Looking out the window of his office on the fifth floor of Chicago Police Headquarters, Captain Mike Rawlingson was watching the throng of people spilling out of offices and shops all along Michigan Avenue bracing themselves ahead of their rush hour commute.

He was on the phone to his wife, Susan, to remind her that he wouldn't be home till late. He was going to work on for another hour before heading to Wrigley Field where he was meeting their son, Keegan to watch their beloved Chicago Cubs. The Cubs were playing the Pittsburgh Pirates and going into tonight's game, the two teams were level pegging at the top of Baseball's National League, Central Conference. The Cubs hadn't been this successful in years, there was hope in the air.

'No that's fine, I was remembering about the game. Keegan told me at breakfast. Make sure you get him something to eat as he's heading straight from band practice at the school.'

'Not a problem. I've not eaten either, I'll grab us a couple of chilli dogs and fries. You don't have to worry about us, we'll not starve.'

Susan laughed ironically.

'Oh, I know you won't. A lifetime of working in the police has given you an addiction to junk food and somehow you've managed to pass that affliction on to our son!'

'Yes darling, I knew you would approve. Anyway, changing the subject. How did you get on with Charlie's present, did you have any joy?'

'Got it in Pritchard's eventually. Most places didn't have it because it's a special edition. Special price too I can tell you. But it's kinda neat. The bottle's the shape of a pot still. We'll need to pack it carefully in bubble wrap, the neck of the bottle is long and thin. We don't want it breaking during the journey.'

'Good effort though. Charlie will be made up. He was always banging on how Willett's made the best bourbon. Fancies himself as a bit of a connoisseur does our Charlie. Bet he couldn't tell the difference between a Willett's and a moonshine in a blind tasting. But I'm glad that's sorted. So, are we still good to go about 4 o'clock tomorrow?'

'Yep. I told your mum we would drop Keegan off about then. He told me this morning he was looking forward to a weekend with his grandparents. I can see why he would, they'll spoil him rotten.'

It was 1815 hrs by the time Mike left the office. It was only a short walk to Grand underground station where he would catch the red line to Wrigley Field. The train was already busy with fans bedecked in the blue, red and white colours of the Cubs, everyone seemed to be heading to the game. Fortunately, the station was far enough from the ground for Mike to be able to get a seat. But by the time the 'L' train, Chicago's famous elevated line, reached Monroe the train was packed,

214

and the aroma of perspiring bodies was in danger of overwhelming the carriage.

The unpleasant smell was mercifully brief, for as soon as the train pulled into Addison most of the passengers spilled onto the platform. The ballpark was less than a five-minute walk away, but as the crush of supporters made their way along the concourse the nervous tension between the fans was palpable. A win tonight and the Cubs would be in pole position for a place in the play offs.

Mike had arranged to meet Keegan underneath the large clock that stood facing the main entrance. As he followed the crowd towards the ground, his pager went off. He pulled away from the swarm of supporters and stood in the doorway of a store. The message on his pager was from Lieutenant Bill Carle, one of his senior detectives. It was asking him to contact the office ASAP.

Mike spied a phone box just across the street. A minute later he was speaking to Lieutenant Carle.

'Sorry to bother you, boss. I know you're going to the game, but I thought you'd want to know. There's been a murder over at Clarendon Hills.'

'It's not a problem Bill, the game can wait. Now what's the story?'

'Still trying to make sense of it being honest. Deceased was found lying face down in his garden by the edge of a carp pond a couple of hours ago. He'd been shot in the back with a crossbow bolt. The locus is Clarendon Gardens, it's part of a swanky gated community, over on the west side, the house is called Allegheny.'

'Hmm, that name's a blast from the past. And it doesn't sound like your everyday type of murder, not if he's been shot with a crossbow. Do we know who the deceased is?'

'That's why I wanted to contact you. The deceased is an 89-year-old male, goes by the name of Eldridge Lawrence. According to the cops at the locus, he used to live in your old patch. He's the oldest brother of the Lawrence dynasty apparently. They owned a coal mine and when they sold that they opened an asbestos factory near Lewisburg. Very wealthy by all accounts.'

'Eldridge Lawrence eh. I never dealt with the family personally, but everyone in Greenbrier County knows about the Lawrences. Do we know anything else? Motive, witnesses?

'Too early yet, but I'm about to head out to the locus, I'll keep you informed of developments. I just wanted to give you the heads up, that's all.'

'Appreciate that Bill. But I think I'd like to head over, it sounds intriguing. I'll need to speak to Keegan first, but he'll understand. He's got used to it over the years, part of being the son of a detective. Anyway, he'll still get to see the game. My only difficulty is I'm stuck here with no transport. Any chance of a lift?'

'Well, if you're sure you want to go, I'll swing past and pick you up. Should be with you in fifteen minutes.'

'Make it twenty and meet me at the corner of North Clark St and Belmont. It'll be a bit quieter there and it will give me time to speak to Keegan.'

'Gotcha boss, I'll see you there in twenty.'

*

A uniformed officer was standing at the barrier at the entrance to Clarendon Gardens. After recording their names in the log, he directed them up the hill to the fork in the road. Allegheny, a sprawling architecturally designed gothic mansion surrounded by a large wrought iron fence stood just back from the road on the right-hand side.

Mike and Lieutenant Carle parked up across the street and made their way to a side gate that was open and led directly to the back garden. A detective clutching a clipboard looked up and gesticulated to the officers to come in.

'We're not in danger of compromising any evidence coming this way; are we?' asked Lieutenant Carle.

'No, you're fine we are using that gate as our single point of entry.' replied Sergeant Patrick. 'It was padlocked shut when we got here. We believe whoever murdered Mr Lawrence left by the gate on the other side of the garden.'

On the far side of the garden the detectives could see a uniformed officer standing on the walkway outside an open metal gate. Yellow barrier tape and been strung across the door to prevent any unauthorised access.

Over to their right, approximately 50 feet away, lying amongst some water irises, by the edge of the pond, was the deceased. He was lying face down with his head to one side. A 9-inch crossbow bolt was sticking out between his shoulder blades. The deceased's cream coloured polo shirt was saturated with a large red blood stain that almost covered the top half of his shirt. Two scenes-of-crime officers, clothed head to foot in white protective suits were examining the area around the body. Another SOCO was busy taking photographs.

'So, what can you tell us Sergeant?' asked Lieutenant Carle as the three officers surveyed the scene.

'I can tell you that someone has painted his hands red!'

'Yep, I can see that from here. Strange thing for anyone to do.' replied Lieutenant Carle wiping his brow.

'You said someone. It's not something he might have done himself then. I mean could he have been painting something and got paint on his hands?' asked Mike straining to get a better look.

Sergeant Patrick shook her head.

'Very much doubt it. We've found drops of red paint on the grass heading towards the gate. My best guess right now is it's dripped from a brush as the murderer made their escape.'

Lieutenant Carle nodded.

'Well, I suppose that would make sense. By the way who found him, and do we have any idea how long he's been dead?'

'Mrs MacLeod found him. She's Mr Lawrence's housekeeper. Officers are with her up at the house. She's a bit shaken up understandably, but she was able to tell us that it was 1615 hrs when she found him. Mr Lawrence liked to sit in the garden in the afternoon if it were a nice day and she always brought him out some coffee about that time.' replied Sergeant Patrick.

'And do we know who the last person to see him alive was? asked Mike.

'Again, we think that was Mrs MacLeod. She says she was taking washing in around 1530 hrs and she could see him standing near the pond feeding the fish. She didn't see anybody else in the garden at that time.'

'That's useful to know. It narrows the time when he must have been killed to a timeframe of what, 45 mins.'

'Yeah, something like that.'

As the other two were still speaking, Mike crouched down and stared at the corpse. Something had caught his attention. Mike turned to his colleagues and pointed at the body.

'It looks to me like there's something in his mouth, can you see it? There, that yellow thing that's sticking out the edge of his mouth, it looks to me like it might be a feather.'

The others came a few feet nearer and stared at the stricken corpse.

'Good spot boss.' said Sergeant Patrick. 'That's what it looks like to me. Anne, if you're still gloved up can you check his mouth for us. We think there might be a feather in there.'

Anne nodded and put her thumb up.

'Can we make sure we get it photographed before I remove it.' asked Anne taking a pair of tweezers and a small plastic bag from her scenes of crime case. 'We haven't really started on the body yet. We only just finished checking the area from where we think he had been sitting to the edge of the pond where he's lying.'

Anne pointed to a garden table and chair that was sitting under a large spruce tree about thirty feet further up the garden towards the house. A used coffee cup and saucer sat on the table.

'Nothing wrong with your eyesight, Captain.' said Anne handing Mike a small plastic bag containing a somewhat bedraggled yellow feather.

Mike held the bag aloft so the others could see.

'Hmm, why would the body have a feather in its mouth. Could it have got in there by accident? Not sure that it could. And what type of feather is it? Could it have come from a bird in this garden?'

Lieutenant Carle and Sergeant Patrick shrugged their shoulders.

'Hope you don't mind me butting in,' said Anne, 'but I know a little bit about birds. I wouldn't call myself a twitcher, but it's a bit of a hobby of mine.'

'Go right ahead.' said Mike, 'we're all ears.'

'Okay then. I'd say it's highly unlikely it's come from a garden bird. Not many wild birds with yellow feathers in these parts. We'll need to test it to be 100% sure, but looking at the size and colour, I'd say that feather has come from a canary.'

Chapter 18

The Friday morning meeting that Charlie held every week with his team to discuss ongoing enquiries, crime figures and detection rates didn't last long. The first few weeks of September had been relatively quiet which, considering tomorrow was the big birthday party, was no bad thing. It meant, that apart from Sam and Chris, who had agreed to cover the late shift, most everyone else in the department could attend the party.

As the other detectives departed the meeting room, Charlie gestured to Angela and Sam who were sitting towards the back.

'Can the both of you hang on for a few minutes? I want a quick chat about where we are with Ella's enquiry. Since you've got a personal involvement Sam, I thought it best we discuss it off table and not in front of the others. We'll also have a quick chat about those dolls you found. I've read your briefing note, but it's an odd one right enough, I'd like to get both your thoughts on it. So, my office in a couple of minutes.'

'Coffee?' asked Angela picking up her folder.

'Sure.' replied Charlie holding the door open.

'Black for the boss then and milk and one for me. Oh, and whatever you're having.' said Angela with a wink.

Sam smiled weakly.

'And don't worry yourself, you're making it because I'm away to find us some goodies, it's Sarah's birthday and there's a cake in the main office.'

Over coffee and a slice of angel cake, Angela explained what enquiries she and Ryan had undertaken to progress the investigation into Ella's assault and the vandalism to Sam's parents' garage.

'Right, I'll start with the graffiti on your old man's garage. We've drawn a complete blank. Ryan did the door to door with a uniformed officer and nothing. No one seems to have seen anything suspicious. Zoe hasn't heard from the lab yet as they've got a bit of a backlog, so I've nothing on the paint. I'm afraid graffiti on a garage isn't a priority. But she'll let us know as soon as she hears from the lab.'

Sam nodded but didn't say anything. He knew from experience how difficult it was to get a result in a case like that. It would have taken whoever did it less than a minute to commit the crime. It had likely happened during the dead of night. It was hardly surprising that they hadn't traced any witnesses.

Sam was more interested in the update about Ella's case. He already knew that the interviews with the Sill brothers and other potential suspects had not turned anything up. But he was pleased to hear that Sergeant Brown was now pursuing another line of enquiry. As she explained, she was now trying to discredit the suspects alibis.

Through cash receipts she had obtained from the bowling alley, she was now attempting to trace other patrons who had been at the alley on the same afternoon the suspects were supposed to have been there. Not surprisingly, none of the cash receipts she had seized referred to the suspects. Theirs had been the first details she had checked. When she questioned Muntz about it, he'd said they were playing on a freebie, as he owed them for helping him dump old equipment at the refuse facility some days earlier. It appeared Riley Muntz had an answer for everything.

It was a painstaking task ploughing through all the other credit card details for the afternoon in question. She didn't have any names, just a series of account numbers that would now have to be checked with the various banks. That would take a while, but Sam was encouraged to hear that Sergeant Brown was still confident of getting a detection.

'That all sounds pretty comprehensive Angela. I can't think of anything that you've not already considered. Muntz sounds like a slippery customer right enough, but you don't need me to tell you that, he seems to have an answer for everything, it's all just a little too convenient. But good work. Fingers crossed that we catch a break with those bank details.'

'If you need any help with those accounts Sarge, crunching numbers is right up my street.'

'Oh, we know that Sam, but we're managing fine, but I'll bear it in mind if we're stuck.'

'Okay, before we get side-tracked any further, either of you got any thoughts about those dolls. I caught the local news the other day and Aiden Lawrence was being interviewed about the collapse of the case against the old asbestos company. It was long before my time, but I'd forgotten that his family owned the Spruce Knob mine as well as the asbestos factory. I'm aware there's some bad feeling in the town towards the Lawrences, so

I wondered if there might be a connection.' said Charlie twiddling the end of his pen.

'You're well ahead of me then. Being honest I haven't given it much thought. Too busy with these other enquiries. But what you say sounds plausible. Someone who bears a grudge against the Lawrence's could well have left them there. But that's not a crime. Maybe they were trying to make a point.' remarked Angela.

'A rather threatening one then! Those nails were pretty menacing. And the red paint, I was thinking that could suggest that whoever the dolls were meant to represent had blood on their hands. It's just a theory, but it's feasible don't you think?' added Sam.

'Hmm.' said Charlie. 'I hadn't considered that, but yeah, I suppose that's possible. Oh, and one last thing about those dolls. When I was talking to Dave Robertson, he told me that corn dolls were often made by Indian tribes. They made them for their kids to play with apparently. Does that ring any bells?'

Angela and Sam shook their heads.

'Okay fine. Perhaps we're getting ahead of ourselves again so, for now Sam, I want you to lodge the dolls with the Production Keeper, under crime not established. Better to be safe than sorry. At least we'll know where they are should we need them.'

*

It was ten minutes to four when Mike and Susan waved goodbye to their son and Mike's parents and got on their way. Lewisburg was nearly 600 miles away and they intended to break the journey with an overnight stop in Florence, a small town in Ohio, not far from the Indiana border. Mike had stayed there before when he had been on police business, and the motel he had booked was two minutes from the highway and just around the corner from a special restaurant which he hoped would bring back happy memories for Susan. But before he could think about that they needed to get onto the I-64 S, the main highway south. Once they got on that they would make steady progress.

Mike and Susan had been married for 23 years. They'd met on the banks of the Shenandoah river near Susan's aunt's lodge at Harpers Ferry when she came to Mike's rescue after he capsized and injured his arm on rocks while white water rafting during a friends buck's weekend. It had been the start of what turned out to be a long and happy marriage and now Mike wanted to surprise his wife. After dating for over a year, Mike had proposed to Susan during a meal in a Red Lobster restaurant. The franchised restaurant wasn't particularly fancy or for that matter expensive, but as they both loved seafood and money was often tight, it became their go to place on birthdays or other special occasions. They often joked about it whenever they passed one of the many restaurants that can be found all over the country.

It had been a while since they'd been in one. Twenty-three years on, money was not the same issue it once was, now they could afford to dine in more upmarket places. They certainly could in Chicago. Those places might be posher and more expensive, but the food wasn't necessarily better. In Mike's book the Red Lobster's seafood platter was hard to beat.

So long as they could get there by eight everything would go to plan. They would check into their motel and then Mike would suggest they head out for something to eat. The restaurant was a two-minute walk away and Mike had arranged for a bouquet of flowers and a bottle of champagne to be on the table.

It had been a rough few years for Susan. The death of Maisie Foster, one of her former music pupils had hit her hard. Then, another of her pupils, Josh Heggerty was wrongly imprisoned for Maisie's murder. It was a difficult time for everyone as Mike had been the lead detective in the murder investigation. Things were starting to look up when Josh was released from prison when fresh evidence came to light, but then out of nowhere, wham. Susan was hit with a cancer diagnosis. She underwent an operation to remove a tumour and endured months of radiation treatment. Now, finally, she had been given the all clear, she was cancer free.

This, then, was the perfect time for a party. She had been looking forward to the weekend for weeks. Mike had arranged to take Monday and Tuesday of next week off, so they could enjoy the party and spend a couple of days relaxing with their friends.

Susan had always been very fond of Charlie and his wife Alison. Charlie had worked with her husband for years and the two were as thick as thieves. Mike looked upon Charlie as a little brother. They had their moments, but most of the time they got on like a house on fire. Mike had been made up when Charlie was appointed to lieutenant after they had decided it was time to move back to Chicago, Mike's hometown. They hadn't been back to Greenbrier County since they'd left more than 15 months ago. And as many of their old friends would be at the party, it would be the perfect opportunity to let their hair down and catch up on all the news.

'Where did you think we would eat?' asked Susan as they walked across the car lot of the motel.

'I've got somewhere in mind.' replied Mike twisting and contorting to relieve the stiffness in his back that now arrived as predictably as a new dawn.

'No wonder your back's stiff. I did suggest we pull over for a coffee break, but you insisted on carrying on. Looks like you're paying for it now. You're not as young as you once were.'

Mike made a face and carried on walking. If he'd stopped for a break, they might not have made their reservation. As it was, they were five minutes late when Mike opened the door to the restaurant. When Susan realised where they were eating, she smiled and started to giggle.

'Ha, I should have known. You old romantic. I can't remember when we last ate at a Red Lobster. But this is great, what a way to start the weekend. I'm going to demolish a plate of jumbo shrimp and Marie Rose sauce, just for old time's sake.'

The waiter greeted them warmly, took their jackets and showed them to a booth by the window. On the table was a large bouquet of oriental lilies and white roses. Chilling in an ice bucket was a bottle of Cook's Californian champagne.

Susan smiled and wiped a tear from her eye. She had been on an emotional rollercoaster recently, and during her dark times, the thought of a romantic meal with her husband seemed a distant prospect. She didn't know what to say, she was overwhelmed by love for the man who had stood with her through thick and thin. Mike had been a trooper throughout her illness. He was her rock and he meant the world to her.

'Well you've pulled it out of the bag again Mr Rawlingson. This is just lovely and such a sweet gesture. It doesn't seem like 23 years ago when you proposed to me in that restaurant. This will be just like old times.'

Mike smiled and poured Susan a glass of champagne.

'Now is that all the surprises over? I need to know so I can enjoy this feast.'

Mike winked and took a sip from his glass.

'Oh, you never know, there's life in this old dog yet.'

Susan started to giggle.

'Well in that case, you'd better go easy on that champagne. That's if past experience is anything to go by. Too much drink has a detrimental effect on your performance.'

'Hey Cheeky. I'll let you know that performance improves with age, but I'll let you be the judge of that.'

Mike clinked his glass with Susan's

'And here's to us and a great weekend, let's make the most of it.'

'I'll drink to that.' replied Susan. 'Now about those shrimps.'

Chapter 19

It was Saturday lunchtime. Sam had to start his late shift at three, but before then he thought he would hang out with Ella for a couple of hours. She had spent the morning at the library going through the Spruce Knob archive as she pieced together the history of the mine. He had arranged to meet her so they could grab a quick lunch.

Sam parked up on the street outside the library and wound down his windows. The Indian summer that had arrived last week showed no signs of going away. The temperature on his dashboard said 83 degrees and unusually for that time of year, there was next to no breeze.

He hoped Ella would hurry up, he was starving, and he'd set his heart on a Big Mac before he had to start work. It was only going to be him and Chris covering the detective side of things at the office, so he couldn't be sure if he'd get much of a chance to eat later. He certainly wouldn't if it got busy for any reason.

A smiling Ella came rushing across the road carrying her bag in both arms. She appeared to be in good spirits.

'Sorry I'm a bit late, hope you haven't been waiting long. But I'm just off the phone to my mother. She's going to search her attic for the letters my grandfather wrote to his mother when he started working in the mine. I knew mom had them; my grandmother gave them to her before she died but I've never read them. It's really fascinating and quite exciting. I keep seeing my grandfather's name in documents, and now that I've started my research, I thought his letters might give some insight into what working in the mine was really like back then.'

'That does sound interesting. Old family stuff like that, especially where you've got such a close personal connection is always fascinating.'

Sam leant across and switched on the CD.

'Thought we'd go grab a burger. And I'm gonna put on some proper music for a change. None of that Ella Fitzgerald nonsense your mom likes to play.'

The first few bars of Harvest Moon started to play. Ella burst into fits of laughter.

'And you were slagging Ella Fitzgerald, Neil Young, you've got to be kidding me!'

Sam laughed as he indicated and pulled out into the street.

'I knew you'd like it.'

Ten minutes later Sam and Ella were in the drive thru queue at the McDonald's on the Fairlea road. It was busier than Sam was expecting. He was four back in the queue and the parking lot was packed with cars. A steady stream of parents and young children were making their way into the restaurant.

As Sam searched through his glovebox for a different CD, Ella noticed two guys carrying take out bags walking towards a cream coloured GMC truck that was parked against the far wall of the lot. The guy in the red t-shirt with '14 Words' written on the front looked familiar. Ella thought for a moment. Then it came to her. He was the guy who crushed the squirrels head the day she'd been attacked. She strained to get a look at the other guy. She couldn't see him clearly as he was shielded by his friend. But he was wearing a grey baseball cap. He could easily be the other guy who'd been carrying the shotgun. Ella nudged Sam's arm.

'You see those two guys walking towards that truck, I think they are the guys I saw shooting squirrels the afternoon I was attacked, and now I can get a better look at him the one in the grey cap looks like the guy you saw talking to your colleague at the diner the other day.'

Sam nodded as he watched the two males get into the truck.

'I had already clocked them.' said Sam. 'The one wearing the red t-shirt has got blue paint all over the toe cap of one his sneakers. Metallic blue paint by the looks of it, much the same colour as the graffiti on my fucking garage.'

'What you gonna do?' asked Ella as Sam bumped the car over the kerb and did an illegal u-turn much to the annoyance of the driver behind who gave him the two-finger salute.

Ella gripped the door panel and sat back in her seat.

'Are you going to chase them? Are we going to be in a vehicle pursuit like the ones you see in the movies?

Sam grinned and shook his head.

'I wouldn't get too excited, this car ain't fitted with blue lights or a siren, so I'm gonna follow from a distance. I just want to see where they're going. Grab a pen from my jacket and write down the licence plate number of the truck. Just in case we lose them. There should be paper in my folder on the back seat.'

The truck turned right onto the main road and headed towards Lewisburg. A couple of miles further on it indicated left and pulled off the road into the bowling alley parking lot. Sam had been following from a few vehicles back, so he slowed down and pulled into a layby opposite the alley.

'Afraid you're going to have to stay here. I don't want either of them to recognise you. They don't know me, so I should be fine. I want to get a better look at those shoes.'

'Just be careful, won't you?' said Ella putting her hand on Sam's arm.

Sam smiled and squeezed Ella's hand.

'Don't worry, I won't be long.'

By the time Sam had crossed the road the truck had parked up in the middle of the lot, but neither of the men had got out. Sam ducked into a bus shelter from where he could get a good view of the truck. It looked as though the men were tucking into their McDonald's. Nearly ten minutes passed before an arm reached out the window and dropped a scrunched-up paper bag onto the tarmac. The doors of the truck opened and both men got out and walked towards the front door.

Sam followed from a safe distance weaving between parked vehicles as he picked a route that let him keep out of sight. As they reached the entrance, the man in the grey cap put his hand in the back pocket of his jeans and pulled out what looked like a wallet. He hadn't noticed, but as he did something else came out of his pocket and dropped on the ground. It was a small piece of paper. The draught from a passing car lifted the paper and blew it under the wheel of a SUV that was parked in a disabled bay.

As soon as the men entered the building Sam ran across and retrieved the piece of paper. Looking at it he wasn't sure what it was. It appeared to be some sort of receipt, either that or it might be a ticket for something. The purple print was quite faded and indistinct, he could just about make out the words, Georgina's Alterations, Webster Street, but that was about it. Not knowing what it was he put it in his back trouser pocket and made his way into the alley. Over at the counter the two men were handing in their shoes. They seemed to know the fat balding guy with the manager badge on his shirt who was leaning on the counter.

That fat lump of lard must be Riley Muntz, thought Sam. He couldn't hear what they were saying but judging by the laughter they appeared to be sharing a joke. Sam went and sat at a table in the cafeteria and watched as the men changed into their bowling shoes. When the three of them had disappeared to the far end of the alley, he made his move. The girl at the cash desk was collecting empty glasses from tables and the manager was talking to the guy in the red shirt while grey cap guy set up the bowling lane.

Sam slipped behind the reception desk and took the pair of white sneakers from its pigeonhole. 'I knew it. I damned well knew it.'

The paint on the left toe cap appeared to be an exact match for the paint on his garage. It was such an unusual colour of aquamarine, and with those flecks of gold sparkle through it, there could be no mistake. It was the same type of paint.

Sam returned the shoes and made his way out to the parking lot. Before he left, he wanted a look at the truck the men had been driving.

233

It was a plain and unremarkable looking truck. It wasn't festooned with any stickers or badges and it didn't look like a works truck as it didn't have any advertising logos on it. Sam peered into the cab. There was nothing to be seen except a dog-eared copy of Hustler magazine that was lying on the passenger seat. Sam was about to return to his car when he glanced down at the rear of the vehicle. There, tied onto the tow bar underneath the licence plate was the end of a piece of rope. He had nearly missed it against the mud splattered tailgate.

The rope had been roughly cut just below the knot and there was no more than a couple of inches showing. The knot appeared to be slightly flattened, suggesting it had been pulled very tight. It didn't look like it would come off easily. Bingo, thought Sam, I've got them. Any money this is the truck they used to pull Ella through the forest. If we can match the fibres that were on her socks to this rope, we can prove it was this truck. Those two fucking assholes are going down for this, and I'll get the others who were with them as well. Wait till Sergeant Brown hears about this.

Back at the car Sam could hardly contain his glee as he explained what he'd discovered.

'Okay, okay great. I hear all that. But what are you going to do, arrest them?' asked Ella.

'For sure.' replied Sam, 'but we won't be doing that today. With Charlie's party, we don't have the resources we need. It'll keep till Monday, if I get a chance today, I'll do a briefing note for Angela. That's only fair, it's her enquiry after all. But don't worry, if they were going to get rid of the evidence, I mean the rope or the paint on the shoes, then they would have done it before now. But they haven't because they're too fucking stupid. You see, Ella, here's the truth about policing, it's not that we're brilliant detectives, it's just that the criminals we're up against aren't very bright. And I'll bet my bottom dollar these ones are particularly stupid. Oh, before I forget, give me that licence plate number, I'll check it when I get in. I want to know who owns that truck.'

Ella smiled and handed over the piece of paper she'd written the number on. She then high fived her boyfriend. Sam Coutts was proving to be cleverer than he was giving himself credit for.

*

Mike and Susan had arrived at Charlie's house on the outskirts of Lewisburg at just after one. Now the four friends were sitting in the back yard enjoying the sunshine and a plate of sandwiches, fruit and a jug of iced tea. They hadn't seen each other in fifteen months, but like all good friends, their conversation had managed to pick up from where they had left off. This was a weekend away from the pressures of work for both Charlie and Mike. And the two former colleagues were desperately trying not to talk shop. So, for the last hour the four of them had discussed their children, recent vacations and the chances of the Cubs finally winning something. Oh, and Susan's health of course. That was the first thing that Alison, Charlie's wife, had asked about when their friends arrived.

As the friends chatted over lunch, Mike produced the carefully wrapped birthday present which he handed to Charlie.

'Gee guys, this is great.' said Charlie unwrapping his gift. 'A bottle of Willett's, and it's their special edition too. Not a bad way to start the weekend. We'll maybe crack it open later.'

'No, don't be doing that just because we're here. Why don't you save it for some other time? I expect there will be more than enough booze at the party.' said Mike.

'That is for sure.' replied Alison.

'Talking of the party, is there anything needing done that I could help you with? Food, decorations, anything at all.' asked Susan.

That's kind of you, but most of it is already done to be honest. But I do need to go to Costco to pick up the platters of sandwiches and vol-au-vents. Oh, and I've balloons and bunting to pick up as well. You're welcome to come along for the ride if you'd like.' replied Alison.

'Love to. Just say when you'd like to go.'

'Great. Well if everyone's finished lunch we could go anytime. It will let us pick up what we need and give us time to get back and relax for a couple of hours before we need to get ready. Then I thought we could head down to the community centre around six, that would give us an hour to put up the decorations and lay out the buffet. I don't want Charlie to arrive before seven. So, I'm relying on Mike to keep him amused until then.'

Susan started to chuckle.

'That shouldn't be a problem. The pair of them haven't stopped chatting since we got here. And I think I'm about ready, I just need a quick visit to the bathroom.'

'Fine, I'll take these dishes into the kitchen and I'll see you round at the car in a couple of minutes.'

As soon as the girls were away, Mike turned to Charlie.

'Got an interesting case to tell you about. We had a murder a couple of days ago and it looks like it's going to be a bit of a whodunit. But when you hear who the victim is, you'll know why I'm telling you.'

Charlie looked around to check no one was listening.

'Sounds interesting. Go on then, who's the victim?'

Mike leant across the table.

'Eldridge Lawrence, he used to own the asbestos factory near Lewisburg. He's been living just outside Chicago ever since he left Greenbrier County. It's a weird one right enough. You don't get many 89-year-old murder victims. Certainly not ones shot in the back with a crossbow bolt and with their hands painted red!'

*

The detectives' office was like the Marie Celeste when Sam arrived. He'd called in at the control room on his way in and got them to check who the GMC truck was registered to. It wasn't what he was hoping for. The registered keeper of the truck was a Rita Garavelli who lived at an address in Marlington. The name meant nothing to Sam and a check against Garavelli's name came back no trace. She had no criminal record. By the time Sam got up to his office the only person still there was Sarah, who was patiently waiting to go over the hand over list. Angela had left twenty minutes ago to go and get her hair done ahead of the party.

'This won't take a minute.' said Sarah handing Sam two pages of A4.

'Overnight there was a break-in to a yard in Addison, but that's now all in hand, there's nothing outstanding. SOCO were just finishing up when I was there and that was two hours ago. Other than that, there's next to nothing to report. A truck broken into in Fairlea and a domestic incident over at White Sulphur Springs, but the uniforms have dealt with those. And that's about it. So, you're starting with a clean slate.'

'Excellent.' said Sam perusing the note. He glanced up and looked out the window. Walking across the yard with what looked like a bag of doughnuts was his colleague Chris.

'Things are off to a good start. No follow ups and a bag of doughnuts to get torn into. Looks like I should get the kettle on.'

Sarah smiled.

'I'll leave it with you then. Hope you have a quiet one.'

Sam nodded.

'Enjoy the party and keep an eye on my dad. You know what he's like after a few beers.'

Sam had just finished making the coffee and was about to take a bite of his doughnut when the phone on his desk rang. It was the front office and the officer on the other end of the line sounded concerned.

Sam put down his mug and picked up a pen.

'Okay, okay slow down a sec, where is the locus?' The Greenbrier Country Club. Yes, I know it, it's just off the mountain road. Fine, that's all noted. Now get a message to the uniforms who are up there that we're on our way. We should be there in twenty minutes. And just confirm with them that they've got the locus properly secured, just get them to tape the thing off till we get there. Oh, and make sure that nobody leaves the premises.'

Chris put down his doughnut. He had been listening carefully to the conversation. Whatever it was it sounded serious.

'And just one more thing,' said Sam, 'see if you can track Zoe Batchelor down, she's the late turn SOCO. Get a radio message to her to meet us at the club ASAP. Oh, and print me off the incident, we'll pick it up on our way out.'

'Guess that's our quiet Saturday out the window then?' said Chris putting on his jacket.

'Looks that way.' replied Sam. 'There's been a murder up at the country club, it appears that someone's been shot in the back.'

'What, shot in the back with a gun?'

'Nope.' said Sam grabbing his folder and car keys. 'With an arrow or a crossbow bolt. Whatever it is we better get up there. With the party tonight we've hardly any resources on, they're sending a uniformed Sergeant over from White Sulphur Springs. They've only got two cops up there and one of them is a new start.'

*

The Greenbrier Golf and Country Club was seven miles from the office in the foothills of the Allegheny mountains. While it was predominately a golf club, there was a spa, tennis courts and even a small pool. There were also bars and an exclusive restaurant for its wealthy patrons, many of whom lived in the expensive designer homes, set back in the mature woods, that ran alongside the clubhouse and the first and eighteenth fairways.

Saturday afternoon was usually the busiest time of the week and today was no exception. A mixed foursome competition was in full swing when the detectives pulled up in the parking lot.

Sam and Charlie got out and walked across to the side of the clubhouse. From there they could see the putting green and the whole macabre scene.

'Whoever that young cop is I'm going to make a point of speaking to her sergeant. She's done a cracking job getting those rubberneckers away from the window. And they've got the whole putting green taped off. Given it's just the two of them they've done a good job.'

'Agreed.' replied Chris. 'And I'll tell you something for nothing, whoever did this wasn't messing about. Shooting him in the back like that, the old boy never had a chance.'

The deceased was lying on the edge of the putting green near to a gravel path that led to the locker room. The man was elderly, at least in his mid-eighties, and he was dressed in golfing clothes. White shoes, blue trousers and a short sleeved yellow top that was now a violent pink colour.

'It looks like he must have fallen face down. His glasses are smashed. I think he's literally been shot right here and gone down like a tree being felled.' announced Sam.

'How can you say that?'

Sam pointed towards two golf balls that were sitting a few inches from a hole about fifteen feet in front of the deceased.

'He's still got his putter in his hand. I reckon he'd just taken a couple of practice putts before he was shot. That's why the balls are lying next to the hole. And then wham, poleaxed by a crossbow bolt to the back.'

Sam stepped over the barrier tape to get a better look at the body.

'What you up to now?' asked Chris who was struggling to follow Sam's explanation as he didn't know the first thing about golf.

'I'm checking if he's got red paint on his hands?'

'Now I'm really confused, why the hell would he have red paint on his hands?'

'I'll explain that in a minute. Anyway, he doesn't so my theory might not stack up.'

'Okay. So, he doesn't have paint on his hands, but you'll be interested in this then.' said Chris crouching down and pointing at the edge of the putting green.

'There are drips of red paint here. Look there's some on the edge of the path too. And there's more here on the leaves of this bush. It looks like there's a trail heading into the woods.'

Sam came over and peered at the line of paint spots that led towards the trees.

'Good spot hawkeye. It looks like my theory might not be so wide of the mark after all. But before I explain that, we're going to need some more resources here. And party or no party, Charlie is going to have to know about this.'

'Already on it.' said Chris taking out his radio. 'I'll get the control room to give him a shout. And I'll get an ETA for Zoe, we could do with getting this photographed soon as.'

*

Mike was washing his hands in the sink when the phone in the kitchen rang. He answered it and confused the caller who thought he was speaking to Lieutenant Finch.

'I'm not the Lieutenant but he's right here. Hold the line I'll get him for you. He won't be a minute.'

Mike opened the kitchen window and shouted to Charlie.

'Charlie, there's a phone call for you, it's the office. The caller sounds quite agitated, must be important.'

241

Charlie came in and took the receiver from Mike who headed back out to the garden to read his paper.

'Lieutenant Finch speaking, what's up?'

Five minutes later Charlie came back out. Mike knew immediately that something was afoot as Charlie had his game face on.

'Problem?' asked Mike putting down the paper.

Charlie grimaced.

'Yep, I think so. Looks like there's been a murder up at the Greenbrier Country Club. Sam and Chris are up there now, an old man has been found dead with a crossbow bolt in his back. Looks like your crossbow killer has come home. We don't have a confirmed ident yet, but I reckon I know who it is.'

'Well in that case you're one step ahead of me. How do you know who it is?'

'Come on get in the car and I'll explain on the way. I take it you don't mind coming along?'

'Try stopping me. But what about the girls and the party? You're supposed to be there in a couple of hours.'

'Sod's law isn't it, but you don't need me to tell you that. This is too serious an incident for me not to attend. I'll phone Alison later, she'll understand. You don't stay married for 17 years in this job without an understanding wife.'

'Never a truer word spoken my friend. But about this murder, why do you think you know who the deceased is?'

Charlie reversed into the street and accelerated towards the junction with the main road.

'It's to do with dolls. Sam Coutts recovered a box of corn dolls lying in a box outside the entrance to the old

242

Spruce Knob mine last week. Each doll had a dirty great nail sticking out its back and their hands had been painted red. Those nails represent a crossbow bolt and each of the dolls represents one of the Lawrence brothers. You've already found one dead, and you told me he had red paint on his hands. This then, I reckon, is number two.'

'Which means that the third brother is next on the hitlist.'

'You've read my mind.' said Charlie. He then scoffed ironically.

'By the way, you've not met our new chief, have you?'

Mike shook his head.

'The man's hopeless. He's a bag of nerves at the best of times, this news will really tip him over the edge.'

*

By the time Charlie and Mike arrived at the country club, several other uniformed officers were already in attendance. Sam had arranged for the sergeant to take the details of everyone that was in the clubhouse around the time of the murder. That was being done in the main lounge. Two couples who had been having a drink in the dirty bar had been spoken to separately by Chris. The side window of the dirty bar looked directly onto the putting green where the deceased was lying. But both couples, who had just come off the course after completing their round, had been having a drink and chatting and hadn't seen anything untoward.

Over at the eighteenth green, a uniformed officer was taking details of golfers finishing their rounds and directing them towards the car lot on the other side of the clubhouse, so they could be kept away from the putting green which was now being photographed by Zoe Batchelor.

Sam and Chris had to check themselves from smiling when they saw Charlie and their former boss come around the side of the clubhouse. Mike nodded towards his old colleagues.

'Sam, Chris good to see you both. Perhaps not the circumstances I was expecting to meet you in, but there you have it, policing has a habit of throwing up the unexpected. Anyway, enough of that. I know you've got your hands full and I'm sure you've got plenty to update Lieutenant Finch about.'

'Still trying to make sense of what's gone on, but we'll do our best.' replied Chris.

'Do we have a confirmed identification yet?' asked Charlie opening his folder.

'Yep, we do boss. The deceased is an 87-year-old male by the name of Mitchell Lawrence. Long-time member of the club who lives in one of those fancy houses just down there.' replied Sam pointing down the eighteenth fairway.'

'And I can see from here that he's been shot in the back. Is it a crossbow bolt right enough?'

Sam nodded.

'And what about his hands, have they been covered in red paint?'

Sam stopped and stared at Charlie. How did the Lieutenant know about the red paint? He hadn't relayed that information to the control room yet. And Lieutenant Finch had only just arrived, so how come he knows about the paint?'

Mike sensed Sam's confusion.

'You see that's why he's the Lieutenant, Sam. He's sharp. It's his job to know these things.'

'I'll explain all that in a moment.' said Charlie stepping over the barrier tape so he could get a closer look at the body.

'What I just found out and what you won't yet know is the deceaseds older brother, Eldridge Lawrence was murdered in his garden in Chicago two days ago. Captain Rawlingson here was just telling me about it this afternoon. Exactly the same MO. Shot in the back with a crossbow bolt and then the killer painted his hands with red paint.'

This was now starting to make a bit of sense to Sam. His theory about the red paint was correct. Whoever killed Mitchell Lawrence must also have killed his brother. It was likely they would also have been the person who left the box of dolls at the entrance to the mine.'

Charlie Looked at Sam. He could almost see the penny dropping.

'You've made the connection to those corn dolls, haven't you?'

'I have sir, yes. And in answer to your question about the paint. There is red paint. It's just that it's not on his hands. Chris here found a trail of paint spots leading from the putting green into the trees. We've not had a chance to investigate that yet. But we reckon the killer must have been disturbed. He's taken off through the woods before he had a chance to paint the old guy's hands.'

Charlie and Mike bent down to examine the paint spots on the edge of the putting green.

'That certainly sounds plausible.' said Charlie standing up. 'And what about witnesses? There seems to have been dozens of people around.'

'It's early days, but we're not aware of any eye-witnesses. Chris here has some positive news though, I'll let him explain.'

Chris took out his notebook and flipped through the pages.

'I've just had a word with a guy called Dave Beckett who works as a waiter in the restaurant. He was just arriving to start his shift. He told me as he was walking up the main drive, he saw a figure running through the woods. Says it looked like he was in a hurry and heading towards the main road.'

'Huh. How long ago was that?' asked Charlie.

Chris looked at his watch.

'About a quarter to three. So, an hour and fifty minutes ago.'

'Was he able to give you any description?'

'Not much of one. He said it was a male and he was wearing dark clothing. Including a jacket which he thought was surprising considering how warm it is. He had a rucksack over his shoulder; and he was wearing a hat. A big black hat was how he described it.'

'That's good work Chris and it's a start. Could be innocent enough, but it does sound suspicious, anyway, it'll need to be checked out. Did you circulate a description?'

Chris nodded.

'Just did it before you arrived. All mobile patrols are aware and looking out for him.'

'Well he should be a stick out, especially with that hat. Not many folks dressed like that around here.' added Sam.

'How are you getting on Zoe? asked Charlie. 'I see you're on your own, and that's partly my fault. Too many people with time off because of my damned party.'

Zoe put her camera down at her side and screwed up her nose.

'Sorry about your party Lieutenant, I take it you won't be able to go now. That's a real shame.'

'Don't concern yourself about that, it can't be helped. I'm going to phone my wife and tell them to carry on without me. The community centres booked and anyway, it would be a shame to waste all that food. If we can get things sorted here, Mike and I might get there before eleven, we might still manage a beer.'

Charlie continued.

'Look, I've got Dave Richardson's home number, I'm going to give him a call. You're going to need some help and Dave won't mind, he's not much of a party animal. He'd probably prefer to be up here getting involved.'

'I think you're right.' replied Zoe. 'He's proper old school. The job always comes first with Dave. I've got his number if you can't find it. But I sure would appreciate another pair of hands, by the looks of things I'm going to be here for a while.'

'I'll sort that for you boss.' said Chris. 'If you give me his number I'll go into the clubhouse and phone him. Expect there are other things you want to discuss with Zoe.'

'Appreciate that Chris.' replied Charlie taking a sheet of telephone numbers from inside his folder. 'Here just take the sheet, his number's on there somewhere. And while you're at it, give Sergeant Brown a call. Tell her I need her to go to the office and set up the incident room.'

'Roger that.' said Chris disappearing into the club-house clutching the sheet of telephone numbers.

Charlie and Mike were now standing on the path just a few feet away from the corpse. It was as close as they could get without contaminating the crime scene.

'Zoe, have you got a mirror in that bag of yours?' asked Mike.

'Sure do. Couldn't do this job without one. What do you need it for?'

'It's not for me. But do us a favour and check the deceased's mouth will you, I've got a feeling you might find something interesting.'

'Hmm, intriguing. Just give me a moment, I'll need to put on a pair of protective gloves.'

'What's this about then?' asked a bemused Charlie.

'Apologies, but I forgot to mention it when we were back at the house. And I've only just remembered. Seeing the body lying there has jogged my memory. You see, when we found his brother dead, we checked his mouth, and in it we found a ....'

Before Mike could finish Zoe blurted out.

'There appears to be a yellow feather in his mouth. It's covered in saliva and stuck to the roof of his mouth, but it's definitely a yellow feather.'

Chapter 20

The following morning Charlie was up early and searching the kitchen for his car keys. It was going to be a quick turnaround as it had been after midnight when he'd left the party at the community centre. At least he'd managed to make it for the last hour and catch a word with most of his guests. This morning he had arranged to meet Angela at the office at 0730 hrs to get an update ahead of the morning briefing.

At lunchtime he intended to head out to the Greenbrier Community, an evangelical Christian group who had set up a church, accommodation, and workshops high in the hills near Huntersville. Given that it was a Sunday, he knew they would be busy with their church services, but it was important that he got to speak with David Lawrence, the youngest of the three brothers, who had been part of the community for the last fifteen years. Charlie had to tell him about the death of his middle brother Mitchell. He wasn't even sure if he was aware that his oldest brother had also been murdered, so it promised to be a difficult meeting, he would have to be tactful.

Last evening, Charlie had tried to get hold of Aiden Lawrence to inform him that his uncle had died. But he wasn't at home. Aiden's son told him that his parents had gone to Chicago to sort out matters regarding

Eldridge's death. He thought they were staying in a hotel, but he didn't know which one. At that moment, there was no way of getting in contact with Aiden.

Anyway, before Charlie could think about any of that, he had to check in with Angela and agree what actions needed to be allocated to the small team of detectives he had put together to work on the enquiry. The first thing he was going to do was check if there had been any update on the figure in dark clothing that had been seen running through the woods. When he'd left the office at ten thirty last night there had been nothing. No one had seen hide nor hair of him.

Before he got into his car Charlie turned and waved to Alison, Mike and Susan who were standing in their dressing gowns at the kitchen window. The weekend hadn't quite gone to plan and given the circumstances, Mike and Susan had decided to head back to Chicago after breakfast. Mike needed to get back to his own force. With a second Lawrence brother now dead, it was important that the two police forces linked their enquiries, to give themselves the best chance of solving the crimes. Mike would be that conduit, the vital link that would ensure that information and intelligence was shared quickly and efficiently.

Angela was writing actions up on a whiteboard when Charlie walked into the incident room. Sam, as usual, had been in for a while and was already primed and ready to go.

'Shame about the party.' said Angela noticing her boss had walked in the door. 'Did you go after you left here.'

Charlie nodded.

'Mike and I called in on our way home, so we were there for the last hour. Managed a couple of beers and a quick chat with most people which was nice. Thanks for the present, I know it was from the department, but I haven't had a chance to open it yet. Maybe later today, I've got dozens in the back room waiting to be opened. And I'm sorry I ruined your evening, nice hair by the way.'

Angela smiled and sat down.

'Not a problem. Someone had to come in and get the ball rolling. By the way, I got all the others on your list except Ryan. Don't know where the hell he is, but the others will be in for a briefing at 0800 hrs.'

'Okay, fine. Even without Ryan we should have enough cover, certainly for today. We can shake things up tomorrow if need be.'

Sam handed them both a coffee and joined them at the table.

'Just before you arrived, Sam was telling me about the feather. What do you think that is all about? The crossbow bolt and the paint clearly link to that box of dolls, but the feather! I can't see any tie in with that.'

Before Charlie had a chance to answer Sam piped up.

'I was thinking about the feather last night when I got home. It's funny, but Ella and I had been discussing it last week.'

'Discussing what?' asked Charlie taking a mouthful of coffee.

'Well, the fact that canaries were often used down mines. You know, to detect if there was any carbon monoxide present. It's an odourless gas you see, but canaries are sensitive to it, they would keel over before it had a chance to harm the miners. A type of early

251

warning signal so to speak. Anyway, the point is, canaries are usually yellow and as the Lawrences owned the Spruce Knob mine where we found the dolls, I wondered if the two things were connected.'

'You're cleverer than you look.' said Angela scribbling some notes.

Charlie tapped his lips with his fingers.

'Hmm. I hadn't thought of that. Seems a reasonable explanation. The lab will be able to tell us what type of bird it came from, but one thing's for sure, a feather didn't end up in their mouths by accident.'

'I don't know about you, but I'm starving. I thought I'd get a couple of rolls from Annie Mack's. I didn't have time for breakfast this morning.' said Sam.

'Not surprised. What time did you get here? I've told you before, we work long enough hours as it is, especially now we've a murder enquiry running, you'll need to be careful, it's not good for your health.'

'Guess I'm just not a very good sleeper, so if I'm up anyway I like to get in and get on with things. Now about breakfast, anyone want anything?'

'Sure.' said Charlie taking a five-dollar bill from his pocket. 'And just for your information, last night I telephoned the Greenbrier Community where David Lawrence lives. They've got services till midday, so I thought you and I would head over there about then and try and get a word with Lawrence. But it means we'll miss lunch, so I'll have two bacon rolls thanks.'

'Same for me then.' said Angela raking through her bag for some money, 'and get some sachets of sauce will you, I like lots of tomato ketchup on mine.'

*

The drive up through the mountains was stunning. There had been rain overnight which had freshened the air and now the trees and fields that hugged the lower slopes glistened in the bright sunshine. The colours of fall were everywhere to see. Orange, reds and golds, the maple and beech trees were a riot of colour. Fields of ripe corn and marmalade coloured pumpkins were interspersed with orchards of seasoned fruit. Wooden crates packed to the gunnels with sweet apples stacked high and waiting to be uplifted and transported to distant markets.

In the background the ribbon of mountains that made up the Allegheny range snaked their way towards the mighty Appalachian plateau that ran as far as New Brunswick in the north and Georgia to the south.

High above their car, stretching their wings on the thermals, a pair of turkey vultures soared, professional scavengers, combing the landscape with telescopic eyes ready to zone in on their next meal.

Charlie looked through the windscreen to the sky above.

'Reckon those turkey vultures have got their eye on that deer carcass we just passed at the side of the road. Nothing if not opportunists are our feathered friends, looking at them up there has put me in mind of old Screech and Eustace for some reason. Expect it's because the pair of them never missed an opportunity for some easy pickings.'

Sam shook his head. He'd better start paying more attention. This was just like being out with Ella. She was forever pointing things out to him. He hadn't noticed the vultures, let alone the carcass at the side of the road, and he wasn't even driving. It was noticing the little, seemingly insignificant things and then making connections, that set Charlie apart from the other detectives in the department. Sam was ambitious, he wanted to get to the top. He had made detective with less than 3 years' service so he'd made a good start, but if he were to make it to Charlie's level, or even captain, then he needed to be able to switch on 100% of the time.

A steady stream of worshippers was coming out of the small stone-built church when Charlie parked up on some hard standing to the side of what looked like a row of single storey dormitories. The worshippers, both men and women, were of all ages. There were even a few children walking obediently in silence at the rear of the group. Everyone was similarly dressed in blue smocks and white linen shirts. The only difference in attire was that the women and girls were wearing long skirts while the men and boys wore three quarter length trousers.

Sam had seen nothing like it before. Well not in real life. He had seen programs on TV featuring Amish and Mennonite communities who seemed to dress similarly to these people, but what was really bizarre was the men's socks. White socks, red Socks, there was even a pair of lurid green socks all sticking up above the level of their plain black boots. It looked completely incongruous with the drabness of the rest of their clothes. The other thing that struck him as strange was that none of the men were wearing hats. In the programs he had watched, the men always wore hats. Broad brimmed hats that covered their faces.

Sam felt slightly on edge as he got out the car and walked with Charlie towards a group of elderly men who were gathered outside what appeared to be a canteen. They were speaking in hushed tones and not paying the slightest attention to the two visitors coming towards them.

The two detectives stood politely waiting for the men to finish their conversation. Eventually Charlie interjected as the men showed no sign of acknowledging their presence.

'Excuse me, sorry to disturb you, but I'm looking for David Lawrence. I'm Lieutenant Finch from Lewisburg police office and this is Detective Coutts.' Charlie reached into his jacket pocket and took out his police badge.

An elderly man with wrinkly brown skin and a neatly trimmed white beard smiled and nodded.

'That would be me.' said the man in a soft velvety voice.

He was aged about 80 and of average height. He had a well-worn but welcoming face and piercing blue eyes that stood out against his tanned skin.

'I got the message that you were coming over this morning. We could talk in our meeting room; the elders won't need in till later this afternoon. We won't be disturbed there. Please follow me.'

The old man led them across a forecourt to a wooden panelled building that stood to the side of the church. Inside was a large table and about a dozen chairs. A carving of Christ on the cross hung on the wall above the fireplace and a large leather-bound bible stood on a plain wooden lectern at the far side of the room. Apart from some threadbare brown curtains that was about it. It was already apparent that the Greenbrier Community didn't indulge in the luxuries of life. There weren't even cushions on the chairs.

'I'm not keeping you from your lunch, am I?' asked Charlie sitting down on a chair.

The old man shook his head.

'I had breakfast at six, so I won't eat till we have dinner at five. The children and some of our younger people will eat a light lunch now. Just some soup and bread. But I don't bother, you don't need to eat as much when you get to my age.'

Charlie smiled and nodded gently.

'Fine then. I'll come straight to the point. Before I start can I ask if you've had any contact with your nephew Aiden in the last few days.'

The old man nodded once.

'And was that to inform you about what had happened to your oldest brother, Eldridge?'

The old man nodded again but didn't say anything.

'Well, I'm very sorry to bring you more sad news Mr Lawrence, but your other brother, Mitchell is also dead. He was shot in the back at his country club yesterday afternoon. In much the same manner as Eldridge was. As I said, I'm really sorry for your loss.'

The old man sat in silence. There wasn't a flicker of emotion on his face, if anything he looked serene, peaceful even.

Sam squirmed on his seat. He was finding all this just a little disconcerting. How could you learn that your brother had been murdered and not show any emotion! Charlie should have told him that his fly was undone, that might have elicited a response. But to sit there in stony silence, it was all just a bit disturbing.

'I don't mean to be rude, sir. But you don't seem shocked or perturbed by that news.' said Charlie.

Again, the man sat expressionless looking straight ahead. Eventually he spoke.

'I'm sorry. I don't mean to appear callous. In the community we are taught not to show our emotions. It's looked upon as being unseemly. We are here to honour God. To do his work. Frivolous outpourings of emotion can get in the way of that. I know that must sound strange because it's not your way Lieutenant. But it is our way. We honour the Lord, no one else.

Each to their own, thought Sam, but I wouldn't call mourning your own brother frivolous, but there you go.

'Would it be alright if I asked you a couple of questions. You see I'm leading the investigation into Mitchell's death, so, if you don't mind, a bit of background information would be useful.'

'Surely, I'll see what I can do.'

'I know you weren't involved in the running of the asbestos company, so my questions are about your time at the mine. I have reason to believe that someone, perhaps someone connected to the mine holds a serious grudge against your family. So serious that they are prepared to kill to get their revenge. Can you think of anyone or any circumstances that could have led to somebody murdering both of your brothers?

The old man lent back in his chair and thought for a moment.

'There isn't any one person I can think of. But if you're asking if I know of anyone that holds a grudge against my family then I'd say yes. Half of Greenbrier County hold a grudge against my family, and the half that don't didn't work for us.'

Sam opened his folder and started to take down some notes.

'You see, it was the reason I left the company. I couldn't stand it anymore. The lying and the bullying. I had to get out. Eldridge and Mitchell, oh, and don't forget Aiden. He was part of it as well. They were obsessed with money. If it didn't lead to profit they weren't interested. It started by cutting corners, then they didn't invest in new equipment. But I finally left when they started to compromise the men's safety. We had a big bust up at a board meeting and that was the end of it. They gave me some money; I suppose it was to buy me out. It wasn't a particularly large sum, but I took it and left. Not long after that they sold the mine. Six months after that, I ended up here. Found God for the first time in my life and gave the community what money I had. I've never been happier. Money can't buy you the love of God, Lieutenant.'

'That's very interesting Mr Lawrence. But can I take you back a minute. You said you finally left when they started to compromise the men's safety, can you tell us more about that?'

The old man sighed and stroked his beard.

'It was a long time ago now. But as I recall there was an almighty row between me and my brothers. Of course, Aiden, who had recently been appointed company lawyer, sided with his father. You see two men had died. Two good men Lieutenant. Joe Jarret, who was the union rep and Tom Hicks. They died in a new seam that hadn't yet been developed. My brothers were trying to keep it secret from the men, they were planning to sell the mine and had been running down the other seams for months to keep their costs down.

The new seam had three times as much coal as the other ones we were mining, but the coal was deep and difficult to extract. It would require expensive new cutting equipment and expertise that we didn't have to get it to the surface, and they didn't want to spend the money. But that new seam was their jewel in the crown. They knew one of the bigger mining companies would want it because they would have the equipment and expertise to mine it. And it meant they had an asset to sell. And that takes us back to money. It's the root of all evil, Lieutenant.'

Charlie scratched his head.

'Yes, I think I follow that. But I still don't see how any of that was compromising the men's safety. Were the men put in danger?'

The old man nodded.

'They hushed everything up. Bribed some of the men to tell lies so the truth about their deaths never came out. They got them to testify that the men who died had gone into the mine without a canary, lamps or their hard hats. Those men died of carbon monoxide poisoning. The gas had been leaking from that seam for weeks. They cancelled a mine inspection because they didn't want to spend money sorting the problems ahead of the sale. But the worst of it was they intimidated some of the men. I didn't know that at the time, but I later found out that my brothers had paid henchmen to threaten a couple of the miners who wanted to speak out. You see Lieutenant, my family were involved with the Klan. That was another reason they wanted me out, they knew I wanted no part of it. But Eldridge and our father and grandfather before him had been Grand Dragons of the Greenbrier Klan. Knowing Aiden, I wouldn't be surprised if he was involved with it too.'

Charlie glanced across to Sam who was busily taking notes.

'And do you think your brothers used the Klan to threaten those men.'

The old man nodded.

'Almost sure of it. And they were two of our best men. Hardworking decent people. Those thugs threatened their wives and children with violence. So, they kept quiet, they had no choice. It was despicable behaviour and I wanted no part of it. And that Lieutenant, is all I've got to say on the matter.'

Charlie looked across to Sam, the briefest of nods confirmed that he had got all that down.

'I'm grateful for that.' said Charlie standing up. 'But I can't guarantee that I won't need to come back to speak to you again. That will depend on how the enquiry progresses. But before we leave today, I must warn you that I believe your life to be in serious danger. If someone has murdered your brothers there is every reason to believe they might come after you. So, this is a formal notification that I've informed you of that threat.'

The old man sat expressionless not saying anything.

'Perhaps there's another community that you could go to meantime. Somewhere away from here. If that were possible, I would advise it. I believe you would be much safer away from here.'

'I won't be going anywhere.' said the old man shaking his head.

'I'm sorry then. But I don't have the resources to provide you with 24-hour surveillance. We will step up our mobile patrols to ensure that we are regularly passing by and, of course, you can phone us anytime. If you have the slightest suspicion about anything, just pick up the phone and call us and we'll respond immediately.'

'Thank you but that won't be necessary. Whatever transpires will be God's will. I'll place my trust in his hands. So please, save your resources for other things, I know your officers must be busy. I have nothing to fear. But I will pray for you Lieutenant, and you too officer. I'll pray that the good Lord keeps you safe as you go about your work. Now, if you'll excuse me, I have chores to attend to. We are harvesting our bean crop this afternoon. In time to have some for our supper. We have much to be grateful for.'

And with that the old man stood up and left the building.

'I still can't get my head around this.' said Sam. 'He's going to pray for us, but no mention of his murdered brothers. I think that fall out runs deep, very deep, even after all these years.'

Charlie looked at Sam suspiciously.

'You're not suggesting what I think you're suggesting.'

Sam shrugged his shoulders.

'Well he does have a motive. And he clearly hates his brothers and nephew. Can't blame him for that, not if they were running the Klan like he said. But if this was any other enquiry, he would be considered a suspect, wouldn't he? And no need to look at me like that boss, I'm just saying.'

261

Chapter 21

The detectives gathered in the conference room awaiting the arrival of the Chief were in sombre mood. It was now Monday afternoon and they had spent the last day and a half interviewing everyone who had been at the country club at the time Mitchell Lawrence was murdered. They still had interviews to complete, but of the 52 that had so far been spoken to, no one had seen anything remotely suspicious.

Chris had spent all day yesterday trawling through CCTV tapes from the country club's security cameras. He had also viewed the tapes from the Sheetz gas station that was only a quarter of a mile from the entrance to the club. Again nothing. The mysterious figure with the black hat had appeared to have melted into thin air.

The door of the conference room opened, and the Chief walked in wearing a pained expression. His cheeks were flushed, and he appeared to be sweating. He took out his handkerchief and wiped his forehead. He placed a sheet of paper on the lectern and put on his glasses. After a few moments of awkward silence, he started to speak never once making eye contact with his audience.

'I've just had a phone call from Assistant Commissioner Mulroy in Charleston. He's asked me to convey how concerned he is about the murder on

Saturday of Mitchell Lawrence, and of course his brother, Eldridge, who, as you know, was murdered two days earlier in Chicago. The Lawrence family are long-standing friends of the AC, so as you can imagine, he's taking a very keen interest in this case.

Small beads of sweat started to trickle down the side of his temples. Chief Bowater took a sip of water from a glass and dabbed his face again.

'To say the AC was less than impressed with the update I gave him would be an understatement. Having received Lieutenant Finch's briefing note this morning I was hoping I would be able to give him some positive news regarding the state of the enquiry. I accept that it's early days but the fact that we haven't found a single witness, despite there being over 80 members at the country club is disappointing to say the least. You will need to do better as I don't intend to have any more conversations with the AC like the one I've just had. Now Lieutenant Finch.'

'Yes sir.' replied Charlie looking up from his notes.

'I understand from your briefing note that, 'A Threat to Life Warning' has been given to David Lawrence.'

'That's correct sir.'

'But I don't see any mention of the same having been done for Aiden Lawrence. The AC is particularly concerned about him as he's a close personal friend.'

Sam glanced at Ryan who was leaning back in his chair on the other side of the room with his hands in his pockets. The self-satisfied smirk on his face was enough to make Sam want to punch him. There was something of the night about Ryan Mulroy, something, thought Sam, that he probably shared with his uncle. He wouldn't trust Ryan as far as he could throw him.

'I've not had an opportunity to speak to Aiden Lawrence.' replied Charlie. 'He's been away in Chicago sorting out things regarding his father. I've spoken to his son who's told me he's due back sometime today. I'll make a point of visiting him later. He's a lawyer, he'll be well aware of the potential danger he may be in. But I'll certainly issue the warning.'

'And make sure you offer him protection from us. Round the clock if necessary.' said the Chief taking another drink of water.

Heads turned and looked at Charlie. Everyone in the room, with the possible exception of the Chief and Ryan knew that was an impossibility. They didn't have anything like the number of officers that would be required to take on such a responsibility.'

Charlie loosened his tie.

'With respect, sir.'

Angela shifted in her seat expectantly. Oh, good she thought. He's used the 'with respect' line. Angela knew that what was to follow might on the face of it seem respectful, but if she knew Charlie Finch, she knew that the Chief was about to be put firmly in his place.

'I don't think that's either wise or achievable.'

The Chief looked up and glowered at Charlie.

'Oh, you don't.'

'No, I don't, sir. We don't have sufficient resources to offer that level of security. I told David Lawrence much the same thing yesterday. And just as importantly, it wouldn't be sustainable. How long do you envisage us being able to keep him under 24-hour surveillance? A day, a week. Sir, we could be there for months. Once you go down that road there's no turning back. It's very difficult to withdraw the support. And if you do, and then something happens, we would look like fools, and that, sir, would be something I'd be keen to avoid.'

Angela and the others looked on in admiration. The weaselly guy standing at the lectern might not be a leader, but their Lieutenant clearly was, and it was oozing from every pore. It had needed to be said, but at the same time it had been done firmly and diplomatically. Surely even the Chief would see the sense of what Charlie was saying.

'Lieutenant Finch, see me in my office now.'

And with that the Chief was gone. Taking off his glasses he slithered out the door to return to his lair on the top floor.

Charlie shrugged his shoulders and picked up his folder. He left the room without further comment. As to what would now follow, well, that was going to be a matter between him and the Chief.

As the others filed out the conference room Sam held back to have a word with Angela who was still scribbling notes at the back of the room. He wanted to update her about what he'd seen at the bowling alley and of course, tell her about the rope on the back of the truck. He was in the middle of explaining things when Zoe Batchelor stuck her head around the door.

'I'm not interrupting, am I? I know you're busy with the murder enquiry but the lab report about the paint on Sam's garage has come back, I've got it here.'

Zoe handed Angela an orange coloured envelope.

'Thanks Zoe. No, you're fine. Sam was just telling me about an interesting truck he's come across. By the sound of it, it might be the one we're looking for regarding the assault on Ella when those assholes tied her up and towed her through the forest. I'll speak to you later about it, but I'm going to need you to try and match the fibres that we got off Ella's socks with the end of the rope that Sam tells me is still tied to the truck.'

'Sure. That won't be a problem. Just let me now when you're ready to make a move on it and I'll see what I can do.'

'Okay great. Now about this report, it'll need to wait till later as we're up to our eyes in it, but is there anything interesting in it?'

'I think there might be. They've been able to identify the paint. It's a metallic car paint that comes in an aerosol. Made by a company called Hood's. The colour's called Sea Blue. I knew you would be busy, so I phoned Home Depot. They don't stock it. They said it's a specialised type of car paint. They thought our best bet would be a car accessory store. The only one locally I can think of is AutoZone, it's on the corner of, ah, the name of the street has gone right out my head. But it's opposite the train station, you'll know where I mean. I tried phoning them, but it was just ringing out. Anyway, I thought you'd want to know.'

'Appreciate that, Zoe. As I said I'll read the report later. We'll follow up on the AutoZone suggestion, but it might be a while before we can get to it.'

Zoe smiled and closed the door.

'Well that's at least some positive news. Look, I'm going to go and stick the kettle on.' said Sam. 'I expect the boss will be needing one when he gets back from sparring with the Chief. What about you?'

Angela laughed.

'I don't know about him, but I'm definitely needing one. So, stick an extra shot in mine, will you? It'll help spark me up a bit. I feel a bit lethargic. I'm not getting enough sleep these days.'

Chapter 22

There must have been at least a dozen family photographs liberally scattered round the ostentatious front
room of the large sandstone mansion. Aiden Lawrence
looked uncannily like his father. There was just no mistaking the sharp chin and Romanesque nose. Aquiline
and with a prominent bridge, father and son were the
spitting image of each other.

Charlie browsed the photographs while he waited for
Aiden to finish his telephone call. It was abundantly
clear who was the star of the show, Aiden Lawrence was
no shrinking violet. Pictures of him were everywhere.
Several showed him dressed in sportswear, wearing
medals round his neck, or clutching some overly large
and garish trophy, reminiscent of the type you often see
in bars, having been won by the local pool or bowling
team.

Dominating the room was a large oil painting in a
gilded gold frame that hung above the fireplace. The
painting depicted a man, dressed head to foot in white
buckskin leather, fighting hand to hand with a red Indian
who was wielding a knife and naked apart from a loin
cloth and some war paint. The white man appeared to
be getting the upper hand as the Indian's knees were
buckling beneath him as he was being forced to the
ground. The plaque at the bottom of the picture read,

Eldridge Gaylord Lawrence 1st
Battle of Spruce Knob
28th May 1869

'That's my great grandfather.' announced Aiden noticing Charlie studying the picture as he entered the room.

'A bit of a character was old Eldridge. The family have a lot to thank him for. He started the Spruce Knob mine all those years ago, without him I might not have any of this.'

Aiden stood with his arms held wide proudly showing off the trappings of his wealth.

'It's a fine house right enough. But I don't fancy having to cut all that lawn.' said Charlie looking out the bay window. 'There must be acres of it!'

Aiden laughed.

'I've got a man who does that for me. Well, two men actually. Anyway, I expect you haven't come to talk to me about gardening. Am I right Lieutenant?'

Charlie nodded.

'First of all, can I pass on my condolences about your father and, of course, your uncle. That was quite shocking. It must have been a difficult week for your family.'

'That is an understatement. But yes, it's been a dreadful week. And putting my lawyer's head on, I suppose you've come to warn me that I might now be in some danger. In my profession I've been down this road many times before. But that was with clients who've found themselves in a similar position? So, I expect you've come to warn me, and of course to tell me that you can't guarantee my safety as you haven't got the resources to protect me. That's how it goes isn't it Lieutenant?'

'Well something like that, yes.'

Aiden smiled and sat down on a green velvet chaise-lounge that was standing in front of the French windows.

'No need to look so sheepish. I understand how this works, I'm a lawyer after all. We all need to cover our asses at times.'

Charlie wasn't quite sure how he should respond to that.

'And what about dad's youngest brother, my uncle? You know the God bothering one up in Huntersville. But perhaps you've already spoken to him. Surely he must be as much at risk as I am.'

'Yes, sir I spoke to your uncle while you were away in Chicago. It won't surprise you I'm sure to hear that he's not going to move from the community. In fact, he's not going to do anything differently to protect himself. He believes whatever happens will be God's will. He was remarkably sanguine about the whole situation if I'm honest.'

'I wouldn't expect anything different from him. I haven't set eyes on him for more than ten years and I'm fine with that. I phoned him out of courtesy to tell him about my father. But that's as far as that will go. I don't regard him as part of the family anymore and I'll guarantee another thing, he won't be attending either of his brothers' funerals, because I won't be asking him.'

'Well that's a decision for you and your family, it's not for me to make comment. But I do have to formally warn you that I believe, given the circumstances, that your life may be in danger. And as a lawyer you'll know that I'll have to formally record that we have had this conversation.'

'Fine. Now will there be anything else? I've got a load of things to be getting on with.'

'Just to say that we will give your house some extra attention. You'll see more mobile patrols in the area, and we'll respond promptly should you report anything suspicious.'

Aiden guffawed sarcastically.

'It's not just gardeners I have at my disposal Lieutenant, I'll be calling in a few favours from some friends, a little bit of added security if you like. But I'll tell you one thing, it's my birthday this Saturday and a group of us are going mountain biking. I won't be cancelling that. I'll be about the oldest there, but I'll be the first down the damned mountain. You don't get to be a winner coming second as you can see from the photographs.'

'Yep, that's quite a collection of trophies you've got there, puts my cycling proficiency badge to shame, but there you go.' said Charlie sardonically.

Chapter 23

Saturday 25th September.

The Greenbrier Chair Lift Company had only been operating for little more than a year. Historically, there had been no skiing in West Virginia as the mountains in the Allegheny range weren't particularly high and snow fall was at best inconsistent. But it was the boom in mountain biking that led many to believe that erecting a chairlift was a viable project.

It could take bikers to the summit of Greenbrier mountain from where they could follow a myriad of trails, of varying degrees of difficulty, back to the bottom. If there then happened to be some decent snow during the winter months, then that would be a bonus and the chairlift could ferry skiers up the mountain to enjoy some winter sport.

The chairlift was the first venture of its kind anywhere in the state, and Aiden Lawrence had been part of a group of investors who had put their own money into developing the project. That now brought certain privileges, as today for Aiden's birthday, the chairlift company had agreed to open early, in order that he and his friends could get exclusive use of the lift and cycle runs, before it opened to the public at nine.

So, they were up early, and if all went to plan, they would have already managed several runs by the time the public were allowed access.

They were about to start loading their bikes onto the specially adapted chairs when Aiden noticed his front tyre was flat.

'Ah, shit.' said Aiden examining his tyre. 'There it is there. A fucking great tack sticking out the side of the tyre. Look, you guys go ahead, and I'll meet you up there. I've got a spare wheel in the back of the truck. I just wasn't expecting to have to use it so soon. It'll not take five minutes to change, I'll see you up there.'

His friends were reluctant to leave him, but Aiden was insistent, and they knew from experience not to question him a second time. So, they loaded their bikes and climbed onto the chairlift. By the time Aiden had changed his wheel, he could just about see the others in the distance as they approached the summit.

Aiden lifted his bike onto the rack at the back of the chair and got on the lift. It was just after seven and the early morning chill was still in the air, but by the look of the blue sky it promised to be another glorious day. His chair swung slightly as it caught the breeze as it soared above the tops of the conifer trees. Underneath, a creek ran slowly over smooth boulders and jagged rocks. A chipmunk, happily sunning itself on a tree stump, darted for cover as the chair clunked over the metal stanchion. The next section was the steepest, and the chair slowed to a snail's pace as it crept its way up the mountain.

At first Aiden wasn't sure what it was. He had heard a whistling sound hurtling passed his ears. What the hell was it? There was no mistaking the second sound.

A loud metallic clang as the crossbow bolt ricocheted off the metal pole that connected the chair to the cable.

'What the fuck.' shouted Aiden turning around to see the dark clothed figure in the chair behind levelling the crossbow for a third shot.

'Oh God, what the fuck man. For God's sake don't shoot. What is it you want? Please I beg you, don't shoot.' screamed Aiden throwing his hands up in surrender.

The dark figure in the black hat spoke calmly.

'You've got five seconds to decide. You can take your chances and jump, or you'll be shot. Your choice, you decide.'

Aiden stared at the ravine below. It must be at least a thirty-foot drop.

The figure behind started to count.

'One, two, three ...'

*

Back at the incident room, the enquiry team were hard at work. Saturday was just another working day. If they were lucky, they might get Sunday off, but that would depend on how the enquiry was progressing, and if today was anything like the first few days a day off seemed a remote prospect.

They still hadn't turned up a single piece of evidence. The only positive bit of news was confirmation from the lab that the feather found in Mitchell Lawrence's mouth had come from a canary. Charlie had called Mike in Chicago to update him about that. As it happened, Mike had been about to phone Charlie with the same news. Their Lab was now confirming that the feather they had recovered had also come from a canary.

Charlie gathered the detectives around the whiteboard to go over the actions for the day that Angela had spent the last half hour writing up.

'Okay, so everyone understands that both victims were found with canary feathers in their mouths. There must be a reason why our killer put them there. When you're out and about today I want you to ask everyone you're speaking to about canaries. Who owns one? Has anyone been seen with one? You all know the script.'

There was a murmur of acknowledgement from all those present.

'Sam, Chris, I want you to check the train and bus stations. Then every bar in the town. And that includes Fairlea and White Sulphur Springs. I want to know if anyone's seen our mysterious man in the black hat. And check their CCTV tapes for last Saturday. Sergeant Brown has a handout with the material times highlighted. And Ryan, I want you to contact the state penitentiary and every other penal facility in the state. I want the names of all those released from prison this year. We might well have to widen that search but let's start local. Then check the database for crimes of violence. I want printouts and photos of every released prisoner with previous for violence by end of play today. Clear?'

Everyone nodded.

'Well don't just sit there, let's get our asses into gear and get out there.'

Chris turned to Sam who was searching the desk for car keys.

'Do you think he's feeling the pressure, the boss I mean? Never seen him so jumpy. Perhaps the Chief's paranoia is getting to him.'

'Nah. That's just a warning shot across the bows for lazy guys like Ryan. That's all that was.'

An hour later Sam and Chris were grabbing a quick coffee at the kiosk outside the train station. They had spoken to the station manager and checked their CCTV for the material times. But they had found nothing. There was no one remotely fitting the description that they could see. The station manager was going to speak to all his staff and get back to them, but neither detective was pinning much hope that it would turn anything up.

Sam looked across the street to the store on the opposite corner.

'I'm just going to nip into AutoZone for a minute while we're here. It shouldn't take long. I've got an enquiry I could kill. You sit and finish your coffee, as I said I won't be a minute.'

There were no other customers in the store when Sam walked in. A ruddy faced man in his forties was behind the counter reading the sports pages of the local paper. He peered at Sam over the top of his glasses.

'Can I help you?'

'I'm hoping you can.' replied Sam taking his police badge from his pocket. 'I'm trying to track down a particular make of paint as part of an enquiry I've got. It's made by a company called Hood's, I believe it comes in a spray can, I'm told it's a specialist car paint.'

The man behind the counter nodded and pointed to the far wall where a rack of aerosol cans were displayed.

'That's them over there. Is there a particular colour you're after?'

The man came out from the counter and met Sam by the rack.

'Yeah, it's called Sea Blue, it's an aquamarine colour and it's got sparkly flecks of gold through it.'

'Not one of our better sellers.' said the man perusing the rows of cannisters. 'But yep, there's a couple here. In fact, I think they're the only ones I've got. Not the most popular colour so no point in holding a lot of stock.'

'Would you happen to know if you've sold any recently?' asked Sam.

'I can check that, but I must have sold at least one. I would never only order two cans. Three maybe, but never just two. If you give me a minute, I can check my receipts. If it was purchased within the last month then the receipt should still be in the office. If it was before that I may have taken it home. I do my bookkeeping in the evening at home. Find it easier that way. I'm in the process of moving everything onto the computer. The old type of bookkeeping will soon be a thing of the past.'

Sam waited at the counter as the man searched a filing cabinet in the back office. He returned a few minutes later carrying a receipt.

'My filing system can't be as bad as I thought it was.' said the man handing Sam the receipt.

'I seem to have sold one about three weeks ago. The guy who bought it paid with a credit card. But he's signed the bottom of the receipt. It's difficult to make out but it looks like Ryan somebody to me. It could be Mulhany, it's something like that.'

Sam starred at the signature on the receipt. He recognised it straight away. He had seen it often enough on the bottom of police reports. It was Ryan Mulroy's signature.

*

Charlie was in his office looking at the photographs and autopsy report of Mitchell Lawrence's murder that Zoe had brought up earlier that morning. It was gruesome stuff. The crossbow bolt had been fired from only a few feet away. It had penetrated both his lung and heart. He would have died almost instantly according to the pathologist.

The phone on his desk rang, it was Sergeant Lang from the front office.

'Gordon, what can I do for you?'

Charlie knew straight away from the tone of Gordon's voice that something was up.

'Boss, I think you're going to want to get over to the chairlift on Greenbrier mountain straight away. Sergeant Joice and a couple of uniforms are there now. We had a report that someone had fallen onto rocks from the chairlift. Sergeant Joice is now reporting that it's Aiden Lawrence and he's dead.'

For a moment Charlie didn't say anything as he tried to gather his thoughts. Shit, not another one. Numerous thoughts and scenarios swamped his head as his brain went into overdrive. Are we certain it was him? Was it an accident? Had he somehow just fallen? Did he have a crossbow bolt in his back? He shook himself to bring himself back to his senses. He needed to be thinking clearly. Now was not the time to be panicking. Panicking never resolved anything.

'Do we know if he's been shot?' asked Charlie calmly.

'We don't think so. Well not in the back anyway. Steve said there's no sign of a crossbow bolt. It looks like he's fallen and smashed his head on rocks. Steve says he's got a massive head trauma.'

'I take it Steve is protecting the locus at the moment?'

'So I understand. They've closed the lift down and got everyone they can into the reception area at the bottom but it's a bit chaotic as you'd expect. He says there are quite a few cyclists still out on the mountain. I've got two other patrol cars en route to give him a hand. Do you want me to get him to phone you?'

'No need. Get a message to him that I'm on my way. I'll be with him in half an hour. I'll get a full update from him then. Oh, and one last thing, nobody phones the Chief. We've got enough on our plate without him going off on one.'

'Roger, that's all noted boss.'

Charlie stuck his head round his door and shouted down the corridor.

'Angela, Angela my office now.'

Angela stepped into the corridor.

'What's up? Not like you to be shouting instructions.'

Charlie rushed along the corridor trying to get his arm into his jacket.

'Grab your folder and car keys. We're heading to Greenbrier mountain; Aiden Lawrence is lying in a ravine with his head smashed in. Looks like we've got our third murder.'

*

Sam and Chris had now made their way across town to the bus garage. The bars wouldn't be open for another couple of hours so they thought they would concentrate their efforts on the transport hubs. Of course, the killer could turn out to be local, but if they weren't, then they must have got to the area somehow.

On the drive across town Sam started to explain what he'd discovered about the paint and the truck that he'd seen at the bowling alley the other day. Chris was an experienced detective and a good friend. Sam trusted him implicitly. He wanted his opinion on what he'd found out.

'At the moment none of that proves anything. The truck and the rope sounds promising though. And I would agree that it all appears mighty suspicious. But I'd tread carefully if I were you. You don't want to be throwing about accusations about a colleague without being 100% certain. You might end up getting your fingers burnt. When you get the chance sit down with Angela and explain what you've got. Don't go running to Charlie just yet. He's got enough on his plate with the Lawrence enquiry. And anyway, Angela is the investigating officer in both those cases, so, I'd make sure that you tell her first. That would be my advice.'

'Yeah, you're right.' said Sam parking up at the side of the bus depot. 'It's just so frustrating. I understand the murder enquiry must take priority, but there are arrests to be made and cases we could solve. I'm itching to give those sons of a bitch the jail.'

'It'll happen. You're just going to have to be patient. Now where do you think the manager's office is?'

'If it's the manager you're looking for then I'm afraid he's not in.' said a lady filing her nails in the ticket office. 'You're not the police, are you? I mean proper detectives like you see on the T.V. Because you look like them, it's the suits you see.'

Sam smiled and nodded. That had done his ego no harm at all. Somebody thought he looked like a detective. He must be doing something right for a change.

Chris produced his badge and explained why they were there.

279

'Well you might want to try the canteen. You'll get some of the drivers up there having their break before they start their next run. One of them might be able to help you.'

Five drivers were sat around a table at the far end of the canteen playing cards when Sam and Chris walked in. They sat and listened politely as Chris explained why they were there. When he was finished the drivers shook their heads and muttered. Nobody seemed to know anything. They were about to deal another hand when Sam butted in.

'You didn't mention the canaries. Sorry, but my colleague here forgot to say that we're interested in anyone who might have a canary. You know either as a pet or perhaps it could be someone who breeds them and keeps them in an aviary.'

The bald-headed driver sitting at the end of the table put down his cards and looked up.

'You said canaries.'

Sam nodded.

'And the guy you're interested in wore a dark hat.'

'Yep, that's correct.'

'In that case it sounds like the guy I dropped off at Spruce Knob a couple of weeks back. Leroy's friend. He wore a black fedora and had a cage full of canaries with him. I remember thinking it was bizarre. Who goes climbing in the mountains with a cage full of birds!'

Sam looked at Chris and raised his eyebrows. Finally, they might be getting somewhere. This sounded like it could be their man.

'I'll come back to the birds.' said Sam taking out his notebook. 'But firstly, who's Leroy?'

'Leroy's a colleague of ours.' replied the man. 'I think the guy you're describing was staying with him for a few days. If he were here, he could confirm that for you but he's on vacation just now, I think he's away to visit his mother but don't ask me where she stays as I haven't a clue. Check with Cindy in the office, she might know.'

'I'll do that thanks. But what can you tell me about the guy in the hat with the canaries?'

The bus driver took a sip of his coffee.

'I remember thinking he seemed like a really decent guy. He was polite, respectful even. I'd say he was around my age, maybe a bit younger and he had dark skin, ruddy, reddish coloured skin. He looked like an Indian if I'm honest. And he wore a black fedora hat. That's all I can remember about what he was wearing.'

'And what about the canaries. What can you tell me about them?'

'Nothing really except that they were in a large cage. Maybe four or five of them. Bright yellow they were.'

'Did he say where he was going with the birds.'

The bus driver shook his head.

'I don't think he really said where he was going. I dropped him at the path that leads to the mountain and we joked about him climbing it. But thinking about it now, he could have been going to one the farms, there are several in that area. I don't recall him saying where he was going. And that's about it. I don't think there's much more I can tell you.'

Sam put down his notebook.

'Look, can I take your name and contact details just now. I'm going to need to follow up and take a proper statement from you, but that can be done later. But what you've told us is going to be most useful, so thanks for that.'

The bus driver shrugged his shoulders.

'Sure whatever. Happy to help. But I'm not off till six and then it's my pool night at Ruby's. I'm off tomorrow and late shift Monday, but I'll be around in the morning.'

Sam smiled.

'I'll be in touch, but I'll bear that in mind. I'll make sure it's not tonight, I don't want to disrupt your pool night.'

'Well that's good news. We're playing Bursley's tonight. Bit of a local derby, I wouldn't want to miss that.'

Chapter 24

Forty minutes after leaving the office, Charlie and Angela had arrived at Greenbrier mountain. Having walked the first section along one of the cycle trails they now had no choice other than to scramble up the ravine as the path they were on was about to take them in completely the wrong direction. There appeared no other way of getting to the locus. It was far from ideal. The ground was steep and uneven, and they certainly weren't dressed for the terrain.

'Well that was damned stupid wasn't it? It's the sort of thing I'd criticise others about. And look at me. These shoes will be ruined by the time we get up to Steve.'

Charlie had forgotten to grab his boots as he'd left the office in such a hurry. He was now paying the penalty. His leather soled shoes had next to no purchase as he scrambled over rocks and damp boulders trying not to slip or get his feet wet in the creek that ran down from the top of the mountain.

'You think you've got problems! Try getting up there in these suede loafers. I think I'll bill you 'cause they're are going to be wrecked. And the pair of us must look ridiculous.' exclaimed an unimpressed Angela. 'But I've got an excuse because I didn't know where we were going. You've got none, you knew we were heading up a damned mountain!'

They could now see Sergeant Joice in the distance. As they paused to catch their breath Charlie glanced above him. The cable car was stationary. From where he was standing, Charlie estimated that the drop from the chair to the rocks below must be the best part of forty feet. You'd have next to no chance of surviving a fall if you fell onto rocks from that height.

By the time they reached where the body was lying, they were shattered.

'Are you pair Okay? You look knackered.' asked a somewhat bemused Steve. 'When I noticed you climbing up the ravine, I wondered what the hell you were up to. You would have been better following the blue trail and coming down from up there. That's what I did.'

Sergeant Joice pointed up the slope towards a chair-lift stanchion.

'The path's only a couple of hundred yards from here, it's just beyond the stanchion. When I looked at the map it seemed the obvious way to get to here.'

Angela who was still trying to catch her breath shook her head in despair.

'A map. You had a fucking map!'

'Yeah. I picked it up from reception. And guess what, they had hundreds of them.' Steve started to laugh.

Angela was on the point of punching someone.

'Boss, we've got forty years police service between us and we didn't think to pick up a frigging map.'

Charlie sighed and smiled weakly.

'I know, I know, and we're supposed to be the detectives, I expect we won't hear the end of this. But that can keep. What can you tell us Steve, any idea what happened?'

The three colleagues were standing on top of a large boulder. About ten feet below the body of a man was lying on its side wedged between some jagged rocks. Most of the left side of the man's head had been caved in, congealed blood and bits of tissue were clearly visible on the rock next to it.

'I wouldn't recommend trying to get down dressed like that.' said Steve. 'Those rocks are real slippery. I've been down and had a look. Other than the trauma to his head I couldn't see any other injuries. I mean he doesn't appear to have been shot. He'll have broken bones from the fall for sure, but I couldn't find any evidence that he'd been shot.'

Charlie nodded.

'Witnesses? Do we know if he was on his own when he fell?'

'No eye witnesses. It appears he had gone back for a spare wheel while his friends headed up the mountain. They waited for him, but he never arrived. Just the chair he'd been on with his bike still strapped on the back arrived at the top station. That's when his friends raised the alarm.'

'And who found him?' asked Angela.

'One of the staff went up on the lift when the alarm was raised. He saw him lying in the ravine. He radioed back and then they called us. I've got the boy's details. You can get a word with him at reception. He's just a young lad and a bit shaken up understandably.'

'And what about his friends, where are they now?' asked Charlie.

Steve took off his cap and scratched his head.

'Well some of them are down at the reception area.'

'Some of them. What do you mean some of them?' asked Angela suspiciously.

'It would appear that some of them have disappeared.'

'Disappeared! How the hell did that happen?'

'Hey, don't have a go at me. There was only me and two uniform cops up until you two arrived. We can't be everywhere. We had to check he was dead for a start and then try and get everyone off the mountain and into the café in reception. It was like herding cats, not easy, so cut us a bit of slack. We were doing our best.'

'Yep. That's enough Angela. No need to have a pop at Steve. Just think of the help he's given us these last few weeks. Let's not make things more difficult than they already are.'

'Apologies Steve. I think I'm just frustrated. I didn't mean to have a go at you or your officers.'

'No need to apologise. I remember how stressful these enquiries can get. But we are all here just trying to do our best. Now about the witnesses, I did notice something that will interest you both.'

'Go on we're listening.' said Charlie.

'Well it was a long way off, but I'm sure as I was making my way down to the body, I saw Riley Muntz arrive in the parking lot. He walks funny and is so fat he's difficult to mistake. Anyway, four or five of the guys that were milling about in the parking area got into his truck and they drove away. Suggested to me that they didn't want to be hanging around when the police arrived.'

'Huh,' said Charlie who was leaning against a boulder removing a stone from his shoe. 'Sounds suspicious right enough. And you're sure it was Riley Muntz?'

'It certainly looked like him and it was a cream coloured GMC truck.'

Angela's ears pricked up.

'Sam was just speaking to me about a GMC truck that colour in connection to the assault on Ella. He said he'd seen it at the bowling alley. But I'm sure he told me the registered keeper's name and it wasn't Riley Muntz. I'm sure it was a female name, sounded Italian if I remember right.'

Steve nodded.

'That would be one Rita Garavelli. She's shacked up with Muntz. God knows what she sees in him. He must have a fat wallet as well as a fat belly. I've stopped that truck before. Several times. It is registered to her and has all its docs, but it seems that every man jack drives it. Been a different driver each time I've stopped it.'

Charlie turned and looked back down towards the parking lot.

'Hmm, intriguing. I wonder who Muntz was picking up?'

'I might be able to help again with that. I'm not certain, because he passed me so quickly, but when I was walking up here, I'm sure Linton Webb went past me on a bike. And if it were him, there's every chance that Perry Blackley and the Sill brothers would have been around too. Those shysters are hardly ever apart.'

Angela raised her eyebrows.

'If it were Webb then I'd say that was very likely. But how does any of that tie in with Aiden Lawrence? Surely, they weren't part of his group! They come from completely different ends of the social spectrum for a start. That doesn't make any sense to me.'

'I know, me neither. But from what I can understand the chairlift was only open for Lawrence and his friends. It was his birthday apparently. People were just

287

beginning to arrive when we got here as the lift doesn't open to the public till nine. So that suggests that everyone on the mountain was part of Lawrence's group. I know it's weird, it doesn't seem to stack up.'

Charlie puffed out his cheeks.

'What a thing to happen on your birthday. That's three members of the Lawrence family dead. And all within ten days of each other.'

It was a sombre thought.

'I've got something else I want to show you.' said Steve scrambling down from the boulder. If you come this way, it's a little less steep.'

Charlie and Angela followed Steve till he came to a stop near to the stanchion. The chair in front of them was less that fifteen feet above them. It was the chair that Aiden had been sitting on before he fell. It still had his bike attached to the back of the chair. The front bar of the chair was hanging free.

'I wondered if the bar being like that meant that it had somehow worked loose. Perhaps this could have been a tragic accident after all. Especially as it doesn't appear that he's been shot.' said Steve.

'Could be.' said Angela looking at the chair. Charlie didn't say anything, he just stood staring up at the chair for several moments. Then he walked further up the hill and stared at the next chair. He then turned and looked at the chair on the other side of the lift that was facing down the mountain.

'He's up to something whispered Angela. I can always tell. You can almost hear the cogs in his brain turning. What are you thinking boss?'

Charlie came back down and joined his colleagues.

'Take a look at the pole which attaches to the cable. There do you see it? about four feet above the height of the handlebars.'

Angela and Steve stared up at the pole.

'I can see a large dent on the left-hand side as we look at it.' explained Steve. 'I didn't notice that before. Good spot Lieutenant.'

'Yeah, that's quite a dent and its chipped the paint.' agreed Angela.

'But if you look at the other chairs, they all appear pristine, there's not a mark on any of them, the paintwork's almost perfect. In fact, if it wasn't for the dent this one would be the same. There's not another scratch on it.' explained Charlie.

'Okay.' said Angela, 'go on.'

'Well, I think I would agree with what Steve said. He hasn't been shot. But I've got a feeling he was being shot at. Somebody was firing at him. Probably from the chair behind. I reckon that dent has been caused by a crossbow bolt ricocheting off the bar. He could have been fired on more than once. That's what I think caused him to fall, or perhaps I should say jump. He either stayed where he was and risked getting shot or he took his chances and jumped.'

'That's brilliant, Charlie.' said Steve. 'I reckon you could well be right. And look, the distance between each chair is what? No more than fifty feet I'd say. Easily within range of a crossbow bolt.'

Angela looked a little sceptical.

'Just one thing. If someone was firing shots from behind him, why didn't Lawrence's friends who were waiting at the top see the attacker? The chair would have taken him right past them.'

'It would have unless he jumped off. The chair can only be about twelve feet above the ground when it passes the path up there. I've been up and had a look. And if you lowered yourself down and held onto the foot bar, the drop would only be about six feet. I don't think it would be much of a problem getting off.'

'Yeah, well I suppose.' said Angela thinking over what Charlie had said.

'Okay, back to the theory. If he was being shot at then we know where he fell. But we can't say for certain where the assailant fired the shots from, but where that dent on the pole is, it must be somewhere below the body. If we could find a bolt, then we could prove your theory. Worth having a quick look just now. The ground's quite open either side of the creek. You never know, we might get lucky.' said Steve who was already scanning the ground.'

'Good idea.' replied Charlie. 'But if we're going to do this then let's try and do it properly. Let's do a line search headed down the mountain. It's possible the bolt could have gone past the body and ended up on the slope somewhere up there. That being the case let's start, say, by that big boulder up there and work our way down. And give yourself ten feet or so either side of each other and let's make sure we move at the same speed, so make it slow.'

After ten minutes of methodical searching they had managed to cover a couple of hundred feet of the ravine. Then, quite suddenly there was a loud shriek. Angela had spotted something.

'Yesss. Oh, you little beauty. Guys,' she shouted excitedly. 'Look at that conifer tree over there.'

Angela pointed to a line of trees over to her right.

'You're smarter than the average bear Lieutenant Finch. Can you see it? The tree in the middle, the biggest one. There's a crossbow bolt in the trunk about twenty feet up. I think it must have deflected off the pole. Old Trevor Wilks was right enough Steve. Always remember to look up!'

Chapter 25

In his office at the university, Professor Foulis was feeling agitated. He had just watched the evening news and now he felt quite sick. There could be no mistake. The detective describing the man he wanted to trace in connection to the murder of three members of the Lawrence family was Chaska. The ruddy complexion, dark clothing and black fedora hat. Add to that his knowledge of the Lawrence family. It just couldn't be anyone else.

Professor Foulis's heart sank. He was struggling to believe that Chaska would do such a thing. It had been less than a month since they'd been drinking coffee with Lilian in this very room. He was torn as to what he should do. He had an obligation to contact the police, but first he wanted to speak to Lilian. If she didn't already know, then this news would come as a complete shock. She would be devastated.

Lilian answered the phone almost immediately. She wasn't her usual breezy self. The professor could tell that she already knew the distressing news. Her voice was trembling; she was clearly distraught.

'No professor, really there's no need to apologise. If you hadn't phoned me then I would have contacted you. I saw the broadcast; I just can't believe it. It's such a shock. You were with me when we were speaking with him. He seemed relaxed and in control. I never for one minute expected this.'

'There's still hope Lilian. Just because they are looking for him as a suspect, doesn't prove he murdered anybody. So please, try and stay positive. It doesn't mean it was Chaska.'

Lilian scoffed cynically.

'No of course it doesn't, but I'm afraid I don't have much faith in our justice system. If he's apprehended, then that's it, you might as well throw away the key. He won't have a hope of getting a fair trial. Look what happened to him the last time.'

'Look Lilian, you don't need to answer this question, so if I'm sticking my nose into somewhere it shouldn't be please tell me. But I was wondering if he's contacted you. It's been more than three weeks, I just thought he might have been in touch, just to let you know how he was.'

There was a deep and resigned sigh at the end of the phone.

'I got a letter from him. It arrived yesterday. It's the only contact I've had. He'd told me his foster mum, Carole Hicks, remember the lady we told you he was going to visit, had died. It was quite unexpected. He said he'd got to see her before she passed away which I suppose was a blessing, but that would have upset him, I know he had been close to her.'

'That's most unfortunate and very sad. But did he say anything else, was there any suggestion that he might go and do something stupid, like killing three members of the Lawrence family?'

'No, honestly, there was nothing threatening about the letter. He did mention the Lawrences, but only in the

293

context of finding out information that could be used against them in a court case. He was telling me how he'd been able to use his librarian's skills to research an old archive that plotted the Lawrences time as owners of the Spruce Knob coal mine. He said he'd found out loads of interesting things that might help in any subsequent prosecution against them. But there was no suggestion that he was going to harm anyone. Quite the opposite. It was very measured. It was what I'd expect from the man I'd got to know.'

'Okay. That does all sound pretty normal. But I think we have to contact the police. I don't really think we've got a choice. I'll do it if you like as I know how difficult this is for you. But we've got a responsibility to tell them what we know. But that's it, nothing more. I'll phone them tonight and try and get to speak to the Lieutenant who was doing the broadcast. I'd expect they'll want to come and see us and take a statement. And I'm pretty sure they'll want a look at that letter. I'm just so sorry about all of this Lilian, I know how close you are to Chaska. But in the circumstances, I don't think there's anything else we can do.'

*

It was 0800 hrs on Monday morning and Charlie had gathered all the team involved in the Lawrence enquiry in the incident room for a briefing. There had been lots of developments over the weekend, not least of which was the death of Aiden Lawrence. Charlie had spent the last half hour with Chief Bowater in his office. He was a broken man. Assistant Commissioner Mulroy had telephoned him at home immediately he'd heard the news of his friend's death. He'd shouted and hurled

294

abuse at the Chief and threatened him with demotion and a return to some meaningless job pushing paper in a cupboard at police Headquarters. According to Bowater, the AC had been incandescent with rage.

The Chief was now a bag of nerves and reluctant to leave his office. The stress of this latest death had caused his eczema to return with a vengeance. His face and neck were covered in an angry red rash which understandably, he didn't want anybody to see. Bowater was at his wit's end and worried sick that the killings hadn't finished. There was still one Lawrence brother alive. Charlie had done his best to reassure the Chief that he didn't believe he would be a target for the murderer. If he was going to be, the killer would have struck by now.

David Lawrence would have been easy pickings. He had been put his trust in God and had been going about his daily business as normal, he wasn't trying to hide away. Anyway, as Charlie had tried to explain, there were only three dolls in the box found at the mine. If the killer was going to strike again there would have been four. Of course, Charlie didn't know that for certain, nobody could know for certain, but he had a gut feeling that the killer wasn't interested in David Lawrence.

His focus now had to be on catching the murderer. And for the first time since the enquiry began, Charlie felt like he was making progress. It felt like the net was slowly closing in on the killer.

'Okay everyone, pay attention. I want to start today with an update on the autopsy that's been carried out on Aiden Lawrence. The cause of death was a massive trauma to the head consistent with falling onto rocks from height. Death would have been almost instant.

And I can tell you that unlike Mitchell Lawrence, there was no feather found in his mouth and his hands hadn't been painted red. Neither of those things are a surprise given the circumstances of his death. Anybody got any questions.'

Everyone shook their heads.

'Alright moving on then, I want to mention a couple of positive developments in the enquiry. Firstly, we are indebted to Dave Richardson and his team who have once again pulled out all the stops. Dave has completed his examination of the crossbow bolt that was discovered in a tree near to the spot where Aiden Lawrence was found. Paint recovered from the tip is consistent with the paint from the pole of the chair we know that Lawrence was sitting on just before he died. There can be no doubt that someone was trying to shoot Aiden Lawrence. Folks, we are now looking for a triple killer.'

A murmur of approval swept round the room.

'Furthermore, and as a result of some good work by Ryan, we have been able to confirm the identity of the person who is now our prime suspect. Most of you will have seen my broadcast and appeal last night. About an hour after that broadcast I took a call from a Professor Foulis, who works at Carnegie Mellon University in Pittsburgh. He told me that he and a friend had recently had dealings with a man fitting the description of our suspect. That conversation has corroborated other information that we have recently obtained from a bus driver and several other witnesses from the local area. Consequently, I am now in a position to confirm our suspect's identity.

I believe the person we are looking for is,

Charles Walker (58) D.O.B, 17.11.35. AKA Chas or Chaska. A native American who now identifies as a member of the Shawnee tribe.

'Ryan, bring up the slide.'

Ryan pressed the keyboard and a picture of a man dressed in prison uniform appeared on the screen.

Charlie continued.

'Walker was convicted of the murder of his foster father in 1952. He was released a month ago from the State Penitentiary in Moundsville having served 41 years of his life sentence. He has a history of violence during his incarceration. From what the professor was able to tell me last night, Walker has a connection to the Lawrence family and we now know that he travelled here to visit one of his former foster parents who was in hospital in Fairlea. That lady has subsequently died.

Sergeant Brown will brief you separately about those circumstances as there are several actions that will need following up on as a matter of urgency. But before she does that, I want to mention an intelligence gap that we have identified that I need your help with. We are trying to establish a link between Aiden Lawrence and Riley Muntz, Linton Webb, Perry Blackley and the Sill brothers. There is nothing on our systems about it, but we believe there is a connection. We need to establish what that connection is.

Sergeant Joice is sure that he saw Linton Webb on one of the cycle trails the morning Aiden Lawrence died. And several men were then seen getting into a truck that we know Riley Muntz uses. At the moment, these men aren't suspected of being involved in the death of Aiden Lawrence, but we are keen to establish what their link to him is. They may well be involved in other forms of criminal activity.

'And lastly,' continued Charlie, 'there is a separate briefing note for you to collect regarding the cream coloured GMC truck that we know Muntz and others have access to. All the details are on the note so pick one up and read it. I want to emphasise that I don't want the vehicle stopped at this stage, but I want reports of any sightings and, more importantly, confirmation of who else has been using the vehicle. Is that clear?'

Sam watched as Ryan Mulroy, who was sitting at the front of the room next to the computer, opened his folder and wrote something down. Strange thought Sam. He'd not written anything else down during the briefing, what was he up to?

After Angela had allocated the actions, the detectives drifted away to begin their enquiries. Sam stayed behind until Ryan had left the room. He then followed him along the corridor and lingered at the door of the general office pretending to be reading the briefing note. He watched as Ryan returned to his desk and immediately lifted the phone. He spun his chair, so he had his back to his colleagues. He spoke in hushed tones. Who the hell is he speaking to? Sam was suspicious. Ryan was up to something; he just didn't know what. Then a thought occurred to him, he'd had an idea. He bounded down the stairs to the front office. He wanted a word with Sergeant Lang.

Gordon was checking custody records when Sam walked in.

'Have you got a minute?' asked Sam sitting down at a desk.

'Sure, shoot. What's on your mind?'

'Itemised phone bills. Do we get them for the office? I'm sure I read a memo about it, but that was yonks ago, so are they still a thing?'

'Oh yes.' said Gordon peering over the top of his glasses. 'It's the bane of my life. They come in at the end of every month and I have to check them all before they get sent to the Chief. Wouldn't be the first time we've had a large bill because someone has spent hours on the phone to their bookie. It's my job to make sure there's no inappropriate stuff going on. But it takes me a whole morning to check the damned thing. There are a lot of phones in this office.'

The slightest of smiles creased Sam's mouth, he might just be onto something.

'So, would you be able to tell what calls have been made from what phone in the office?'

'Absolutely, that's why it takes so damned long to check. Every call that is made from each extension is recorded. And it's broken down by the number that was called, the duration of the call and the time and date it was made.'

Sam was now grinning like a Cheshire cat.

'What are you looking so pleased about? Wait till you have to check them, it's a complete pain in the butt.'

'I'll tell you later, but just to confirm you said the next one is due at the end of the month?'

'That's what I said.'

'And all calls made this month will be on that return?'

Gordon sighed wearily.

'Yep, every damned one.'

*

It had been another long day. Sam and Chris and had been tasked with checking all the farmsteads that were

299

located within a two-mile radius of Spruce Knob mountain. There were twelve of them in total and they were spread out around the base of the mountain. They had spent the last nine hours trekking round all of them, and like a lot of police work, it had proved to be fruitless and frustrating. They had been given a recent photograph of their suspect to show people, but all they had received back were blank faces. Nobody had seen anyone matching the description in the area. It had been another unproductive day.

It was quarter to eight by the time they got back to the office. Only Angela, who was busy updating the action log was still at her desk. Even Charlie had gone home for the night. Chris gave Angela their return and put on his jacket.

'Are you meeting Ella tonight? asked Chris.

'Not tonight.' replied Sam. 'She's doing a weights class at the gym; I won't see her till tomorrow.'

'In that case do you fancy a beer on the way home. Just a quick one, it's an early start again tomorrow.'

Sam tilted his head and pulled a face.

'I'd love to but I'm sorry, I can't manage tonight. I've something on that I can't really get out of. Next time maybe.'

Chris snorted ironically.

'Not a problem, it can't be helped, but who knows when the next time will be. If today is anything to go by, it might be a while before we track down our man.'

The two friends chatted as they walked across the rear yard to their vehicles. Sam made sure that Chris had left before he drove away. He had somewhere to go and for now he didn't want Chris or anyone else to know what he was up to. He was starving, so he picked up a KFC as he headed out along the Fairlea road. A couple of miles further down the highway he pulled into the layby across the road from the bowling alley. He was in luck. The GMC truck was parked on the far side of the parking lot near the perimeter fence. The car lot was quiet, half a dozen cars and a dilapidated old minibus and that was about it. There was nobody about but he daren't risk being seen, not at this stage, there was too much at stake.

He looked at the bucket of fried chicken sitting invitingly on his passenger seat. But this was important, his dinner would have to wait. Sam removed his penknife from his pocket and ran the edge of the blade along his thumb. It felt sharp, it would need to be, that rope wouldn't cut easily.

Using the shadows of the fence as cover, Sam made his way to the truck. He moved quickly and skilfully. It was all done in seconds, but he had what he'd came for. He tucked the plastic bag containing the strands of rope into his pocket and made his way back to his vehicle. Mission accomplished. He was about to celebrate with a piece of his chicken when he noticed a short fat figure shuffling his way across the parking lot towards the truck. There was no mistaking that gait, it was Riley Muntz. What a stroke of luck. Sam put the chicken back in the bucket and watched as Muntz drove out of the parking lot. He turned left onto the main road; he was heading towards Fairlea. But where was he going? Sam followed from a safe distance.

Half a mile outside the town Muntz pulled into a small industrial estate. Sam couldn't risk his car being seen, so he parked up under the cover of some trees and continued on foot. He knew there was only one way in

301

and out of the estate so the truck would need to come back this way at some point.

Suddenly from behind him came the growl of an engine and the glare of headlights. Sam darted for cover behind some bushes. Seconds later an orange coloured truck crawled past him. On board were Sean and Darren Sill. As the truck disappeared round the corner, Sam did a quick check to make sure that no one else was coming. With the coast clear he sprinted along the side of the road. He needed to know what both those trucks were up to. As he reached the corner, he could see the orange truck parked outside a row of industrial units. Staying within the shadow of the buildings, Sam crept forward to get a better look. But where was Muntz and the GMC truck? There was no sign of either of them.

A security light went on and into the brightness stepped Muntz. He was carrying a bunch of keys and a large padlock. He slammed the metal door shut and secured the padlock before getting into the rear of the orange truck. Sam stepped back into a door recess as the truck drove past. He waited a minute or more to make sure they weren't coming back. Then he made his away to the units. He wanted to be sure which one Muntz had left the GMC in. Muntz had come out of the second last one, that was unit 9. Sam stared up at the sign above the door.

Mulroy Alarms, manufacturers of high-quality security alarms for home and business use.

Sam stood back and scratched his head.

'Well I'll be darned!'

Chapter 26

The following morning Sam and Chris were sitting in Charlie's office. They had just been tasked by Sergeant Brown to go to Pittsburgh to get a statement from Professor Foulis. After that they had to call at the State Penitentiary in Moundsville and interview Lilian Taylor who had reluctantly agreed to provide a statement. The round trip was more than 600 miles, so Sergeant Brown had arranged for them to stay overnight in Moundsville.

Charlie was going over some of the key points that he wanted them to cover when they spoke to the witnesses. He had chosen them both specifically for the task. Chris was one of his most experienced detectives and young Sam was as keen as mustard. They made a good team and they could be trusted to do a good job.

Yesterday had been a frustrating day for everyone but at least there was some positive news. During door to door enquiries, officers had traced the lady who had given the suspect her old birdcage and they'd obtained a reasonably detailed statement from the bar man in Ruby's. He had suggested that the officers should speak with Dan Tomkins, the permanent fixture sat at the end of his bar, as he had spent time speaking with the man they were now looking for. That conversation did not go well. Tomkins had a healthy disregard for the police, and he didn't mind who knew it. He didn't believe for one minute that the man who'd bought him several beers a couple of weeks ago would kill anyone. He told the cops he didn't seem the type. There wasn't much the officers could do. They couldn't compel him to speak. So, they'd left without his statement.

They hadn't had much more success when they tried to interview Mary Winters at the library. She'd seen Lieutenant Finch's broadcast over the weekend, but now when the officers tried to speak to her, she kept breaking down in tears. She was distraught, but she shared something with Dan Tomkins. She was finding it hard to believe that the man she'd grown fond of could have killed three people. It was hopeless trying to take her statement, she was far too emotional. They would have to leave it for another day.

Every murder enquiry has its share of frustrations. This one was proving to be no different. They just needed a break, a stroke of good fortune that could turn the enquiry in their favour. Charlie knew that his best chance of getting decent statements lay with what Professor Foulis and Lilian Taylor might be able to tell them. They knew the suspect better than anyone. What they had to say could prove crucial to the investigation. It was certainly their best hope of tracing their suspect's whereabouts.

*

Sam had phoned before they left the office and told Professor Foulis that they hoped to be with him by one, but it was just before two when the detectives arrived at the university. Sam got out and stretched his arms and shoulders. His back was stiff after the long drive, so he did a series of bends and rotations to try and loosen it off.

'First thing I need to do is find a restroom.' announced Chris getting out the car. 'Been desperate for a pee for the last half hour.'

They made their way through a large stone arch that opened into a rectangular shaped quadrangle that was surrounded by grey limestone buildings. It even had cloisters and a central lawn. The university had been built in the style of ancient Oxbridge colleges, the stone buildings came complete with turrets and flying buttresses. Sam stood for a minute gazing at the impressive architecture. Wow, he was blown away. This couldn't be more different from West Virginia State, where Sam had studied for his statistics degree.

'I can't stand and gawp at buildings, if I don't get to a bathroom soon, I'm going to wet myself!'

The pained expression on Chris's face suggested he wasn't joking.

'Hallelujah, there's a sign for the reception, there must be one in there, I'll be back in a minute.'

Sam sat down on a bench as Chris hurried off to find a restroom.

Over to his right a small group of students appeared to be having some form of tutorial on the lawn. The lecturer, a lady in her fifties with short curly grey hair was dressed in a long flowing tie dye purple dress which she wore with a large brown leather belt. She sat crossed legged on the grass with her sandals next to her. All her toenails were painted blue, except her big ones, which were bright scarlet. She was reading aloud from a book held in front of her. From what Sam could gather, she was reading poetry. It was like a scene from F. Scott Fitzgerald's novel, 'This Side of Paradise.'

There were other students milling about. Some carrying books and folders on their way or returning from lectures. Others gathered in small social groups, laughing and flirting, like students do the world over. They were young and full of hope and expectation of what life might bring them.

Sam wasn't much older than most of the students here. There were one or two who were clearly mature students, but it wasn't the age profile that had got his attention. It was more the racial diversity that was so noticeably on display. While the gender balance looked about 50/50, it was the number of black, Asian, and Oriental students that was fascinating. Right there in front of him was a mix of races that he'd rarely, if ever, encountered before.

His hometown looked nothing like this. Nor, thinking back, did his own student days. It hadn't been exclusively white. There had been several black students on his course and a few from China. Sam remembered them alright, not because of their appearance, but because they were always near the top in the exams. They were his competitors. The oriental students had a gift with numbers.

What was different was not so much the number of students from different racial backgrounds, it was the way they were interacting. This was obviously a diverse and racially inclusive campus. Sam didn't want to label his former university, but what he was witnessing was not what he had experienced. He had stuck solidly to his own racial group. Whether that was by choice or by chance he wasn't sure. But thinking back, he had made little or no effort to integrate. Perhaps he hadn't needed to. Much the same as it had been throughout his life, it had never been on his radar, it was just so straightforward and easy.

He thought back to the exercise he had done with Ella in the restaurant, and the conversations they'd had about the causes of discrimination. Looking at the scene in front of him it was all starting to make sense. How could you begin to understand different races and cultures if you were never exposed to them? His upbringing had been typical of the kids he grew up with. He had never had to worry about being different as he was just like everybody else. He'd never given it a minute's thought. He did now, and that was all down to Ella. She was introducing him to a whole new way of looking at the world and he liked what he saw. These last few weeks with Ella had been an awakening. There was no going back. He couldn't now unsee what she had taught him and that made him feel good.

None of that meant he was going to excuse what the Sills and the Linton Webbs of this world had done. They had been violent and racially abusive. But he was now beginning to understand why they behaved as they did. They felt threatened and inadequate. Their experience was a million miles from what he was watching in front of him. The racists didn't want to engage or understand, their instinct was to attack, crush anything that threatened their beliefs and values. Their behaviour was a sign of their insecurity. They would never admit to that, but that's exactly what it was.

*

The interview with Professor Foulis didn't last long. An hour and a half later they were on their way to Moundsville with his statement in the bag. He had been

307

polite and accommodating and over coffee and a sandwich he had explained how he'd got to know Chaska. But it was clear from what he had told them that Lilian was the key witness. She had known him for more than ten years and worked closely with him these last three.

Lilian had informed them that she would be working a backshift today, so she would be at the library till nine. The drive south to Moundsville should take them little more than an hour if they could avoid the worst of the rush hour traffic. As it was the traffic was light and by the time they had been checked through security, it was just before six. A prison guard escorted them across the exercise yard. Suspicious eyes lasered in on them as most prisoners stopped to stare. That didn't faze Chris or Sam. They were used to visiting prisons, it came with the territory. And just as every con would swear that they could tell a cop from a hundred yards, every cop worth their salt could return the favour. Not that that was a challenge today. If you were a con, then you were wearing an orange jumpsuit, and if you were a cop, then you were the guy in the suit.

The interview with Lilian was fraught and at times strained. She appeared detached and reluctant to engage. She got quite defensive when Chris challenged the veracity of what she was saying. Their suspect, the man who was wanted for the murder of three men, sounded too good to be true. Chris had done his homework; Chaska was no saint. Chris knew all about his conviction and about the beating he had meted out to a fellow prisoner. Chaska had a history of violence, and just because some do-good librarian thought he was rehabilitated, that didn't make it so. If Chris had believed every witness he'd interviewed who'd spoken up for an accused person, then nobody was guilty of anything. He had heard it all before and he was beginning to run out of patience with Lilian's pleadings. Sam was a little more conciliatory. He could see how genuinely upset Lilian was. This was no act. Her pain was heartfelt and raw. It was clear that she couldn't comprehend Chaska doing such a thing. But there was little mileage in talking about feelings, it was time to deal with the facts. Sam wanted to know about the letter that Professor Foulis had told them about.

Lilian produced the letter from a drawer in her desk. She explained it had arrived two days ago but that had been the only contact she had had with Chaska since she dropped him at the bus station more than three weeks ago. Sam put on a pair of protective gloves and removed the letter from its envelope. The first page was taken up with the usual pleasantries you'd expect from a letter of a personal nature. Hope you are well and managing without your assistant. I'm doing okay and settling into life on the outside. That kind of thing. There was also effusive thanks for all that Lilian had done for him. It was standard fare from someone who was close to the person they were writing to. Pages 2 and 3 were a little more interesting. They described what had happened to Carole Hicks and explained the significance of the Spruce Knob mine archive.

Sam stopped and thought for a moment, for some reason this was ringing a bell. Then it came to him. The letter was referring to the same archive that Ella had been talking about when she was doing her research into her grandfather. What a strange coincidence.

Sam continued reading to the end. He would need to read it again more carefully and take some notes, but on the face of it he could see nothing that suggested that Chaska would seek to harm the Lawrences. Sure, he made mention of them, and it was clear from his tone that he didn't much care for them. Aiden and all three brothers were named in the letter. But there was no direct threat or abusive language. He had concluded the letter by suggesting that the relevant authorities might be interested to hear what the Lawrences had been up to. But it was all a bit underwhelming. The letter was not the silver bullet that Lieutenant Finch was hoping for. Sam would get Chris's opinion on it later, but on first reading he couldn't see how the letter would assist their investigation.

After noting her statement, Sam explained that they would need to take the letter with them. It was potential evidence and may be needed if there were to be any subsequent court proceedings. Lilian looked unimpressed. She was naturally suspicious of the police. Her views had been jaundiced from years of working in a maximum-security prison. Too often she had seen prisoners get shafted by the justice system. Her earlier spat with Chris hadn't helped her mood. It was time for them to leave. It had been another long day.

'Right, no excuses tonight. It's time for beer. Beer and a great big steak. And then perhaps another beer. What do you say?' asked Chris as they handed in their security passes at the front entrance.

'That sounds like the best idea I've heard all day. I noticed we passed a place not that far from the motel that looks like it might be just the job. We'll be able to walk. But a quick freshen up first and I'll need to phone

310

Ella. It's been a couple of days since I've seen or spoken to her.'

'That love bug must have got you bad. Seems to me like you're pretty keen on her.'

Sam blushed. Ella was his first proper girlfriend, and he still felt awkward talking about her. But Chris was right, he was keen on her, in fact his was smitten.

The drive to the motel only took minutes and five minutes later they were checked in.

'Okay, quick wash and a change of clothes and I'll see you in reception in twenty. That enough time for you love birds?'

Sam scoffed.

'That will be more than enough. I said I was keen on her, but I'm keen on that steak and beer too, I'm famished.'

Twenty-five minutes later, Sam opened the door into reception. Chris was already there reading a paper. Sam had a troubled look on his face.

'What's up? Don't tell me you've had a row and she's put the phone down on you.'

Sam shook his head.

'No, no, nothing like that. But she was really upset on the phone. She's never been like that before. Not even when she was in hospital after being assaulted. But I don't know what's wrong, she didn't want to talk about it on the phone.'

'That's not so good.' said Chris trying to sound supportive. 'But I wouldn't worry about it too much. If it had been really important, she would have told you. Let her sleep on it. It'll probably not appear so bad in the morning, and you'll see her tomorrow so you can find out what was wrong then. Now, there's two beers with our names on them just down this road. I say we go and acquaint ourselves with them. How about it?'

Sam sighed and shrugged his shoulders.

'Yep, you're right. If it was that important, she would have told me, I'm sure she would.'

Chapter 27

Thursday 7th October

The morning briefing was far busier than usual. Angela had moved everyone into the conference room ahead of Charlie's arrival as the incident room was too small to accommodate all the additional uniformed officers who had been called in to assist with today's operation. Every seat was taken, and officers were standing shoulder to shoulder against the back and side walls. Everyone was dressed casually in hillwalking gear and boots.

'For the second time, will someone open those damned windows?' shouted a crimson faced Sergeant Joice from the back of the room. 'It's like the black hole of Calcutta in here. I'm dying. So, get them open, pronto like.'

'You would have thought one of those young officers sitting down might have given the old man a seat. He's not as young as he once was and he's clearly feeling the heat.' laughed Sam who was standing a few feet away.

'Hey, if I could reach you, I'd slap you. And less of the old codger bit. I'm as fit as most in this room.'

Before Sam could reply, Lieutenant Finch walked in and stood at the lectern.

'Okay, morning everyone. And thanks to our uniformed colleagues who will be assisting us today. I'll keep this brief as it's like a furnace in here. Can we have those windows open please.'

Steve turned and made a face at Sam.

'They are open sir.' came a voice from the side. 'Well the two that will open are. The catch is broken on the other two, can't seem to get them open.'

Sergeant Joice snorted and made a theatrical play of dabbing his head with a hanky.

Charlie continued.

'Right, as I said I'll try and keep this brief. You'll all be aware that we are still trying to establish the whereabouts of our suspect. Having spent the last few days following up leads at addresses across the town and further afield, I'm now convinced he's not currently in the Lewisburg area. What information we have suggests that he might be holding out, somewhere on Spruce Knob.

We know that he got off a bus at the footpath that leads to the mountain, that was more than a fortnight ago, and it was also the last confirmed sighting of our suspect. The bus driver who dropped him off doesn't think he had a tent with him, but he can't be 100% sure. What he is sure of is he got off the bus with a cage full of canaries.'

A ripple of laughter went round the room.

'Yep, you did hear that right, our suspect was carrying a birdcage containing canaries. All of this suggests to me that our man might be living rough somewhere on the mountain. He wouldn't be short of cover as there are woods, caves and plenty of fresh water. With wild berries still in season and numerous wild goats up there, he wouldn't be short of food either. And with the hot weather recently, he could be surviving quite happily. Any questions before I move on?'

Steve put up his hand.

'Two quick ones Lieutenant. Firstly, I know canaries are usually yellow so that being the case, are you presuming that the feathers that were found on Eldridge and Mitchell Lawrence came from the birds our suspect had with him? And secondly, other than the bus driver, do you have other information that suggests the suspect might be on the mountain?'

Charlie leant forward on the lectern.

'To answer your first question let me be clear that I'm not presuming anything. The lab is working hard to try and establish what type of birds those feathers came from. But until I see their report, I'm not prepared to say anything more at this time.

With regards to your second point, we have been in contact with another witness. A man by the name of Professor Foulis, who claims he was speaking to our suspect three weeks ago. He has told us that they had been discussing the Spruce Knob massacre. Some of you might remember hearing about that in history lessons at school. Well, for those of you that aren't aware, around 30 members of the Shawnee tribe lost their lives in a battle with white townsfolk who were trying to throw them off the mountain and claim the land for themselves so they could open a coal mine.

Those townspeople were led by Eldridge Gaylord Lawrence the 1st. He's the grandfather of the Lawrence brothers and the great grandfather of Aiden. And it's that connection that makes me believe our killer is on the mountain. We know our suspect identifies as a member of the Shawnee tribe and the massacre, well that cements the link to the Lawrence family. So, we know he had a motive. To right the injustice that he believed his people suffered all those years ago.

I want that mountain searched from top to bottom. That's why I've brought you here today. We must ascertain, one way or another, whether he's up there. So today I'm asking for your help to find him. Now I know you're all carrying sidearms but remember he may be dangerous. If you set eyes on him, call for backup. I've got a firearms team standing by.

Jerry Curran, our search advisor, has divided the mountain into eight search areas. Detectives and uniformed officers will be neighboured up and those who have areas that include more challenging terrain like forest and rivers, will have a bigger team. I want every inch of your sector searched. Sergeant Brown has organised water and some sandwiches, so pick them up on your way out, you'll be dining al fresco today. We'll be travelling up in two minibuses which will leave immediately after Jerry's briefing. He'll allocate your neighbour and give you maps of your search area. I'll be heading up later after I've briefed the Chief. So, I'll catch you then. Oh, and there's a bottle of Old Mister for the team who finds him.'

'That will be me then. I've just finished the last of my bourbon, another bottle will do just dandy.' said Steve rubbing his hands.

*

Both minibuses had parked on the dirt track leading to the entrance to the mine. It was as far up the mountain as you could get by vehicle. Some of the teams had been dropped off on the lower slopes, and now the only ones still on the bus were the teams allocated sectors towards the top of the mountain. Sam picked up his bag and got off the bus.

'Well what were the chances eh?' said Steve slapping Sam on the back.

Sam sighed and gave Steve a knowing look as he unfolded the map of their search area.

'Could have been worse. At least they didn't neighbour me with that idiot Mulroy. That would really have pissed me off. Right young fella, no point in lugging two bags up this mountain, leave yours on the bus and put your lunch and water bottles in mine. There, see the things us old boys do for you young uns.'

'Appreciate it.' said Sam stuffing his lunch bag into Steve's rucksack. 'Now if I'm reading this map right, we're searching the south slope from the summit down to this area here, which is called Yellow Rocks.' Sam pointed to the feature on the map. 'It looks like a fair chunk of land, but it doesn't look nearly as steep as the rest of our area. The contours flatten out noticeably. It looks like it's a bit of a plateau.'

Steve took hold of the map which he studied carefully. He then made a loud snorting noise.

'Expect you're right.' said Steve starting to chuckle.

'Perhaps that's why it's called the Yellow Rocks Plateau.' he said sarcastically pointing at the map.

Sam blew out his cheeks.

'Okay fine. I hadn't noticed that. Anyway, once we get up there, I don't think it will take us that long. There don't appear to be any trees, it all looks fairly open.'

'Agreed, it looks that way. But there could be caves up by those rocks, so just as well the experienced old Sergeant has remembered to stick a flashlight in the bag.'

Steve grinned and patted the side of his rucksack.

'You mean you've got one like this.' said Sam taking a small flashlight from his trouser pocket.

Steve laughed and shook his head.

'Okay, fair enough. Let's call a time out. I reckon that makes us about even. Right, time we made a move. You lead the way; you're in charge of the map.'

Sam had decided that the best route looked to be a well-defined footpath that meandered between outcrops of rock on its way to the summit.

Forty-five minutes later they had reached the top of the mountain. They each placed a stone on the cairn and stood back to admire the spectacular views. To the north they could see the vast expanse of the Appalachian range disappearing into the horizon, while far to the west the terrain flattened into fields of corn and apple orchards. The two colleagues rested for a few minutes, soaking in the magnificence of this beautiful part of the world. After a drink of water and a call of nature for Steve they were ready to begin their search. Visibility was superb and progress swift as they made their way down the southern slope. Other than the occasional area of scree, where loose stones slipped underfoot slowing their progress, it was mostly plain sailing.

Away to their left and further down the mountain, they could see their colleagues inching their way through thick forests. It would take them all day to complete their sector. Sam and Steve had won a watch, at the rate they were going, theirs would be done in a couple of hours.

At the start of the plateau they stopped for a rest and a drink of water. It was hot thirsty work. The unseasonably warm weather had rolled on into October and it still showed no sign of abating.

'You can see why it's called Yellow Rocks.' said Steve wiping the sweat from his forehead. 'They are almost the colour of lemons, a bit paler maybe but you know what I mean.'

Steve rubbed his hand over the rock.

'And the stone is surprisingly smooth, I wonder what type of rocks they are.'

Sam didn't answer. He put his finger to his lips and made a shushing sound.

'There listen. Do you hear it? There it is again. Can you hear it?'

Steve looked confused.

'What am I supposed to be hearing? The only thing I can hear is some damned bird singing.'

'Yeah, that's what I mean, you can hear it singing then?'

'Sure, but what about it? It's just a bird singing. I've seen dozens of birds since we've been up here.'

'It's not just any bird singing.' replied Sam who was now scrambling down through the rocks trying to see where it was coming from.

'That's the song of a canary. Ella told me how to recognise it. Listen, there it is again. It's soft and melodious and then, there, a series of deeper clicks. It sounds like water dripping into a bucket. That's how she described it. And it does, it sounds just like that.'

'Okay it does.' said Steve trying to keep up with Sam as he slithered down the rocks. 'So, what are you saying?'

'Well firstly, you don't get wild canaries round these parts and secondly, our suspect was supposed to be carrying a cage full of them when he got off the bus. And look, look, over there, underneath the overhang.'

319

Sam stopped suddenly and pointed towards a slab of rock that hung out like a canopy from the side of the mountain.'

'Well I'll be darned.' said Steve catching up with Sam. 'You're right enough, that's a birdcage alright, but look at the bottom of the cage, looks like the birds are all dead and dead birds don't sing!'

Sam made his way to the overhanging rock.

'No, but a live one does.' said Sam staring into the cage. 'There's one perched on a branch in the top corner and it's very much alive.'

The canary sang again. Soft and melodious like the sound of water rolling over rocks.

The birdcage was standing on a ledge and partly shaded by the overhanging rock. Four birds lay dead at the bottom of the cage. Sam glanced at the two metal feeding trays; they were both empty. There was no seed or water in the cage. Someone had placed some sticks and pieces of vegetation in the cage. To give the birds some cover and a place to perch. But the vegetation had withered and was now a strange brownish colour. It didn't look as if anyone had been attending to the birds recently.

While Sam examined the birdcage, Steve started rooting about underneath the overhang.

'Well, well looky here.' shouted Steve. 'There's a ruck-sack and some clothes. And here look, there's a notepad and some papers. They look like academic papers, this one's called 'The History of the Ghost Dance' and its got Carnegie Mellon University written at the top.'

Steve flipped through the paper. He then bent down and picked up a book that was lying underneath the notepad.

'And there's even a book here from Lewisburg library called 'Massacre at Spruce Knob.' I think it's safe to say that our man has been living up here. The Lieutenant was right enough. But it doesn't look like he's been here for a while, not judging by those dead birds.'

'I better radio the Lieutenant and Angela. And get them up here.' said Sam who was now examining a leather thong that was hanging over a spur of rock. It had some feathers and dried up flowers still attached to it.

'They're going to want to see this, but there's no hurry, our suspect appears to have disappeared again.'

By now Steve had emerged from underneath the over-hang and had made his way to a large boulder about thirty feet away. He was staring down at something.

'Well you were right about there being no hurry, and while you're on the radio, tell them I'm claiming that bourbon, 'cause I've found our man and he's very much dead!'

Lying spread-eagled on a rock approximately twenty feet below where Steve was standing was the body of a man. He was fully clothed and hatless. Next to his head was a large pool of what appeared to be congealed blood. It was the colour of dark chocolate and contrasted vividly with the yellow coloured limestone.

Steve scrambled down the rocks followed closely by Sam.

'Jeezo, he's in some state. Birds or a fox or something has been at him, and he don't smell too fresh.'

Steve put his hanky over his face as he approached the corpse.

'I'm not getting any closer, he's clearly dead and I don't want to contaminate any scenes of crime. But come round here and take a look at this.'

Sam made his way over to Steve who pointed at the man's head.

'Forget the damage to his ears and hands, I'm pretty sure that's been done by a critter after death. But I don't see any obvious injuries, I don't think he's been assaulted. And look the area around his mouth and nose. It's covered by that same brown stuff. It doesn't look like blood but what else could it be? It's pretty gross, look there's lumpy bits in in, and there's more over here on the rock. I reckon he's coughed this lot up. I'm no doctor, but it looks to me like he's had some sort of massive haemorrhage.'

*

Dave Richardson and Zoe had already arrived by the time Charlie and Angela eventually reached the locus. They had been side-tracked by the discovery of a cage by a team searching the forest on the western side of the mountain. Although the cage had been empty, if the truth be told, it didn't look too dissimilar to a large birdcage. However, it turned out it was an old squirrel trap. Charlie knew it wasn't what they were looking for immediately he saw it. It was completely the wrong shape. But that frenzy of excitement had delayed them for nearly an hour, so by the time they got to see the body most of the photographs had already been taken.

Dave was busy assembling a SOC tent with the help of Sam. He was keen to get the body protected so he could begin his examination. There were reports of thunderstorms in the area. It still didn't look like it would rain anytime soon, but it was feeling more humid, and if it did rain, they risked losing vital evidence.

Especially the congealed blood and lumpy matter that might easily be washed away.

Noticing that Charlie and Angela had arrived Dave came over to join them. The three colleagues stood on a boulder above the body studying the grisly scene.

'Any initial thoughts?' asked Charlie as he wrote some notes in his folder.

Dave scratched his head.

'I've got a feeling Steve may be right about this one. The only injuries that I can see appear to have been made by birds and perhaps an animal. Most likely a fox. There is no evidence of violence that I can see, and he doesn't appear to have fallen. The blood looks like it's come from his mouth or nose. Could be both of course. The autopsy will tell us for sure, but it looks like he's haemorrhaged.'

'And what might cause that?' asked Angela.

'Could be a variety of things. But it's almost certainly some underlying health issue.'

'What, you mean something like cancer?'

Dave nodded.

'Something like that, but it would need to be something very serious to cause him to haemorrhage as badly as that.'

'Hmm.' said Charlie chewing the end of his pen. 'Not sure how helpful any of that will be to our investigation. Finding out how long he has been dead would be useful. Any thoughts on that?'

Dave smiled wryly.

'You know me. I don't like to speculate on these things. Got caught out recently doing just that.'

Charlie gave Dave a knowing look.

'But if you were pushing me, I'd say quite some time, at least a week but maybe more.'

'And why do you say that?' asked Angela. 'The body's not badly decomposed and it's lying out in the full sun and its been roasting for weeks now.'

'That's true, but there is still some decomposition. And I'm no expert on entomology but look at the number of flies that are around the body.'

'There's always flies around dead bodies, certainly ones that are discovered outside. The flies don't hang about, they make themselves right at home.'

'Okay, as I said, I don't want to speculate, but all of that will need to be checked out. But this will be a priority, I Know how important this investigation is. The Chief was biting my ear about it just yesterday.' explained Dave.

'You and me both my friend. The man's under stress, he's desperate for us to get a result. Right I'll let you get on; I'll catch you back at the office later and you can give me a fuller update then.'

As Dave went to bring down the tent, Charlie and Angela clambered back up to where Steve and Sam were going through the clothes and books that they'd found.'

'Anything of particular interest?' asked Charlie.

Sam nodded.

'lots of bits and pieces, we'll need to spend some time going through it all. Most of the clothes in his rucksack appear to be dark coloured which fits the profile. And there's a paper here written by Professor Foulis. He told me about it when I went to get his statement. It's about a ritual dance that some Indian tribes, including the Shawnee, used to perform. It might be significant but then again it might be nothing. Same with this book about the Spruce Knob massacre that appears to have come from Lewisburg library. It's all going to need to be checked.'

Sam put the book and papers down and picked up the notepad.

'This on the other hand, might be the evidence we've been looking for.'

Sam handed the notepad to Charlie.

'It's stuffed with notes about the Lawrence family. Pages and pages of them. Although there are some pages that seem to be missing. Look, you can see the ragged edges where somebody's torn them out. But most of it seems to be here and it appears to be a history of the time when the Lawrences owned the mine. But have a look at the back. It's about the third last page.'

Charlie flipped through the pages while Sam looked over his shoulder.

'There, that's it, stop there. You've gone past it.' said Sam.

Charlie turned back a page. Written in large black capital letters at the top of the page were the words, 'THE GUILTY PARTIES.' The names and addresses of Eldridge, Mitchell and Aiden Lawrence were written underneath and highlighted in green fluorescent pen. Underneath that, someone had written, 'What goes around comes around.'

Charlie thought for a moment.

'The three members of the family who are dead are all mentioned on that page. But I don't see David Lawrence's name.'

'Yep, I noticed that too and he's the only one still alive. And another thing boss, the handwriting looks identical to the writing in the letter that was sent to Lilian Taylor. And that was signed by our suspect. I think we can be pretty certain that the writing in this notepad is his as well.'

Charlie nodded.

'Seems like it, but that can be easily checked by the lab. And make sure you get that birdcage back to the office. I want those feathers examined as a matter of urgency. If we can prove the feathers found on the victims came from these birds, then we may be onto something.'

'Right, last thing before I go. Any trace of the crossbow? It would be a big help if we could locate the weapon.'

Sam and Steve both shook their heads. There was no trace of any weapon amongst the belongings they had found.

'Okay then. Once Dave and Zoe have finished and the body's been removed, I want a fingertip search done of this entire area. Make that a priority for tomorrow, will you?'

'Not a problem.' replied Angela. 'And I'll make sure we've got the locus protected overnight.'

'Yep, fine. Oh, And I nearly forgot. What about his hat? Most of the witnesses mentioned that he wore a black fedora, any trace of that?'

Sam and Steve looked at each other and shook their heads. They hadn't found any trace of a hat.

Chapter 28

The following morning Angela was in early, but she was not the first to arrive. As she parked her car, she noticed that Charlie's office light was on. Sam of course was already at his desk when she walked in the office. That was no surprise, Sam was invariably first in in the morning. He had the kettle on and was making coffee.

'You making one for the boss as well?' asked Angela as Sam passed her a mug. Sam nodded.

'Do you know if he's been in long? Not like him to be in this early.' Angela looked at her watch. It was only twenty-five to seven.

'Well he was here before me and I got in at quarter past. Why you asking? Do you think there's a problem?'

'Don't know; but grab his coffee and we'll go and see shall we.'

Sam picked up the mug and followed Angela along the corridor.

'Morning boss.' said Angela breezily as Sam handed Charlie his coffee.

'You're in early today, something up?'

Charlie looked up and raised his eyebrows. He lent back in his chair and put his hands behind his head.

'Didn't sleep well. Too many things going on in my head so I thought I'd come in and make a start. Here, I want you both to have a look at this.'

Charlie handed Angela two sheets of paper.

'They're photocopies, it's okay you can touch them. The original is away being tested for prints. But take a close look, do you notice anything?'

Angela stared at the paper, holding it to the side so Sam could also see it. It was a copy of the last page of Lilian Taylor's letter complete with Chaska's signature. The other page was a copy of the front of the envelope. Angela looked at it blankly. Then it dawned on her. Sam had noticed it too. He now felt stupid as he had been the one who had seized the letter in the first place. He had even read it, yet he never noticed it. The writing on the letter was different from the writing on the envelope. They didn't look like they'd been written by the same hand.

Sam puffed out his cheeks and shook his head.

'Sorry, sir. I should have noticed that, but somehow I didn't.'

'Is it necessarily a problem?' asked Angela. 'I suppose there could be an explanation.'

'Fire away then, 'cause I can't think of a plausible one.' said Charlie getting up and looking out the window.

'Why would someone else's writing be on that envelope?'

Angela screwed up her nose.

'Maybe someone found the letter and posted it for him.'

'What. And they wrote the name and address on the envelope before they mailed it!'

'Oh, I don't know, I was just talking out loud. But it doesn't mean he's not our killer. We've got other evidence.'

'Yeah, but it's all circumstantial. We don't have the critical pieces of evidence, like the weapon or any eyewitnesses. Jeezo, we don't even have his hat!'

'No, but the initial report from the lab says they're pretty confident that the feathers found on Eldridge and Mitchell are canary feathers from the cage we found. Another couple of tests and then they'll be able to say for certain. And if that does prove to be the case then it places our man at the locus of two of the murders.'

Charlie gave a weary sigh and shook his head.

'Afraid not. It only proves that the feathers from the cage were at the locus. It doesn't prove that our suspect put them there. As I said, it's all circumstantial.'

'Well, I can't see who else could have put them there. And cheer up, it's not like you to be so despondent. We've still to conduct a proper search around the area where the body was found. Who's to say we won't find the weapon or even his hat. So, come on, it's not all bad news.' said Angela trying to sound upbeat.

'Oh, but there's more.' said Charlie sitting back down. 'I tried to tell him not to do it, but he couldn't help himself. After I briefed him last night, the Chief was straight onto the AC to tell him that we had found our murderer and solved the case. How naïve can you be? I told him that there were discrepancies around the weapon and hat that we hadn't resolved, but he wouldn't listen. He was just desperate to get the investigation over and off his desk.'

'And what about the letter, does he know about that?' asked Sam.

'No and that makes it even worse. I think that's why I couldn't sleep. Zoe only gave me these copies when I was heading out the door. She'd only just discovered it herself. So, the Chief knows nothing about the letter.'

'Have we got any positive news?' asked Angela.

'There may be one glimmer of hope. I spoke to Mike in Chicago last night to tell him about the letter. He told me they'd found a partial fingerprint on a railing just outside Eldridge's garden. It's smudged and covered in red paint but he's checking it against our suspect. Being a convicted prisoner at least we've got some decent prints, so that's getting analysed right now. And I'm waiting on the autopsy results, they are going to be key. Dave hopes to have them for us by tomorrow.'

*

Later that evening, Ella was sitting on a park bench waiting for Sam to arrive. Other than speaking on the phone, she hadn't seen him in three days. The reality of being the girlfriend of a busy detective was starting to kick in. Work had to come first. She just had to get used to the fact there would be times when he couldn't be there. At least she was no longer crying. When he phoned the other night, she'd been very upset. Her grandfather's letters that her mother had found hidden away in a box in her attic had arrived and she'd taken them with her to the library to read. It had been a chastening experience.

Heroes aren't meant to crumble. They are meant to stand strong and firm, be resolute and determined in the face of adversity. Heroes don't have the same frailties that we have. That's the reason they appear heroic. They are invincible. Ella's grandfather had always been that man. In her eyes there was nothing he couldn't do. Walter Massie was heroic in everything he said and did.

It had been her grandfather who'd taught her to swim, ride a bike and identify bird songs. He was the one who always encouraged her to study and work hard. And it was most certainly her grandfather who had told her to never be ashamed of her black skin or who she was.

Ella closed he eyes as the tears welled up. She had cried enough; she was determined that she wasn't going to cry again. Her mind drifted back to the car park in Denny's where she'd been assaulted and had her money stolen, it had been the words of her grandfather that had sustained her through that ordeal.

Don't run, stand firm. Stay strong in the face of adversity. That why they don't get to touch your dignity!

Reading his letters in the library those words now seemed hollow, hypocritical even. He'd told a lie and ran away. His friends had died down a mine shaft and he knew what had happened. But he told a lie and fled. It was clear in the letter he'd written to his mother that he'd felt ashamed of what he'd done. So where was his dignity now? He'd done it, he'd told his mother, to protect his wife and children. But he'd told lies and run away. He hadn't stood strong; he had deserted his friends just when they needed him most. And for what? To protect himself and save his own skin.

It had all started to make sense to Ella. She'd read the documents in the archive and the altered minutes. The cover up was obvious. The meticulously ordered box had exposed the truth. The two men who'd died had been sold out, and now she knew her grandfather had been part of it.

Ella hadn't written a word or opened a book since she'd read the letters. Her heart just wasn't in it at the moment. But at least now she would get a chance to get things off her chest. Tell someone her feelings. Sam hadn't seen the letters yet, but as she saw him walking through the park gates, she knew this would be her opportunity to talk it through with him. Just seeing him lifted her spirits. It may only have been three days, but she had missed his company and his strange ways. He was a good man with a caring heart. And much smarter than he gave himself credit for. The thought of being able to share her feelings with her soulmate was comforting, she was already starting to feel a little better.

For the next twenty minutes, Sam listened as Ella explained what she'd discovered in the letters. He didn't say much, his role was to listen, to give a sympathetic ear, so that's exactly what he did. He just sat and listened. There had been one particular letter that had greatly troubled her. So, when she had finished speaking, he read that letter. He thought for a few moments. He was recalling his meeting with Charlie and David Lawrence at the Greenbrier Community. He remembered what Lawrence had said. While he hadn't referred to Walter Massie by name, there was no doubt in Sam's mind that it was Ella's grandfather that Lawrence had been talking about. He'd told him that two of their best men had kept quiet because they had been threatened with violence, their families had been threatened too. Those men didn't have a choice, they'd been forced into telling a lie.

Sam took hold of Ella's hand.

'I'd like you to meet someone. An old man I had dealings with at work last week. He's got first-hand knowledge of the mine and I know he knew your grandfather. I think he might have some interesting observations to make. Can I also say, while it's not for me to judge whether what your grandfather did was right or wrong, I'm just sorry I never got a chance to meet him. Hearing you talk about him; I wish I had. He sounds like a great man. But what I can tell you is this. There are always two sides to a story Ella, and right now, I'm not sure that you're hearing both sides.

Remember what you said to me. These things can be subtle and not immediately obvious. You taught me a different way of looking at the world and now, using a bit of my police experience, I'd like to show you that there may be a different way of interrupting this. So, what do you say? Would it be alright if I give this guy a phone and set up a meeting? I think he could throw a whole different light on these circumstances.'

Ella smiled and hugged Sam.

'Sure, why not. It can't do any harm. You've listened to me often enough these last few weeks, it's probably time I returned the favour.'

Chapter 29

'Ah ha.' said Gordon noticing Sam coming in the front door of the office. 'Just the man I want to see.' He glanced up at the clock. 'And it's gone seven. There are at least three detectives in ahead of you.'

Sam rubbed his nose.

'I know, I slept in this morning and that's something I never do.'

'Clear conscious you see.' said Gordon laughing. 'Anyway, I'm glad I caught you. I've had a look through the itemised phone bill you asked me to check. Nothing too exciting to report. No one's been spending hours on the phone calling people they shouldn't be. Well, not that I can see. Looks pretty straightforward for a change. And I've marked all the calls made from extension 2310 in blue highlighter just to make it easier. That was the extension you were interested in wasn't it.'

Sam nodded as he took the report from Gordon.

'Thanks Sergeant appreciate it, this is just what I was looking for, that's a beer I owe you.'

Sam started to scan the report as he headed upstairs. Sitting at his desk he studied the print-out more carefully. There it was. Four entries from the bottom on page seven. Monday 27th September, 0843 hrs, a 3-minute call to 304-278-1455.

Sam lifted his phone and called the control room.

'Hi, is that Amy? Good. Hi Amy, it's Sam Coutts speaking. I was hoping you might be able to check a telephone number for me. The number is 304-278-1455. Sure, a couple of minutes, I'll be at my desk I'm not going anywhere.'

Three minutes later the phone on his desk rang.

'Yes, Amy, Sam speaking, what you got?'

'That number you're interested in is registered to a Riley Muntz, 458, Primrose Gate, Addison.'

Sam clenched his fist and punched the air.

'Much obliged Amy, you've just made my day.'

*

Charlie was in his office with Angela going through the murder enquiry action log. Yesterday's search of the mountainside where the body had been discovered had not found anything of significance. There was no trace of any crossbow or the hat the killer was thought to have been wearing. The only thing the team had found was the name of Chief Malakai carved into the trunk of a red cedar tree.

Charlie was not long off the phone to Mike. Their possible fingerprint had come back negative. The print was smudged and there was insufficient detail to allow a positive identification. The air of despondency was palpable. This was turning into a nightmare. They had three bodies, they thought they had a motive, they just didn't have the evidence to prove that Chaska was their killer.

There was a knock on the door. Charlie looked up. It was Dave Richardson and he was carrying a large envelope.

'Coffee?' asked Angela getting up to give Dave a seat.

'Why not.' replied Charlie. 'Black with an extra shot, I'm needing all the caffeine I can get right now.'

Dave smiled.

'Just milk for me thanks.'

By the time Angela returned with the coffee, Dave and Charlie had gone through the set of photographs which were now sitting piled on the floor. Well, all of them were except one.

Charlie and Dave were leaning over the desk studying one of the photographs in great detail.

'Calliphora Vomitoria. Better known as the common bluebottle.' announced Dave pointing at the photograph.

'I had my suspicions when I first saw the body, but I didn't want to commit myself without being sure of my facts. But Howard Epstein in Charleston has confirmed it. He's our go to man for all things entomological. Those white things you are looking at are bluebottle maggots and those copper coloured things next to them are its pupa. The first pupa don't appear on a corpse until 15 days after the female fly lays her eggs. I'm afraid, Charlie, your suspect had been dead for more than a fortnight, and in all probability, it is likely to be nearer three weeks. I'm sorry that's not the news you were hoping for.'

Charlie slumped down in his chair and looked up at the ceiling as the significance of what Dave had just said sunk in. He shook his head and sighed wearily. Chaska wasn't their killer.

'And what about the cause of death, what did the autopsy show?'

'Loss of blood through the haemorrhaging killed him. But he was suffering from stage four cancer. His body was riddled with tumours. Primary site appears to have been his lungs, but it had spread to his colon and liver as well. He wouldn't have survived long even if he hadn't haemorrhaged. And another interesting thing, his stomach and colon were empty, it didn't look like he'd eaten in days.'

Charlie bit the end of his thumb nervously. If he were being honest, he was half expecting the news. He'd had nagging doubts ever since they'd discovered Chaska's body. There were too many things that just didn't fit. This was just the icing on the cake. For the first time since he'd taken over from Mike, he felt deflated. The case he had been building had just collapsed. Right now, he hadn't a clue what he should do next. It was back to the drawing board. He needed to re-set and start again.

He'd had plenty of unsolved crimes in his time, but he'd never had a serious case, like a murder investigation remain unresolved. He needed some time to take stock and decide what to do. Of course, to make things even worse he still had to tell the Chief the news. Just how he would react was anybody's guess. But one thing was certain, he wasn't going to take it well.

'Right decision made, and thanks Dave for getting that done so quickly. But tonight, we're finishing at six. I'll be in Bursley's by ten past and the first round's on me. Angela spread the word. I'm needing a beer and I'm sure the rest of the team are. So, I hope to see you there. We need to take a time out, the team's morale has taken a knock, and there's nothing like a bit of teambuilding over a beer to build it back up.'

Angela nodded and smiled.

'I'm up for that, I'll go tell the others. It will certainly be one of your more popular decision's, I can guarantee that.'

*

'What a really nice man.' said Ella as she walked back to the car with Sam. 'He had such a kind way about him, and that voice, so soft and warm, I could have listened to him all day.'

Sam put his arm around Ella's shoulders.

'And such a strange set of coincidences don't you think? I mean him knowing your grandfather and being involved in the running of the mine. And now you doing your research for your master's and finding that old archive of documents. Even me coming across him as part of our enquiry. It's a funny old world at times.'

Ella smiled.

'It feels like a weight has been lifted off me. I don't know what got into me. Thinking about it now, it was really just that one letter that made me doubt him. But I shouldn't have. The man that Mr Lawrence just described was the grandfather I knew. Strong and principled. And now hearing Mr Lawrence tell me that he'd been threatened by the Klan, then I don't blame my grandfather for what he did. He was just trying to protect his family. I would have done the same if I'd been in his shoes.'

Sam opened Ella's door to let her get in.

'I think you also have to consider what you've been through this last month. I think it's a factor in how it affected you. Reading that letter in the library was just the final straw. It all became too much. That letter was the catalyst, but it had been building up for weeks. It just all came tumbling out. That outpouring of emotion was just the result of everything that's been going on. I'm convinced of it.'

Ella smiled and leant across and kissed Sam.

'You're a good man Sam Coutts. I'm mighty glad I met you. Do you have time to grab a bite to eat or do you need to get back?'

Sam's face lit up in a beaming smile.

'Lieutenant Finch wants the team to meet in Bursley's for a couple of beers at six. Just to boost morale as it's been a tough few weeks. But I don't have to be back at the office before then. So, I've got a surprise for you.'

Ella's eyes opened wide.

'How exciting, what sort of surprise?'

By now Sam was grinning from ear to ear.

'Do you know the dress shop in Fairlea, the boutique on the corner of Webster street whose name I can't remember?'

'Sure.' replied Ella looking slightly suspicious. 'It's called Boudica. I've never been in it, but I've looked in the window. It's got some lovely stuff but it's quite upmarket, it does evening gowns, stuff for weddings, that kind of thing.'

'Exactly.' said Sam starting the engine. 'Well I thought we might drop by and see if we can get you a dress for your sister's wedding.'

Ella sat back in her seat and started laughing.

Sam had no idea what was so funny.

'Nice thought! But two things Mr Detective. Firstly, it's way out of my league, I can't afford to shop there. And secondly, I was rather hoping a dress might come with the gig, usually does when you're a bridesmaid at a wedding.'

Sam looked embarrassed. He hadn't even considered that Ella would be getting a bridesmaid's dress.

Ella could tell that Sam was feeling foolish. But that was just typical of him and in many ways the reason she liked him so much. There was a naïve innocence about him that she found endearing.

'Never mind, it was a lovely thought and very sweet of you.'

Sam wasn't going to be defeated.

'It doesn't have to be a dress; we could get something else. And I should have explained better, this is a gift from me. So, is there anything else you might like?'

Ella pondered for a moment.

'Well now that you mention it, there was a rather funky kantha jacket in the window the other day. It's yellow with dropped shoulders and three-quarter length sleeves, it's gorgeous.'

'Sounds like we should check it out. You always look great in yellow.'

An hour later it was a done deal. The jacket Ella had tried on looked fabulous but was a little on the large side. The shop assistant told them she could order a smaller size and it would be there within the week. Ella was made up, and as they walked back to Sam's car she felt as good as she had done in months.

Sam was searching for his car keys when he noticed a middle-aged woman sitting on a bench across the road. She was rummaging through a large shiny white bag that had 'Georgina's Alterations' printed in purple letters on the front. The woman was Mrs Sill, Sean and Darren's mother. Sam had met her before when he'd gone to her house looking for her sons. She didn't much care for the police as her colourful language and frequent use of expletives made abundantly clear.

Sam watched as she removed two white cotton robes from the bag. After a quick examination she folded them carefully and returned them to her bag. She looked up and noticed Sam watching her from across the street.

'What you gawping at?'

Sam didn't reply. He was thinking back to when he'd last been at her house with Steve Joice. They'd been there to interview her boys, but Sam remembered seeing a similar white robe hanging on the back of a bedroom door. Sean had got quite defensive about it. In fact, Sam was sure that he'd said the robe belonged to his mother who used it with her amateur dramatic club. Sam thought it a strange comment at the time. Now seemed like a good time to validate the truth of what Sean had said.

'Are those more robes for your amateur dramatic club Mrs Sill?'

Mrs Sill glowered at Sam. Her stare could have cut glass.

'Amateur dramatics! What the fuck you talking about? I wouldn't be seen dead doing that stuff, I've better things to waste my time on. Anyway, what's it got to do with you? It's none of your fucking business.'

'Fair enough.' said Sam, 'I was just trying to be neighbourly.'

He was about to get into his car when there was a roar from an engine further down the street. It was Sean Sill driving his orange Ford pick-up. Sitting on the flat bed in the back were Linton Webb and the guy with the grey baseball cap. Sean gave Sam the one fingered salute as he drew up by the bench. Mrs Sill picked up her bag and got into the passenger seat.

Sam smacked his forehead and turned towards Ella.

'I know where I've seen that name.'

Ella hadn't a clue what he was on about.

Sam started searching the back pocket of his trousers.

'I'm sure I put in here. Yep, gotcha.' said Sam holding up a small piece of paper.

'I'd completely forgotten about it, but here it is.'

It was the receipt he'd picked up in the car lot at the bowling alley. Sam squinted at the faded purple writing. He could just about make out, Georgina's Alterations, 97A, Webster Street, Fairlea.

'Fancy coming on a police enquiry?' asked Sam opening Ella's door.

'You bet. Never done that before, will it be exciting?

Sam laughed.

'I doubt it. But as it's just along the street, I don't want to miss the opportunity. It shouldn't take long.'

97A was up a steep set of steps. The bell rang as Sam opened the door. A smartly dressed lady in her early sixties was standing behind the counter.

'Good afternoon.' said Sam producing his badge and introducing himself.

'Are you by any chance the owner?'

'That's me, Miss Georgina Main, pleased to meet you.' said the lady taking off her spectacles.

'And my goodness, you're now the third detective I've had visit me in the last twelve months. I had a Detective Brown and her colleague, Chris, something, I can't remember his surname, come to see me last year. They had an enquiry about Marsco College. They were both very nice. Polite and professional, not like some of the ones you see on T.V. Fortunately I was able to help them with their enquiry. I take it you know them?'

Sam chuckled.

'Indeed, I do. Angela Brown's a sergeant now, in fact she's my boss and Chris is a good friend, I'll make sure I tell them I was speaking to you.'

'She's a sergeant now, that's marvellous, yes, please pass on my regards.'

As she was speaking, Sam noticed several white robes hanging on a rail at the rear of the shop. The last robe on the rail was red and made of satin. All the other ones looked like they were made of cotton. Sam pointed to the rail.

'I think it might be those robes I'm interested in. Can you tell me what they are and who they belong to?'

Miss Main put her spectacles back on.

'I'm not really sure what they are. Funnily enough a lady was in just ten minutes ago. She was picking two of them up for her sons, I'm sure she muttered something about a drama club. It was something like that.'

Sam, who was now standing at the rail examining the robes, scoffed.

'Have you made these? This one looks new, but the others don't. They are a slightly darker shade as well.'

'You've got a discerning eye detective. I did make that one from new. As you can see its much shorter than the others. Between you and me the man was a really strange shape. Squat and very wide. I couldn't just shorten his, it was much easier to make him a new one. Oh, and the red one's new too. And it's made of satin, the others are all cotton. But that's what was requested, and I always do what the customer wants.'

'So, these other ones have just been altered then?'

'That's correct, and some of them had to be repaired. They are quite old and were in a bit of a state when they were brought in, smelt a bit too, so I had to wash them first. Don't think they'd been used in years. And some were ripped, fortunately it was mainly at the seams, so they were easily repaired.'

'And the red one, why is it a different colour?'

'No idea but that's what the man wanted. Although, I don't know what I'm going to do with it now.'

'Why do you say that?' asked Sam.

'Because, well I'm sure you'll be aware, and it's a very sad story, the red one was for Mr Lawrence. You know the man who fell off the chairlift and was killed. It was all over the news last weekend.'

Sam nodded respectfully.

'Yep, that was a sad set of circumstances. But I'm sure one of his family could pick it up, and settle the account, so you're not out of pocket.'

'Well that's another strange thing. I'm not going to be out of pocket. Mr Lawrence paid the account in full when he came in to get measured for his robe. He was the last to come in. Several weeks ago now. But when he was here, he paid for everyone else's too.'

Sam took out his pocketbook and took down some notes.

'Do I take it then that everyone who has one of these robes came in here to get measured, to make sure they fitted properly?'

'That's correct. I think there was only one that was the perfect length, but all the others either needed let down or taken up. Well except for the two I made from scratch.'

'I see. You don't happen to have a list of names who the robes belong to, do you?'

344

Miss Main nodded.

'I certainly do. It's in the back shop. Give me a minute and I'll get it for you.'

Sam turned to Ella and smiled. He could sense he was on to something.

Miss Main returned with a large black notebook. She opened the book and handed it to Sam.

'The names of everyone who had a robe fitted and their measurements are listed on that page.'

Sam scanned down the list and smiled. It read like a who's who of every redneck in the district.

Sean and Darren Sill, Linton Webb, Riley Muntz they were all there. And there right at the bottom, just above Aiden Lawrence's name was the one he was hoping for. Ryan Mulroy.

'Fuck me, I knew it. I just knew he would be involved.' whispered Sam under his breath. It was like an awakening. The clues had been there all along staring him in the face, he just hadn't linked them together. Mulroy had body swerved the enquiry Sam had with the Sill brothers. It was clear now that he didn't want to be involved. Then there was the meeting with the guy in the grey baseball cap at the restaurant and the phone call to Riley Muntz. Sam hadn't been able to make the connection before; it wasn't obvious why they were friends. It was now. These were Klan robes, and Ryan Mulroy was part of it.

Sam scribbled all the names into his pocketbook. There were only two he didn't recognise. Carter Hayes and Bubba O'Brien.

'Can I ask you another couple of questions. Firstly, these two names, Hayes and O'Brien, can you tell me anything about them?

Miss Main rolled her eyes.

'I don't remember too much about Hayes. If I recall he didn't come in to pick his robe up. Linton Webb picked it up for him, said Hayes was his cousin. But I remember O'Brien alright. He was a surly individual, extremely rude too. Insulted one of my customers who was in the shop at the time. A black lady like yourself ma'am.' said Miss Main acknowledging Ella.

'He insisted that he kept his stupid baseball cap on during the fitting. Even when I was putting the robe over his head. It was filthy. I'm sure there were things living in it. I didn't care for him at all.'

This was almost too good to be true. Sam now knew the identities of everyone in Miss Main's book. This was the break he'd been looking for.

'Quick question, I know you said you don't remember much about Hayes, but I was wondering if you could recall whether he'd been wearing a red t-shirt or what type of shoes he had on?'

Miss Main sat down and thought for a moment.

'Can't say I remember him having a red t-shirt, but now you mention it, I do recall his shoes. He had a pair of white sneakers on and one of them was covered in bright blue paint. Yes, I do remember that.'

'Excellent.' replied Sam trying to supress a smile.

'And one final question if I may. I see these are just plain robes, there's no insignia or hoods with them. I take it they didn't bring in any of those?'

'There were certainly no hoods, but that's maybe not so surprising, they wouldn't need altered to the same degree, but there was some insignia. But it was only for the red robe. Mr Lawrence brought them in. They're in a drawer somewhere.'

Miss Main searched through a drawer underneath a sewing table.

'These are the ones.' she said holding three patches aloft.

'This confederacy flag is to go on the left shoulder. It's the only one I recognise. Don't ask me what these other two are. Some form of white cross and this triangular one, it looks like a triangle within a triangle. These two were to go on the front of the robe.'

Makes sense thought Sam scribbling more notes. David Lawrence had said that Eldridge and his grandfather had been the Klan leader, the Grand Dragon he called them. That's why Aiden Lawrence's robe is red, he's the Grand Dragon, just like his father and grandfather before him.

'Miss Main, you've been most helpful and I'm very grateful to you. Can I ask, what time do you close?'

Miss Main looked at her watch.

'Just as soon as you've gone. It's after half five and that's when I usually head home.'

'Okay great. And what time do you open in the morning because I'm going to have to come back tomorrow.'

Miss Main looked puzzled.

'I open at nine thirty. But have I done something wrong officer?'

Sam smiled.

'You've done absolutely nothing wrong; I can assure you of that. But I'm going to need to come back and take these gowns and this notebook away. It's part on an investigation I'm involved with. It's actually Sergeant Brown's enquiry so with any luck she'll be with me tomorrow, so you'll get to meet her again.'

'Well that would be just lovely, I'll look forward to it. Now if you give me a minute to get my jacket and handbag, I'll follow you out and lock up.'

*

'Do you want me to wait and give you a lift to the gym?' asked Sam as he parked up outside Ella's digs at the other end of the town.

'No, you're fine. I'll just walk. It's not far and it's a lovely evening. Anyway, aren't you going home to drop the car? I thought you said you were going to meet your colleagues for a beer.'

'Change of plan. I'm still going to meet them for a drink, but I'll stick to Coke, I'm going to head back to the office afterwards, after what Georgina Main told me I've got some things I need to do ahead of tomorrow.'

'Well don't stay too late. I know what you're like, but you're not invincible, you'll need to get some rest, oh, and make sure you eat some proper food. Something healthy and green you hear me. No more KFC.'

The others were already there by the time Sam walked into Bursley's. He was twenty minutes late and had missed the first round. He got to the bar just in time to catch Angela ordering the next round.

'Just a Coke, are you sure? You've not brought the car, have you?'

Sam nodded.

'Afraid so, I need to go back to the office after this for a bit. Something's come up.'

Angela leant back and stared at Sam.

'Really. Remember what I told you about working all those hours, it can't be that important. Won't it keep till tomorrow?'

'Nope.' said Sam shaking of his head. 'It won't take me long, but I need to get it done while it's fresh in my mind. I'll tell you about it tomorrow, I promise.'

'And is it, good news?'

'Think it might be that's why I'm keen to get it done.'

'Sounds intriguing, I'll look forward to hearing about it in the morning. Could do with some good news for a change. The last few days have been torture. But remember what I said, don't stay too late. Gordon's late shift Sergeant, I'll be checking with him to see when you left.'

Chapter 30

Sam looked at the clock, it had gone 2am. He had been writing his briefing note for more than three hours. It ran to five pages, but it was now done. When he arrived at the office, he had dug out the relevant paperwork and prepared meticulous notes to make sure everything was accurate and in chronological order. This needed to be precise and persuasive. Writing reports did not come easy to him, his dyslexia meant they were always a challenge and progress was painfully slow. But he had put his heart and soul into this one. It was important and it needed to be right. The catalogue of events together with the names of the suspects and supporting evidence would, he hoped, be enough to convince Lieutenant Finch that there was sufficient evidence to arrest the perpetrators for the abduction and assault on Ella and the criminal damage to his parents' garage.

He knew that the matter of the KKK might have to wait. But with the burnt wood fragments, the scorched tree and now the robes he reckoned he could prove there was a Klan operating in Greenbrier County and Aiden Lawrence was its leader. But this was all new to him. He hadn't encountered anything like it before. He wasn't even sure if the Klan was a proscribed organisation or whether it was an offence to be a member of it. He knew it was for Ryan Mulroy. It was against the police's code of conduct to be a member of a white supremacist group. The information he had obtained from Georgina Main would be enough to nail Mulroy. But Sam wanted more.

Mulroy's corruption went way beyond being a member of a racist organisation. He was complicit in other ways too. His phone call to Riley Muntz proved that. Muntz had only moved the truck to Mulroy's father's business unit because Ryan had warned him that the heat was on. Sam just hoped that the truck was still there. He still had the rope fibres in a bag in his desk. But he knew what Charlie would say. That wasn't evidence. Well, not evidence that could be submitted in a court of law. He'd been alone when he'd taken the fibres. Any lawyer worth their salt would discredit his testimony in seconds. Those fibres could have been obtained at anytime, anywhere. Sam knew all that. He'd taken them because he'd wanted to have them checked against the fibres that were recovered from Ella's socks. When they came back as a match, as he was sure they would, well then, they could obtain a warrant and go and get another sample. One that could be corroborated and be admissible in court.

But there was more. Mulroy was right out of wriggle room. Sam could link him to the racist graffiti on the garage through the purchase of the spray paint, and his association with Carter Hayes. He could now prove that they knew each other. He would be the first to admit that most of his evidence against Mulroy was circumstantial, but there was now so much of it, he wouldn't be able to just explain it away. And anyway, Mulroy didn't have the brains for that.

Sam had done as much as he could. He would give his report to Angela in the morning and hope she would agree to discuss it with Charlie. But for now, he needed some sleep. He thought about driving home, but if he did that, he would get less than four hours sleep. He decided to stay at the office and save himself the drive. He could catch a few hours on the couch in the Doctor's examination room, there were blankets and it would be comfy enough. He might have to wear the same shirt for a second day, but he could grab a shower and still be at his desk for six thirty. Nobody needed to know he'd been at the office all night.

*

There was no sign of Sam when Angela arrived at the office. She made herself a coffee and read through the overnight crime reports. She was updating next week's availability roster when Charlie walked in. It was now after seven and there was still no sign of Sam.

'Anything I need to know crime-wise?' asked Charlie picking up the file. Angela shook her head. 'Another quiet night, nothing out of the ordinary. A number of thefts, two assaults, and a break-in to a nursery over in White Sulphur Springs and that's about your lot.'

'Well at least that's something. Can you come through once you're done? I've something I want to discuss. Oh, and bring Sam with you, it's going to need a couple of officers to check it out.'

'Sure, but I might be on my own, I haven't seen Sam this morning, not like him to be late.'

Liz the cleaner's ears pricked up. She was busy emptying the office trash cans, but she'd overheard what Angela had said.

'Oh, he's in alright. He's sleeping like a baby on the couch in the doctor's room. Well he was ten minutes ago when I went in to collect the trash.'

Charlie raised an eyebrow and smiled.

'I'll let you wake him up, give him fifteen minutes to find his feet and then I'll see you both in my office.'

Angela was about to head down the stairs when a dishevelled looking face appeared at the door. Sam had clearly just woken up. He still had his bed hair, it was sticking up everywhere, and looked like a burst mattress. He'd skipped his shower and quickly got dressed. Rather too quickly as he'd missed several buttons on his shirt.'

Angela blew out her cheeks.

'I despair. The last thing I said to you was to make sure you didn't work too late. That fell on deaf ears I see. I take it you've been here all night?'

Sam nodded sheepishly. There was no point in lying.

'Okay fine, you're here now. Grab yourself a coffee and a notepad and get through to the boss's office. He wants to see us first thing.'

Sam about turned and headed off to get himself organised. He made himself a coffee and picked up his folder. Inside were three copies of his report. It didn't matter what it would take, he was determined that Angela and Charlie would read his report. This was important and he knew from the conversation in the bar last night that the murder enquiry was likely to get scaled back. Without a suspect, they didn't have the work to justify the number of detectives who were working on the case. There would now be capacity to take on the Sill brothers and their cronies, Sam knew that, and his girlfriend was banking on it.

Since that day at Denny's when he'd first set eyes on her, he'd seen how people treated and judged her because of the colour of her skin. He'd watched her suffer. There were serious wrongs that needed to be put right. Like her grandfather and the wider black community, Ella was tired of being ignored, pushed to the back of the queue, and told to wait. She'd spent her entire life being treated like a second-class citizen. Sam was angry. Not with Angela or Charlie. He was frustrated with them, but not angry. It wasn't their fault. His anger was directed at the system. The government, the police and other power brokers that allowed such discrimination to go on. Time and again it went unchallenged. That, or it was brushed under the carpet. Either way they tolerated it. It may have been out of sight, but it hadn't gone away, it was still there festering away, never far from the surface. And as these last few weeks had proved, you didn't have to scratch very deep to find it. He had witnessed it with his own eyes, the way they treated his girlfriend was abhorrent, truly disgusting.

It maybe more than 30 years since Lyndon Johnson signed the Civil Rights Act, but right here, in his hometown, there were white supremacists ready and willing to spread their hate. Not much had changed, racism was still rife, Ella could testify to that. Sam was angry, he had had enough. Right now, he couldn't care less about what it might do to his career. Turning a blind eye to the discrimination was the main reason why society was still in such a mess. It had to stop; he was determined to make a stand and teach those scumbags a lesson.

Angela was sitting in Lieutenant Finch's office when Sam came through. Charlie was on the phone, so Sam sat down, put his folder on the table and sipped his coffee.

'I see my name's at the top of that report,' said Angela peering at the folder. 'I take it that's what you've been doing all night? Preparing a report.'

Sam nodded.

'It's a briefing note regarding the assault on Ella, and the racist graffiti on my old man's garage. I've got new evidence, a whole bunch of it and the names of who was involved. I didn't want to bother you before now because I know you've been up to your neck with the Lawrence enquiry. But now the suspect is out the frame, I thought there might be time to take a look at this.'

'Sure.' said Angela taking a copy of the report. She was about to start reading when Charlie put down the phone. He scoffed ironically shaking his head.

'That was the sergeant at the front office on the phone. Apparently, our illustrious leader has gone off sick. His doctor has signed him off work with stress. Looks like we won't be seeing him for quite some time.'

Angela raised her eyebrows and groaned.

'He must have had another roasting off the AC. That will have tipped him over the edge. Anyway, no loss. I don't mean to sound unsympathetic, but the man is as much use as tits on a bull!'

Charlie spluttered trying to suppress a laugh while Sam nearly choked on his coffee. But Angela was right. The Chief was a liability and having him out the way for a while, might just make things a little easier.

'Well I don't think there's much I can add to that. I think you captured the essence of the man quite succinctly Sergeant. Now on to more important matters. I'm starving and you can't have eaten.' said Charlie producing a $20 note from his wallet and looking at Sam. 'Get yourself to Annie Mack's and get whatever you want. And I'll have a bacon roll, what about you Angela, what are you going to have?'

'I'll have that same roll, ta. And remember the tomato sauce, or there will be trouble!'

Sam smiled and took the note from Charlie. The boss was right, he hadn't eaten, and he was famished. But now he was in a quandary. He wanted two rolls, but as the boss was paying, he didn't want to appear greedy. He mulled it over as he headed to the store.

Half an hour had passed by the time he got back to Charlie's office. Annie Mack's had been queued out the door. There were six people ahead of him waiting to be served. Anyway, he'd decided to bite the bullet and go for two rolls. He needed to be bold, especially if he had to defend what he'd written in his briefing note. He hadn't held back, but as far as Sam was concerned it was a call to arms.

'Sorry about the wait. Don't think I've seen the place so busy so early in the morning. The good news though is the rolls are still hot.' said Sam handing over Charlie's change.

'Well it's also good news for you.' said Charlie taking a bite of his roll. 'You were away so long it gave Sergeant Brown and me a chance to read your report. I'll say one thing. Your report writing skills have come on. Seriously, it reads well, although you weren't messing about, it's pretty direct. There's no flowery language, and it's succinct and to the point. It's a good report, evidence based, well except the fibres that you took from the truck without corroboration. But we can fix that. We'll get a warrant and do the thing properly.

But it's a cracking piece of work. It's all there. Evidence, suspects the lot.

The bit about the robes and Aiden Lawrence and the others involvement with the KKK is particularly interesting. It certainly cements that there was a racial element in the other incidents, including the first one in Denny's car lot, you were right all along about that. And it also answers a question that had been bugging me. I couldn't work out why Linton Webb and the others were on the mountain with Lawrence the day he died. But now I know. They were supposed to be his security. When I spoke to Lawrence in his house, he said he was going to organise his own protection. He clearly meant them. He obviously knew them from their Klan meetings.'

'That makes sense, they've got all the necessary qualifications to be henchmen.' said Angela. 'But the even better news is these jokers will now be going to jail because of your report. Hopefully, for quite some time. And I agree with the boss, it's an excellent piece of work. We knew there was a detective lurking in there somewhere.'

Sam tingled all over. He'd never felt so good since he'd joined the job. It was vindication for all his hard work, but more than that, it was a reward for everything that Ella had taught him. Without her, he would never have opened his eyes to what was really going on. He owed her a lot. But at that moment he felt proud. This was the detective he wanted to be. He was setting the agenda not just following it, and that made him feel pretty damned good.

'A couple of things that we need to discuss before we can make a move on any of this.' said Charlie.

'Well three things in fact. Firstly, as soon as we're finished here, you and Sergeant Brown are going to Fairlea to seize those robes and notebook. That evidence needs to be secured before we do anything else. And on your way back you can stop at the DA's office and pick up a search warrant for Mulroy Alarms and get a sample of that rope. No, cancel that. Here's an even better idea, just seize the whole damned truck. That way we can deprive them of having any use of it.'

Angela and Sam nodded approvingly.

'Okay, and secondly, and this is really important Sam. You can't speak a word to anyone about this. One of our colleagues is now a suspect and his uncle's the AC, so it's sensitive. There are procedures to deal with this type of situation. And believe me, I'll be dealing with it. But you can't say anything to anyone, do you understand?'

Sam nodded but didn't reply. Angela looked up.

'And the third thing? You said there were three things.'

Charlie leant back in his chair.

'The third thing is to do with the Lawrence enquiry. I was going to get you and Sam to check it out. But I'll get Chris and Sarah to do it. You two concentrate on giving the Sill brothers and their friends the jail. It was your enquiry after all.'

'If it's only one action we could maybe do both.' suggested Angela.

Charlie shook his head.

'It's really two things and it might take a while. But I've just got a feeling about it. I think it could be important. I re-read the letter that was sent to Lilian Taylor. The one you brought back from Moundsville,

Sam. One of its recurring themes is the Hicks family. There are numerous mentions of Carole Hicks, the lady who recently passed away, and her husband who died in an accident at Spruce Knob mine in 1953. The year after Chaska had been sent to prison. But there's also at least two mentions of their children in the letter. The Hicks had a daughter called Julie and a son called Eric. They are roughly the same age as Chaska. You see the thing is, when I checked their names against our statement log, they weren't there. We don't have a statement from either of them. They just appear to have been missed.'

Angela thought for a moment. Something was ringing a bell with her.

'I'll dig you out the statement from Screech Jarret, I was reading it a couple of days ago. It stuck out from all the others cause he'd written it himself because he doesn't have speech. It wasn't very long, but I'm sure he mentions being with the Hicks family at the mother's funeral. He might know their whereabouts, it's definitely worth pursuing.'

'That's a good shout, I wasn't aware of that.' replied Charlie. 'Make sure you action it before you head out, we need it bottomed out one way or another.'

'Anything else before we go?' asked Angela.

'Yep, one last thing. Find Ryan Mulroy and tell him to report to my office immediately. And make sure he's got his badge, sidearm and pocketbook with him. And give Steve Joice a shout on the radio, I need him to come in as well.'

'On it.' replied Angela as she headed out the door.

'What was that last bit about?' asked Sam as they walked along the corridor. 'Why is he wanting Ryan to have his badge and pocketbook with him.'

Angela looked around to make sure no one was listening. She put her finger to her lips and whispered.

'For someone who really is quite bright, you've still got a lot to learn. The boss is going to suspend Ryan from duty. He needs to seize his badge and other appointments to do that. And he wants Steve to come in to corroborate the process, and if I know Lieutenant Finch, he'll want Steve to assist him to interview Ryan. Steve's an absolute rottweiler when he interviews suspects. It'll be the classic good cop bad cop routine. Steve's wasted in roads policing if you ask me, he would have made a terrific detective.'

'Well I know that's true; I've seen him in action. A wily old dog is Steve. Don't fancy being Ryan. Not facing the pair of them in an interview. No thanks, you can have that one all to yourself Mr Mulroy.'

Chapter 31

It was late the following evening and Charlie, Angela, and Steve were talking in the detective's main office. They were waiting for Ming's to deliver their Chinese takeaway. Spirits were high. It had been another long and tiring day, but at least for a change, it had been a fruitful one. Well, in terms of the case against the Sill brothers and their redneck friends it had. The Lawrence enquiry remained stubbornly frustrating and they were still no closer to catching the killer. Thanks to Screech, they had been able to trace and interview Julie, Carole Hicks' daughter, but they still had no idea where her brother Eric was. Julie couldn't help. She'd told them he'd left immediately after the funeral and now he could be anywhere. He was probably picking fruit on some farm somewhere between Pennsylvania and Florida, but there was just no way of telling.

Ryan Mulroy had folded like a cheap suit when Charlie had confronted him about his involvement with Carter Hayes and the others. He had tried to back track when Steve had challenged him about his association with the KKK. He tried to claim that he'd only been at one meeting at the clearing in the forest where the wood fragments and scorched tree were discovered. He then tried to say that it wasn't really his thing and he'd now given it up. But he kept contradicting himself and tying himself in knots telling lies. Mulroy hadn't seen it coming, he was totally unprepared and now he was up to his neck in it. Not even his uncle could help him now. He was way out his depth trying to take on experienced interviewers like Charlie and Steve. Realising that the game was up he had resorted to self-preservation mode and now he was singing like a bird.

Steve's interrogation had been a master class. After getting Mulroy to confess, they went and arrested Linton Webb. With the Chief out of the way, there were no new custody procedures to worry about. This was back to the old way of doing things. Arrest and interrogate. Steve had been right again. Webb had proved to be the weakest link and when he realised the game was up, he burst like a ripe peach.

Both he and Mulroy were now trying to save their own necks. But Charlie was in no mood for brokering any deal. The youngest member of his department had been right all along. He should have listened and paid more attention to what had been going on. It was a schoolboy error. He'd become so absorbed with the Lawrence enquiry that he'd lost the grip of other enquiries. No detective wanted an unsolved murder on their watch. It might be an occupational hazard, but it was still an unwanted one. There was no getting away from it, Charlie had taken his eye off the ball and it had nearly cost them dear.

Perhaps he wasn't as good as he thought he was, this last month had proved that he wasn't the finished article, not by a long way. The best detectives, the very best, like Mike Rawlingson, would not have made that mistake. You need to learn to spin the plates to be a great detective. Keep them spinning, just enough so the plates don't smash on the floor. Reflecting on it now, Charlie knew he had got away with one. In other circumstances this could really have backfired on him and had serious consequences. The Klan had been operating under his nose. He had been too quick to dismiss Sam's concerns when he'd first come to him. Those rednecks could easily have killed someone. They nearly killed Ella. It was a sobering thought.

'So boss, same again tomorrow then? asked Steve handing round the boxes of food that had just been delivered.

'Yep, that's the plan. You, me and Sam will go and get the Sill bothers first thing, then we'll go get Muntz. Angela, Chris and their team will pick up Blackley, Hayes and O'Brien. Once we get them in custody, we'll decide the interview order. But Sean Sill will be last. Nasty piece of work is Sean, but he does have half a brain. That's way more than the others have got. But if we save him till last, we'll have the benefit of knowing what the others have said, they'll give us enough rope. If he decides to play hardball like he usually does, then it might be a straight caution and charge. But it won't matter either way. We've got enough to charge him from what Mulroy and Webb have told us, but the real bonus was getting the rope and the truck. They didn't even have the brains to get rid of it. Excuse the bad pun, but that ties them into the abduction of Ella. It's physical evidence that can't be explained away. So, when you consider all of that, whatever he says tomorrow will just be a bonus.'

'Can't wait.' said Steve taking a mouthful of chow mein. 'And thanks for asking me to be involved. I haven't had this much fun in ages.'

'Not a problem, and we appreciate your help. You've got a lot of knowledge about the case, so it seemed sensible to keep you involved and make use of those razor-sharp interviewing skills.'

'And tell me this Steve, does it beat being the Chief's bagman?' asked Angela grinning as she wiped sauce off her chin.'

'Is the Pope a Catholic?' replied Steve starting to chuckle.

'I'll take that as a yes then.' said Charlie with a wink.

Epilogue

May God bless and keep you always
May your wishes all come true
May you always do for others
And let others do for you
May you build a ladder to the stars
And climb on every rung
May you stay forever young.

Lilian switched off the CD and wiped away her tears with a tissue. She closed her eyes and took several deep breaths. Her heart ached with sadness but now she needed to compose herself.

Lilian had specifically asked for the last appointment of the day. Thursday was late night opening so when she drove up and parked in the quiet side street opposite Ink Envy, it was after seven and already getting dark.

Lilian sat for a few minutes staring at the studio on the other side of the street. A light was on and she could see the figure of a man sitting behind a desk. Lilian swallowed hard. This was unknown territory. Perhaps surprisingly for a woman her age, she didn't have any tattoos. Neither did Marion, her partner. Up until two weeks ago she would never even have considered getting one. But life was different now. She had been devasted when Professor

365

Foulis had telephoned her to tell her the news about Chaska's death. She had cried for most of that first day. Now, nearly two weeks later she was venturing out for the first time and she felt nervous. Her chest felt tight and her mouth was dry. She was apprehensive, but she was determined to do it. She owed it to her friend.

The tattoo studio had been recommended by one of Marion's friends who had used it before. It had a reputation for the quality of its artwork and after thinking about it for several days she had finally made her mind up. In many ways it provided the perfect solution. Lilian didn't just want to mark Chaska's death, she wanted something permanent, something that wouldn't fade away. The tattoo would be that constant reminder of the friendship they had shared. Other than Marion, he was the person she felt closest to. They had a bond that wouldn't be easily broken.

She had been numb for days after hearing of his death. How much suffering did one man have to bear? After 41 years in prison he had been released for less than a month. Her only solace in her grief was that he'd died a free man. Looking back, she should have seen the signs. The hacking cough and loss of appetite, the blood speckled tissues in the trash. Not that it would have made any difference. The cancer was too advanced, they would not have been able to treat him. She took some comfort that he'd died on Spruce Knob, in the shadow of Yellow Rocks, the spiritual home of his ancestors.

Tonight, she was going to honour her friend and pay homage to the Chief on the Shawnee people.

Lilian opened the passenger door and released the child's seatbelt. Her offer of a hand was declined. The boy seemed reluctant to get out. The promise of some candy later eventually did the trick and the boy climbed down from the seat and held her hand as they crossed the street to the studio.

They were greeted by a man in his late twenties. He was sporting a neatly trimmed beard and moustache. He wore a silver nose ring and his arms were muscular and heavily tattooed.

The young boy grinned and pointed to the blue and red fish that wound its way round the top of the man's left arm.

'You like the fish eh. It's Japanese, it's a koi carp and these here are water lilies.'

The young boy smiled again as the man offered him a lollipop from a jar.

'Always keep a stash of these for the youngsters. You'd be surprised how many kids we get in. And it can be a long wait, especially if it's a complicated tattoo. But that shouldn't be the case tonight. You said on the phone it was just some words.'

Lilian smiled and nodded.

'And have you decided where the tattoo is going?'

Lilian undid the top three buttons of the blouse she was wearing.

'I'd like it here, just above my heart.' replied Lilian pointing to her chest.

'Not a problem. That should be quite straightforward. And the wording, have you decided on that?'

Lilian handed the man a sheet of paper.

'Chaska, Chief of the Shawnee, forever in my heart.'

'Cool.' said the man showing Lilian to a leather reclining chair.

'Just open your blouse, you don't need to take it off. This shouldn't take very long but it will hurt a bit. Not excruciating, but the needle is sharp and you'll going to feel some discomfort. Just so you're aware. I tell all my customers who haven't been inked before that you can't get a tattoo without there being some pain involved. But as I said it shouldn't be too bad. If it does become too much tell me and we'll take a break. Okay, you ready?'

'Let's do it.'

Lilian leant back in the chair and shut her eyes.

Half an hour later and it was all done.

'There's a full length mirror over there if you want to jump down and take a look.'

'It's perfect.' said Lilian staring at the mirror. 'I love the style of the lettering and the size is just right. I love it.'

'Cool.' said the man removing his latex gloves.

'The redness and swelling will go down overnight, but you'll need to keep it covered and dry for a few days. This is just a cellophane cover I'm putting on now. It'll help keep it clean and stop any infection getting in.'

'I suppose I shouldn't shower with it then?'

'Preferably not for a few days. You can have a bath though. Much easier to keep the water off it that way.'

'Fine, a bath it is then.'

The man turned to the young boy who had been sitting drawing pictures with some crayons.

'Right my friend, it's your turn now.' said the man with a big friendly smile. 'Here let me give you a lift onto this big chair.'

The man lifted the boy onto the chair which he reclined to an angle of 45 degrees. He turned to speak to Lilian.

'And just to confirm what I told you on the phone, you'll need to sign this consent form. Even though it's just a henna tattoo, he's much younger than anyone I would normally work on, so I just want to make you fully aware of that. It's not illegal, but it's certainly not very common, so if you don't mind.'

The man handed Lilian a form and a pen.

'And it's completely painless, it won't hurt him will it?

The man shook his head.

'It might tickle a bit, but it'll not hurt. That's the benefit of a henna tattoo. It will only last him a couple of months but it's painless getting it done.'

'That's good to know.' said Lilian signing the form.

'Now young man. I don't think we've been properly introduced. My names Joe, what's your name?'

The boy appeared shy and looked away. He was aged about four and of average height. For a boy his age he was sturdily built and had olive coloured skin and dark brown eyes. His hair was thick and black and sat neatly on the top of his shoulders.

'Go on son,' said Lilian gently, 'tell Joe your name, go on, you can do that.'

The young boy smiled and leant back in the chair holding onto the arm rests. Then he announced.

'My name's Jamey Chaska Taylor, and I'm nearly four!'

'Well that's a mighty fine name.' said the man tying back the boy's hair with a scrunchy band. The boy giggled and wriggled on the chair.

'And you said it was going to go on the side of his neck?'

Lilian nodded.

'Have you brought your design?'

'I've got it here.' said Lilian handing Joe a piece of paper.

'Hmm,' said Joe studying the paper. 'Interesting design. I don't think I've ever done one of these before. What's the significance of the three arrows?'

Lilian sat down on a stool next to Jamey. She leant over and held him by the hand.

'Those three arrows, mean that my boy is the son of a Shawnee Chief.'

*

One week later

The Indian summer that had baked the eastern seaboard for the last six weeks had finally broken and now it had been raining heavily for much of the last week. Carter Memorial Hospital sat in nine acres of deciduous woodland on the western edge of Savannah.

Doctor Saul Finklestein was at his desk in his office on the ground floor of the Gwinnett building. He had been head of psychiatric medicine for the last eleven years and tonight he was working late, trying to catch up on a backlog of paperwork after a busy week of case conferences and board meetings.

Under the shelter of a scaly-bark hickory tree, the figure in dark clothing had been watching Doctor Finklestein for over an hour. He was soaked to the skin and hungry. He hadn't eaten a hot meal or any proper food in days. He had survived on nuts and fruit picked from trees and scavenged bread that had been left out for the foxes. He was cold, shivery and weak from the lack of food.

Travelling mainly at night, he had covered the 500 miles in just twenty days. He'd kept to the side roads and followed the course of rivers. He daren't risk being stopped. One false move and it would be over. The last week had been the worst. The change in the weather had slowed this progress and for two days it hadn't stopped raining. The cold and wet had seeped into his bones and sapped his energy. The sole of his left sneaker had split, and blistered feet made him wince with every step. Not one part of him was dry. His soaking clothes clung to him like a vine on a tree, chilling his kidneys. He ached all over.

The tap on the window was barely discernible. It was reverential, polite in its unobtrusiveness. It was the tap of a man who didn't want to intrude. He'd known the Doctor a long time, he knew how busy he was.

Doctor Finklestein looked up from his desk. At first, he didn't recognise the dishevelled looking man who stood expressionless staring in the window. He wasn't expecting to see him. It had been a while, maybe more than a year. But the man at his window clearly wasn't well, his appearance told him that. But what of his mental health? That had always been fragile. He gestured for the man to go to the side door.

'Come in, come in.' said the Doctor opening the fire exit door. 'And get yourself into my office I've got some hot coffee on the go. You must be freezing you're soaked to the skin.'

The man stood for a moment not saying anything. Then in a quiet voice he spoke.

'I've done a bad thing Doctor, a very bad thing. I need you to sign me in, I need help, I need you to lock me away.'

Doctor Finklestein smiled and gently nodded.

'Okay, I understand. Everything's going to be just fine. But remember what I've told you before, we need to take one thing at a time. Come and have a seat over here and you can tell me all about it. I'm going to phone the ward and get Lionel to come over. He's your friend, and Lionel and I are going to look after you. Now before we do anything else, you're going to need to get out of those wet clothes. I'll put the fire on and see if we can't get some heat into you. I'll get Lionel to bring some warm pyjamas and a dressing gown. So, give me your jacket and we'll hang it up. It'll dry quicker that way.'

The man took off his jacket and handed it to Doctor Finklestein.

'And you'd better give me your hat while we're at it. It's a great looking hat, I don't think I've ever seen you wearing a hat before, where did you get it?'

Lightning Source UK Ltd.
Milton Keynes UK
UKHW041032281020
372367UK00001B/59